WATCH AND REACT

MEMOIR OF AN OFFICER OF GREAT DARING AND CHARM.

Kevin Healy

WATCH AND REACT

FOREWORD

You don't just walk out of the gates at Hendon and onto the back seat of an ARV. For that very reason, I make no apologies for talking about my youth and the decade spent at the Hill learning my trade. I am in no doubt that those formative years are the reason I passed the course and had the career I did. Along the way, I worked alongside so many amazing people, some of whom are mentioned here; to each and every one of you, thank you for everything. I wouldn't have made it without you.

WATCH AND REACT

For my little FI

Thank you for keeping me sane

(it's a term of affection)

WATCH AND REACT

ON THE POINT

"WATCH AND REACT," the instructor barks the command, you've been here a hundred times and know the drill, you feel your heart beating faster; pressing your chest against the wall of your body armour. You're sweating, you have a quiet word with yourself. The targets turn to face; the image of a man holding a gun, a sheet of paper stapled to a wooden board. Your hand has already released the sentry on your holster. You take hold of the pistol grip, the Glock rising smoothly, once free of the holster you punch out towards the target, both hands now holding the weapon. Sight picture, sight picture, squeeze, squeeze, bang! A 9mm hole appears on the target. You aim for the centre of body mass, you shoot to stop, not to kill. You cover the target; the target turns away, you re-holster your Glock, sentry on. The target turns to face…. repeat.

"Watch and react," the command every firearms officer on the point hears as they prepare to shoot. Everything you learn on the point is designed to preserve life. The paradox: Are you prepared to take one to save one? We shoot a two-dimensional enemy who never shoots back, we train for speed and accuracy, we train relentlessly 'for the day of the races,' 'the big one.' You don't hear a lot of laughter on the point, it's a serious business my chosen line of work. One day the threat will be real, it's just a matter of time.

Watch and react, this is my story.

WATCH AND REACT

THE HOW AND THE WHY

I had no desire to be a copper. The sight of a police car in our street usually meant one of my family was for it. I didn't long to help the weak, the poor, the disadvantaged. In fact, I would say I had no strong social conscience at all. My family tree, if examined closely, was a miserable specimen. My father could best be described as a practising alcoholic, and boy, did he put in the practice. My mother, abused and beaten by him, raised the five of us kids alone and in poverty, instilling in us survival skills Bear Grylls would die for. No pictures of war heroes, long dead, hung from our living room walls. However, I did have a great uncle shot dead by the British Army. It was alleged he was part of an IRA active service unit, but as my Uncle Shotgun sagely pointed out, "They would say that, wouldn't they, the Brits?" I didn't mention my links to early Irish Republicanism on my application form; there was no point getting off on the wrong foot now, was there? Talking of the wrong foot, Uncle Shotgun was so called after a wee accident with a loaded firearm, leaving him with a limp and minus a few toes.

"I bet you were bullied at school!" What Copper hasn't had that thrown at them? School, of course I was bullied at school; it was the 1970s, but that's not my reason for joining the Thin Blue Line. Listen, everyone got bullied in a Catholic school; it was written into the curriculum by order of the Holy Father. Put-downs, sarcasm and random acts of violence followed you from assembly to double home economics to PE and rounding off the day with RE. In between attempts at breaking my spirit and teaching me to bake scones, they occasionally attempted to educate yours truly. When you're poor, badly dressed and lacking in self-confidence, a faith school does a great job of destroying your faith in just about everything. As for role models, do me a favour; in fact, the only person I looked up to, quite literally, was the Scottish skinhead who lived next door. Seeing me in my school uniform was a red rag to a Scottish Nationalist bull with a personality disorder. Grabbing my tie, he would lift me off the ground, leaving me teetering on my tippy toes. Was he attempting to avenge hundreds of years of Scottish humiliation at the hands of the English, or was it my dinner money he was after? You, the reader, decide. Staring into his half-crazed brooding eyes, the smell of Iron Brew on his breath, I learnt the greatest of life's lessons: LIFE AIN'T FAIR.

My only escape from the day-to-day terrors of home and school came in the unlikely form of the Regal Cinema. Movies and my overactive imagination became my escape module. Sitting in the dark, my imagination ran riot; I was free, if only for a brief moment, from the bullies and the petty humiliations that life bestowed so willingly upon me. I fell in love with Westerns.

It was whilst watching men being men, and the cavalry riding to the rescue, that my love affair with the heroic failure, of one man against many probably took seed. Throw in a pinch of Irish melancholy, a big dollop of sarcasm, half a tablespoon of utter rage and it's clear to see this council house kid was a very square peg in the roundest of holes. Being attacked on my way to Scouts by the local thug Johnny Agga was the final straw. Agga was born with a harelip that dominated a face best described as interesting. The good lord compensated Johnny by bestowing on him superhuman physical strength combined with a cruel sense of humour. Chasing me down the road screaming through a heavy lisp, "I'm going to kill Frank Spencer," I had no choice but to run for my very life. My beloved beret and woggle incited in him an uncontrollable rage, a rage that would eventually book him an extended holiday in Broadmoor.

A week later I joined the local karate club; it was the summer of 77, and I was ready to kick some ass. Unfortunately, being a white belt, it usually meant I was on the receiving end. Karate changed my life; within three years I was a black belt, going on to become national kumite champion. That's fighting, just in case you are wondering why I've gone all Enter the Dragon. I grew up in that Dojo; I learnt bad decisions led to bad outcomes. Never be late, always train in a washed clean Gi, never complain or show weakness, be polite and courteous to 'everyone'. I loved the harsh often brutal environment. I wasn't a natural, but through sheer hard training I began to excel. Within no time I had a six pack, not an ounce of fat remained on a body that could absorb physical punishment and dish it out. Nothing made me happier than a new black belt showing up, wanting to prove a point. I would batter them, and then lesson learnt I would offer them my hand. Lessons I should have learnt in the home and at school, I leant in the Dojo. My instructors were hard men, we called them Sensei, roughly translated meaning teacher. One was a bouncer at the local nightclub. When he wasn't beating seven shades out of punters, he was beating seven shades out of students paying 50p for the privilege. Dressed in his uniform of blue velvet blazer, matching bow tie and frilly shirt, he struck an uncanny resemblance to one Peter Sutcliffe, though no one ever dared point this out to Sensei.

Mr Miyagi, he wasn't, but what he lacked in communication skills, he more than made up for with his relentless desire to push us to our physical limit. This was a man who understood violence and its role in forging character. Controlled aggression, not wild rage or immature anger. Channelled, focused violence that I would learn to turn on and off like a switch. It gave me a warm feeling inside knowing I could knock someone out with my hands and feet. Karate changed my life; it instilled in me self-discipline, resilience, physical courage, and humility, I was filled with a confidence and self-belief that my peers and teachers found quite disconcerting. School was now just something I did when I wasn't training, and home, well, let's just say I wasn't around much. My education suffered, but I couldn't care less; this urban Samurai had found a real home, and that home was the Dojo. I made friends, met people who lived 'good lives,' I earned respect and gave it in return. Leaving school, I had no plans other than to train and teach karate; looking back, it wasn't really a plan, more of a dream, really. So how does someone like me end up in the Metropolitan Police, elite Firearms unit SO19 and an Operational Firearms Commander to boot? Bloody good question. The story begins when I decided to supplement my wages, working as a labourer for a local builder, who in turn promised to teach me the trade.

A series of unfortunate misadventures scuppered my career in the building game, the most notable of which involved burning down a house that I was helping to renovate; this led me to be interviewed at Acton Police Station on suspicion of arson. Fortunately for me, the Detective investigating believed me when I told him I was a terrible builder; he had no choice. All the evidence confirmed I was a terrible builder. My dreams of a trade went up in smoke very much like the house. Now, coppering was not my first choice; I initially considered life as a Marine in the Royal Navy. "Jesus, they would be mad not to have you; feck, they will rip your arm off!" My ever-supportive mother exclaimed, over the moon that her son was finally looking for a proper job, no more running around in my white pyjamas. Though what use a one-armed Marine would be open to debate.

Arriving at the Royal Navy Recruitment Office, I was met at the desk by a naval rating who smiled through gritted teeth and then asked why I had interrupted his morning. I stood to attention. I wish to become a Marine. With that, he stood up and walked out. Not the reaction I was expecting, to be fair. Moments later, a giant of a man wearing a Green Beret squeezed through the same door the rating had disappeared through. "You want to be a Royal Marine." This was clearly rhetorical. "Ok, follow me." Bloody hell, it can't be this easy, I thought as we headed for the display window. The giant marine now pulled back some green sheets and camouflage netting that made up part of the window display to reveal a pull-up bar. "Hop up and give me eight good ones, and I will do your paperwork; any less and you can go join the Air Force. Fair enough." I was up and knocking them out double quick time; I was on my tenth when he told me to jump down and follow him. It was only now that I noticed the little crowd that had formed on the pavement watching my efforts. I gave them a bow in polite recognition, to which they started to clap. This being a Marine was going swimmingly. Sadly, swimming was far from my strong point; to be honest, I could hardly swim a stroke. After passing a few exams and an interview, the swimming issue raised its head; it became abundantly clear I was not best suited for a life in the Marines. Fortunately, I had a plan B. Friends of mine from Karate had joined the force, as in the police, and were banging on about it, telling me to forget joining the military and join them. I took their advice and set about applying.

Weeks later the letter arrived, giving me a date for my fitness and medical screenings. If I was successful, I would be interviewed on the afternoon of the second day, and if I passed that, I would be offered a start date. For the first time, I started to believe this thing could happen. My younger brother did not react well: "Every family has a black sheep." Up until then I thought it was him, but now that I had applied to be a copper, I was the bad guy. My younger brother had a love-hate relationship with the police; he loved to hate them.

He had a criminal record and did everything in his power to increase his record collection. Only weeks before my assessment, he was arrested for the theft of a pedal cycle. He was drunk and didn't fancy walking home from the pub. He may well have got away with it, if he wasn't so well known to local Old Bill. The fact he called two of them some choice names as they drove unwittingly past him didn't help his case much. To say this latest brush with the law had me worried was an understatement. Would it, could it sink my chances? I didn't have a clue, but it kept me awake at night. I must add that little brother straightened himself out joined the Fire Brigade and had a stella career, and I one proud brother.

My big day arrived, and I found myself at the security gates of Peel Centre Police Training Hendon. A guard checked my paperwork whilst my attention was drawn to the recruits immaculately turned out marching from block to block; I fell in love with the place there and then. To someone who had been practising Karate from the age of 14, this was a wonderful sight. I loved order; I loved discipline, which must make me sound like some kind of masochist. Then again, anyone who trained in the martial arts in the 70s would know a thing or two about embracing pain and discipline. The lessons I'd learnt in the Dojo over the last 13 years would come in very handy at training school.

The potential recruits gathered in a hall on the cadet side of the estate; we were not allowed anywhere near constables in training, lest we infect them with civilian attitudes, and they made a break for it. The recruiting staff issued paperwork, checked documents, explained the stages of selection, warning us that we were constantly being assessed as to our suitability to join the Force. I felt eyes peering at me from all directions. I sat up straight, fixing my gaze on a portrait of some long-retired, possibly dead Commissioner of the Metropolitan Police. He stared intensely back at me; I felt we were bonding. Paperwork and motivational chat over the real work began. Were we fit enough to become coppers? Fizz, as the instructional staff called the PT tests, was a breeze. A mile-and-a-half run, some push-ups, some sit-ups and some standing jumps. Shazam, easy. I was amazed, however, at how many candidates, as we were called, turned up overweight and unprepared. If you really wanted this, why had they not sorted their fizz out?

For the medical, we were bussed to Paddington Green Police Station, where a doctor had us strip. He checked my joints, teeth, eyes and even my butt with the dreaded bend over and cough routine. God knows what that was all about! The doctor was surprised at the number of teeth I had missing. I put this down to rugby, not karate. The Met loved rugby, so no dramas there. The kindly old doctor even informed me that if I was lucky enough to get accepted, police officers got free dental treatment. The medical was again a piece of cake, and so I was sent to get dressed and wait in the obviously named waiting room. Time passed slowly; no one appeared to be in the slightest bit of a hurry to get us into uniform. Being somewhat naïve for my age, I was blissfully ignorant of what was to come. I sat in calm silence, not knowing what to expect, and all the more relaxed for it.

Eventually, a very tall man in a suit of clear military bearing, the man, not the suit, entered, read my name from a clipboard and asked me to follow him. We walked along a long narrow corridor; I followed a few steps behind; he said not a word. Suddenly, I became aware; I could feel my heart beating, and for the first time, I felt fear. I wanted this, really wanted this; over and over in my head I repeated my mantra, "Please God, don't let me fuck this up." The man stopped abruptly; then, turning to face me, he smiled a warm smile and said, "Good luck, and remember to sit up straight." In one sentence, this stranger had just given me more life advice than my own father had ever proffered. I smiled back; I liked this serious-looking tall man. He opened the door; I entered. A short while later, I was informed that I had passed the interview. I was joining the Metropolitan Police; I was going to be a copper. Over the next few months, whilst I awaited my start date, I forced myself to watch The Bill for any tips on my new profession but can't say I enjoyed the experience. Now the SWEENEY, that was another matter; it was right up my street. "Nick him, George," criminals were "slags," robbers with shooters; it was brilliant. I actually found I rather liked the bad guys more than the cops, that is, apart from the two main leads, who seemed mostly preoccupied with pulling birds and downing a few pints followed by a chaser, all done on duty! Shit, if this was coppering, my dad should have joined; he'd have made DI (detective inspector) easy.

My search led me to my public library; remember, these are the dark ages before the WWW. The only book I found was a Ladybird book called 'The Policeman', a day in the life of a police officer, very enlightening! What it failed to cover were such topics as sudden deaths, road accidents, delivering death messages, being assaulted, working shifts, mountains of paperwork, attending court and a few of your colleagues being plain batshit crazy. All this and more I would learn the hard way doing 'The Job,' just like every other copper before me. THE JOB: does any other profession describe itself in such a way? If it does, I've never heard it. You go to bed a copper; you wake up a copper. In uniform or off duty, you are a copper. Soon, most if not all of your friends are coppers. Civvies, i.e., everyone else who isn't a copper, including family, don't get it. The job takes over your life, and in truth, it must be that way. You couldn't do the things you were asked to do if you didn't live and breathe The Job.

Wives and children suffered under the demands of the job; marriages broke up, affairs were commonplace, heavy drinking was the norm. All of this was part of the accepted normality of doing the job. Being new, I didn't have a clue about any of this, but sure enough, I would succumb to the lure of The Job. We all did. I soon came to believe I had joined the best profession in the world. Ok, the pay wasn't great, but what the job lacked in financial rewards, it made up for in moments of sheer excitement, horror, and tragedy, sometimes all three rolled into one eight-hour tour of duty. There would be days when you couldn't wait to get up to go to work and days when you didn't want the shift to end. You joined a relief; they became your family. Soon you were seeing more of them than your own flesh and blood. Like all families, reliefs had their issues, confrontations between officers were not uncommon, but if a colleague shouted up for assistance, not a soul would be left in the nick. That was the bond you formed with your colleagues and that bond started the day you walked through the gates of the Peel Centre.

WATCH AND REACT

HENDON 91

They say you never forget your first arrest; how right my Hendon instructors were, but not for the reasons they envisaged. On the night in question, I was on foot patrol in Portobello Road, Bravo Hotel sector, Nottingham Hill, one of my first night duties with my new team. A white Bedford van with POLICE stencilled on the side in fading blue letters pulled up alongside me. The driver's door slid back, as was the way with the old Bedford van, the driver, a fresh-faced kid in his mid-twenties called Alan, called to me, "Healy, get in." Thinking I was going to be the operator on the van, my heart skipped a beat. This was some promotion for the new boy, the probationer, the FNG (fucking new guy). As I started to make for the passenger's seat and a night of being driven around, Alan shouted, "Where the fuck do you think you're going, in back?" The illusion of acceptance was shattered, and with cheeks reddening, I turned for the back of the van. I opened the rear doors to be met by the official operator on the van, a constable called Ken. He was sitting in the darkness on the hard wooden bench, looking down at a middle-aged man. Ken was an old sweat, a team daddy, a man of few words and not someone to mess with. Ken now gave me the good news: "You arrested Clarence for possession of crack in Westbourne Grove ten minutes ago, ok?" Holy shit, I knew Clarence; he was a well-known dealer and petty criminal. He knew the system inside out, and he was never going to play along with this stitch-up.

Was this the moment that Hendon instructors had warned us about? "Things will happen out there on the streets, things that shouldn't happen but do; say no more." Ok, it wasn't exactly the most insightful of warnings, but I read between the lines, or so I thought. The fact my instructor was only at Hendon because he was barred from contact with the public, because of his many and varied complaints, should have told me he knew a thing or three about 'real' policing. "Things can get pretty grey out there," he told the class as we stared back utterly confused. As I stared at Ken and Clarence, I thought to myself, this certainly looks black and white to me. My philosophising was called to an abrupt halt when Clarence shouted, "Are you going to nick me or what?" With that I climbed into the van, and with a shout of "let's go" from Ken we headed for custody at the Hill. The journey only lasted a few minutes, but during that time, Ken offered no more helpful advice on the nature of the stop that led to the arrest. My mind was busy going through the scene in custody when Clarence kicks off screaming "fit up." I saw myself behind bars doing an 8-stretch for perverting the course of justice, sharing a cell with a guy who thought I had a pretty mouth. Mine could be the shortest career in the history of the Met. So yes, my first arrest was memorable, mostly because I wasn't even there. Welcome to The Met. Welcome to the Hill. This was policing in Notting Hill in the 1990s. I should now add that as the van came to a halt and the doors opened, I was not in the back yard of the station but a car park at the top end of the ground. Utterly confused, I climbed out of the van, not knowing what to expect. Suddenly, I realised I wasn't alone; a few of the relief were appearing from the darkness. My heart was pounding, my mouth dry; Clarence now appeared at my side, laughing a deep, booming laugh, "Relax, son, chill out, it's a wind up." It was a fit-up all right, and the joke was on me. Clarence, still laughing, wandered off into the night. I was left none the wiser, half a mile from my beat, thanking God it was a wind-up. Pranks like this were the norm, and as the new guy on the team, I was expected to see the funny side, which of course I did. Humour at the Hill was of the dark kind; as for Clarence, he continued with his life of crime but always had a nice word for me when our paths crossed.

I joined the Metropolitan Police as a recruit on red intake in April 1991. I arrived at Hendon on a miserable Sunday evening; the weather was lovely, but I was miserable. What the hell was I doing at Hendon? It was classic fear of the unknown, fear of failure. The induction letter congratulated me on my success and informed me I was to parade in the dining block and await the arrival of training staff. Entering the canteen, clearly, I wasn't early; the room was already packed full of potential future coppers. I quickly identified that my intake contained a high proportion of young ladies and, in some cases, not-so-young ladies. There were several Black males, a few Asian, but the vast majority were white Anglo-Saxon types. I sat down at a long table and tried to avoid eye contact. Sadly, the guy opposite me was one of those people to avoid on long-haul flights, continental coach journeys or Mediterranean cruises. Within 5 minutes he had unburdened himself of his family history: uncle a cop, dad a cop, mum a nurse; "it's in my blood to serve." Great, in that case, go get me a pint and a packet of pork scratchings, Garçon. He had achieved three A levels, saw university as a waste of time, wanted to be a detective and lived at home with Mum and Dad. He did have a girlfriend, but she was on hold; his career came first, lucky girl I thought. All of this without taking a breath or any punctuation. Staring back at him, I smiled and, in the tradition of all prisoners of war, declared my name and informed him that under the terms of the Geneva Convention, I was duly bound to move tables if he continued to bore me to death; ok, I didn't, but it was a close run thing.

Thankfully, before my new best mate could tell me about his pets and favourite episode of The Bill the room was called to attention. Names were called and after much confusion, we were divided into our classes and sent off for processing. By 6 pm, I had been allocated my room, high in the clouds in one of the three towers that housed recruits. This was my new home, 20 weeks of initial training started right here. Feeling shell shocked I wandered the corridors, discovering toilets, showers, and an ironing room. On my travels, I bumped into other lost souls as confused and nervous as I was. Eventually, a group formed and being the oldest and a natural leader I made my first command decision in the Metropolitan Police, "I need a drink who's coming?" A man giant by the name of Ray smiled a yellow tooth smile and said, "thought you'd never ask." A short fat male wearing glasses, later to be nicknamed Penfold, interjected, "do you think alcohol is a good idea?" "Yes, but only if you want to get drunk," I replied, as our merry band crammed into the lift and headed for the Peel Bar, named after Sir John Peel, the Radio 1 DJ.

My memories of the next 20 weeks are a jumble of faces, exams, marching and physical exercise. The older recruits were almost all military types or failed entrepreneurs, their words, not mine. The military could be subdivided into wankers and non-wankers. Ray the Giant was an ex-Royal Marine, enlisting at 16 as a boy marine. Ray had fought in the Falklands and had stopped being a child around age 5. I liked him a lot; he drank too much, he smoked too much, and he showed me sexy pictures of his Norwegian wife. No one ever fucked with him, least of all the training staff. He was very clearly in the non-wanker camp. Firmly rooted in the wanker camp was the brown-nosing, ass-kissing military. They fought to be class captains, to take us for drill and who looked upon any misdemeanour by a classmate as worthy of informing the relevant authorities. The older recruits or failed entrepreneurs were mostly okay. Civvy Street had not made them millionaires, so here they were bringing their 'life experience' to a street near you. Joining up had everything to do with wives, children, mortgages, etc., etc. Oh, and a pension. In their defence, many of these people did make excellent cops. The younger recruits were just that: young, naïve and well-educated. Their motives were decent and honest, just like the families they went home to each weekend. How could I not like these young men and women who could have chosen a better-paid, less dangerous path?

Where, you ask, did I fit in? I wasn't a Uni type and wasn't ex-military. I wasn't a failed entrepreneur, and I clearly wasn't a young buck just out of school, raring to go. I guess I was just me, a suspected arsonist not sure what I had signed on for, but here's the thing: from day one, I loved it. God knows what I brought to the party, but clearly, I brought something. My instructors liked me; the exams I found a doddle, and the gym sessions, log runs, etc., were a total piece of cake. I was 27 and weighed in at just over ten stone. I was in great physical shape and loved being in a disciplined service, and the best part was I was getting paid to go to school. The instructors were mostly excellent, in complete contrast to the uninspiring, often cruel bunch that called themselves teachers at my school. I loved every second of my time in training. Hendon in those days was looked upon as the pinnacle of police training. Our instructors informed us that for every one of us who made it, thousands had failed. Looking around the canteen, one had to wonder at the suitability of those failed hordes because there were some total fuck nuts sitting amongst our merry band.

It was weird being back in school after so many years, but here I was. Days followed a set routine of breakfast, then into uniform, parade and inspection. If we passed inspection, never a done deal, it was off to class for lessons.

It was here students came face to face with the dreaded white notes. Each day we would study a topic, and these topics would be covered by the pre-read white notes. Lessons on theft, burglary, robbery, drink driving, criminal damage and going equipped. Alongside law, we learnt about our powers as sworn constables. The power to arrest, the power to stop and search and the power to use force. We also had notes on ethics and diversity. At the end of every week, we sat an exam; at the end of every month, we sat a bigger exam. Sprinkled amongst all this book learning, we were also assessed in role plays, where we played the cop against an instructor being a victim of crime, a witness to a crime, a suspect or a total bloody zoomer. We were warned London contained many zoomers and it was their destiny in life to make you look an idiot or hurt you or both.

After our care in the community and mental health white notes, I felt I had a greater understanding of the complexity of the issue and some degree of empathy; however, we still called them zoomers. Race and religion were discussed in class; me, I was more than comfortable with race issues. Karate was full to the brim with superb black karateka. My favourite instructor and personal hero was a guy called Billy Higgins. A Black instructor from Manchester, World Karate Champion and a bloody legend. I loved that guy; he was a role model and father figure rolled into one. I am proud to admit some of the best beatings I ever took in a Dojo were from vastly superior black Karateka. I respected these guys; we were friends, race, religion, or colour meant nothing. We all wore a GI; that was our uniform. We shared the same hardships, the same pain, and the same risks. I assumed swapping from a white Gi to the blue uniform of the Metropolitan Police would be just as easy a transition, or as it turned out, maybe not. What I didn't realise, sat in the safety of the classroom, but quickly hit upon as I patrolled the streets, was that THE GREAT BRITISH PUBLIC, will say and do just about anything to ruin your day.

I swore the oath to serve without fear or favour; I took possession of my new uniform, learnt about the law, about Parliament, about what was expected of me as a cop. Every day was a school day; I loved Hendon. Our study material AKA 'white notes' filled binder after binder; Sting would have shed a tear or two for the rainforests we destroyed in our thirst for knowledge. While at Hendon, I first came face to face with my arch enemy, technology. Sat in front of a computer, studying for my weekly exams, I felt I was trying out for the space programme. I could barely log on, but somehow, I triumphed; I never got below 95% in any exam. Fizz, or physical exercise, was a doddle; my only real match was a guy from South London called Ray; he was ex-military, a PARA, but younger than me. We matched each other in running, push-ups, sit-ups, everything; the only activity separating us was the fact he was a shit-hot boxer, and the physical training staff loved boxing, so they loved Ray. Ray had an Achilles heel, Ray couldn't swim a stroke, the PTIs overlooked this and eventually awarded him the Baton of Honour for Sporting Prowess. It was a close run thing (or so my ego told me), that Baton of Honour, but Jap Slapping as martial arts Were comically known, did not cut the mustard with our white-vested, tattooed gym instructors.

The Physical Training Instructors (PTIs) were the Gods of Hendon; like a scene from Monty Python, they would jog around the site in skin-tight jogging pants and even tighter white vests, sporting moustaches last seen on the Somme. A few absolutely worshiped themselves, which did make us smile, but to be fair they did a great job getting as fit. I actually enjoyed the sarcasm and put downs; it was all a

WATCH AND REACT

game to get us to perform I decided. Hendon had a superb pool, it's purpose to teach recruits how not to die in the Thames, or indeed any of the myriad waterways that flow through our great metropolis. The ultimate goal of the twice-weekly swimming lessons was to pass your Gold Lifesaver Badge. I may have mentioned I too had an Achilles heel. I was an even worse swimmer than Ray. As a child, I discovered I had a fear of washing and, as a result, shied away from all water-related activities.

Swimming lessons had not got off to the best of starts. The girl I was seeing at the time became jealous when she heard I was swimming with young ladies. Like I was on the bloody French Riviera, skinny dipping and calling everyone darling. I asked my sweetheart to purchase me some blue Speedos, as these were the only garments allowed. Being not only jealous but also a comedian, she purchased said Speedos but, in a size, small, for a ten-year-old child. Well, come the first swimming lesson, yours truly unpacks his kit bag, removes the trunks from their wrapping and proceeds to squeeze into the tightest budgie smugglers known to man. My classmates looked on in stunned amazement, turning to horror as both my balls popped out, one on either side with a snap of elastic. My pubic hair pushed in all directions, looking like Leo Sayer was being held against his will inside my trunks. All was lost; I couldn't escape. Sometimes you just have to front up, literally.

As a class we paraded by the poolside; the instructors would march out single file from their changing room, to inspect us prior to us entering the water. Everyone felt awkward, body conscious and shy. My heart went out to the poor girls standing to attention in swimsuits; did the staff enjoy our discomfort? Staff Porter screamed, "Oh my God, Healy, what is that? "Pointing at my trunks. "A testicle staff." With that, the second testicle, clearly feeling lonely, decided to make an appearance. I was frog-marched from the poolside for a quiet chat. After much explaining, they accepted that I wasn't a sexual deviant; I was allowed to change back into uniform and ordered to visit John Lewis and purchase appropriate trunks. After that I felt I had a closer bond with my class, especially the ladies. I went on to fail my life savers badge in true Healy style, having to be saved by Alison, a wonderful swimmer, who realised I was no longer treading water but drowning. Fifteen years later I would bump into this fantastic officer in the parade room at Lambeth. A new recruit to the ARVs, she hadn't changed a bit.

With so many young men and women living in each other's pockets, it was important to keep us busy. Idle hands and all that. With that in mind, you never got a moment to yourself. If you weren't on parade, marching between classes, in the gym, on the track or in the dojo, you were studying your white notes. After the evening meal, we had inter- class competitions, be it cross-country running, orienteering, log runs or team-building exercises of dubious value. Finally, after all these distractions, recruits would head for the bar. The Peel bar is gone now, flattened like the rest of Peel Centre by the developers wrecking ball. But to generations of young coppers, that bar was where you formed friendships that last your whole career. Boys and girls who'd been dumped drank their sorrows away surrounded by supportive classmates. Had a bad day, failed an exam, go to the bar and have a singalong. Got humiliated in a role play; see you in the bar. Feeling lonely? Let's have a beer. That bar did more good than a hundred hours with a councillor. You blew off steam and got whatever was doing your head in sorted with some good old blah blah blah with mates. I loved that bar, and I loved every second of my time at training school.

WATCH AND REACT

It was whilst in training that I had my first contact with the world of firearms and boy did I get off to a great start! Keen to be ready for whatever the streets threw at me, I decided to join the wrestling club. Dressed in my white plimsolls, white knee-length socks, white shorts, creases ironed in with copious amounts of starch, topped off in my blue vest with HEALY written in large black letters, boy was I ready to rumble. Walking into the Dojo, I was met by a group of men all in their forties dressed in blue coveralls. Most, but not all, had grand Mexican-style moustaches, which made them look like 70s porn stars. One or two were smoking roll-ups stood in the fire exit looking out over the running track, the rest lay scattered across the mats, staring rather quizzically at yours truly. I instinctively knew that whatever came out of my mouth next could define the rest of my career. "Hi guys, is this a wrestling club?" I couldn't have sounded more like Julian Clarey if I tried. The roars of laughter lasted as long as it took one of the group to call out in a broad Scottish accent, "Away son, this is the Met police crochet club; wrestling's next door." This had them in stitches. Unsure how to proceed, I stood my ground. That was until a very tall man wearing coveralls and a blue beret marched in. "And who the fuck are you?" I didn't get a chance to reply; the assorted selection of porn stars informed him I was there to wrestle.

A warm grin broke out across his face. "Son, this is PT17 training. You can help push the armoured Land Rover if you want, but no wrestling today." PT17 was the home of firearms training, the forerunner to SO19. These guys were a level one team, SFOs to you and me. I now made a tactical withdrawal, cringing as I heard roars of laughter behind me. Later that same day, I was walking to class when I saw the same group of hardened individuals pulling an armoured Land Rover around the car park. I had a feeling they wouldn't forget the guy in the white socks in a hurry.

All good things must come to an end, after twenty weeks of indoctrination into the ways of the Met, we were ready to be released on an unsuspecting public. The last few weeks flew by, what with the passing-out ball, final exams and waiting to see where you were being posted. Everyone swore to meet up; I didn't buy into that side of things. Maybe I was a little cynical, or was it because I was a bit older? Once we hit borough, we would have enough to worry about just surviving, let alone reunions. I was right; within months, almost the whole class had lost contact. In those days, pre-computers and e-mail, it just fell into the too-difficult box. The day of the postings arrived, and a typed sheet was stuck to the notice board informing our intake where we would be heading. I can't remember my preferences; I really didn't mind which borough, but many did, and many were disappointed. It appeared that the vast majority of us were going to work in inner London, places like Brixton, Kennington, West End Central and Notting Hill. I got the Hill.

I didn't have a clue where it was, but my instructors did and joked about the fact it was lucky I did Karate. I took their leg-pulling in good spirits; I just couldn't wait to get out and start doing the job for real, and if the Hill was full on, then the more the better. I was a lamb to the slaughter, but in truth, I was a very willing lamb with the shoulder number 266 BH, the BH referring to the station Bravo Hotel, Notting Hill police station, 101 Ladbroke Grove. Over a decade I would police the Hill. Over that period, I would marry and divorce, have four children and learn a lot of life's lessons the hard way. I would watch people die, and I would see lives being saved; I would be assaulted, and I would receive commendations for bravery. I would come close to losing my job through malicious complaints, and I would come face to face with the best and the worst that humanity has to offer. To get your pension, you had to do 30 years; looking back, it's a miracle any of us make it.

THE HILL

The best way to learn is through experience. All the book learning in the world does not prepare you for the day-to-day reality of policing. Your instructors in truth take you as far as they can on the journey, but like mothers everywhere, there comes a time when they must let their little brood spread their wings and fend for themselves. My class instructor, shaking my hand at my passing-out parade, smiled, "It's up to you now, son."

I arrived at Notting Hill Police Station as green as any probationer that ever walked through the front door. I introduced myself to the desk sergeant, who, looking rather jaded, stood up, shook my hand and led me through the building down some stairs to the street duties office. I sat alone in silence for half an hour before the next probationer arrived, a girl called Jill. I knew the face from training school, but our classes didn't hang out much. She was as nervous as me; we shared awkward glances, she then blurted out, "My husband hates me being here; I almost didn't turn up." Soon after, two other probationary constables arrived: Steve and another guy called Kevan with an A. Jill resigned a few days later. This was not a great start to our six weeks of street duties, a course designed to get us up to speed with policing the Hill. On the hour, the door opened, and in walked our instructors. The skipper in charge was called Crumpler; he was softly spoken and completely at odds with the constables who were going to teach us the ropes.

Sergeant Crumpler welcomed us, wished us well and then handed us over to his team before departing. I didn't know it at the time, but I would go on to become great friends with PS Crumpler, a lovely man and a great skipper. He left

WATCH AND REACT

behind a selection of coppers who could quite easily have been on the poster for the Dirty Dozen. They stood in stony silence, eyeing us up. Our instructors, of which there were five not counting the skipper, all had service. Service being time in the job. They were all male, two ex-military. All had been at the Hill five or more years and were men of few words, but you could bet one of those words would be the C bomb. From the second we became their charges; I knew the next six weeks were not going to be a stroll in the park. The lead instructor, Chris, was Scottish; he radiated pent-up aggression. He made it very clear that unless we came up to scratch, we would never make it out of probation. Ok, enough of the beanbag stuff, you old charmer. Tell me something I don't know. He covered stop and search, it was expected we would be putting our hands in our pockets from day one. It was explained that the Hill had a reputation for a reason, and we had better switch on, starting yesterday. Instructor Phil relayed the story of the street duties PC stabbed in the stomach in Notting Hill Gate day one out of the box. He survived, but only because his street duties instructor, Kathy, was an ex-nurse. She kept him alive until the arrival of the LAS. In short, shit can happen without warning, so stay frosty.

These street duties instructors were brutal in their appraisal of our daily performance. They were not Hendon instructors passing out shiny probationers; these guys were turning us into cops – cops that they were passing on to work side by side with their mates on relief. It was in all our interests that we knew what we were doing because life on relief depended on each officer bringing something to the party. Each relief took great pride in its reputation, and there was little will to carry people. Over the next six weeks I made my first arrests; I booked prisoners into custody under the watchful eye of the custody sergeant, who would stare across the desk at you and ask, "Why has this man been arrested?" I attended my first sudden death, then another, then another; dead people take some getting used to. My first was an old chap dead on the toilet. Quite common, I was told at the time. My next was a girl who hung herself in her bedroom on the back of her door. Why? She has split up with her boyfriend. She was a pretty girl about eighteen with long black hair. Mum and Dad were at work and had to be informed; thank God I didn't have to do that. What did I learn there? Well, with a hanging, always cut them down above the knot; you don't tamper with the knot. What else? Well, suicide isn't pretty; a young girl with everything to live for shouldn't be hanging by the throat in her bedroom, hoping her lost love will burst in and save her.

Being a bit older, death didn't really shock me or upset me; it was just part of doing the job. Sudden deaths usually follow a similar pattern: a neighbour or family member not seen for a while and a strong smell coming from the flat or house. We would arrive and look for anything suspicious; finding nothing, we would force the front door or window. Once inside, the smell would hit you. You made your way cautiously through the building until you found the deceased. In bed, on the toilet, in the bath. A look at the body to make sure there is no dagger in the back or gunshot wound, no signs of foul play, as they say in Miss Marple. Happy that it wasn't a crime scene, you set about informing relatives, the duty officer, CID, the coroner's office, Uncle Tom Cobbly and all.

Job done, you sat and waited for the undertakers to arrive. While awaiting the men in ill-fitting grey suits, it was your job to go through the dead person's effects, looking for valuables, a passport, and stuff that the next of kin or the coroner may need. At one sudden death, with a crusty old-timer who hated the job almost as much as he resented being posted with a street duties bod, I found a cool-looking air gun with ammo. Quick as a flash, my colleague had set up a target in the bedsit and was firing pellets at a frying pan whilst sat beside the poor old dead geezer. The undertaker's arrival was a grim affair as they appeared to break each limb in turn trying to get his body into the body bag. These men with grey-lined faces didn't smile; I guess their line of work does that to you.

Probably the only sudden death that did affect me in all my time at the Hill was an early morning call straight off parade to something suspicious hanging in a school playground. As I drove to the scene, more information was coming to light. Patients on a ward in St Mary's Hospital had woken to see an object swinging from the climbing frame in the nearby school playground. Sent to investigate, I walked through the school with the probationer I was now puppy walking. Arriving at the entrance to the playground, the look of horror on the caretaker's face said it all. Hanging by his neck from some monkey bars was a slim-built male about twenty years of age of Arabic descent. I knew this because I knew the lad. His name was Mustafa, and he had been a prolific street robber at the Hill for all my time on the team. When I first met him years before, he was an overweight youth with a bad attitude and a real hatred of the police. Over the years I had bumped into him in custody and on the street. Because I never messed with him unless he gave me cause, we got on OK, even sharing a few jokes, usually about his weight or my lack of height. Now he was dead; lying at his feet was an envelope. Later I would find out the note was his apology to his family for the shame he had brought on them. Mustafa had contracted Aids through his drug use. I stood and stared at this lad, then getting my shit together, I took hold of his legs, and the guy I was with cut him down. Later CID would ask why I hadn't awaited their arrival, I didn't give a monkey's what they thought. He was dead, and I wasn't leaving him hanging there for all the world to see. Even though he was a street robber, I actually rather liked him, and the truth was, he wasn't going to be robbing anyone any time soon. I had watched this lad grow up, and now he was dead, and that was that.

Being a probationary constable lasted two years. During this time, you had to pass a series of exams as well as navigate the day-to-day novelty of being a copper. I was one member of a team of officers, known as B Relief. We had an Inspector, 6 Sergeants, several senior constables and a larger number of officers with 4 to 8 years. Finally, you had the bottom of the barrel, the probationers, of which I was one. Everyone on the relief had their eye on you. Your fellow probationers were your rivals, all vying for the role of top dog. The rest of the relief watched you and weighed you up. What they all wanted to know was, did you have a bottle, and could you be trusted? The only way to find out the answer to these questions was to watch you under pressure. Well, in those days you did a lot of single patrols, which meant you often walked into trouble with no backup. Now don't get me wrong, when things went pear-shaped, the team would break their necks to get to you. It's when you're on your own that your mettle is truly tested. Every day was a school day.

All through my career I have watched, copied and stolen the best ideas on how to police from my colleagues. There is no stereotypical great cop. They come in all shapes, sizes and genders. My first real inspiration was a guy called Paul Daniels who gained the nickname MAGIC for obvious reasons. Now Magic was the area car driver at the Hill, which made him the team daddy. Slim of build, about six feet tall, he knew the law inside out. Knowledge is power, but it also helped that he was a fine boxer and didn't believe in taking a backwards step. I took an instant liking to Magic and watched how he dealt with both the public and Slag. Slag was the name given to the criminal fraternity. He was calm; he was polite, and when necessary, he had a degree of menace about him that shocked me the first time it made an appearance. His demeanour of calm professionalism accompanied by his boyish good looks made him a supervisor's dream. Skippers and inspectors trusted him; he was their go-to guy.

However, there was a side to my wonderful colleague they did not see. Upon leaving the backyard, Magic would morph into a combination of Robocop and Mad Max. He was a brilliant driver and would slide the Ford Sierra around Notting Hill like he was Mika Hakkinen. Screeching tyres and burning brakes would always announce our arrival: "The public expects this shit; best we don't let them down." Being on the area car in those days, in the 90s, meant you only went to the most serious calls. "Don't tie up the area car" the motto used Met wide. For some reason, even though I was young in service, I was posted on THE CAR far more than was normal. Call sign Bravo 3. I loved every second of my posting and often didn't want the shift to end. My first real test was being flagged down by a cab driver in the early hours; he ran to my window, saying he had been robbed at knifepoint; the suspect had run into a house. With that, Paul leant across and asked the fateful question, "Which house?" Sure enough, the cab driver had followed the suspect and saw him enter a crack house off Lancaster Road. Now, Notting Hill in those days had more crack houses than just about anywhere in the Met. Not good for the residents but great if you were young and wanted action. Paul shouted, "Put it up," which I did, calling for more units and giving our location.

Paul was already out of the car and approaching the front door. I ran up behind him; the front door opened, and standing in front of us was our suspect. I knew this for two reasons: one, the victim shouted, "That's him," and two, the suspect ran to slam the door. Paul and I wedged our bodies into the door frame to stop him, and let's not forget in those days, no CS, no body armour, just a nice big shiny pair of Met issue balls. The occupiers of the crack house were now raising merry hell, putting all their efforts into forcing the door closed. Suddenly, I felt a thump on my head. I saw a very large, overweight lady in hot pants and a bra swinging a frying pan in my direction. She got in a couple of blows before I could extricate myself. Magic's reaction to this assault was to draw his stick and start smashing all windows of the drug den. Mayhem ensued; screams and shouting rose from inside the crack house. All hell was kicking off inside as I stood rubbing the lump on my head. The crackheads were not best pleased; then again, neither was I.

Sirens wailed, the cavalry were on scene, in a flash the front door was smashed in, and a team of pumped-up coppers stormed the crack house. The suspect fled into the garden, onto a wall, onto a flat roof and, sadly for him, straight through it. Perspex looks solid in the dark. He crashed onto the garage floor, smashing his hip. There he lay writhing in agony while we arranged for a ladder. Success, one in the bin for robbery. One crack house raided and put out of action, for a day or two anyway. The lads were all smiling, and I was one step further to being accepted.

My next run-in with Magic resulted in both of us being hospitalised. Driving around Sheppard's Bush Green, it was kicking off outside a local nightclub. We could see the door staff were coming off second best, so we stopped to fly the flag. As I approached the brawling mass, I suddenly felt a terrible pain in my eyes and face; one of the group, a huge South African dude, had gassed me with some concoction he had brought from his homeland. It would have stunned a rhinoceros; it certainly did for me. My only thought was to nick this guy with the long blonde hair. Half blinded and spitting up bile, I grabbed his hair and wrestled him to the ground. I couldn't see a thing; neither could Magic, but between us we kept hold of this mad, violent South African and cuffed him. Locals soon arrived and took over the scene while we were shipped off to the hospital.

Now, in those days, no one had a clue about toxic incapacitants such as pepper spray or CS. So, when the pretty nurse handed us both soaking wet towels and told us to wipe our eyes and face, she was acting in good faith. WARNING TO READER: DO NOT ADD WATER TO CS CRYSTALS AND DO NOT, UNDER ANY CIRCUMSTANCE, ATTEMPT TO WIPE YOUR FACE AND EYES. Being uninformed 90s cops, we did as we were told. Soon the screams of two tormented cops could be heard all the way to Johannesburg. It was excruciating. The nurses quickly realised something was not cool, i.e., our faces, and stopped us in our tracks. After a while the effects started to wear off; I could see and breathe again, and with the realisation I was free of long-term damage, I did what all injured cops throughout time have done in a hospital: I chatted up the nurses. Soon the Duty Inspector arrived and shook our hands. "Great job, boys." Within a few minutes, he was doubled up crying like a baby suffering the effects of the CS.

Little dramas such as these played out daily at the Hill; not only were they great fun, but they were also a great learning experience. The ground was so varied it offered everything. Notting Hill Gate (NHG) was still lively in those days. Second-hand stores sold used vinyl alongside retro clothing. Shops dealing in used electrical goods, often the proceeds of a burglary or car crime, littered 'the gate.' To add to the eclectic mix, NHG was home to some great bars and a fantastic Greek restaurant that wasn't averse to late-night drinking. As you headed south, the environment changed; the properties grew grander, and by the time you hit Kensington High Street, we were talking very wealthy indeed. At one call to a criminal damage at an address in Phillimore Walk, the lady owner requested I use the tradesman's entrance. North of the Gate, which today is uber trendy and prosperous, was slowly starting to move that way, but by the time you reached Westbourne Grove, you were seeing crack houses, prostitutes, known as Toms, and an assortment of street robbers, drug dealers and crackheads wandering the streets. Portobello Road ran the length of the ground from the Gate to Golborne Road, acting as a magnet for every element of the criminal fraternity, try as I might, I never saw Julia Roberts. As a probationer, I walked everywhere, every day, and in time learnt every inch of the ground. I knew all the faces, and they got to know me. I made friends with the shopkeepers who would invite me in for tea when they saw me patrolling in the pouring rain. I was your traditional bobby on his beat, visible and approachable. I went home at night, bloody shattered, ten thousand steps a day; you can double that and some. This was my early life at the Hill; it was daunting and sometimes scary, but like all those movies I loved, I was now the cavalry, and "Yee ha", I loved it.

WATCH AND REACT

MOVING UP THE FOOD CHAIN

With seven years' service, I passed the advanced driver course. I could now drive the Area Car. Now, in the dark ages of policing, the Area Car was the only car with a main set radio, and so to 'old sweats,' the Area Car was known as the RT car (radio transmitter). I passed my advanced course at Hendon Driving School in 1997. It was a huge day in my career; like the Bible says, many are called, but few are chosen. In those days the course lasted 3 weeks, and before attending, you had to pass a response course lasting two weeks. The course was unbelievably tough, and the failure rate was very high. Being an RT driver in the Met held huge kudos; you were a breed apart. I loved driving the Area Car, call sign Bravo 3; every 6 weeks, I would be posted a new operator who would act as my wingman or woman. To be posted as the operator was a huge pat on the back, and only the sharpest pencils in the box ever got the posting.

My driving police cars did not get off to the best of starts. After I had passed my probation, I was allowed to drive a Panda, a little Ford Fiesta with a blue light and no two tones. These Pandas were not response vehicles; they allowed us to get to calls that were less urgent, such as reporting crimes, missing person enquiries, collecting McMuffins for the control room, road traffic accidents, that kind of stuff. In truth, we 'basic drivers' with no training drove like mad men and women to get to the calls the response cars were running to. Police cars in those days were not fitted with black boxes or computers that recorded your speed, braking or acceleration; as a result, all of us young cops drove like Michael Schumacher, or so we liked to think. It was brilliant fun, and even though no one admitted it, you learnt a hell of a lot about driving, chucking it around the streets of London. That is, of course, if you didn't 'stack it.' 'Stack it,' meaning to crash. If you had a prang, you would come face to face with the most dreaded force in the universe. No, not the Death Star; I refer, of course, to traffic cops. Known as rats, traffic cops with their signature white caps are feared by both the public and cops alike. No sight is more likely to turn a tough street cop's legs to jelly, than the sight of a traffic Skipper with a clipboard. Traffic officers are a unique breed; it is not my intention to mug them off, but nothing warms the heart of these white-hatted guardians of the highway more than the sight of a dented police car, its driver awaiting his fate.

My first accident, and yes, I have had a few in the 28 years I drove cars responding to calls for help, happened on a winters evening as I drove along Notting Hill Gate towards Bayswater. Chatting away to my skipper, the same Marc Crumpler who had run my street duties course, a call came out, a Saab involved in a recent Rolex robbery. It was heading towards Notting Hill from Lancaster Gate; looking ahead, there it was, the silver Saab heading my way. Reacting and not thinking, I spun the car round to give chase, when BANG, a motorcycle coming up on my offside drove straight into the side of me. I braked and skidded to a halt. I sat in silence as Crumps turned to me and smiling said, "Nice one, Kev; I think you may have killed him." Panic pulsing through my body, I threw the door open only to hit the prone rider straight in the head with the door. With a horrible groan he collapsed to the ground and with an even greater groan I crawled from my car a broken man. I knew what awaited me. The accident was totally my fault; it did not matter that I intended to try and arrest suspects for robbery; I had broken the golden rule of driving. No call is so important as to cause an accident. If you cause an accident, you must stop. As a result, you don't get to the call; in reality, you let everyone down. Picture the scene, if you will: one injured rider, one wrecked motorcycle, one damaged Panda car and one police driver about to get it with both barrels.

The ambulance arrived on the scene; I watched in horror as the rider was placed on a spinal board and carted off to hospital. The Traffic Sergeant arrived; he was very tall and clearly enjoyed looking down his nose at me. I must admit in those early years I was intimidated by guys like this, but that wore off a long, long time ago. My 'sod' traffic attitude would not take hold for a few years yet, and so when he told me he was going to breathalyse me, as was Met policy, I felt complete panic. After failing to blow correctly into the device a second time, the rat skipper informed me that if I failed one more time, he would arrest me for failing to provide a sample of breath at the scene of an accident. "What the fuck?" Crumps looked even greyer than I did. Fuck me, I didn't see this one coming out of the long grass. I took a huge breath, filled my lungs and blew and blew until the rat said, "Thank you; well done, you can stop now." The little device did its magic, confirming I was stone-cold sober. The rat then handed me the tube. "You keep this as a memento of our meeting." He then suspended me from driving and informed me he was off to see the 'VICTIM' and check on his condition; he would report the POLAC (police accident), and I may, in the very near future, be prosecuted for a host of serious driving offences, which would directly affect my private driving licence. With a nod of the head, he turned and left. The only thing missing was the click of the heels.

Traffic was never my bag; at Hendon I met lots of officers who dreamt of joining a traffic unit. Personally, I had no interest whatsoever. This apathy towards traffic policing would follow me to the Hill, where I avoided going on a traffic attachment like the plague. Sadly, one day I was spare and got posted with a traffic officer. Sat in the car, he proceeded to tell me what a great driver he was and that I was in for a fun day. I'll be the judge of that, I thought. Turning on the engine, he turned to me and said the immortal line, "Let's make this baby dance." He then proceeded to drive around all day doing 8mph, ignoring calls. The low point in a day filled with so many low points came when he told me about a fatal accident he was investigating. The cause had him dumbfounded; he couldn't sleep; he was obsessed with finding out why. In his desperation to solve this riddle, he sought out a fortune teller, tea leaf reader, Mystic Meg type. He now started to tell me about the séance they held; I opened the car door and with a "See you later," walked back to the station. So no, traffic wasn't my cup of tea.

Nowadays, they are interceptors, on the telly indeed." Hi, my name's Dave, nickname Red Route, favourite road, the B190673, favourite holiday location, Brands Hatch, favourite offence, opening a car door to danger, best day in the job, Gary's wife leaving him, he goes sick, and I get to drive the IMPREZA, win, win, smash, BOOOOM, pet hate, ARV officers. To all the traffic cops out there, my tongue is firmly in my cheek. Take care; you're doing great. job.

I was suspended for six long months but thank the gods I was not prosecuted. When I did return to driving, I was uber cautious for roughly a day, and then my 'Sod it' attitude kicked in, and I was back on the horse. Calls needed responders, and so I carried on the same as before, driving to the best of my limited ability, trying to do my job, in other words, fast. Somehow, I avoided further accidents and set about trying to build a reputation as a good cop. Being single crewed in a Panda car, it was amazing how much 'stuff' just happened in front of your eyes. Stuff that demanded you jump out and 'deal.' This grounding, dealing with confrontation on your own, thinking fast and reacting appropriately would be the bedrock that I would later base my career in firearms upon.

Driving along Ladbroke Grove one rainy Sunday afternoon, a call came out to a stabbing in Portobello Road. I was nearby, and as I started to head in that direction, I suddenly saw a male fitting the description of the suspect sprinting towards me. I couldn't get on the radio to tell my team I thought I had the suspect in sight, as the radio was busy with officers calling for the LAS and more support to the scene. I followed the suspect as he sprinted across Ladbroke Grove and onto an estate. I had no choice; I got out of the car and gave chase. I called to the male to stop, looking back at me, it was clear he wasn't having any of it. He ran into a block of flats with me a few feet behind. I saw the doors to a lift start to shut and without thinking leapt into the lift. Not a good idea!

I was now trapped inside a tiny lift with a very large, very angry male who may have a knife. I looked at him; he looked at me. It was a Mexican standoff and not a sombrero in sight. Well, it was until he threw a punch straight at the side of my head, it was now 'all off at the races' as the saying goes. I made a tactical withdrawal jumping out of the lift, before the doors closed trapping me inside. I wasn't beaten yet I now ran up the stairwell following the lift from floor to floor. I just missed him as he ran out of the lift, on his 'dancers' again, running to a flat banging on the door. Seconds later the door opened, and he was joined by two other large males who were clearly not part of the neighbourhood watch programme. For a moment, we stood in a standoff, and then, calm as anything, they all went back into the flat, closing the door as they did so. Gasping for air, I called for help, explaining what had just happened.

WATCH AND REACT

Very quickly, I was joined by a large part of the team. After listening to my tale of woe, the Skipper decided he was going to knock at the door, make contact and see what he could find out; the rest of the team was to remain on the landing awaiting his directions.

The Skipper knocked, the door was opened by two lovely old Jamaican ladies all dressed up like they had been to church, and being a Sunday, they probably had. The Skipper explained what had happened, and the ladies listened very politely, all of which made my story sound very improbable. Then out of the blue, the subject appeared behind them wearing a nice clean change of clothes. He was soon joined by the other males who had let him in. The mood was darkening as they began to shout abuse at the Skipper, while the two old ladies attempted to keep order. Without warning, the suspect stepped forward and headbutted the Skipper straight in the face. Negotiations were now put on hold, as ten or more police officers witnessing this assault poured into the flat; what ensued looked like a barroom brawl from one of the westerns I loved so much. After much screaming and even more violence, the three males were arrested and taken to the Hill. My man, as it turned out, hadn't robbed anyone; he was a drug dealer with pockets full of drugs, and when he saw the blue lights and police in Portobello Road, he was spooked and ran, and that's where I came in. He told all this to the detectives who dealt with him. I hadn't captured a knife-wielding attacker, but I did learn a tonne about chasing suspects and always knowing exactly where you were in case you needed help. As for the confrontation, I rather enjoyed the whole incident, as did my team. That dreary Sunday wasn't so dreary after all.

At the end of a long night duty, I was heading back to the Hill, tired and longing for my bed. As I drove past

Ladbroke Grove tube, I saw a bus with its alarm lights flashing. In the best tradition of cops worldwide, I pretended I didn't see it, but sadly a member of the public started shouting and pointing; reluctantly I did my duty and stopped to deal. Now, it's about 5 am, I am tired, dog tired, and my brain had turned to porridge, so I strolled up to the double-decker bus and, without thinking, hopped on board. The driver, safe behind his plastic security screen, pointed to the rear of the bus. The first thing I noticed which did make me smile, all the passengers had squeezed onto the bench seat at the rear of the bus, like sardines in a tin. It was only then I realised why. Sitting with his back to me was a male dressed in combat trousers, a camo jacket, big black army boots and sporting a head the size of a small fridge. My smile was fading fast.

The passengers were staring at this male, their eyes as big as saucers. Noticing my arrival, they started to look in my direction, the male, realising he had company, stood up and faced me. The big camo-clad dude was holding a large knife that looked tiny in his huge hands. Standing only a few feet in front of me, he was stooped forward; his head was touching the ceiling. I hope I am painting a vivid picture here; he was a big, big dude. Feelings of tiredness evaporated as adrenalin rushed around my body; a voice in my head screamed, "Nice one, Healy." It's at times like this one realises the power of the spoken word, especially if you have left your new acrylic baton in the car. That voice again, "You twat." Looking directly at this man mountain, I realised this dude was clearly not the full ticket. In as calm a voice as I could muster, I began talking the guy down. I didn't close with him; I asked his name and told him mine. I did everything I could to gain his trust and build a rapport. Later, when I joined firearms, I really came to learn how vital it is to be able to communicate, and that sometimes means shutting up and listening.

For a good few minutes, I talked about getting him a hot meal and that I didn't want anyone to get hurt, namely me. I promised he could ring his mum; I told a white lie that he wouldn't go in a van, but in truth, no one in their right mind was putting this guy in a Panda. Eventually, he placed the knife on the floor and walked off the bus. I handcuffed the giant, sat him on the bonnet of my Panda car, something I immediately regretted, as the bonnet crumpled under his weight. He clearly had learning difficulties and was childlike in his responses, which made me think of my own son. I looked at this giant, and I was glad no harm had come to him. The van arrived, and he was carted off to custody. Walking back on the bus, not one person would provide a statement. No one said thank you or good job, and the driver stayed locked safely in his little cabin. The giant had boarded the bus and started asking passengers for money for food; when he got no joy, he produced the knife, as you do. Would he have hurt anyone? I don't know but thank God he didn't. On that day, I got away with acting without thinking. I was lucky; never again, I swore to myself. At 19 you always have a plan; some are complicated and involve multiple cars and resources. Sometimes, however, it's just "on me, emergency search, let's go." Always have a plan.

All these experiences, good and bad, were essential in my development. I learnt to make decisions and to stand my ground, and I learnt that one guy on his own without backup is not a good idea, so call for help and always let people know where you are. Experience is everything in this job, and to gain it, you have to make mistakes. The golden rule: mistakes happen; learn from them, but make sure you don't repeat them. After several years of getting myself involved in all sorts of scrapes, my Inspector approached me and gave me the good news: I was to go to

Hendon on an advanced course. Being given the course ahead of guys and girls who had been in longer than me put a few noses out of joint, but it was the boss's decision and a real thumbs up for me. I had seven years in the job; it was normal to wait a decade. Hendon Driving School was famous for good reason; it produced superb police drivers. It is one of the few courses you will take as a cop that directly translates into your everyday life. I would happily say that whether you pass or fail, you leave driving school a far better driver than you arrived, fully aware of your capabilities and, more importantly, your limitations. The driving instructors were all class one advanced drivers who had driven in anger all over the Met before taking on the dangerous task of teaching police officers to drive police cars at very high speeds and to engage in pursuits.

From the moment you arrive, you enter a world of old-school policing. Every day you would parade in polished shoes and immaculate uniform; if you passed inspection, you were allowed to prepare the cars. They would be washed and hoovered. Before you could turn the key in the ignition, you had to give a cockpit drill explaining the role of every single button, knob and lever inside the vehicle. Only when the instructor was happy would you eventually be allowed to start the engine. Mother of God, these guys and girls worshipped at the altar of Top Gear. The attention to things seemingly non-driver related blew my brain; they, the instructors, had to be some of the most anal people ever placed on God's earth. On the upside, they were brilliant drivers, and their methods worked. Each car had three students under instruction and one instructor. The day would commence with the instructor giving a demonstration drive. Demo over, he or she would turn off the engine and then turn to us aspiring advanced drivers and ask for comments and observations. We three students would then pour our hearts out using phrases such as smooth, progressive, great vision, and fantastic commentary, basically telling him or her they were up there with the greats like Jackie Stewart and other blokes who drive fast whose names I didn't know. Maybe that was my problem; I was no petrolhead. I didn't learn to drive until I was 27. On day one of the course, each student was asked what car they drove; the replies were as I expected: a Subaru Impreza, a Golf GTI, Escort turbo bastard. Finally, it was my turn: a ten-year-old Renault Espace. French crap, made of fibreglass, seven-seater. From the look on their faces, expectations were set too low.

Now it was our turn to impress. My car had John, aka 'golden bollocks,' a driver destined to be a top driver; next we had Terry, a really good driver who would pass as a class one, and then came me. I was the worst driver in my car; nothing I did impressed the instructor. Crashing the Volvo Turbo on a pursuit was a low point, but somehow, I didn't get the boot. I was the weakest link, but after three weeks of driving school, I was put forward for the dreaded Final Drive. The Rover 827 my chariot for the day, with the turning circle of a cruise liner, the drive so low it felt like you were sat on a skateboard, it did the job. Broken into two elements, first a run lasting roughly half an hour where you demonstrated the skills you had honed over the weeks. Pursuit came next, chasing an instructor who did everything in the book to lose you. It's unbelievably tense, but somehow, lo and behold, I passed. My score got me a class two, not for me the status of a class one. I couldn't care less, as a mate pointed out a class one just has better crashes. I returned to the Hill an advanced driver; I felt ten feet tall. My status on the team rose to giddy heights. The Skippers asked who I wanted as my operator and sought my opinion on team matters. I was invited into the circle of trust, the Skipper's meetings and even got invited to have drinks after work, if they needed to talk about a relief issue.

I thrived on this new responsibility and rose to the occasion. I loved nothing more than driving Bravo 3, getting to the calls fast and safe and then taking charge. Senior officers would comment that when they heard my calm voice on the radio running a job, they knew it would be dealt with properly. The more trust I was shown, the more I wanted to repay that trust.

The saying goes, those the Gods wish to destroy they first make Area Car Drivers. My ego during this period probably got a little bit ahead of me and one day I crossed the line. One of my mates, who was a Sergeant in custody, asked if I would watch the shop while he went to the toilet. Alone, in custody, I realized he hadn't logged off his E-mails. Well, quick as a flash I was sat in his seat and e-mailed the new probationer called Lauren. Writing on his behalf, I informed her that he had a huge crush on her from the moment he laid eyes on her. Her boyfriend, also on the team, was an idiot and that she could do far better and why not date him instead? Hilarious, I thought, as I hit send. Lauren would guess it's a wind up and we would all have a great laugh.

What I didn't know was Lauren's boyfriend had her logon details, and being a jealous soul, he would routinely check her messages. Well, he read my email and blew a fuse. Storming into custody, he offered to bang the sergeant out on the spot. My mate, who didn't have a clue what was going on, told him to 'do one,' suddenly they were being pulled apart. After both parties had calmed down, the story unfolded, and my dear old mate realised in a flash who the likely culprit was. Being a mate, he kept mum. Sadly, Lauren's boyfriend wanted blood and demanded action. Within minutes the Chief Inspector arrived and, realising the message was sent from a computer in custody and that

WATCH AND REACT

custody had CCTV, decided to seize the film and identify the culprit. The game was up!

Hearing of the unfolding drama, bad news travels fast; I headed for custody; it was time to fall on my sword. I marched straight in, removed my flat cap and stood to attention in front of the Chief, an officer who had always treated me very well and whom I respected. "Good morning, sir, I believe you are looking for me." My feet didn't touch the ground; I was marched double time from custody across the yard and into the main building where the Chief Superintendent lived. The Chief Inspector looked like he was about to explode. Moments later I was sitting outside the Chief Supers office; his secretary was looking at me like the condemned man I was. The door opened, and I was up and in. What followed could be heard on neighbouring boroughs as I was well and truly ripped a new one. In between the shouting, the fist banging on the table and the finger jabbing in my face, I stood to attention and sucked it up. Boy, was I screwed, or so I thought.

Bollocking over, the Chief Superintendent invited me to sit down. Being old school and a real gentleman, he smiled and informed me that the performance he had just given was to placate two probationers' who wanted my head on a spike and to ward off other officers from such future behaviour. Data protection act offences, of which this was one, were not being taken lightly by the job, and at some point, someone would get the sack. The Chief Super had 29 year's service and was proper old school. I apologised profusely, and with a shake of the hands, we parted ways. As I opened the door, he shouted after me, "Now get out of my sight." Still in role, you had to give it to the guy. Cheers, Boss. Ego destroys many a good lad; always keep it in check no matter how far up the food chain you rise. Another one of those golden rules learnt the hard way. This wasn't to be my last brush with authority by any means. Somehow, I always survived; maybe it was luck of the Irish. In truth, I think it had more to do with the way I policed and how I treated my colleagues. I never threw anyone under the bus to advance my career, never basked in someone else's glory; I just did my job, leaving others to blow their own trumpet. Karate had taught me humility; in truth, I had a lot to be humble about.

WATCH AND REACT

A HISTORY OF VIOLENCE

The first real hiding I ever took, happened in of all places the family home. After my dad was declared MIA (missing in Acton; he went out drinking and never came home). Our house was repossessed, and so my mum, with her five children in tow, moved into a miserable-looking council house on a miserable-looking estate in West London. Heathrow airport was in touching distance. The garden backed onto the Bath Road, which in turn ran parallel to the runway used by Concorde. When Concorde took off, the windows in the house fell out; it remains one of life's great mysteries, that we as a nation could develop supersonic flight, but failed to master the installation of secondary glazing. The back garden was so thoroughly overgrown it resembled a jungle. An emaciated Japanese soldier would eventually offer his unconditional surrender in spring of 1984.

Coming home from school, I noticed a strange man standing in our front garden. As I drew closer, I saw it was a copper in a white shirt, tie and flat cap. He was pointing a gun at my neighbours' front door. Seeing me, he offered superb tactical advice: "Get down, you bloody idiot." Heeding his advice, I sat down behind a Ford Capri that had been abandoned in the street some weeks earlier. My next-door neighbour was an alcoholic, drug-using layabout. With his giro spent, he decided he needed a payday loan. Arming himself with a gun, he walked into the high street and robbed the local corner shop, taking the till with him for good measure. He made good his escape, followed by one disgruntled shopkeeper, who, having 'housed' the thief, called police. I sat and watched as the cops talked this criminal mastermind into surrendering. I wasn't the only one; an array of single mums dressed in short skirts and skimpy tops now appeared on the scene, offering the officers tea and cake. And yes, this was a euphemism. Moving slightly off script, I would like to add this was the only good thing about my new surroundings. The amount of female flesh on show bore no relation to the weather conditions. Every cloud, I told myself as I admired Debbie from number 63, mother of four, school dinner lady and HOT.

Eventually 'Moriarty' staggered out into the street in his underpants and a Bob Marley T-shirt. Pissed, stoned, maybe both; he acted like he didn't have a care in the world. His wife stood in the doorway; she was clearly distraught. Only having time to apply full makeup, squeeze into hot pants, a bikini top and high heels. I was in love.

My armed cop smiled, threw me a salute, and departed with the line "Good luck, son, you're going to need it."

He wasn't wrong, to make matters worse, my mother took in a lodger. This individual charmed my poor mum into believing he was a hard-working Catholic lad; just over from the old country and in need of a place in the short term to get himself organised. How she met him, I haven't a clue, but meet him she did, and sure enough, one fine sunny day, he appeared at our front door. Within a few days, he had his feet well and truly under the table. I was suspicious of this man from the moment I laid eyes on him. I knew nothing of him, but he was trouble; I knew it in my gut. I tried to avoid him; not easy in a tiny, terraced house, so small that if I was taking a bath and left the door open, my mum could hand me my tea from the tiny kitchen next door. Very handy for the washing up, we all agreed.

Within weeks he set about putting his stamp on the family unit. He was a big man, over 6 feet and strong, bloody strong, as I found out. He drank too much, and when he did, the bully in him was revealed. He was the kind of man who looked like he would be a handful, but in truth, he was a coward, a scared, insecure coward who only picked on those he knew he could get one over on. I say this now in my sixties after a lifetime spent looking at people and working them out. I make my mind up about people usually in the first few minutes, and in truth I'm rarely wrong. It's a gift, sadly not one my mum possessed. One evening in the living room he was throwing his weight around, and I gobbed off at him – nothing too severe, just a bit of back chat. He reacted so violently it took my breath away; he slapped my face so hard I was seeing stars. I responded in the only way I knew; I told him to "fuck off."

The next thing I knew, I was pinned down on the sofa, his long bony fingers clamped around my throat. I could barely breathe, but I did manage to repeat my advice: "Fuck off." He hit me in the face again and again, and after every blow, the same response: "Fuck off." I knew it would stop if I surrendered, but I just didn't have it in me to quit. Eventually, his cowardly rage spent, he released his grip and stood up, his whole body shaking. I dragged myself to my feet and made to leave, but still I couldn't shut my mouth. I insulted my mother for allowing this monster into our home. Bam, he went for me again, but my mum, my tiny mum, blocked his path. I staggered out of the house and into the dimly lit street; it was pouring down. Suddenly, I became aware my face was on fire. He hadn't punched me, but those bloody big bony hands of his had done a great job of smashing my face to smithereens. I could hardly speak; my throat was raw from being choked. I walked to my mate Marco's house; he took one look at me and ran for his mum. She knew what to do. No one called the police; why would you? In those days they did fuck all.

I tell this heart-warming tale because it was another significant moment in young Healy's life. Fuck this for a game of soldiers; I swore never again would I be a bloody victim. After that I trained with a passion and a motivation bordering on obsessive. The reason known only to those closest to me. When I joined the police, I was amazed at how many recruits had never been hit. The first time I got hit on duty was a real eye-opener. A call came out of an elderly female wandering in and out of traffic. I was on foot patrol nearby, so I volunteered to assist. Walking along Notting Hill Gate, I saw the lady. She looked like the Fletcher lady out of 'Murder, She Wrote.' Walking into the road, I put out my hand to stop the traffic. Just like the training manual says. Then turning, I stopped the traffic from the other direction. I was in control; look at me, I thought to myself rather smugly. Reaching the female, I said in my most condescending manner, "Are you alright, dear?" She stared blankly back at me. Someone beeped a horn, impatient to be moving. I turned to identify the driver, and turning back, little Miss Fletcher punched me straight on the nose. She pushed past me shouting, "Get out of my way, you idiot," with tears streaming from my eyes; she was gone. All the cars were now beeping their horns, and I was looking pretty stupid. I didn't go after her; I had no intention of arresting a little old lady, so I quickly made myself scarce from the scene.

Karate was brilliant; it taught me to use my feet, hands, elbows, and even head as a weapon, though not on little old ladies. It also taught me that getting cut, the odd broken bone or the sudden exiting of teeth from your mouth wasn't the end of the world. Often, the thought of getting hit is far worse than the reality, though I must add not always. Fear of getting hurt is branded deep into human DNA, but that doesn't stop people from fighting, does it? Here's the rub: most cops are nice people, so fighting and violence are not always something they are comfortable with. That said, I have worked with some beasts who I was glad were on the right side of the law. One such officer was John D, a Welsh lad on the team; he was huge, he was brave, and I loved working with him. One evening just as I was about to go off duty, a Rolex robbery came in. I grabbed my operator Ben, and we blue lighted it to the scene. The victim was French, but we didn't hold that against him. what was really shocking was the fact that even though he handed over the watch, one of the suspects still attacked him with a hatchet. Leaving the victim with a reporting car, I started an area search. Driving along Oxford Gardens, I found the suspects. Ben and I were out in a flash; the one with the axe ran up some stairs banging on a door to a house. I grabbed his jacket pulling him back towards me. He was still holding the axe; I grabbed his wrist to stop him from taking my head off. As we fought, we fell from the steps into a basement. Suddenly I heard a Welsh voice, "Healy, stop fucking around; let me have a go." John was on the scene and about to deliver some street justice with a beautiful looping right hand that put my opponent to sleep.

A few weeks later, John stopped a car north of the ground; the suspect got out and shot my friend. The suspect now decamped; John did not like being shot and gave chase, catching the shooter in Ladbroke Grove. A violent struggle ensued, which resulted in John calling on the radio for an ambulance. The control room concerned for John's health asked about his condition, to which he gave the immortal reply, "Don't fucking worry; it's not for fucking me." For his outstanding bravery, he received the Queen's Gallantry Medal.

WATCH AND REACT

That hiding I took at 14 taught me it can happen anywhere, any time, and as all good cops know, if it can go wrong, it will go wrong. Not everyone is cut out for this kind of lifestyle. I worked with a guy called Adam; now Adam was two feet taller than me and weighed the same as a small family car. Adam had presence; what Adam didn't have was a clue what he had let himself in for. I had heard rumours he was a bit shaky, but when we stopped a group of lads who may or may not have committed a robbery, Adam was nowhere to be seen, opting to stay in the car. Eventually, he joined me, one of the lads said, "Hey mate, are you cold?" Adam replied in the negative, to which the lad said, "Then why are you shaking so much?" Looking at Adam, he was indeed trembling.

Posted with him, my heart sank; it was like being single-crewed. I knew if the shit hit the fan, he would be 'upstairs collecting fares' – job speak for going missing in action. What shocked me the most about Adam was the fact he couldn't accept he had a problem. Skippers, even the boss, had words regarding his choice of career, but to no avail. The final straw came when a violent suspect was kicking off, and Adam just couldn't bring himself to lay hands on. He just stood there watching me struggling with the suspect. Eventually, when the suspect was secured in cuffs, Adam grabbed hold of him, but it was way too late to make a difference. In the best traditions of the service, the Skippers wrote Adam a brilliant appraisal and supported his transfer to a county force. Another golden rule learnt, don't go judging books by their covers. Big bad Adam was a paper tiger; he had no heart. Sorry, Adam.

I think it's important I set the record straight; I am no MMA cage warrior or ninja master, and I'm certainly not saying I haven't come off second best, because I have. There have been occasions when I have stopped people who clearly could have taken me apart with one hand tied behind their back. When this happens, you must rely on the vital art of bluffing. I like to think I would have received several Baftas and possibly an Oscar for my portrayal of the cop who doesn't give a damn, the guy with nothing to lose. I received a commendation once for tackling a guy with a knife on market day in Portobello. Sitting in my panda, eating an ice cream, as I liked to do on a warm summer day, I heard screams, and still holding my 99, a cone with a flake, I got out of the car to investigate. What should I walk into but a guy having just slashed another guy with a knife? The injured man was on the ground doing an excellent job of bleeding with his attacker standing over him. Armed with a cornet and a flake, I said the immortal line, "Don't make me drop my fucking ice cream." Unbelievably, the suspect dropped the knife, and a stallholder offered to hold my cone whilst I cuffed him. I knew I was lucky to pull it off, but who doesn't love a bit of theatre, eh? And ice cream isn't cheap.

Passing by one of the new trendy bookshops now appearing in Ledbury Road, I heard quite a commotion coming from inside. Stopping the car, I wandered into the shop to be met by a very distressed young lady who explained a couple was having a "domestic," her words, not mine. No copper worth his salt uses the D word, unless they wish to bring a tonne of paperwork down on their head. Walking to the rear of the store, I saw a very athletic, tall male pointing a knife at a female and making some very nasty observations about her character. She looked terrified. Hugh Grant wouldn't have stood for this in his bookshop, I can tell you. The guy with the knife turned, took one look at me and was out the door. I gave chase, as one is meant to in these circumstances, calling for backup as I did so. After a few hundred yards of sprinting, he stopped at a parked van; what followed next must have looked pretty daft. He was tired, I was tired, I couldn't catch him, and he couldn't get away from yours truly. I now chased him round and round a parked van selling German sausage. The tourists awaiting their bratwurst were at a loss to tell who was chasing who but enjoying the free street entertainment. It was better than Covent Garden. I was told later by two attractive Brazilian ladies who asked what I did for an encore!

Eventually, the sheer ridiculousness of the scene must have dawned on my chap; that or he was knackered because he suddenly came to a standstill, I didn't. I hit him chest high with a flying tackle, knocking him to the floor, and with a brilliantly executed headlock, I pinned him down, awaiting the cavalry. As we both lay in the road with him wrestling to break free and yours truly strangling away to my heart's content, I looked up to see two very smart young Black men in suits and bow ties. The Nation of Islam had arrived on the scene, just dandy, looking like two youthful Malcolm X's in their black heavy framed reading glasses. I asked if they fancied giving me a hand. They politely declined but did film the incident on a camcorder, probably to be played at the Nation of Islam Christmas party in Dungeness. I was very impressed with their manners, but their social responsibility needed a bit of work. As the struggle played out an elderly lady stood watching. Dressed in sturdy shoes tweed skirt and matching jacket, miss Marple was on scene. Her Prescence typified the Hill, every social class mixing, living side by side and somehow getting along. Eventually units arrived, I arrested my new bestie and watched as he was driven away in the van. Miss Marple now approached me and handed me a bottle of water from her wicker shopping basket with the words "Well done young man, well done indeed." This interaction was typical of the life I chose, and I loved it: the sudden unexpected moments when you're chasing a suspect with not a moment's thought for your own safety, just reacting, knowing it's going to get messy and loving it all the more for that.

The radio came to life. "Bravo 3, Bravo 3, suspect on foot, Talbot Road." It was the Proactive team. "He's running; he's running. " I didn't have a clue what was going on, but I drove to intercept the male and sure enough located him in Powis Square. He was a white male in a suit, heavy build, aged about 35 to 40. I tried to block his escape using the car, but I was too slow, so now I was out on foot chasing, my operator at my shoulder. As we gave chase, the male looked back, and without stopping, pulled open his jacket to reveal he was holding a silver handgun. Did he intend to shoot us? I never found out because in the act of looking back at us, he completely lost his footing and tripped over a kerbstone, sending him sprawling to the ground; the gun went flying through the air, God knows where. Later it was found a few feet away on a grass verge behind some railings. He, of course, denied ever having it in his possession.

My colleague and I were on him in a flash and cuffed him. Moments later the proactive team arrived. The gunman was Eastern European and had been sent to demand protection money from a bar. What he didn't know was that the bar owner had called the police, and what the police didn't know was that these guys were Russian and played rough. As the proactive team swooped to arrest, he was on his toes, as you would do if you were packing heat, as they say in America. Well, it was tea and medals all round for the proactive team, but me and my buddy didn't even get a thank you. It went to the Old Bailey for trial; it was the only time I ever got to the Bailey. I was terrified of giving evidence in case I blew the job. I needn't have worried because the suspect pleaded guilty. He may have been an East European gangster, but he knew nothing about forensics. When he loaded the magazine on the SLP, Self-Loading Pistol, he forgot to wear gloves, each time he pressed a round into the magazine, he left his thumbprint on the shell casing. Basics, old boy, basics. His defence that the gun was planted on him by London's finest looked pretty ropey when his fingerprints were on the bullets.

After the incident was put to bed, I went for a pint with my teammate. He admitted that upon seeing the gun, he had a holy fuck moment; I admitted I did too. Would he have shot us, or was he trying to throw the gun away? Who knows? Only Oleg can answer that, and he wasn't much for small talk. As Boney M put it, "Oh, those Russians." From confrontation in the home to battles in the dojo to chasing suspects at the Hill, I had become adept at dealing with life's little dramas. Which was handy because I was about to jump out of the frying pan into the fire.

NO TWO DAYS

If you ever speak with colleagues who have reached the happy hunting ground known as retirement. The one thing they all agree on is that they miss the people. No, not you, the public; you lot keep us in work, but trust me, we don't miss you. No, we miss the real people, the boys and girls we worked alongside. During my time at the Hill, it's fair to say I worked with so many huge characters. Scott was a fellow RT driver but with about 4 years' service more than me. He was one of those wiry guys who looked like an anatomical chart. He loved his weight training, and it showed. He sported a healthy tan all year round offset with a crew cut that shone silver. Scott never aged, never put on weight and never took a step backwards.

Now, on this specific evening, as we drove lazily up and down the ground, a call came out to a pub in Portobello Road, a male causing a disturbance. We arrived on the scene, but the suspect had departed. The barman explained the suspect was a bit of a face in the area; he was demanding free drinks and hassling guests. We left, but sure enough, a short while later, the same call, same location. Once again, we returned, but he had gone. The barman explained this time he had a few mates in tow.

Are you with me so far? Well, sure as eggs is eggs, another call, same bar, same problem. However, this time as we entered the bar, who should we meet but the suspect! I wasn't destined to be a detective, but I knew he was our man by the way he called out. "Can anyone smell pork?" He was aged around 25, was fit looking and was sat in a booth with a group of other boys and girls, who clearly enjoyed him goading us. Now it's times like this when discretion is the better part of valour, but Scott had never

WATCH AND REACT

heard of that expression, and so without a second's hesitation, walked up to the booth. To say you could have heard a pin drop would not put too fine a point on the matter. "You are coming with us." The smile and cockiness disappeared from the guy's face. "I'm not going anywhere." Scott then explained very calmly that he appreciated this was going to turn nasty and that the lad was mob-handed. He accepted the likelihood we would both get a battering, but he assured the chap that no matter what happened, no matter how badly he got hurt, he would make sure our suspect left this bar on a fucking stretcher. Scott's matter-of-fact attitude and utter calm were a thing of beauty.

We stood in silence staring at the group; Scott didn't ask for backup; he never spoke another word. Without warning he was over the table and dragging the suspect out of his seat. Scott's incredible strength and speed shocked both the suspect and my good self. Beer glasses went flying, the table turned over and our bad boy was launched through the air. In a flash, he was being pinned to the floor and cuffed. Rent a mob didn't have time to react and clearly didn't have the stomach for a war. We dragged the suspect to his feet and nicked him, and with me covering our retreat, we exited the bar. I looked at Scott's face; the smile could have lit up the street. He loved his job, and he loved dealing with bullies.

Probably the worst bullies you meet are the wife beaters', as they used to be called. Domestic violence is now the catch-all phrase for trouble in the home. I came to love going to domestics because you were always guaranteed two things: an arrest and confrontation. Working with Scott week after week, we developed a kind of sixth sense. I learnt to anticipate when he would make his move, and trust me, he always made his move. Domestics followed a familiar pattern. We would arrive, and if the husband or boyfriend was still present, we would separate them from the victim. The female would invariably deny anything had happened, deny calling us and ask us to leave. The male would be belligerent and stomp around the room pumping himself up for the inevitable confrontation. Critical mass was reached at the point one of us said, "Your nicked shit head." Just prior to giving the suspect the good news, Scott and I would position ourselves in such a way as to have the tactical advantage, or to put it another way, the suspect couldn't hit both of us at once, so if I copped one, Scott would let rip and vice versa.

Just because we understood how each other worked didn't mean we always got it right. At one memorable domestic in a flat on Dalgarno Gardens, Scott went to handcuff the suspect; the suspect decided to pull a large fridge freezer down on top of me. The fridge toppled on top of us; a huge bundle ensued. In the melee, French for clusterfuck, Scott handcuffed me. Which even the suspect found amusing in between attempting to batter his wife and relocate my head into an icebox. Of course, we came out on top, if a little bruised; the bedsit would need more than a 60-second makeover, but the attacker did get arrested, and that's all that matters in the end.

Scott and I worked together on and off for several years before he moved on to pastures new, he was a fantastic copper and a great role model; he was married with kids; he worked shifts, but he never went sick, and he always looked like he had just walked off a parade ground. He was fit; he trained every chance he could. I can hardly ever remember him complaining about anything; he was the sort of cop the Met needs. Shit, he was the sort of cop everyone needs. Not interested in promotion or commendations or indeed what the skipper wrote on his yearly appraisal. He just got the job done, and in doing so, he inspired those around him. That's leadership, and what's so fantastic about it is that Scott was oblivious to the aura of confidence he created on the team. Sadly, Scott is gone now, far too early and greatly missed by all who had the honour to work alongside him.

For every day that goes swimmingly, there are those you wish you could hit the rewind button on. A memorable low point for me personally occurred on a miserable night duty in February. It was freezing cold and raining sleet. A warrant was to be executed at a crack house in Golborne Road, the top end of the ground. Crack was the new drug, and the papers were having a field day whipping up hysteria. "One puff and you're addicted." Where you had crack, you had crime, and the Hills robberies and burglary stats were going through the roof. The plan was to shut a crack house as fast as it opened. The one in question was a basement flat in a Victorian block. Observations on the address made it apparent that by the time we would have forced the front door to the block and then forced the door to the flat, the drugs and the crackheads would have been long gone. Constable D, a man who liked to think outside the box, decided on a cunning plan. Dressed in his NATO helmet (riot helmet) and flameproof coveralls, he would dive through the living room window at the front of the flat, causing a distraction while the team forced the external front door and then the door to the crack house. His plan was nuts, but that was then; in the dark ages of the 90s, crazy shit happened like that. No one had ever heard of a risk assessment or health and safety legislation. Remember too that this is a time before body armour, batons and CS spray. In those bygone days, we wore white shirts, clip-on ties and Doc Martens boots. However, what we lacked in kit we amply made up for with daring and cunning.

The big day arrived; D kitted up, wearing as much protection as possible. At the allotted hour, without hesitation, he dived headfirst through the living room window. Simultaneously, the team smashed the outer door and then the front door to the crack house. Pouring inside, we found a row of Portuguese crackheads lying face down on the floor with Constable D standing over them, barking orders not to move. D was a bit of a legend at the Hill; still in his early twenties, he was like some rogue cop. The criminal fraternity came to know him as Satan with the blue eyes. With his mop of blonde hair and thick northern accent, D was easily identifiable at calls and so accumulated complaint after complaint. He didn't give a monkeys, and neither did his Skippers, who saw a young, hard-working cop. They knew the golden rule: if you were getting complaints, it's because you were stopping the right people. Ds arrest rate was one of the highest on the borough, and his stop and searches always got results. He was a criminal's nightmare; his unorthodox approach was legendary. One of his favourite escapades was to wear the Superintendent's raincoat on night duty, turning up at calls on surrounding boroughs. He would direct officers, ask awkward questions before slipping away into the night on Bravo 3. So here he was, single-handedly taking on a crack house, but why did it go so wrong for me? Well, boys and girls, I did a very stupid thing. While searching the address for drugs, I ran my hand along a picture rail. It was pitch black in the flat, so I was searching with my torch. As I stretched to search a recess, I felt a sudden pain in my hand. Pulling it back sharply, I saw a needle attached to a syringe sticking out of my right hand; I cursed in anger at my stupidity.

Torches were shone on my hand, and sure enough, I had managed to stick a needle deep into my skin. The syringe was full of dark fresh blood; I looked on in horror as blood started to appear around the wound. Well, Kevin, I thought to myself, you have gone and done it this time: the looks on my teammates' faces told me all I needed to know. Like a scene from a gothic horror, their faces illuminated by the torches, looked macabre in the dark of a miserable crack house. The dead zombie eyes of the addicts staring at me added to the nightmare scenario unfolding before me. Was I now like them, a dead man walking. I may well have contracted Aids. So much for a thirty-year career. In no time I was being driven on blue lights back to the Hill; from there I was driven to St Thomas' Hospital virology ward. Blood was taken, and then the charming doctor informed me I wouldn't get the results for six months. "Six months? Shit, I might be dead by then." I was never one to miss an opportunity to overreact. The doctor smiled and patted my shoulder, "No, it takes much longer, maybe a year." Ah, that dark humour I loved so much. Cheers, Doc.

I drove myself home, sat on the sofa and allowed myself a moment of calm reflection (crying like a baby). My wife was due to give birth in a couple of months; what a nightmare. To say there was little or no information available is an understatement; these were the days when the public was convinced you could catch Aids, from a toilet seat. I told my wife, who told all her friends, though God knows why, and very soon invitations for drinks or dinner dried up. Me being me, I brooded on the nightmare scenario for a couple of days and then locked it away with all the other nightmares I had endured. I returned to work, and cops being cops, life carried on as normal, which meant everyone said I would be dead by the summer. I loved my team for that. Well, I didn't die; I didn't contract Aids. It was all part of doing the job. Like they say, if you can't take a joke, you shouldn't have joined.

Some calls stay with you forever, and one I am reminded of highlighted the power of the human spirit. I was posted walking with a good mate when an alarm call was put out. Not being far off, we cancelled the response car and headed for the address. Knocking at the front door, it was opened by a female in her mid-twenties. I am guessing at her age because this young lady had no recognisable face. She wore fashionable clothes, and her hair was cut in a trendy bob style. Her face, however, had been burnt away; deep scars crisscrossed her face. Being a total twat, I stared in shock, totally blown away by this woman standing in front of me. The young lady broke the silence and asked if we were there about the alarm. I nodded we were, she went on to explain she lived in sheltered accommodation; she had accidentally set off the alarm when cooking. Her voice was so gentle, and it was obvious she was doing everything she could to put me at ease. I now overcompensated, trying to make conversation and not lose eye contact, but the more I spoke, the more awkward the situation became, and that was when the young lady reached out and touched my hand, and I shut up. The three of us stood quietly for a moment, and then the young lady said, "Now you two take care, and don't worry; I'm fine." She wished us a good night, then shut the door. I don't think we spoke very much after that. I never saw that young woman again, but her courage, dignity and kindness are something I will never forget; it was a humbling experience.

As my career developed, I gained, through my actions, the trust of both my peers and the people in charge of me, the skippers and the inspectors. I was changing; it was first pointed out to me by my mother over Sunday lunch. Out of the blue, she told me I was different these days. I asked her what she meant; she said I had become more serious; I didn't laugh as much and wasn't so carefree. I remember her comments like they were yesterday, and out of respect for my lovely mum, I bit my tongue. I was changing; I had changed: Cal, my son, was a game changer. Discovering my son was disabled was the worst day of my life. The consultant, realising I was in denial, went to great pains to get through to me that Cal had severe learning difficulties. Cal would never marry, he would never go to a normal school, he would never talk. With these random examples, he took my world and ripped it to shreds. I stopped listening; I stared at this doctor and thought I would kill him if he didn't shut his mouth. I had such dreams, so much hope for my son's future, now my son's future filled me with fear, fear of the unknown. We had named Cal after my younger brother who died of pneumonia. Had I tempted fate? No one in the family said as much, but it played on my mind, what, if anything, could I have done differently? It tortured me. Late at night, I would sit in his room looking at him wrapped up in bed, so innocent, an innocence he would never lose. A crumbling marriage, a son I couldn't protect – yes, I had changed. I had good cause; who wouldn't?

My wife and I met a few years prior to my joining the job; by the time I had ten years' service, we had agreed to go our separate ways. I have no intention of dissecting the whys and the wherefores; shit happens, we separated and later divorced. In both our defence, the pressures of raising a disabled son, not to mention triplets, would have tested the strongest of marriages. In a blink I would find myself homeless, single and broke, Life, however, does not stand still. Now more than ever, I needed to work hard, do my job and pay the bills.

What my family didn't appreciate was how unforgiving I had now become. I was tough on myself and tough on those around me. I hated people making excuses or whining about their lot in life; I stepped up, and so should they. This harshness manifested itself, both at work and in my personal life. After chasing down a suspect in Ledbury Road, the lad I was with bent over and then fell to his knees exhausted. The fact he was years younger than me and overweight filled me with anger; I told him to get up. "What the fuck is wrong with you? Never show weakness on the street, NEVER." He looked at me expecting sympathy; he found none. On another occasion, I was responding to a call that abruptly got cancelled. Turning off the lights and two tones, I turned into a side street; coming directly towards me was a funeral procession, like something out of the Krays. Huge black horses, the guys with the top hats and a cast of thousands following on foot. My operator suddenly looked at me and said he wanted to throw up; he had been out drinking the night before, and me throwing the car around had left him rather queasy. I looked at him, I looked at the funeral procession and told him in no uncertain terms that he would not be throwing up in the street in front of all these mourners. My solution, "use your fucking hat," I was deadly serious. He picked up his shiny flat cap and threw up the contents of his stomach. The funeral procession passed; I nodded my head in respect. In the old days I would have saluted, but no one saluted anymore. The smell in the car was toxic, as was my mood; I drove my operator back to the Hill and exchanged him for one that wasn't a total clusterfuck.

How we portray ourselves is vital in the day-to-day struggle, trying to win hearts and minds. Policing by consent, as it's fondly known. The one thing a cop cannot be is weak. Weak in the face of hostility, weak in his decision-making. We are meant to turn up and fix shit while everyone else is running around like headless chickens. 'Keeping face' was a Japanese concept that applied equally as well in the Dojo as it did on the street. Karate taught me how to conceal pain or fear, to control my emotions, and to remain in balance. This 'keeping face' offered no chink in your armour to your enemy. Once, when I got kicked in the stomach and felt like all my internal organs had been suddenly vacuum-packed, I kept it together, somehow; 'I kept face.' The same attitude was present when all my bottom teeth were punched out; my reaction was to smile a toothy grin at my opponent and ask, "Is that it?" I knew the importance of poise under pressure; I prided myself on never, ever flapping on the radio or when dealing with an incident. The French have a word for someone who embodies this ethos, panache. I would be the embodiment of panache, a certain style, no matter how much shit was hitting the fan.

My body and mind were strong for a very good reason. During my many years of karate training, I pushed myself to my absolute limit. I fought the biggest and the best. I competed in championships with no weight categories and won. I faced my fears and demons daily; in doing so, I learnt to cope with the stress, the ups and downs that life throws your way. Taking up karate so young and having a somewhat romanticised view of how men should behave, I embraced the martial values of strength, dignity and poise under pressure, all of which I learnt through hard training. I learnt about humility, I learnt about loyalty, and I learnt the value of a person's character. Take these values and shove them inside a police uniform, and you got me, not that I always lived up to them, but I tried.

Being a copper on the streets is a rollercoaster ride. Going to work each day, never knowing what's coming your way, is one of the best things about the job. The downside to this conveyor belt of highs and lows is that you often have little or no time to get your head around what you're dealing with and its impact. I was lucky; my ability to keep on taking these little shocks to the system and laughing them off kept me sane. My pension was my pot of gold at the end of the rainbow; it was one of the few things I had to look forward too. I chose not to dwell upon the bad stuff or try to process events; better still, put all the chaos and all the pain in a box marked too difficult and move on. This strategy comes at a price; it did help that I loved what I was doing for a living; the years I patrolled the streets of Notting Hill were some of the best years of my life. Eventually, however, you pay the price.

WATCH AND REACT

THE LONG GOODBYE

In the summer of 2003, I was posted to SO19. I applied to join the previous year, and after much jumping through hoops, I was finally accepted. The selection process was lengthy, involving a written application with a paper sift. The application was to be handwritten, your answers to fill the space provided and no more. My paperwork was infamous across the borough for being terrible, I needed some help, and this I found in the form of a female colleague whose handwriting was a thing of beauty. Add to that she could spell, something that had alluded me until the introduction of computers; even then, my dyslexic attempts often left Google spell check baffled. Next came the board, an interview in two parts, first a practical assessment followed by an interview.

The big day arrived, the first part being a paper feed exercise, run by two ARV instructors, which was pretty intimidating, I have to say. The Sergeant had a face that wouldn't go amiss on Crime Watch, and the other, a PC, looked at me like I'd met his mum on Tinder, whatever that is. I was not feeling the love. I was handed a map book and asked to read a document detailing a theoretical incident involving a stabbing with a victim, suspects, witnesses, and street locations. The document overwhelmed me with information; it was meant to. Once I had finished reading, the pair started hitting me with one question after another. Each answer I gave was challenged, attempting to see if I would buckle or fight my corner. I was tested on police powers and policy, my knowledge of first aid, my map reading, "Find an RVP for Trojan, and "show us where you would land the air ambulance." They tested my ability to think on my feet; to say it was intense was an understatement. The scenario eventually concluded. I was about to take a deep breath when bam, double bam, the PC thanked me and then said, "Ok, it's now real-time; we have arrived on scene. The Skipper wants a full IIMARCH over the bonnet briefing. Go." More of IIMARCH later, but to the uninitiated, it's a standardised format for briefing an operation beloved of the Met.

I information, I intention, M method, A administration, R risk assessment. C communications, H human rights.

The briefing was as stressful as they hoped it would be. Upon finishing, I asked, "Any questions?" I wasn't prepared for the deluge that hit me. What struck me was the detail they expected, and what about the contingencies, the "what if' factor? Even if I had failed, I would have left that office with some good lessons learnt; every day's a school day at 19. With a hint of sarcasm and a smile, I was told I was now about to be boarded next door, so best I jog on. Ah, the warmth of firearms instructors, a breed apart. I walked along the corridor, taking a few moments to collect my thoughts, knocked and entered. Sitting behind a desk were a Chief Inspector, an Inspector, and a very smart-looking lady who informed me she was head of personnel at 19. I took a seat, and so it began. Questions about my career up to this point. They asked about courtroom experience and if I had given evidence at coroner's court. They asked questions on legislation and then the big ones: why I wanted to join SO19 and what I would bring to the party. Did I realise what I was letting myself in for? After each of my responses, the interviewing panel would scribble a note in their pads and then look at me very seriously. All apart from the personnel lady who smiled a lot and didn't seem to write much down.

Then, like a moth to the flame, she hit me with, "What does diversity mean to you? Can you give me some examples of when you have challenged inappropriate behaviour and the outcomes? Ho lee Fuck, I thought she liked me; I tried not to squirm in my seat. The faces of the two senior officers in front of me were a picture. If I could have seen the thought bubbles over their heads, they would have read, "Ok, smart arse, get out of that shell hole." I took a deep breath, calmed my nerves and did what everybody does at some point in a job interview: I was a tad economical with the truth. By the time I had finished, Hollywood wanted the script, the personnel lady wanted my kids, and the two senior officers stared back at me wondering if even half of this is true; I should be the next Commissioner. The interview concluded, as I waited to be released, the Chief Inspector said, "Unusual choice of tie if you don't mind me saying. "Not at all, sir; it's my lucky tie."

"A purple Barney the Dinosaur tie is your lucky tie."

"Yes, sir, it's a family thing."

I didn't go into detail, but Cal loved that bloody dinosaur. When Cal got ill, which he did a lot when he was very little, the only thing that would calm him down was watching Barney. I would take him downstairs, turn on a video, place him between my legs and nod off as Cal chuckled away to the music and dancing. One day, out of the blue, I saw the tie in a shop and just had to have it; I knew it would bring me luck.

The panel smiled back at me, and with that I was out the door. I didn't have a clue if I had passed or not. I knew one thing: they wouldn't forget me, the guy with the Barney Dinosaur tie. A week or two passed before I got the call giving me the good news, I had passed and informing me of

WATCH AND REACT

my course dates. To say I was ecstatic would be an understatement; the failure rate for 19 applicants was the stuff of legend. To have made it onto a course filled me with pride. However once that initial feeling had worn off, the reality of what I had let myself in for started to become clear. First a Glock course; if successful, then onto an ARV course, and if I passed that, then a search course. Then, and only then, could you call yourself an ARV officer. I told myself one step at a time, don't think too far ahead; that's how you screw up. What I didn't appreciate was that the course, no matter how brilliantly it's run, only teaches you the basics that allow you to sit in a car and patrol London. What you do when you get boots on the ground, well, that amigo is all up to you. Them's the rules, and it will forever be so.

Back at the Hill, my success was met with much piss-taking and friendly leg-pulling. I had passed where others, many others, had failed, so no matter what happened in the future, at least I couldn't be accused of taking the easy option. Which brings me to what prompted my change in career path. One sunny summer's day, I was sat on the bonnet of the area car catching some rays when a skipper from the proactive unit approached me. We had never spoken before, but I had heard only good stuff about him. He was tall with cropped black hair, athletic-looking and always dressed immaculately. He was a pretty cool guy who had worked several squads around the Met and would go on to higher rank and even more prestigious roles. We spoke for only a couple of minutes, but in that time, in his soft calm voice, he pointed out to me that I was treading water: I was the big fish in a small bowl. Was driving the area car all I ever wanted to achieve in my career? He said some nice stuff about the way I operated on the street but reminded me it was easy for me now; the challenge was met, and it was time for a new one. As he walked off, half of me wanted to shout out something abusive, but the other half was hurting. The skipper was spot on.

I had got comfortable, too comfortable, it was time to move on. So, Skip, if you ever read this, thank you. Within a few months, I had passed my ARV course and got my start date. More of the course later. Leaving the Hill after 12 years was huge. I had made so many friends, built a reputation for myself and knew the ground inside out. I loved going to work, and even though it would be fair to say my private life was a mess, professionally I was firing on all cylinders. The ability to leave your bullshit at home and not let it interfere with your job was never something I had much trouble controlling. I learnt a long, long time ago that everyone has a story; yours isn't so special. Your average relief will have guys and girls who are divorced, unhappily married, having affairs, drinking too much, court cases to fight regarding child access or maintenance (and that was just me). Then you have the ones with sick kids, parents dying or a loved one with cancer; the list goes on and on. So, like I said, what makes you and your problem so special? The public don't care when they dial 999 for help. The jury in court don't care, and Mrs Miggins, whose cat is stuck up a tree, doesn't care because guess what, they've got shit going on too. The wise copper puts their problems somewhere nice and tidy out of the way; when they book on for duty, there isn't time for a hug and a bean bag session. Like I said, my private life was a mess, but I kept it under wraps, and as the good book says, "Suck it up, son, suck it up."

My final few tours of duty were full of nostalgia. Each street I drove down was a fond memory, a foot chase, a stabbing, a domestic, a pursuit, a punch-up. So much confrontation, so much experience hard-earned. I didn't appreciate it fully at the time, but I had been truly blessed

WATCH AND REACT

to arrive at the Hill when I did. I arrived, a green FNG, and left a daddy. Not my words, thank God; my skipper at my leaving drink decided on that epithet. In true Met tradition, I got wrecked, as one should, spent a fortune buying everyone drinks and eventually passed out unconscious on some bin bags outside the Notting Hill Arts Club. "You're a legend, Healy," I was told more than once. If only they knew the real me; the truth is I was already yesterday's news, to be replaced by younger officer's keen to fill my shoes. I wished them well. I came in on my day off, emptied my locker, and with one last look back, I was gone. 19, here I come.

TOP GUN, BACK TO SCHOOL

Milton is home to the Met's firearms training. It is here that anyone who wishes to be an AFO, an Authorised Firearms Officer, must first come and pass their 'shots course.' It doesn't matter what firearms path you choose, be it ARV, diplomatic protection, aviation security or indeed rifleman, better known to the public as a sniper. Before you can call yourself, a shot and carry your blue card (the little blue book that details your firearms authorisation), you must first get past the instructors at Milton. Up until recently you could only become a firearms instructor if you came from within 19. This meant that the instructors all had the common bond of serving on the ARVs. This cadre of instructors produced superb firearms officers; I can say this without fear of contradiction. Over the 18 years I 'carried' (firearms slang for being a shot), I have worked with some of the most dedicated, switched-on and highly motivated people you would ever care to meet in any walk of life.

Now may be a good time to give a very brief potted history of armed policing in London. Prior to 1991, a small number of borough officers were trained in the use of firearms and basic tactics. If a spontaneous firearms incident occurred, suitably trained officers would rush back to the station and book out a Smith and Wesson revolver. That is after obtaining suitable authority from a senior officer. This all took time, putting the public at risk. The Met finally concluded that armed support to unarmed colleagues and the public had to be addressed. A course was designed, officers trained, and by the summer of 1991, the first ARV rolled out the gates of Old Street. Crewed by three officers, this mobile armoury provided round-the-clock firearms support to every borough in the capital. The safe held two MP5s; the crew were armed with revolvers. Soon these would be replaced by the Glock 17. These first ARV officers had no blueprint to guide them; they made it up as they went along, building a reputation as dynamic, aggressive problem solvers. Over the following decade, tactics were refined, the numbers of ARV officers grew, and 19's reputation went from strength to strength. Ok, back to the plot.

The Milton training facility is based in Kent, just outside Gravesend. A charming location twinned with Chernobyl. The choice of the location was a drag, being miles from London, wasting valuable training time, having to travel to and from. To add to its charm, it was built beside a railway line, a cement factory, industrial units and the Thames. The Met, being the Met, cut costs by giving away half of the facility to Public Order Training (riot training). What should have been a state-of-the-art, purpose-built firearms establishment, solely for the training of armed officers, was, with one fell swoop, cut in half like a bloody big cake. This compromise would create huge issues further down the road as 19 grew and grew but didn't have the facilities to cope with the increased number of ARV courses, let alone continuation training for the reliefs. As a result, ARV reliefs were shipped all over the South Coast, housed in ever more expensive hotels close to the military bases they now trained at. Once again, the Met's inability to plan for the future would end up costing them dearly.

Milton opened its doors in 2003; it comprised sleeping accommodation, a canteen, classrooms, ranges, gyms, the worst bar in the UK and 'the site.' The site is a mock-up of houses and street furniture that mimic everyday street scenes across the country. The site allows for the armed containment of buildings, vehicle options and pedestrian foot strikes, all to be carried out under the watchful eyes of the instructors. These three strands, buildings, vehicles and pedestrians, are the bread and butter of ARV work. The ARV course teaches you the tactics and skill set to deploy onto the streets of London with loaded firearms 'ready to deal.'

I arrived at Milton for my ARV course on a Sunday evening. I collected the keys to my room and set off in search of my new digs. I knew what to expect because I had already attended my Glock course, as it was called in those days. So here I was again, round two. As I entered my room, I saw my new roomie sitting on the bed nearest the window, the best bed, not a good start. My bed was the one nearest the door. We exchanged pleasantries; my new roomy was called Mike. He was married; he was once a Royal Marine; he worked in Hackney as a PC; and he had just failed the ARV course but had been invited to try again. This was about as rare as my dad pitching up for parent's evening sober. I quickly came to realise why Mike was offered a second chance when so many others were not. Mike was one of the most genuine people you would ever care to meet. The instructors loved him, and so did we, the students. Mike was as posh as he was huge; we should have had nothing in common, but we hit it off from the moment we met. Our ability to laugh at ourselves and take the piss out of one another would serve us well over the coming weeks. I was older than Mike, but this didn't get in the way; we soon became very good mates. I owe him a huge debt of thanks for helping me pass the course. Each time I had a mare, as in nightmare, or got a bollocking, I would return to my room to find Mike lying naked on his bed or, worse still, on mine, with a tale of woe from his course that was far worse than my moment of madness. Remember he once said, "In the land of the blind the one-eyed man is king." Wise words indeed, but could you please not piss in the sink? For some reason, police officers see a sink in a bedroom as ensuite facilities, especially for anyone who couldn't be bothered to traipse to the toilets at 2 am.

Mike remained for a second course and went on to qualify. In my humble opinion, one of the main reasons he was successful was his attitude. He passed the unwritten rule all instructors ask of a student, "Would I be happy to sit on an ARV with that guy or girl?" The answer was a resounding yes. Mike was pure gold; like all of us, he made mistakes, but he was sound, someone to have at your side. He learnt from his mistakes; if you wanted to pass, you had to. The instructors were constantly probing to see what made us tick. As the course progressed, they raised the stakes; it was a steep learning curve. We had so much to learn and only four weeks to get up to speed. Inevitably some crumbled; that's just the way it is.

Day one, week one, a meet and greet in the classroom. At 8 am I found myself sitting in a room with 11 other hopefuls. We 12 eyed each other nervously; apart from Mike, I didn't recognise a soul. Without warning, the instructors marched in. They lined up in front of the whiteboard and smiled back at us, and guess what, they were rather a friendly bunch. Sadly, this mood did not last long; the Sergeant now entered and joined the instructional staff. He was about 40 years of age, tanned with jet black hair; he introduced himself as Sergeant J. Sergeant J welcomed us, then introduced his team. He then went on to explain that joining SO19 was the pinnacle of an officer's career. He expected the highest standards in everything we did. The rules were laid down, the classroom would always remain immaculate, our uniforms always clean and pressed, and boots polished; the schedule was tight, and lateness was totally unacceptable. If we drove to locations outside of the facility, anyone caught falling asleep in a car would be gone the same day. Our dealings with staff at the facility were always to be polite and professional; we were on show, and we were always being watched, on or off duty, and that included the gym and the bar. No one said a word; all eyes were fixed on J, who had one very striking feature: one of his ears stuck out like a wing nut. We would soon learn his nickname was OBE, one big ear. Not that any of us would have dared use it. J then introduced the Inspector who led the training team. He surveyed the group and wished us well before informing us he was off to Africa, joking as he left that most of us wouldn't be here when he returned. Ouch!!!!!

On the table in front of us were blue folders in which all material concerning our performance would be stored. If you did something wrong, you would receive a comment sheet. Rumour had it two red ink comment sheets and you were history. Over the next four weeks, we would learn to dread coming into the classroom and opening the blue folder. OBE laid out the format for the next four weeks, and without further ado, we were up and running. Now any ARV officer reading this will have their own story of how their course was run. Over the years, 19 has changed just about everything that can be changed. All to select the most likely people to pass the course. This in the hope that they will improve the pass rate, but as I write, I am reminded that a recent course had a 100% failure rate, so much for reinventing the wheel.

The course and its structure have been tinkered with so many times that you can sit in a car with your crew, and not one of you has gone through the same process. The skill sets taught are the same, but the similarity ends there. To put it bluntly, ARV courses cost a lot of money, putting twelve officers through the now nine-week course only for a few to pass upsets the top brass, pen pushers and bean counters. In their defence, they haven't been there; they don't appreciate that being a Trojan officer is unique. Not everyone is cut out to carry a gun; it's an environment where life-changing, split-second decisions are made daily. Every call you run to has a critical incident stamped all over it. 19 is the sharp end of firearms, and all other firearms commands fully accept this. Officers go to Heathrow and carry a firearm; officers go to the Diplomatic Protection group and carry a firearm. These roles are vital, but it's not responding to armed criminality or terrorism anywhere inside the Met and, on some occasions, outside it. 19 is the ultimate test of your determination to perform at the highest level; it is a very unforgiving environment. Only a fool would want it any other way.

What follows are a few highlights from my course.

Sometimes the training would take an odd turn. Training at Uxbridge RAF, all the students had to share a dormitory for the duration. As we commenced unpacking, one of the instructors marched in, called a name, and out our colleague went, only to reappear twenty minutes later, red-faced and not very chatty. I was next up, "Healy." I left the safety of the dorm and followed the instructor to an office. As I walked in, I was faced by six instructors, all seated in a horseshoe formation. I was asked to take a seat facing them, not intimidating in the least! I'm not sure how long I was questioned, but time did not fly by, I can tell you. It was time for the proverbial Met Police 'shit sandwich.' This involves telling you something good about your performance, the bread, then hitting you with a world of shit about you and your underperformance, the filling, and lastly something positive to leave you with some self-respect, the bread. A shit sandwich. It was brutal, and I returned red-faced and silent to the dorm, feeling sorry for my mates who still had it to come.

Why did they do it? God knows, theories abounded, one being that we as a group were doing way too well; our teamwork was getting us through. The instructors thought, not so bloody fast. Let's throw a hand grenade into this happy band and see how they deal with the fallout. God knows what the game was, but it bruised some egos and deflated the team, but only for as long as it took to get a few beers down us in the Sergeant's mess. On a personal level, this mind-bending exercise caught me off guard but only helped to steel my resolve to pass.

Bad admin is almost done for me, and a lad called Sam. We were so near the end of the course and passing out, that maybe we took our eye off the ball. Kitting up a car to go out on a vehicle exercise, we both thought the other had put the bag containing the 'stooge weapons' in the boot. The bag contained deactivated guns to be used by the instructors in the role plays later that day. On this occasion, a shotgun and a couple of revolvers. When we stopped to get petrol in Gravesend, one of the team asked about the bag. That was the moment both Sam and I had seizures. Sod the petrol; we drove at warp factor 10 back to Milton into the yard to find the bag full of guns sitting on the wall where we left it. If it had been discovered, we would have been out the gate that night. Ok, they were deactivated and inside a secure police location, but so what? We had royally screwed up, no excuses. Thankfully, the Gods were with us that night.

The course was brutal in its treatment of failure. The open country search is a compulsory element, it's a good indicator of an officers' teamwork and fitness. The scenario commenced with two ARVs running to a job; the armed suspects drive into a car park located at a remote location. The Trojan officers carry out an armed stop; one or more of the suspects escapes into the countryside. The officers must now search for the armed suspects in dense woodland, moving tactically as they do so. It's no easy task, because along for the ride is a police dog and its handler, to assist with the tracking. Fido is off like a rocket; it's the officer's job to keep the pace relatively achievable by reining the dog in. and the enthusiastic handler. Dressed in boots and body armour, carrying an MP5 and belt rig, it's a challenge. Of course, the dog drags you up and down Dale until at last, you get a 'contact,' which invariably involves someone getting shot.

Now we get to the good bit: the team carried out first aid on the wounded person, all of which is assessed; next, roll out a stretcher from the first aid kit, and once the wounded party is strapped in, it's up and at 'em. The team casevac'd the injured party back to the RVP and a waiting ambulance. Six people run with the stretcher; the remaining officers run alongside, providing armed security, rotating roles, as officers tire, or so you would hope. The day after the open country search, we were told to be in the gym at 7 am for PT. Everyone attended, and we were duly beasted for an hour or so before breakfast. However, at the end of the gym session, four of our course were invited to sit in the canteen and await the training staff. Four instructors duly arrived, each holding the student's dreaded training folder; this was going to end badly, and within the hour, the four were off the course. Why? What was their crime? The training staff had filmed the open country search and identified that these four officers had avoided carrying the stretcher, letting their teammates suffer as a result. That was it for them; in the eyes of the instructors, they were not the right types to sit in an ARV. Maybe these four were already on the instructor's radar; maybe the stretcher run was the final straw, confirming their unsuitability. As for me, I gave 100% every day, kept my mouth shut and hoped for the best.

Whilst in a containment position watching a house with an armed suspect inside, I became aware an instructor was approaching. I had all my answers ready. I am at point 2, black/red containment. I had an escape route planned; I knew where my nearest support was if I need help. I had a surrender plan if the suspect came out. I hear the instructor beside me, "Don't look at me, Healy."

"My kids do karate; don't think because you wrote a book on the subject that anyone is impressed."

"Absolutely not."

"Ok then, I said, don't look at me." With that, he was gone, was he pulling my leg, probably, well that told me! Little interactions like this happened daily, leaving me bewildered as to my progress. No one ever patted you on the back or gave you a big thumbs up. This lack of positive feedback is totally at odds with society today. Young people seem to crave a constant flow of positivity and affirmation; 19 did not function on those lines. Debriefs brought up learning points, lessons were learnt, no one was fist bumping. The Friday one-to-one with an instructor always made me smile. Sat facing one another in the canteen, my weekly appraisal went something like this: "Keep doing what you're doing; get some rest at the weekend. Big week next week." That was it. Fortunately for me, I had low expectations; my Karate instructors were men of few words, and those were mainly in Japanese. I knew not to expect praise; in fact, quite the opposite was true. If your Sensei was beating you black and blue, it usually meant you had promise, but don't expect a big hug and a balloon.

One of the best days on the course, for me anyway, was on the range, firing from vehicles. The range was huge and allowed ARVs, two BMW saloons, to manoeuvre at speed and engage targets. If the Alpha car broke right, Bravo broke left and vice versa. Depending on where you were sitting, you could find yourself engaging a target with live rounds from inside the vehicle or 'bugging out' – getting out of the vehicle and finding suitable ballistic cover, be it over the bonnet or behind the engine block. This officer would now engage the target, getting some rounds downrange. This cover fire allowed the rest of the crew to get the hell out of the car. It's fast, and it's dangerous with lots of moving parts. Heaven forbid you move with your selector lever to fire or sweep a buddy. It was pure adrenaline; everyone was soaked with sweat by the end of the exercise. Years later, an ARV would arrive on the scene at the murder of Lee Rigby and use the same training drills to save their lives. Just another reason 19 was 19: the training was second to none. Testing your shooting, tactics, use of cover and weapons handling.

Live fire, cover and movement, this is the one day on the course that really ups the ante. Moving in pairs up and down the range, to and from cover whilst engaging the targets with live rounds. It's intense but fantastic fun. Weapons handling is everything; never move with your selector to fire, always know the condition of your weapon, dealing with stoppages and tac reloads, identifying cover before you move, and of course, make sure you hit the bloody target. It's noisy; everyone is shouting "COVERING, MOVING", "STOPPAGE, BACK IN", "MOVING". The atmosphere on the range is electric but pray to God no one goes off script. When it's over, you can see the staff breathing a collective sigh of relief. This exercise really does pressure test your skill set; you cannot switch off, not for one second; it's that intense. I loved every second of it; we all did.

WATCH AND REACT

The final memory I shall share is perhaps the moment I feel I was accepted into the fold; someone the instructors would choose to work with. Those of us who remained after the Open Country search were told to parade in the Dojo. We had no idea what awaited us. The instructors filed in along with the Inspector who had disappeared off to Africa. This should have set a few alarm bells ringing, but of course it wouldn't have helped if it did. So commenced the hardest gym session I can remember. We punched the bag, did sprints, squats, rugby tackled the punch bags, wrestled, did more sprints, sit-ups followed by push-ups until you couldn't move your arms. On and on it went, no water breaks, no let-up; the beasting had no end. Pushed on by the training staff, each one of us in our own personnel hell. Suddenly it stopped; we were ushered into a tiny room, and the door slammed shut behind us. We sat in silence, staring at one another. Suddenly booming dance music was drowning out our heavy breathing; the noise was ridiculously loud, the music awful. The door opened, and M was dragged out. He did not return.

The door opened, a hand grabbed my arm, someone put goggles on me, which were blacked out; I couldn't see a thing. The noise, the goggles, the exhaustion left me disorientated, and that was just what they wanted. Someone shouted, "Defend yourself," and with that, I was hit in the chest, then the back; a hand went to grab the training Glock in my holster. As per my training, my right hand dropped to protect my sidearm while I fended off my invisible attackers with my left. More hits to the chest, back and legs, not full on but enough to make you react. The noise was deafening; I was shouting, "Get back, get back." More attempts to grab my gun, the strikes getting harder and with fewer intervals in between. It was like being in a karate class; I kept on my toes shouting the police mantra "Get back, get back," when in reality I wanted to shout, "Come on then, and your fucking mates." I had trained against multiple attackers on a host of occasions, though, in truth, never blindfolded and never with the 'Now that's what I call disco 98' CD playing at max volume. The hits kept coming faster and harder, and I don't mean from that bloody CD. I was beginning to tire; out of nowhere, I was grabbed in a bear hug and ran backwards and smashed into the padded wall. 20 years of karate now came to my rescue; I managed to get an arm free and struck my attacker in the face with a palm heel strike. I hit the plastic face guard; he was wearing a protective 'fist suit.' I now went full Jean-Claude Van Damme, smashing elbow strikes and palm heels into his face. BANG, I dropped in a head butt. All my strikes were making contact; I felt my attacker physically weaken and then fall backwards to the floor. I was on top of him in a flash, totally in the zone, striking full power to the head, my attacker pinned beneath me. Blow after blow I rained down until he lay limp, offering no resistance.

I felt hands grabbing at my body armour; I was pulled violently up and backwards, but I was still in the fight, ready to go on. I was going down fighting. It was then someone had the good sense to pull the goggles off; I was surrounded by the instructional staff. Someone shouted, "YAME, YAME, STOP." I put my feet together and bowed. That's muscle memory for you. To a man, the instructors were pissing themselves. Some clapped, some bowed, everyone was smiling; that is, apart from the poor guy on the ground. I stood and watched as the padded helmet was removed. Shit, it was OBE, and he did not look a well man. The test was over; I was sent to wait in the canteen. Looking back, to my mind that was the moment I passed my ARV course, not that I knew it at the time, sitting dreading seeing OBE later.

My last taste of 19 humour was typical of the department that I love. It's the final day; we surviving students are sat in the canteen waiting to discover our fate. My name was called, I made my way into a small office where six instructors sat, stony-faced. I was asked to take a seat and handed a comment sheet, the dreaded comment sheet, every word of it typed in bloody red ink. I was crushed. I sat staring at the sheet of paper. Fuck reading it, I thought. What's the point? Reading my mind, one of the instructors told me to read the document. Line after line pointed out a mistake; I was crestfallen. Then I got to the last couple of lines, which gave me the news I had passed; this was them having a wee bit of fun. I looked up from the sheet; they were all smiling. I wanted to cry; the relief overwhelmed me. We shook hands, and some nice words were exchanged. I walked out the door a nervous wreck, but a Trojan nervous wreck.

That, ladies and gents, was my course and my welcome to life on 19. It was maybe the proudest day of my life. As a footnote, the skipper who ran the course was brilliant with me after the Dojo incident. He was tough, uncompromising and typical of the skippers on 19, back in the day. He kept every one of us on our toes; you never switched off because if you did, he would appear as if by bloody magic, and your day would get a whole lot more 'interesting.' The training team was fantastic, but two stood out: Neil and Martin, both SFOs attached to ARV courses. They were funny, chilled-out individuals with nothing to prove. They made learning an enjoyable experience, constantly pointing you in the right direction. They got you to think outside the box, to use your initiative. They knew that very soon we would be set free on an unsuspecting London, and we had to be ready.

WATCH AND REACT

WAY BACK WHEN

It probably makes sense if I put some structure to the SO19 I joined in those long-gone days of 2003. The department has changed so much that new guys and girls joining today would barely recognise the ARV world I joined. Ok, where to start? Recruitment: applications went out once a year, and the lucky few, and it was the few who made it, eventually landed on relief. The reliefs ran from A to F. Recruitment being once a year and failure rates being very high meant that once you landed on a team, you could be the new kid on the block for quite some time. In my case, just under a year. That's a long time running the tea club, especially if you have 12 years in the job and you're no spring chicken. Fortunately, my ego was firmly in check when my new skipper, also called Kevin, asked my length of service and if I was an advanced driver; I was ready for a knockback. Though I didn't expect him to pinch my cheek so hard that it bruised, he informed me in no uncertain terms, "Don't even think about getting in the driver's seat." Radios or maps, that was me for the next few months.

The relief was run by one Inspector, call sign Trojan One. He was ably supported by a cadre of Skippers. Two Sergeants based North at Leman Street and two at the South base, Trojan 97.97 was a deactivated police station, not open to the public, a station completely unfit for purpose, located on a housing estate in Clapham. Leman Street, call sign Trojan 99, was where it all happened. Set over 5 floors, it housed the senior leadership team; it was the home of the SFOs (Specialist Firearms Officers); this was before they became CTSFOs. The building had a firing range, kit stores, locker rooms, several gyms, admin offices, an intel unit and the legend that was Dave Mate the armourer. So-called because he called everyone mate; do try and keep up. This man was a walking, talking encyclopaedia on firearms. He fixed what we broke and gave many a new ARV constable wise words of advice on making a weapon safe. These are the days before you could Google or YouTube how to unload an Uzi or Mac 10. Also living the dream at 19 was the duties office, which shared floor space with the personnel department.

The building was overcrowded and hectic. The department's growth spurts had swamped the small building; it was not uncommon to be standing in a corridor talking to a colleague when two of your team would amble past, naked except for the world's tiniest bath towels, which appeared compulsory on 19. Because of this overcrowding, you quickly got to know everyone, which added to the great sense of camaraderie; you were part of something special, a small elite group. The nerve centre of 99 was the base room, staffed by a Skipper who was a Tactical Advisor (TAC AD) supported by a base PC, and that was it. Between them, they answered the multitude of phone calls from squads needing armed assets, SFO operations and ARV calls coming out over the main set. The Skipper gave Tac advice on the phone to Uncle Tom Cobbly and all, whilst the base PC made the tea, answered the phones, directed the cars to calls and gave updates on tactics, etc. The base room was hectic; when a few jobs were running north or south or both, you could feel your brain starting to melt. To add to my confusion, nicknames were the norm; being asked to call up Magic, PT, Johnny Orange or Ecky made life difficult to start with. Sadly, the base room is no more, moved to a secure central location, staffed by a team that would fill the deck of the Starship Enterprise. With its removal went the heart of the building; back in the day, it was buzzing with gossip, rumour and the latest news on jobs. Even though I thought I would hate it, I loved my 6-

week posting that all newbies got on arrival. One Sunday afternoon the phone rang; I answered, the woman on the other end was not in a good place. "Is that the base Sergeant? Can you call up to the SFO office and tell my husband X that if he does not come home this week, not to bother coming home ever again?" I informed the base Skipper; he told me to hold the fort as he ran up to the third floor to speak in person. That was not the last call I took of that nature; 19 really did become some officers surrogate family.

North officers were called Northies, and so it followed that South officers were called Swampies, South London being perceived to lack critical infrastructure such as fast roads, Starbucks and Leicester sq. If Trojan 99 was the Hilton, then Trojan 97 was Fawlty Towers. The good-humoured banter between the two bases goes back to early cave paintings. The North officers would argue they went to more calls, stayed out on patrol longer, and were generally more professional and competent than their brothers and sisters from the South. The South base officers would respond with, yes, you may run to more calls, but South ones tend to be the real deal. I was never sure if either side was right; in truth, it mattered not. The rivalry was good fun and kept everyone on their toes. However, bring the two halves together at training or on a job, and the team worked like clockwork.

Trojan 97 was a mess, a glorious mess, based in the old Clapham Police Station, which was no longer open to the public. The upstairs offices were used by squads, but we never saw them. The local home beats and PCSOs used rooms at the front of the building, and again, we had nothing to do with them. We, the South ARV Reliefs, were housed in the old custody suite area. The armoury where we stored our weapons, loaded and unloaded, was a cell.

My locker was a broken MFI wardrobe with no door. We had a small kitchen which was home to several mice and probably a few other nasties; needless to say, the kitchen was underused. The parade room doubled up as the TV lounge and resembled a 1970s living room with moth-eaten armchairs and worse-for-wear furnishings. Downtime was spent reading newspapers, watching DVDs and engaging in general banter, often directed towards the North. Mounted on the wall was a large animal skull with horns; God knows what creature it had been in a previous life; several arrows protruded from it at irregular angles. On first entering the base, I must admit, I loved the lack of corporate identity; the South Base was an anachronism, a throwback to better times.

In 2003, 19 ran five cars per shift, 3 North and 2 South, for a city with a population of 7.5 million people; as of writing, that number is now in the high twenties for a population nearing 9 million. Extra cars were put on if a borough was having abnormal issues with gun crime, to fly the flag, so to speak, or to cover an operation, but day to day, 5 cars covered London. That's just fifteen ARV officers; throw in the kit vans, (BMW estate, carrying shotguns, ladders, ballistic blankets and a host of other kit) both double crewed, that's just 19 armed officers facing everything and anything that can possibly come their way. This was a win-win in my opinion because never a day went by that didn't see you deploying to an armed incident. A normal day could drag you both north and south of the river to a dig out, a vehicle stop or siege, a foot strike or to support the SFO teams on a job. A busy day could see you doing a number of these tactics back to back. Dinner was often eaten at the roadside, hot refs (a hot cooked meal, preferably eaten sat at a table with a knife and fork) a joke.

By the time I retired, the proliferation of cars, the advent of 5 bases if you include Heathrow and the now hated phrase from the Pod, "not declared", meant you could go weeks without pointing your weapon at someone. This lack of activity can and does lead to de-skilling and apathy, traits you do not want to creep into armed ops. Back to 2003, In a word, it was bloody brilliant, amazing, better than it says on the tin. Did I mention it was bloody brilliant? Yes, brilliant. You deployed; you did what you were trained to do, backed up by supremely professional colleagues. What was even better, you would often be tidying up the scene, getting locals and the Duty Officer down to take over, and boom, another Trojan call on the main set, and, with a thumbs up to the local Skipper, we would be off. High tailing it to some unknown street in some corner of the Met, all three of you furiously multitasking, getting the details of the job, which car was running comms, what was the radio link, what was the map grid reference, did the driver have a clue where he was going otherwise, "can he slow the fuck down and give maps a chance?"

The dress code in 2003 was still traditional London bobby. We didn't wear hats or ties, but we did wear white shirts and Met-issue wool trousers. Compare that to today; what a contrast. Patrolling in body armour was not routine; the crews drove around with the 3 sets lying on the back seat. No one drove around fully kitted up; to be honest, if you did, the nickname Tackle Berry would have soon followed you. Each one of us was issued with a blue baseball cap known as a plot cap. On E relief they were called c… caps, and no one ever wore one. Staying with hats, I was getting into a containment position on a job in Sydenham when I heard a voice behind me. "Where is your hat? Get your hat on, NOW." It was ten o'clock in the bloody morning, on a busy bloody high street. Some clown in a flat was pointing a rifle at pedestrians, and some bigger clown was worried about my fucking hat. It was time for the famed Trojan diplomacy: "We don't wear fucking hats; now fuck off into cover, whoever you are." He was a borough Skipper, and proof if proof were needed, idiots do get promoted.

Finally, gun nut reader, we arrive at weapon platforms. In 2003 we hadn't yet gone all Seal Team Six. Firearms were firearms; the first time I heard the words 'weapons platform', an SFO instructor was teaching a class converting us to the new SIG 'weapons platform.' Someone foolishly asked what it was like in the cold; his response confirmed this lesson was a one-way street: "How the fuck do I know? Why don't you take it home and put it in your fridge?" Whoever said there's no such thing as a stupid question had never trained at Milton. I thought the department had invested in a Black Hawk helicopter, imagine my disappointment. I kept that to myself. The ARV officer routinely carried a primary weapon, the MP5 Carbine (carbine, a short barrelled rifle invented for cavalry), which fired 9mm rounds. The MP5 in my humble opinion was a fantastic bit of kit. Stripping and reassembly could be done blindfolded. It was indestructible, you couldn't break it. No tricky reassembly of gas parts and no recoil of note. I loved using the 5, it was perfect for the ARV role, with it's folding stock it was design perfection. On your hip, no leg holsters for nearly a decade. You wore a holster which secured your Glock 17. This also fired 9mm rounds. The Glock was carried in condition one, one in the chamber, loaded and ready to go.

Having never fired a gun in my life prior to my joining the department, I was amazed at the simplicity of the Glock. As with the MP5 it was engineered to be police proof. Though I was devastated to learn it wasn't made of Porcelain, bloody John McClane. The MP5 was placed in the safe; it wasn't loaded but had a mag inserted into the mag well.

You carried two spare mags on your belt, both 9mm, one for the Glock and one for the MP5. If you looked closely, you would have noticed most officers' holsters had strips of black adhesive tape attached, known as 'black nasty' (it stuck to bloody everything) this innocuous tape was a life saver. I have lost count of the times it was used to create an improvised chest seal on victims with sucking chest wounds. That was us. No Taser: nope, only the driver wore that box of tricks. To modern eyes we must have looked very conventional, and that is exactly what the politicians and the big brains at Scotland Yard wanted. Guns on the streets carried by cops just did not compute to them. If we were to be armed, we would bloody well still look like your traditional London bobby, and that was an end to it. The war on terror would change that mindset forever.

In time, the arrival of weapon-issuing officers and loading and unloading booths would come as a huge surprise. This to us was the world of the DPG, the Diplomatic Protection Group, as they were once known. Each day they would count out their rounds, charge their magazines, load and make ready, and at the end of the day, they would unload the magazine, etc. We were 19, we didn't need any of that tosh slowing us down; we got our own weapons, loaded and unloaded them unsupervised, and that was that. As for cars, no one ever went to a skipper and informed them they had found damage on the vehicle. The cars were battered, no one asked any questions, the state of the ARV fleet drove traffic skippers apoplectic, but no one cared what they thought. Staying on the cars, we drove BMW saloons and the legendary Vauxhall Omega. German engineering may have produced a brilliantly functional car; Vauxhall, on the other hand, gave us a car that was fast, had a mind of its own, and, if you hit a big enough bump, could end up on its roof. The computer on the BMW was programmed by a German scientist, intent on removing human error; by contrast, the Omega was programmed by an eighteen-year-old boy racer from Swansea out to impress his girlfriend. Obviously, everyone given the choice voted British when booking out a car.

The SFOs, Specialist Firearms Officers, inhabited a 'base room' on the third floor. In 2003 you could only become an SFO if you came from the ranks of the ARVs. Which made perfectly good sense to me. In those halcyon days they wore black coveralls; nowadays it's urban grey (if I am in error, forgive me). They carried an MP5 and Glock, but nowadays it could be lightsabres; they are constantly evaluating new, more sophisticated weapons platforms and kit. The ARVs live in the world of the spontaneous; the SFO's bread and butter is the pre-planned operation. However, their remit goes so much further: hostage rescue, counter-assault, marine operations, counter-terrorism and a great deal more I can't write about. In 2012, with the Olympics looming, the SFOs upskilled to a new accreditation, CTSFO. Counter-Terrorism Specialist Firearms Officers. In 2003, SFO instructors regularly taught on ARV courses as well as continuation training. This was fantastic for breaking down barriers; ARV officers interested in making the leap to the third floor actually trained with the very officers who had done it and who could pass on words of wisdom. Even though there was a lot of playful banter, they were approachable; a them-and-us culture did not pervade Leman St. One final observation, it was a widely held belief that to become an SFO you had to fulfil one if not two essential criteria, 'muscles or medals.' To put it another way if you wanted to join the 'Teams' best you were a gym monster or ex-military or both. I decided to keep my three years as boy scout under my hat.

Lastly, continuation training was all done on site at Milton. Arrive Monday afternoon, gone Tuesday by lunch. The two bases trained together and drank together; SFO instructors mixed with ARV instructors, making sure that we were getting up-to-date relevant training. We classified every twelve weeks, and overtime was mostly green ink. That's double time. It was always sunny, the commissioner loved us, and life was good. OK, I lied about the sunny bit, but life was good on the 19.

This was the SO19 I joined in the spring of 2003. I was 39 years of age, divorced, living in a 'job flat,' Johnson House, located in Ebury Square at the back of Belgravia police station. The flats have long since been demolished, the land sold to property developers, more's the pity. Three bedrooms, a threadbare sofa, a second-hand telly and a fridge containing bottles of beer, and my dear friend Jack Daniels – this is where I called home. I wasn't big on interiors in those days; if someone had suggested Feng Shui, I would have asked if it came with rice. Divorce can do that to a man; to say I travelled light was an understatement. Living alone, that flat was the sole witness to the highs and lows of my early years on the cars. Many were the nights I would roll in from work, grab a pack of beers from the fridge, slide down the nearest wall and ponder my career path, elated or crestfallen. All to the soundtrack of police cars screeching out of the Belgravia nick, two tones wailing, engines revving, and sometimes, if you listened very, very hard, you could hear me wailing too.

WATCH AND REACT

INDUCTION

Arriving at Leman Street, I met the guys who had passed the course with me. Each of us was clearly nervous, the awkward smiles and forced conversation a clear giveaway. The fact everyone, including the cleaner, was staring at us newbies added to the tension. This was our induction day; by the time I retired, I think new recruits got a week to settle in. We were afforded no such luxury. One of my new relief, Mr B, told me that on one of his rest days, he had dropped into the base to meet his team, who were on night duty, just to say hello and introduce himself. Within a few hours, he had check-zeroed his Glock and was out on a car taking calls. One of his team had gone sick, and his mentors thought, sod it, no time like the present. Trojan One agreed, Mr B rang his wife to say he wasn't coming home; he was doing a night duty. This can-do attitude earned him a tonne of brownie points with his team, though less so with his wife.

Talking of brownie points, as a new ARV officer, the value of your stock rose if you brought with you some respected credentials. Coming from the TSG, the Territorial Support Group, was a biggie. A huge swathe of the 19 officers had done their time on a borough and then moved on to 'the group', where they tended to get involved in a lot of confrontational policing. Which was great preparation for the next obvious career move, SO19. If you were not ex-TSG, you still had the ex-military route. 19 had its fair share of Paras, Marines and, would you believe it, Guardsmen. Being an ex-serviceman went a long way to getting you accepted, and if you were ex-TSG as well, you were a 'made man.' The only other fast track to being one of the lads was the borough where you worked. Inner or outer. If you were the area car driver from Tottenham, Hackney or Stokey, Stoke Newington, you were seen to have worked a tough inner; the same went for Brixton or the Hill. Mr B was a classic example of this, ex Guardsman, he did his time policing the G, as Hackney was known. I would soon learn he was an excellent ARV officer, unflappable and direct. However, if you worked an outer, the Richmond's', the Kingston's, etc., well, let's just say you probably had a little more to prove. Not fair, but that's just how it was.

The day commenced with meeting the Chief Superintendent. He was softly spoken and relaxed and did his best to put us at ease. He informed us of the fact he was an AFO(Authorised Firearms Officer) back in the day, so he understood the pressures we were volunteering to take on. He clearly was proud to lead the department and told us he expected that within five years we would be instructors or SFOs, and some of us both. 19 was not a department you left easily after fighting so hard to get in. As with all meets and greets, he wished us good luck and told us his door was always open. In the middle of the general chit-chat, he did unload the fact that SO19 was a world-renowned department, and if we didn't cut the mustard, we would be exiting stage right; there was no room for passengers on the 19.

Time now to sort out my admin, this was the day I changed my profile on the Met computer; no longer PC 266 BH, now I was 4335 SO. Thinking this rather dull, I added AN OFFICER OF GREAT DARING AND CHARM. Over the next eighteen years, this description of yours truly raised a few eyebrows in high places but made me a lot of friends along the way.

After the Boss, I was met by my mentors, who took me off for a wee chit-chat regarding expectations – theirs, not mine. In truth, Mick and Hugh were brilliant, both funny and charming and more than willing to help. They sorted my locker, my operational kit (Ops kit), and then went to the range to check zero on my Glock. This is the point at which you show your mentors you can shoot while you check the weapon works correctly. Now, 19 officers have their own personal issue Glock. "This is my Glock; there are many like it, but this one is mine." To say I was nervous is an understatement. Hugh was an instructor, and once we hit the range, his relaxed mood instantly changed. I was being assessed, and how I performed was going to go right back to the team I was joining. This wasn't my first rodeo; this is how the job works. Suck it up. What I thought would be ten rounds in your own time turned into an hour of shooting and drills. Pressure was applied, with Hugh and Mick watching my every move. Correcting my finger placement on the trigger, my grip, my draw, basically taking my shooting apart. By the end I was soaking with sweat, so much so that I could hardly pull the slide back to do a live round unload.

Departing the range, I went to clean my Glock; both followed and watched as I stripped, cleaned and reassembled the weapon. As I did so, they critiqued my performance, and they didn't pull any punches. A natural shot I was not; I lacked an essential tool: consistency. They approved of my fast shooting close-up, but my long-distance shooting was messy. This is the stuff from 20 metres and beyond. Yes, I hit the target, but I also threw a few rounds off. The rounds that did hit the target showed no group, no pattern; in their words, "like a wild woman pissing in the snow." More than a little downhearted, I set off home for the first of many soul-searching sessions. Now, on the surface, I appeared assured and confident, but this day one reality check was a shock. I was a published author, a 5th Dan in Karate, and I had made it on to the toughest police department in the country, SO19. I was a success story, right? Wrong. However much I portrayed myself as a happy-go-lucky individual, deep down I was always fighting the demons in my head. That little voice saying you're not good enough, you will be found out. These voices plagued me my whole career, an insecurity bred from a very dysfunctional childhood, I guess. It meant that I never felt I fitted in. Yes, I made friends, great friends. I loved the teamwork and comradeship but always felt I was on the edge, never completely secure. Today it's got a fancy name, Imposter Syndrome; it happens in all walks of life. I was far from unique; sadly, I didn't know it at the time. It may have saved me a few sleepless nights.

This feeling of being an outsider, manifested itself socially, when we, as a group, were off duty. I would always try and attend team drinks, leaving do's, etc., but I was never completely at ease; after an hour or two, I would slide off into the night. This was in no way a slight on my comrades, who I bloody loved being around, but remove the structure and hierarchy of work and my place in the food chain, and I was lost. Over the years my disappearing act became a joke on the team; they knew what to expect. Maybe they thought I wanted to avoid getting drunk and embarrassing myself, but I had been doing that for years, just not in front of them. In truth, I was and still am a social misfit, an outsider, just like being back at school and dreading those days when we went on outings, getting to wear our own clothes. I was often ashamed of my appearance, looking and feeling a total numpty, the butt of just one too many jokes. Poverty shamed me; feelings I can hide but never escape.

If you grow up in a home where violence is the norm, you grow up fast; you have no choice. My father often announced his return home from work by crashing the car into the garage doors drunk. This was our alarm bell to make ourselves scarce. If, however, he managed to get indoors before we fled, we then had to sit and witness the ritual of the flying dinner plate. Being the 1970s, my mother's attempts at keeping a meal warm, without burning it to a crisp, were less than successful. The gravy could easily have been the forerunner for No Nails. The evening would play out like so. My father would slump into his armchair; my mother would carry out a tray with a plate of meat, two veg and potatoes covered in a brown oil slick, the plate so hot it glowed red. My father, just about conscious, would stare bewildered at his evening meal, pick up the plate, burn his hands, then launch it at the wall where it would cling to the flock wallpaper, like a piece of modern art, sometimes for hours. Tracey Emin would later use this scene as inspiration for her work titled "What's for dessert, dear?" I joke now at this tragic scene played out in front of our young eyes, but it wasn't very funny at the time; to be honest, it broke my heart.

I tell my kids sanitised tales of my youth to amuse them. Secretly, though, I hope they gain some insight into the madness of my formative years. Through it all, my mother was a rock, always smiling, as fast as you like with a quip or one-liner. Nothing daunted her, like the time she attempted to make me a sleeping bag for my first Scout camp. She couldn't afford to buy me one, so using bed sheets, rubber matting and some bin liners, she set to work. Her design would later go on to be banned under the terms of the Geneva Convention. Camp arrived; I went to bed snug and warm; by morning I had to be helped out of my sleeping bag by the other scouts. I was so dehydrated from sweating all night inside my bin liner coffin. Mysteriously, it went missing, one of the leaders finding me a second-hand one. Or the time my mum knitted me a school jumper, she couldn't afford to buy five new ones. Trying it on, I looked and felt like I was wearing chainmail. It was so heavy I could hardly stand, and God forbid it got wet. She basically invented an early form of body armour. Hanging down just above my knees, I looked like a member of the Battle of Hastings re-enactment society. She would later sell the patent to Kevlar. It went down a treat at school, I can tell you.

I love my mum dearly; she tried so hard, and meant so well, all the time battling to keep our family unit alive, against a backdrop of violence and abuse that beggar's belief. This was how life played out; maybe all families behaved like ours. I learnt to cope; there wasn't much this kid couldn't bat off, with my big gob, and a healthy dose of sarcasm. These two defence mechanisms pissed off all the wrong people and resulted in yours truly attending the headmaster's office, for adjustment therapy, in the form of the cane. I treated each stroke as a badge of honour; this was my rite of passage and may explain my healthy mistrust of the teaching profession, knitting and Baden-Powell.

"The past is never dead. It's not even past".

YOU CAN NEVER MAKE A SECOND FIRST IMPRESSION

The day of my first shift arrived. That night I didn't sleep a wink, terrified I would miss my alarm; I was so wired I was out of bed and out the door before it rang. I entered the base and found it deserted; I headed upstairs to my locker, the room again deserted. It was at this point I decided to look at my watch; it read 4 am. Under stress the mind plays games with you; I was so focused on getting in early I hadn't even noticed I was the only person awake in London. For the next hour I sat in the locker room awaiting the arrival of my team and hoping no one from night duty would discover the early bird.

At the duly appointed hour, 0515, I headed for the armoury, got my Glock and went to the loading bay. I placed the mag in the mag port, released the slide and made ready, condition one. As I turned to walk away, Hugh, my mentor, appeared from nowhere and asked me to unload my Glock. Confused, I drew it from the holster, and as I did so, I noticed the mag wasn't secured properly. Inexplicably, I had caught the mag release button; I took it out of the magazine well and then proceeded to carry out a live round unload. As I pulled the slide back, thank God a 9mm round appeared from the chamber. Hugh smiled, "Ok, reload, and from now on, tap the bottom of the mag, give it a tug and be sure it's sighted properly, ok?" I reloaded my Glock under Hugh's watchful eye, calm and controlled, but my brain was screaming, What the fuck were you thinking? In all my training this had never happened, and it never happened again. What a start, and in front of my mentor. Later, over a coffee, Hugh added to my discomfort; if that Glock had not been loaded, I would have been up in front of Trojan One and possibly out the door. As crimes go, going on patrol with a weapon that isn't loaded, is pretty much at the top of the list. Over the course of my career, I heard of officers who committed this crime, and most of them bid 19 a fond farewell.

That first morning Hugh and Mick taught me how to kit up the car correctly. Body armour placed on the back seat. Radios, fresh batteries, kit bags containing your ballistic helmet (lid) and your field suit, a raincoat that didn't keep out the rain, but was great for concealing your MP5 if you were out in public, and not wanting to draw attention to yourself. Goggles attached to lid and lastly gloves. That was it; to say ARV officers travelled light was not an exaggeration. On gloves, everyone seemed to have a different style; some were on trial, some were from the distant past and some were straight out of Soldier of Fortune Magazine. Shooting in gloves was not compulsory but seeing as the MP5 got bloody cold in winter, it was advisable to wear them, lots of officers cut off the trigger finger and yes, it did look sexy, and yes I did.

One of the strangest items we took out with us, was a brown leather briefcase, that wouldn't look out of place on the arm of a city gent. Inside the case you found a map book and some radios. The first rule was checking the map book was in one piece. For some inexplicable reason, people ripped pages out; God knows why. It wasn't like you could use the sat nav because the cars didn't have sat nav. You quickly realised certain pages were more well-thumbed than others; you can guess the areas: Hackney, Tottenham, etc. On close inspection the cases were as battered as the map books. Kitting up the cars also involved checking the two MP5s and the mags in the safe, this was known as a hot handover, the 5s stayed in the cars. They were accessed via a metal trap door on the back seat. Turning the handle, the guns would slide forward on rails.

The designer of the safe clearly hated police because the safe was bloody deadly.

Every part of the sliding mechanism was razor-sharp; getting the guns out on a job, in a car being driven by an advanced police maniac, being thrown around like a rag doll was quite an experience. Over the next few months, I lost count of the times I cut my fingers or trapped them in the bloody safe. Loading the MP5s in a fast-moving car was no mean feat, the ARV course reflected this. Each student was placed in the back seat of an Omega and driven around Milton at daft speeds while the driver, an instructor, threw the car around. Over and over, you repeated the drill: get the guns out, check the safety catch, load them, make ready, condition one, hand one forward to your operator. I developed a set routine: tap the operator on the shoulder, await their acknowledgement, pass it forward muzzle down. Job over, you unloaded guns, put them back in the safe, and off you went again. Good job I liked roller coasters, because it was not uncommon to see green-faced officers crawl from the car on the verge of throwing up. Foolishly I thought, I'm ok; not so. Map reading would leave me a physical wreck after a long run to a call. Car sickness was the stuff of legend, and tales of 'maps' arriving on the scene, getting straight out of the car and throwing up in front of their borough colleagues were not uncommon. Did I do it? Yes, I did, and nothing helped. Boiled sweets, window open, lucky heather, car sickness tablets, etc., etc. – a total waste of time. As the new guy, I just knew I had to tough it out and suck it up, and I mean this quite literally.

The final bits of kit were absolutely essential: the first aid kit and ballistic shield. The ballistic shield was something I was used to using. Being short, I was often number one on a search team, commonly known as a stick. Number one

WATCH AND REACT

involved carrying the long shield, pointing your Glock and protecting the team behind you. Your number two, armed with an MP5, covered over your shoulder, so you really didn't want a number one that was too tall. Like everything over the years, the shield evolved; it's bigger and heavier; it's a lifesaver.

Last, but by no means least, was the first aid kit. Before you attend an ARV course, you must first attend a ballistic first aid course, and boy, this was intense. Well, it was if, like me, you couldn't open a box of plasters, let alone stop a catastrophic bleed. The two-day course was brilliant and got you prepped for the injuries we WOULD face. Stab wounds, gunshot wounds, crush injuries, etc. Obviously, on borough I had seen my fair share of grisly shit, so I wasn't in the least perturbed at the thought of seeing the public with bits missing. I once took a call to Westbourne Grove station a male under a train. Walking onto the platform I saw a leg lying on the track. Severed at the hip, still wearing a shoe and sock the flesh exposed. Boarding the train, the guard explained the victim was directly beneath us. I assumed he was dead, until I heard his voice, just a whisper really, how was he still alive? He didn't make it. I don't wish to sound blasé, but my ability to see nasty, messy, real life up close and deal with it calmly was something I was very proud of.

The first aid kit contained oxygen, bandages, and tourniquets; all the usual suspects. It was the last thing to go in the boot because it had to be easily accessible. I forgot to mention, the course also pointed out that we may well be the ones being treated and may even be treating ourselves, so it had to be ready to go. Over the years the first aid bag got bigger, the training more extensive, but the injuries remained the same. It was also stressed to all officers that we had a duty to preserve life, all life, so come the day of the races, if a suspect was shot by police, we would be expected to do everything in our power to save their life. There were no good guys or bad guys in this situation; it was our duty, I have lost count of the times I found myself kneeling in a suspect's blood, attempting to keep them from checking out. Self-preservation is no bad thing; every officer carried a tourniquet as well as at least one field dressing, which is another way of saying a bloody good bandage. Both had to be easily accessible, because if you took a round or got stabbed, you do not want to be wasting precious lifesaving seconds fumbling around.

I joked I was rubbish at first aid but in truth the training I got was put to good use, not just on duty. One day out shopping, a lady fell down a flight of stairs and went into cardiac arrest right at my feet. Of course, being an off-duty experienced officer, my first thought was getting the hell out of there; I am joking, next thing yours truly is cutting off clothing and calling for the defib. Soon the LAS were on scene, and I was doing a handover before continuing my shopping trip, and yes, I did call the base and book on.

Car kitted, it was time to meet the team and parade. Entering the parade room, I was met by the Boss, the two skippers and my new team, E relief. Around 13 officers, all males, were scattered around the room chatting quietly. I pulled up a chair and attempted to blend in. My anonymity lasted as long as it took for one of the elders of the team to shout across the room in a thick northern accent. "How far away is he?" alluding to my lack of height. Ecky, the oldest team member and from up north, was a day one SO19 original from 1991. Probably one of the most outspoken coppers it was my enormous pleasure to work with. He then burst into "Hi Ho, hi Ho, it's off to work we go." Ice well and truly broken, he shouted, "Who the fuck are you?" Conversation ceased as all eyes fell on me. Kev the skipper, still laughing as he spoke, called for me to introduce myself, and so in time-honoured fashion, I stood up and gave my life story. The team smiled kindly back at me, all apart from a very large lump of a PC called D. D didn't like me from the moment he laid eyes on me, full stop. In all the time I served alongside him, he never once looked happy to be in my company. Some months later, I was chatting in the yard with the Boss, D strolled over and pointed out I had gel in my hair and what the fuck was 19 coming to? The following day on parade, the boss informed the relief he would not allow "boy band haircuts on his relief"; I was nearly 40 years of age, but a dab of gel had made me a member of Westlife. Admonished, the gel disappeared from my locker.

Trojan One, M, was the Boss; he was a top-notch leader, totally hands on. Running jobs, briefing ops he was the real deal. The Skippers, sorted out admin, also ran jobs, and were either in the base or out on the kit van. They kept everything running smoothly, they knew their role inside out and it was best to stay on their good side. That said, the reliefs policed themselves. I discovered this on my first parade. Trojan one finished what he had to say; the Skippers said their bit, parade over, up stood one of the team known as Johnny Orange. I came to learn he was ex-TSG and a bloody brilliant ARV officer. John was also 'fines master.' Each relief ran a fines club. Fines were dished out for small screw-ups such as wrong call sign on the radio, being late on parade, swearing on parade, getting 100% on your shooting classification, known as showing off. Getting your photo in the paper or being on the telly, known as being 'papped,' from the word paparazzi. The list of crimes was endless. If the offending officer didn't agree with the fine, they could appeal, and then a kangaroo court of their peers would listen carefully to their argument, weigh up the evidence and then confirm that they were indeed guilty. It was only a few pounds per offence, but it all went into the pot and paid for drinks at the Christmas party, so it was a win-win.

As the new kid, I was being mentored for 6 weeks, which meant I could screw up for six weeks, and my mentor Hugh would pay my fines. When I say screw up, I mean the small stuff, like forgetting to sign for your kit or bad admin. If I screwed up on a job that was outside the fines club remit. I would be dealt with by means of the infamous SO19 debrief. After 6 weeks all my misdemeanours would come out of my own pocket. The fines clubs ran on all reliefs, included the Boss and the Skippers, and made for a lively end to each parade. Sadly, over the years, the fines club system has come into disrepute and was even called a device for bullying, which was total claptrap. There is no stereo typical ARV officer, but some traits ran through the team, a sense of humour, the ability to take joke, ownership, robustness, loyalty to name but a few. These qualities clearly still exist on 19 but sadly some officers have now joined the department who believe THEY are the story. I saw being on 19 as a privilege, hard earned. I loved the fines club, even though it cost me a few quid I could ill afford each month.

Kev worked hand in hand with the Gareth, the other Skipper. Personality-wise, these two were chalk and cheese, but one thing they had in common was the high standards they set and expected. I was never far from their gaze, and they made sure I knew it. Nothing got past them. I had been operational less than a week when I found myself up in front of Trojan One. I knew I was in the shit when, after the parade, the Boss, as we called him, nonchalantly said, "Oh, Kevin, can I see you in my office?" As I stared blankly back at him, he added, "Now." 19 being 19, everyone in the room knew what I had done, all apart from little old naïve me. My crime, I soon discovered, was wearing half blues to work. Half blues? This is travelling between home and work, partially wearing uniform. In my case I wore my job trousers and white shirt to work disguised by a civilian jacket to complete the ensemble. On the borough, this was no big deal and very common; however, at 19, this was a big, big, big deal. The Boss informed me I had been spotted travelling in half blues; this was unacceptable and would never happen again. As I was being ripped a new one, I nodded my agreement but didn't have the heart to tell him that I would have to travel home that day in job shirt and trousers. He concluded our friendly chat with the advice, I drive home and get a change of clothes. Like I said, they didn't miss a thing. Obviously, this screw-up cost Hugh £2; he was not best pleased.

What was surprising about 19, was how friendly everyone was. On a job or at a debrief it was brutal, however, the rest of the time everyone was so relaxed and friendly. This downtime between calls was when you got to learn about the lives of your team. Kev the skipper was exceptionally fit and expected everyone else to be the same. One day I was on the running machine in the gym, when out of nowhere he was standing beside me watching me. Without warning, he placed his finger on the keypad and proceeded to increase the speed, to the point I was in a flat-out sprint; on and on it went. Just as I was about to jump off before I fell off, Kev took the speed back down to jogging mode. Staring at me with a fierce look in his eye, he said, "If you're going to run, then bloody run." Point taken; I looked around to see the rest of the gym users cracking up. That was Kev; he was everywhere and knew everything. A few weeks later, I was his base PC; suddenly deciding he was bored, he leapt out of his chair and wrestled me to the floor. Attacking whilst I was sat watching the telly, I was utterly unprepared for the onslaught. Within seconds he was choking me out, ignoring my taps. When he did let go, it was only because the phones began ringing. In a blink he had reverted to SO19 Tactical Advisor while I put the kettle on, convinced he had broken my neck. The whole incident was typical of the department; Kevin was 100% pure testosterone. The department attracted 'big' characters; they came in all shapes and sizes, though none bigger than Kev.

Gareth was his polar opposite: quiet, calm, softly spoken and an SFO. Having passed his Skippers, he moved to the ARVs for a year before returning to the third floor. Well, that was the plan. I got on well with Gareth, and, if time allowed, he would take me on the range for extra shooting practice. These sessions were fantastic; we did SFO shoots, bodyguard shoots, and even Sky Marshall shooting drills. These lessons really stretched me, and in doing so, my Glock shooting began improving immeasurably. These were my skippers, the team I would get to know over the following days and weeks as I got to work with all of them. The two constants were Hugh, who was always by my side pointing me in the right direction, and the high standards my team expected of me. I should probably now address the elephant in the room. In the eyes of my team and every single ARV officer before me, I wasn't a fully trained ARV officer, and this led to misunderstandings and, in some cases, outright disdain. To understand the issue, we must delve into the confusing world of ARV courses. The historically high failure rate was a huge bone of contention. The course costs a lot of money, and the Met expects to get something in return.

There was constant pressure on the instructors, from those in high places, who counted paper clips and worried about the next rank, to get more officers through the course successfully. In the good old days, the final week or two of the course was built around searching buildings. Training staff, well, some of them anyway, identified that students were possibly failing the search element at the end of the course due to overloading them with new skills. It was argued in some quarters that if searching was removed and made a separate module, the students could, upon passing a newly designed course, go to a team and, in a few months, return to Milton to complete their training. Fresh and full of confidence, these armed officers would hopefully breeze through the search element. The problem with this was you were sending officers to reliefs who, in the eyes of the team, had not yet passed the course and who could only partially carry out their role. Plus, there was an inference that we couldn't cope with the old course and needed a more user-friendly new one. This enraged a lot of guys and girls who had passed under the old system. Some officers called for tabs to be worn, denoting search trained, and non-search trained. We newly trained Officers didn't ask for the course to be changed; we turned up and passed everything that was put in front of us, and guess what? Even with searching removed, we lost four out of our twelve, so much for the remove searching theory.

It's fair to say a proportion of ARV officers who passed the 'old course' were not happy to have us amongst them; it was to them the start of dumbing down the course to get bums on seats. D, my nemesis, was one such officer and was happy to let me know of his disapproval at every opportunity. I must add, however, that I was lucky, because the people around me, my new team, treated me brilliantly, and I will never forget their kindness and honesty. This training system stayed in place for some time until, once again, Milton reinvented the wheel, and the search course became the final two weeks of the course. Today the course bears little resemblance to the one I passed, and no doubt it's being rewritten as I sit here in front of my typewriter.

Looking back on that first parade 22 years ago, I am filled with a huge amount of pride. That room contained police officers. From the Boss down we were coppers, coppers who also happened to be armed. Coppers first and last. I had 12 years on the street as my credentials. I had earned the right to be there, as had they. This was a time when a Sergeant was a Sergeant, not a bloody supervisor. Did I go to bed one night a police officer, waking up to find, I stacked shelves in Tesco. By the time I retired, I would see in the media, male officers in women's shoes and nail varnish, in support of what exactly? Officers would be posted as part of a 'dance troupe' to engage with the crowd at Carnival, though I'm not sure what a 'slut drop' has to do with policing. To do this job you must have credibility. The officers on parade that first day were credibility personified. It was an honour to be amongst them.

So dear reader, you are now up to speed. The moment you have waited for, I am about to hit the streets, partially trained, nervous as hell but buzzing to get started. It didn't take long.

Arriving for the early turn, there were no night duty cars waiting to hand over. This meant they were out on a job; word spread they were at a siege and would need to be relieved. Cars kitted, double-quick time, we headed out in convoy, blatting across a sleepy South London. On route I got the story. Police called to a domestic; arriving on the scene, they knocked at the front door, which was opened by a male armed with an assault rifle. He threatened the officers, who took this as a good time to make a tactical retreat. We arrived on scene and started getting briefed by the control. I was given white containment, acting as the less lethal option, supporting an officer with a conventional firearm (a Taser was only issued to drivers at this time).

The front of a building, be it an aeroplane, train, tent or intergalactic spaceship, is designated the white; the back is never the back; it's, you guessed it, the black. No one in firearms has a back garden; they have a black garden. This plotting of a venue into colour-coded segments is called TI, target identification. The right side is red, the left the green. TI is further improved when an imaginary clock face is placed over the venue, with me so far. So, the 12 o'clock position is directly in the middle of black. 6 o'clock is the centre of white. This use of colours and numbers allows a containment officer to give their exact position to control. Easy, really. Well, it is on paper. Try doing it at night while trying to be covert, climbing garden fences and avoiding ponds and a myriad of other obstacles. It's very easy to get disoriented and give the wrong location.

This was an interesting job; it was a siege, an armed subject refusing to come out, but was it a hostage situation because his wife was still in the address? It was she who called police on her husband, though she did leave out the teeny weeny bit about him being ex-military and armed with an automatic weapon. Anyway, here we were, the address was contained, negotiations were under way to get him to come out. His wife was free to move around the house, even coming to the phone. This scenario played out for several hours until he went all Rambo on us. The suspect informed the negotiators that he would not surrender to police; that was below him, but he would to a military officer he had served under. Let me guess, Colonel Trautman Fort Bragg. Phone calls were made, a few more hours passed before a military dude in uniform arrived at the RVP.

Information came to light that the suspect was ex-special forces; now I don't know if this was cobblers or not, but the arrival of the SFO team meant some sort of intervention was being planned to rescue the female, if things got a little crazy inside the house. The SFO team, wearing their signature balaclavas, set off, checking the address, its tactical openings and all the other stuff they need to know to gain entry rapidly, facing a dude who, in theory, knew his shit. The military officer who was in his late twenties, wandered over to a group of us, I expected him to say, "I'm not here to save him; I'm here to save you." He didn't, sadly, but he did inform us the wife was coming out, and hey presto, she did. I remember thinking at the time, should Trautman be so bloody close to the action seeing as he wasn't even wearing body armour? More calls were made into the address, and the suspect agreed to leave the house via the front door, hands in clear view, leaving the firearm inside. So far so good; this was going swimmingly. The negotiators were happy; he was calm and cooperative.

The door opened with Rambo now getting a good look at us all. An armed officer started directing the suspect, what to do and where to go; suddenly, with a roar, he rushed directly at my containment position. I was the less lethal option armed with a taser, supporting two guys with carbines. In an instant he was on top of us; boy, could he shift? Fortunately, so could I. The moment he was in range, I zapped him. Rambo collapsed in a heap, screaming in pain. I was glad I wasn't dealing with him; I didn't fancy being sat across from this maniac in an interview room. He was quickly handcuffed, nicked and disappeared in a van. The army officer, smiling, quipped, "Best laid plans eh, all the best now chaps," shook his head and took his leave.

Interesting fact time, Taser only went live in 2003 and this incident was one of the first occasions it was fired in anger. Myself and a colleague who also discharged his Taser were now shipped to Trojan 99 for a post incident procedure (pip). I was examined by a doctor and went through the lengthy process. The highpoint of the day free pizza. A

WATCH AND REACT

photo of the moment the suspect was dealt with now hangs on a wall on the third floor, taken by the police helicopter I believe. Oh, how times have changed.

What lesson should I have learnt from this job? Don't trust negotiators; trust your eyes; trust your instincts. Not some anonymous suit who has done a course and likes to tell his university friends he's a hostage negotiator. Over a decade later, I would find myself outside an address in Brixton, number two on a stick, as a negotiator got things wrong, very, very wrong.

IF YOU GO HUNTING TIGERS

The first time I heard this expression I was sat in a classroom at Milton. My team had carried out a stop which resulted in most of us getting shot. Why? Because whilst we were focused on the threat, we failed to identify the third suspect who relishing the opportunity opened on us on full auto. As paint rounds exploded on my already paint splattered body armour, my mind wandered to the final shoot-out in Sam Peckinpah's The Wild Bunch. An orgy of slow-motion murder and mayhem, washed down with gallons of blood and gore. As we sat awaiting the inevitable 'beat up' debrief the door flew open and in strolled instructor X. "Well ladies, how do you think that went" Before anyone was stupid enough to respond to this rhetorical question, he continued "Guys if you go hunting Tigers don't be fucking surprised if you find one." With that he did an about turn and disappeared. In layman's terms, if you set out to confront bad people, don't be surprised when one leaps out at you.

We are on patrol, Muggins in back reading the map. Hugh was on comms (radios), chatting away to the driver and occasionally throwing the conversation my way to check I was awake. All was peace and calm, until the main set came to life, with the words you long to hear. No, not a 10% pay rise better "Any Trojan unit any Trojan unit" In that split second the car goes quiet. Hugh reached for the hand mike, calm as you like accepting the call, giving our call sign, location and asking for a map ref. I scribbled the page number and grid ref down on my clipboard and furiously began searching for the address. The driver already has the lights and two tones wailing and not a clue where we are heading well that makes two of us.

WATCH AND REACT

The above scenario played out daily over the following days and weeks. Sometimes Hugh would drive, and comms would fall to someone else John, or Mick, or Stu, or Paul, but never me. My fate was to sit in back read a map and don't screw up. In truth I wasn't itching to drive I was wise enough to know that it would come soon enough and with it the expectation I could throw an ARV around as quick as the next guy. Hand on heart I wasn't relishing the prospect. Driving Bravo 3 around the Hill was a piece of cake compared to punting a car around the length and breadth of the metropolis. In my previous incarnation my longest emergency call was never more than a few miles on roads I knew inside out, not anymore. What added to the pressure was being lead car in a convoy. Protocol demanded you never overtake the car in front, chance would be a fine thing, at the speeds we went at. Convoy driving was a real challenge, no one trained you how to do it. 19 was the ultimate in on the job learning. I watched, I copied, I got better, Before I knew it, I could get a car to Hackney be redirected to Harrow and end up in Heathrow no problem.

It was all going so well, that was until I told D, my new best friend, to turn right into a three lane one way traffic system off the A40. The only problem, it was no entry, head on, into oncoming traffic. For the next 30 seconds, he was driving like he was in an asteroid storm. The air in the car turned blue as he explained he intended to locate the map book up my backside. An hour or two later, Job done we huddled together for a quick debrief, everyone was smiling at me and then "So what's this about you trying to kill D," All the crews were laughing, I was glowing red with embarrassment. Later that same night we took a call up to East Ham. I shouted over the two tones, "Next left," expecting D to turn left at the junction, to my horror he pulled a sharp left into the car park for the City Airport. What a colossal fuck up, I now had to direct us out of the

WATCH AND REACT

world's most confusing car park, in the dark, with my driver calling me every name under the sun and Hugh desperately trying to talk on the radio over the swearing. The tension in the car was unbelievable, eventually we arrived at the RVP to discover it was a stand down. I was soon being asked where D and I were flying on holiday. He was not amused. On the drive back to the base I prayed we wouldn't get another call, in truth, I think the other two did too. You guessed it "Any Trojan unit."

Coming off Hammersmith flyover, we joined our sister car; now in convoy, we headed towards Ealing. Two suspects in a car were involved in a gunpoint robbery. The local duty officer authorised an option two stop. This was the manual talking, to us, in the cars, it meant a hard stop, a bash-up. A local unmarked unit was behind the suspects, but how long they could remain there before they got blown was anyone's guess. Being the Bravo car, I wasn't lead on maps, thank God, and then suddenly Alpha called up on the back-to-back radio. "Maps is lost; Kev, take it." For fuck's sake, not me; we overtook the lead car and now became Alpha. I was now in the hot seat. Reading a map, playing catch-up with a suspect vehicle is tough. Add to the equation, I was receiving a pretty poor commentary from the unmarked car, that was the icing on my bloody cake. D chipped in helpfully, "Don't you dare fuck this up," all to a backdrop of radios, sirens and chit-chat between cars in my earpiece. Thanks for the moral support, bestie. This was the reality of three coppers in a car racing to stop bad shit from happening. Each with their own roles and responsibilities but somehow working as a team.

What no one knew, was that Muggins here had lived in Ealing for years, so I had good local knowledge. I grabbed hold of maps, did a few rat runs, and hey presto, we were behind the locals. No lights, no noise, silent approach.

Hugh shouted, "Crack the safe." It was already done; the two MP5s were out, loaded, and in condition one. I tapped Hugh's shoulder, "Coming through." With that, I passed his 5 forward muzzle down in a safe direction; Hugh leaning around smiled and took the 5. He waited for a suitable location, then called for the locals to step aside, we were now in pole position, directly behind the bandit vehicle. Darren turned on the lights and noise, and with that, the Bravo car flew past us doing a two-car overtake. The stop was going in.

The next few seconds are an explosion of movement and controlled aggression. The Bravo car cuts across the path of the bandit vehicle, forcing it to come to a halt. Our Alpha car drives right up its backside so that it's wedged between us and can't force its way out. The doors of the ARVs fly open; each officer has a place to be and a role to perform. The cars hardly stop moving and, in many cases, still are as your boots hit the deck and you are sprinting to where you need to be. No one has a clue what anyone else is doing; I know I didn't. I was so focused on carrying out my role. I reached the car that was supposed to contain two suspects. Well, guess what? If you go hunting tigers? Sat on the back seat was a third, and he was pushing open his door to escape. I'm not sure who was more surprised. I raised my five, the folding stock jammed into my shoulder selector lever to fire, finger on trigger, and said the words I would repeat a thousand times over 18 years of living the dream. "Show me your fucking hands."

Suspect three raised his arms doing a jazz hands action that even at the time made me smile. Suddenly a Trojan officer was at my side, grabbing my subject by the shoulder and arm. Dragging him from the car, shouting "Down, down, down." As he did so, I covered my subject. Face down, he was cuffed and searched, patted down for weapons, only when I heard "prisoner secure." I placed my selector to safe, finger off trigger, and came off aim. I only now realised the search officer was D; he looked up at me with a beaming smile, which disappeared as quickly as it arrived. The car was cleared, the boot last; only then did the call go up, "car clear."

If you had a drone hovering overhead (not that they existed in 2003), you would have seen three suspects prone, face down, handcuffed. The front of their vehicle would require someone who knew a thing or two about panel beating. Our car had a lovely dent running down the car door to add to the hundreds of other dents, all scars from other armed stops. Lastly, you would have seen six armed officers doing their job; no dramas, just professionals at work. Scene secured; local officers called forward. Hugh spoke with the local Skipper, giving him a full handover of the job, our actions and the fact the suspects were detained, not arrested. They had been patted down for weapons only; as such, they should be treated as unsearched. Job done, I headed for the car, back to base, notes to write, debrief, off late, who cares? What a great way to end the evening. "Any Trojan unit, any Trojan unit." Hugh grabbed the mic, and off we headed into the night; it looks like my notes would have to wait.

I remember this day well because I wrote it all down in my diary. When I got divorced, I started one as a way of remembering what the kids and I did together. This then evolved into me giving my children an insight into what their absent father did for a living. The idea being that I would leave the diaries to them after I depart this mortal coil, and that is still my intention. The diaries ended when I retired, buried now under a mountain of boxes in the barn, hidden from prying eyes. No one has ever read them; maybe if I go first, Kerry, my wife, will read them, though maybe she shouldn't. The pages are not my attempt to excuse bad decisions and dubious behaviour. Nor are they my shot at redemption from beyond the grave. Just a story, a story that I hoped may go some way to explaining why their sometimes tough but always loving, proud dad was the man he was. Will they ever really understand me? Maybe, maybe not. I know this: when they were with me, they always felt safe and loved. That's a father's job description right there.

Back to the stop, we learnt later a handgun was found in a bum bag stuffed down the back of the seat. One gun was recovered and three in the "bin" as custody was commonly known, a good day's work all-round. If anyone reading this today is living the dream jumping out of cars and pointing guns, they may be a bit confused. Nowadays tactics and terminology have evolved. Vehicle stops involve three cars Alpha, Bravo, and Charlie. The names for the stop have gone from option one two or three and occasionally something called a traffic stop to wordy, teach you to suck eggs tactics. We must thank the College of Policing for "non-compliant stop, armed extraction," in old money an option two. For me this is a slippery slope, what's next, telling you when you can or cannot point your weapon? To put it bluntly, in 2003 the Met and principally SO19 wrote the book on armed operations. We did what worked and threw out the stuff that didn't, live operations were our education and lessons learnt were passed on to training who fed this into ARV courses. The instructors had all been on the cars and would in most cases return to the cars. This system worked brilliantly. Who needs 20 words when you can say option one, two, or three? Over the 18 years I carried a gun, the College of Policing got more and more involved in firearms training and procedure. In 2003 the Met didn't give monkeys what the counties did, we were doing it for real, every single day and doing it better faster and harder than anyone else. Quite often at training, county operations would be used as examples, of how NOT to do the job. This always led to much merriment, especially if we had county transferees in the room. Of course, offended or not they couldn't argue the point, why else had they moved to the Met and 19?

That stop in Ealing was not my first job, but I mention it to highlight what life on the cars was like. It was hectic and sometimes brutal. Crews did shout and swear at one another, and fallings out did occur, though they were usually resolved quickly. You as an individual could go from zero to hero in the course of one good job and back to zero by the end of the next one. I had screwed up twice on maps that night; D wanted my head on a spike, and Hugh had fines to pay for my mistakes. Then, in a flash, all was forgotten as I map-read us to the suspects and did my job. Suddenly my credit rating was up again. If 19 had a motto, it would be You're only as good as your last job.

Vehicle stops are arguably the most complicated, dangerous and exciting tactical option you carry out on 19. Why? Because there are so many moving parts. The Bandit vehicle is armed and heading to a location often unknown; it may have any number of occupants, and which one is in possession of a weapon? possibly more than one subject; are there innocents in the car, like a cab driver? Two ARVs must somehow rendezvous, travelling often huge distances from opposite ends of London, then get behind the Bandit Vehicle, the location is constantly changing. On route, the cars are talking to each other as well as the base, discussing tactics and contingencies, and spare a thought for the poor sod on maps. Once behind the Bandit, you now have three cars moving through crowded London streets, busy with innocent members of the public, happily getting on with their lives. Oblivious to the fact that armed officers are about to ruin someone's day.

All the while the lead car operator is looking to choose a suitable location to activate the plan, a 'safe backdrop' is essential, not in front of a primary school, a crowded bus stop, or a busy pub. Not at a set of traffic lights, not at a junction allowing the bandit to turn off just as the stop goes in. Add to this hive of activity loading the MP5s your Primary weapon, the fact information can change raising or lowering the threat, add the weather, is it pouring down making driving conditions more difficult and reducing vision. The list of factors affecting the stop is endless. It's a bloody nightmare, a fantastic roller coaster ride that tests all your skill sets, and then, when the stop goes in you must make split-second decisions about the suspects you're confronting. These moments create unbelievable stress, stress the course attempts to replicate to see if you can cope. Many can't, hence the high failure rate. Just before I retired twelve of a course of twelve dipped out You do the math on that one.

The stress, the decision-making, the pressure to perform and keep on performing meant only the very best officers cut the mustard, and I am proud to say over time I grew to cut the mustard with the best of them. My mentoring period was now a distant, distant memory; job after job came my way, my experience of firearms ops growing, and experience in this game is everything. The base called over the radio, "Any unit near Brixton, SCD behind a car, both occupants wanted for a murder in America, and here is the best bit: they are professional hitmen." Well, you don't hear that every day, and even though it's all very serious, all three of us in the car burst out laughing. Hit men, indeed, I'm sorry, this is Blighty; we don't have hit men. As luck would have it, we were on the borough; I put us up for the call, the base then gave us the cherry on the cake. We were it; no other cars were available, all dealing with other calls. My brain now went into overdrive. We were going to stop two guys wanted for murder, potentially armed, and we only had our car to deal. Normal tactics were now out the window, so in the finest traditions of 19, we made it up on the hoof.

Within a few minutes, we were behind the unmarked surveillance car, which was acting as 'one for cover.' I was comms, at the agreed moment, it pulled aside, letting us now take pole position behind the suspect vehicle. My MP5 was loaded, condition one. My driver went for a big overtake: no sirens, no blue lights, just shock and awe. As we flew past, I covered the suspects with my 5 through my open window; the look on the suspect's face was priceless. Pulling the ARV hard left, we cut in front of the bandit car, forcing it to come to a shuddering halt. Before we had even come to a standstill, I was out and sprinting to the driver's door, my MP5 up in the aim selector lever to fire.

"Show me your fucking hands," I screamed the command; the driver was massive, clearly some sort of bodybuilder pumped full of animal growth hormone. "Hands on the fucking wheel and don't fucking move." The driver slowly placed his hands on the steering wheel, all the time looking directly at me. Suddenly the door was pulled open, D grabbed hold of the driver's wrist, dragging him from the car and driving him face down into the tarmac with one hell of a thud. I kept the firearms cover on as D cuffed the male, but his back and shoulders were so big I had to unstrap my cuffs from my body armour and throw them to D; this guy needed two sets linked together to secure him properly. D shouted "Male secure"; this was my cue to run round to the passenger's door, where S was covering the front seat passenger. Just like the driver here was another bloody monster. I slung my MP5. I pulled open the door. "Stay calm, man; I ain't going to hurt you." I ignored his attempts at a negotiated surrender. Grabbing hold of his wrist and collar, I pulled him out and down, smashing my palm heel into the back of his shoulder for extra leverage as I drove him face-first into the tarmac.

S was already ahead of me, throwing me his cuffs to secure the suspect. Thank God this guy was a bit more flexible in the joint department, one set did the job. Cuffs on, I patted him down for weapons, happy he was secure and unarmed I shouted, "Suspect secure." We quickly cleared the car and with a collective sigh of relief called the plainclothes units in. The squad guys were over the moon, arresting both suspects on suspicion of murder, Trojan never arrested in the old days that's just how it was. The SCD skipper shook my hand "Fucking hell Trojan, I almost creamed my pants when you put the stop in." I didn't know what to say, what can you say, it was a job well done, not textbook, high risk and not something we trained for, but one car stops were a reality, that "Never say never" adage again. Initiative and flexibility are two traits every good ARV officer must have. It also helps if the person at the other end of the gun believes you will pull the trigger without hesitation, if they pose a threat to life. The swearing and verbal domination were a vital tool, used to overwhelm the suspect. As someone amusingly pointed out to me "If this is the fucking Jungle Healy, then best we are the fucking lions." His tongue was firmly in his cheek that or maybe too many Guy Richie films, who knows, fortunately no one took themselves that seriously on 19. That said, the bad guys had to know they faced officers who would do their duty, on Trojan I was lucky to be surrounded by officers who relished the risks they faced.

CARNIVAL AND CHRISTMAS

I had worked twelve Notting Hill carnivals, all on foot, as a local officer. Not anymore, now I was on the cars dealing with any issues Carnival threw up. E relief was nights; on parade, we were briefed that late turn and day duty had been full on, so cup of tea and let's get out and about. My probation was over the six weeks, a blur of ups and downs, but Hugh signed me off, and that was good enough for me. I was making friends and fitting into the E relief vibe, which I can describe as being super chilled; it wasn't a gym monkey relief, nor was it full of giant egos. The guys, because they were all guys, were mostly mature married men with kids. My crew that night was Rob, who had a voice straight out of EastEnders, and Mark, who was soon to quit the police for a career with the family firm. I was maps for a change, and it wasn't long before my services were called upon. A call came out to Harlesden, North London, not far from the Carnival footprint. A Black male was seen walking down the street with a female. He was believed to be holding a handgun. Rob took the call; I plotted our route. We were flying solo; the other cars already on calls were busy. The Duty Officer at QK (Kilburn) authorised our deployment, we were to carry out an area search and armed stop on a subject if located. Note, dear reader, no convoluted wordy tactic. We were trusted to make our tactical assessment based on what we faced.

Arriving on scene, we were met by a row of terraced Victorian houses with small front gardens with high hedges. All three of us got out of the car. It was a warm summer evening; the street was dead, not a soul in sight. Rob walked one kerb; I took the other, with Mark acting as tail end Charlie. Without warning, a figure appeared on the kerb in front of me about twenty metres away. Rob must

WATCH AND REACT

also have seen him because he was crossing the road to join me. The male walked towards us, calm as you like. I spoke first, "Hello mate, can you keep your hands in view please? I went on to explain why we were there. As I spoke, he interrupted a few times, it was clear when he spoke that he had been drinking or was high or both. He was clearly getting agitated at us stopping him and kept repeating, "I don't have a gun; search me." He then decided the only way to convince us was to strip naked.

Standing in front of me was a naked male aged about 40; when I say naked, I mean butt naked. He told us to "Fuck off and leave him alone" and then started walking back the way he came. We followed him, calling for him to stop; I ran to get in front of him just as he stopped by a garden gate. Looking into the front garden, I saw a partially clothed Black female slumped on the doorstep; the look on her face told me something was very, very wrong. In that moment I saw the gun, a silver SLP, self-loading pistol, placed on the doorstep. The slide was locked back but a loaded magazine was in the mag well. What happened next happened fast. The naked male pushed open the gate and headed towards the gun; Rob and I raised our 5s, shouting for him to stop, and in the same split second, Mark tasered the suspect. In a flash, I was in the garden getting between the gun and the now-prone naked suspect. Rob was on top of him, cuffing him, and it was over just like that.

The locals were called, and the suspect handed over to them. The poor girl was the victim of attempted rape at gunpoint. We three had stopped a rape and recovered a viable firearm. As we prepared to leave, the local skipper approached me. "Good job, lads. Imagine the shit that would have hit the fan if Trojan had shot dead a naked man on Carnival weekend." We three mounted up and headed back to base for a debrief and notes. As we drove in silence, each one of us dealing with our own private thoughts, the skipper's words struck me. If I had shot the suspect before him picking up the gun the media would have had a field day. I would have been totally justified; the gun had a loaded mag. All he had to do was hit the slide release, and he was ready to rock. Action beat's reaction: I was ready to shoot, but only Marks's speed with the taser prevented me from using potentially lethal force. Such were the margins within which we operated. Sadly, the media and sections of the community don't get it or choose not to.

Walking into the base, Trojan One was all smiles, as was skipper Kev. The local Duty Officer had rung 99 praising us to high heaven, which didn't hurt my credibility one iota. This was the closest I had come to pulling the trigger so far, and I was remarkably chilled about the whole deal. Years later I was in a car with a new guy, an experienced cop just starting his Trojan career. A call directed us to a street in Wandsworth, where a white male, wearing a cowboy hat was seen with a gun, walking down the middle of the road; it was broad daylight, and multiple calls were coming in. Arriving on scene, members of the public directed us towards a local park. We got out of the car and headed after him. Within seconds, we located 'Woody,' a very thin, clearly pissed male, aged about 50, who could not be described as one of life's winners. He was holding a silver plastic cowboy revolver, the kind we all had as kids, straight out of Toy Story. He was told to drop the gun, and of course he did. Led from the park, I think he was arrested, but in truth, it was just a sad drunk with a toy gun being stupid. What shocked me was the fact that the new guy was banging on, "I could have shot him; I could have shot him." I looked at his mentor, and we both shared a "What the fuck" moment. This new guy was clearly disturbed by the incident. Me? I thought back to that street in Harlesden, when I was a new guy. I thanked the gods of war I was wired the way I was.

The summer rolled into the Autumn; the Rugby World Cup in Australia was upon us. I had never seen the base so excited. England had a great team, and everyone was sporting England shirts. Kev decreed it was a fineable offence to be on parade without an English red rose on your uniform. The rose had to be homemade by you, not some cheap knockoff from a shop. I didn't have the heart to tell him I supported Ireland so went along with the shenanigans. The rest, as they say, is history. The year ended with me cooking a meal for the team. It was a tradition that each new officer would, on a chosen evening, feed the team, both bases North and South. Kev and Gareth informed me after the parade that I was to have the honour in two weeks. I was to make the meal myself, provide plates, tableware, beverages and 'entertainment,' whatever that meant.

George was the last person to organise dining in night, and he went all out. Patriotic music, Union Jacks, candelabra – it was like the last night of the proms. It was a huge success, and at the end of the evening, everyone left a donation; this usually covered the costs and then some. I chose a Mexican theme and gave it my best shot. I didn't own a car at the time because of my divorce settlement. I say settlement; it was more like the Versailles treaty, and I was Germany. As a result, I ordered a cab and transferred my Mexican fiesta from my flat to Leman Strasse in the boot of an old Toyota. The driver kicked up a bit of a fuss, but a couple of wraps later he was on board. Carrying pots and pans, I headed for the kitchen and laid out my wares. Suitably happy, I headed to the base room, the skipper put out the call, Dinner is served. The cars arrived one by one until all were seated; even the base Skipper was upstairs joining in. I waited table for the next hour or so until a call came out South, and the Swampies departed, but not before leaving piles of cash on the table, and so it went with the North leaving me all alone to clean up. The cash easily covered my outgoings, so I must have done good. The problem now, what to do with the pots and pans; I didn't need them. I left them in the kitchen for the canteen lady as an early Christmas present. On dining in night, you were not posted on a car, so with the kitchen spic and span, I headed home. Everything was a test, and this evening was just another one. It was all about logistics and organisation. Could you pull it off, on time, with enough food, cooked to a good standard and create a dining night that the whole team would enjoy; on one of the few occasions, we were all together socially? It all went towards your credibility, and at 19, I was realising credibility was everything.

I mention that night over twenty years ago for two reasons. First, it no longer happens; the department is too big, and the will isn't there. Sadly, when organisations grow at the speed 19 did, some of the invisible fibres that held us together get lost along the way. Old-school Skippers and Governors understood how important these bonds of trust and loyalty were, and so wearing a handmade red rose or cooking a dodgy paella (that's not Mexican) for thirty guys were things that made us all just a little bit tighter as a unit. The other reason I mention it is because George, who did a great job with his prom night, would soon fall foul of training and leave us. The manner of his departure was brutal; I stood by as a silent witness, not experienced enough to comment on his actions or the severity of the punishment meted out.

His crime, on a siege exercise at training, was to challenge an escaping armed subject with a baton gun. He should have ditched the less lethal weapon and reverted to his MP5 or Glock; he did neither, the subject escaped. The suspect escaping from an armed containment was bad; however, if this had happened in 'real life', the consequences could have been catastrophic. George could have been shot, and the lives of the unarmed officers as well as members of the public were put at risk. Trojan officers were often described as containment experts, and this fiasco was not to be tolerated. George brought a baton gun to a gunfight, and there was no way back from that bad tactical decision. At the debrief, a room full of instructors, dog handlers, even the negotiator cell, plus his peers, he was challenged regarding his actions. He was completely blindsided; maybe he thought because everyone liked him, his mistake would be glossed over. Maybe he thought it was training, and you should be able to make mistakes at training, learn from them and move on. Sadly, for him, that wasn't the case, and what followed left him visibly shaking and close to tears. The room was deadly silent as the chief instructor ARV continuation training tore him apart. George attempted a defence, but as I soon learnt, when training has you in their crosshairs, it's game over.

George left the room that day never to carry again on 19. I really liked him; he was a lovely man. He was shipped off to the DPG, the diplomatic protection group, to stand outside embassies in the pouring rain, losing his mind. When the dust had settled, I mentioned George to Hugh, saying what a nice guy he was. Hugh replied, "The graveyard's full of nice guys." I didn't raise the subject again.

The summer was now a distant memory; every job seemed to be in the pouring rain or freezing cold. One night as we drove to a call in the snow, the driver lost control completely. We did a 180-degree turn, bounced off a kerb and slid to a halt. The three of us laughed; the operator shouted, that's a fine, and with that, we were back on route to the call. Christmas was upon us; I wasn't seeing my kids, so in truth, it meant little or nothing to me. The north and south bases had Christmas parties, one with the wives and one just for the lads. I attended both, but the other half's black tie affair really was something.

A hotel was booked and a DJ for dancing. I arrived at the hotel to find the relief members, as I had never seen them before in a word, restrained. All the wives were so friendly I was at a loss to their kindness. OK, I was on my own; maybe they knew about my divorce and my access problems seeing my kids. As we sat down to dinner, boy-girl-boy-girl, I was clearly the odd one out. I was getting slowly drunk and enjoying the Christmas spirit when one of the wives who was enjoying the wine as much as I was said, "Do you mind if I ask you a personal question?" Somewhat confused, I nodded. Ok, where is this going? "Are you gay?" Suddenly the jigsaw was complete; no girlfriend, no wife, 40, single and wearing hair gel, I had to be, surely. I approached a few of the team who confirmed my suspicions; there was speculation as to my sexuality amongst the ladies, not that anyone could care less. Everyone treated me just fine, so please, no screaming homophobia. I didn't give monkeys; I got to dance with all the wives, all apart from D's misses. When she invited me to the dance floor, he put an arm across my chest and, in his thick Yorkshire accent, "Kev doesn't dance. "The crowning glory of the evening was AD, an ex-Marine, cornering me in the toilets and handing me a blue Viagra tablet. "I've pissed the wife off son, I don't need it now. Good luck." He spoke as if sending me on a mission; maybe he was. As he staggered back to his table, I stood on the edge of the dance floor playing with the blue tablet in the palm of my hand. One of the wives saw it and, smiling, said, "Who's the lucky fella?" Merry bloody Christmas.

Christmas Eve arrived; we were late to turn, the two-to-ten shift. Everyone was hoping to be off a bit early, rushing home to wives and kids, and who could blame them? Kitting up the cars, everyone was in that mood that grabs you at that time of year – friendly banter, spirit of goodwill to all men – I loved it. I was the opposite of my fellows; for me, working Christmas was a lifesaver. One, it kept my mind off my kids and what I was missing. Secondly, Christmas meant double time, and I needed all the money I could lay my hands on.

We left the base and, as tradition demanded, headed straight for Leicester Square and Fiori Italian restaurant. Cars, be they north or south, could always be found in Leicester Square, drinking a coffee and trading gossip. Tonight was no different. A south car containing Jules driving; he always drove, and boy, did he drive it like he stole it? Magic, my old friend and mentor from the Hill, was comms, and Larry was maps. The two cars parked side by side, windows down, and the six of us set about fixing the Met, the country, and the universe. The atmosphere was great: the Christmas lights, the tourists who seemed to love an 'English bobby,' the carols and Christmas music blaring out of speakers. All was well until our operator took a call on the job mobile from the base.

We were heading to Hackney on the hurry up; there we would meet Kev on the kit van and two other cars. That was the info, so no point second-guessing. We arrived at Hackney and headed to the conference room. Walking in, you could cut the atmosphere with a knife. Sitting around the edge of the room, every chair taken by local uniformed officers, dog handlers, local CID, and detectives I guessed were from Op Trident, a task force set up to deal with shootings in the Black community. Add to this motley crew eight wary ARV officers. The door opened, and in walked the local DI, Detective Inspector. He was wearing a rather dishevelled suit over the top of which he wore the world's most ill-fitting body armour, what a sack of shit. The room was packed, the heating was on, and tensions were running high. I thought it might be wise if he took off his bod, as we called body armour. However, after he briefed us, I realised it was prudent to leave it on. What follows is my recollection of events. I apologise if I get the exact dialogue wrong, but, in my defence, I couldn't believe my ears.

"Good evening, everyone, and thank you for coming. We have source-led intelligence that X intends to visit Club Y tonight and shoot Z. My intention is to deploy armed assets to that location and arrest X in possession of a firearm. The club in question opens its doors around midnight and closes around 7 am. I have considered the option of telling the club to remain closed and disrupt the actions of X. However, I don't think the Christmas revellers attending the club tonight should have their evening ruined because of the actions of one bad man." Rob stood up. "Sir, with respect." This was a bad start; nothing good ever came after those three words. "This is total bollocks." Rob really emphasised the word bollocks. "Shut the club; it doesn't bloody open till midnight. You do realise we have lives too; what about our Christmas plans?" Before Rob could say another word, Kev was putting forward the shut the club and flood the area with marked cars plan, disruption being the safest course of action. The DI was having none of it. When it was pointed out we were late turning, and this operation would run into the early hours, he dismissed bringing in night duty cars because it would involve a second briefing causing delays, and he was too busy to mess around. Rob looked like he was about to kill his first DI.

WATCH AND REACT

As we walked back to the cars the mood was sombre. All the guys were on their phones calling wives and loved ones trying to explain the fiasco that was unfolding. All we could pray for was an early resolution. I spent Christmas Eve in a car park on a rat-infested industrial estate. No food, no hot drinks; we sat in silence, each of us alone with our thoughts. As the hours dragged, the night got colder, and the club opened. Over the back-to-back radio, Kev wished everyone a happy Christmas. Everyone got out of the cars, shook hands and smiled through gritted teeth. Then someone I can't remember who said the police officer mantra "You shouldn't have joined if you can't take a joke." Everyone cracked up, and as if by magic, a local unit arrived with coffee, and suddenly life looked just a little less shit.

The sun had risen, our saviour was born, and the suspect finally arrived; seated in the back seat of a minicab, he was armed with a handgun and bad intentions. Kev ran the job; sharp as a razor, he talked our cars in "Strike, strike, strike." The option two was textbook. I reached the door where the suspect was sitting; I pointed my MP5 and called him every name under the sun while also asking him to "Show me your fucking hands." The door was pulled open, the suspect extracted, and that was that. Oh, I should mention he had a pistol in a bag he wore round his neck. We never saw the DI, which was probably a good thing. We arrived back at base tired but still had notes to write, but the debrief was for another day. Paperwork sorted, a group of exhausted coppers wandered out to their cars for the long drive home, praying not to fall asleep at the wheel. I waited in the locker room until I was sure the team had left. I didn't have a car, and no way was I asking any of my team for a lift home. I was still the new guy, and I wasn't up for asking favours, especially after the night we had. If we had finished on time, I would have got the train home to

Sloane Square and a nice stroll to my flat. Now it was Christmas Day, no public transport, and to make matters worse, it was pouring down.

I left the base and headed towards Tower Bridge, turned right and hugged the river all the way home, the streets deserted. It's roughly five miles; I felt I was on a death march. I stopped at the local corner shop and bought Christmas dinner, Jack Daniel's, a bag of ice and a party pack of Monster Munch, pickled onion flavour. It was Christmas after all. Entering the block, I was soaked to the skin, so glad at last to be out of the December downpour. I took the lift, as I got out, I heard the spirit of Christmas emanating from behind each door. Every flat was home to a policing family; I was the only single occupier in the building. Lots of laughter and music, as it should be on such a magical day. I can't say I was suicidal, but upon entering my flat, I walked into the living room, opened the window and threw my Christmas tree out. Watching as it crashed nose-first into the patch of sodden grass that was laughably described as a communal garden. From a flat below a huge cheer rang out; I wanted to cry but found myself laughing instead. I poured myself a drink and allowed my thoughts to drift to my young children, probably awake now and opening presents. Wrapping paper thrown everywhere, the dogs, Strawberry and Bon Bon, revelling in the mayhem. I whispered my kids' names, wished them a merry Christmas, then climbed into bed.

WATCH AND REACT

DIG-OUT

The armed containment and call-out of a subject by means of limited entry, also known as a dig-out. ARV officers are often described as containment specialists, and rightly so. The three-crew system allows for a control to be set up while the other two head out into the unknown to 'put in containment'. The good book says IDENTIFY, LOCATE, CONTAIN AND THEREBY NEUTRALISE THE THREAT. Failure to contain an address is unacceptable. In 2003, Google Maps and iPads were the stuff of George Lucas, so spare a thought for the two officers tasked with the role. Countless times I found myself with a house number, a road name, maybe a sketchy description, "It's got a red door", or the "Front gate's broken", and that's it. Often in the dark on a hostile estate with everyone 'eyes about.' Dressed in your field suit (a heavy raincoat), your MP5 concealed underneath, you did whatever you had to do to get in position, often with time working against you. Climbing walls, creeping through gardens, sometimes carrying a folding ladder or ballistic blanket, and all the while being tactical, no wonder you had to be bloody fit; it was taxing both physically and mentally. If getting the white in was hard, that's the front of the venue; try getting the black in, often with no landmarks to assist other than "Trojan, it's the 6th chimney along," ok thanks for that. Add dogs, security lights, barbed wire, broken glass and, on one occasion, a bloody great canal. The truth is dig-outs test your ARV skills to the max.

The boss came over the hailing group (Trojan radio channel), asking for three cars to Walworth Nick on the hurry-up. Arriving in the backyard, we did the usual musical chairs routine, trying to find a parking space, in a car park designed for half that number. Trojan One arrived along with the kit car, a BMW estate; that car was so overweight that driving it at high speeds required nerves of steel. In the wet, it was a death trap. Speaking of death traps, a few months later the car made one final bid to kill me when it burst into flames outside Waitrose in New Malden. The car came to a sudden stop, flames started licking the bodywork, the Skipper and I had one thought: the guns and ammunition in the back. What a sight we must have been to the middle-class shoppers watching us furiously de-kitting the car of anything that may go bang. A backup car was called, and the LFB (fire brigade) took great pleasure in saving our bacon.

The job was fast time, the briefing over the bonnet. X was wanted for murder; he had been housed in a flat on the Heygate estate on The Old Kent Rd. This high-rise rambling lump of concrete was clearly designed by someone who hated the poor. We were going to dig it out. Kev gave the briefing and stick order. I was number one; my number two would be Big N. N was huge; no one ever said his name without the word 'Big' coming before it. He was one of those dudes who never hit the weights, whose idea of a protein drink was a McDonald's milkshake. He was big, strong, aggressive and very, very funny; everybody loved Big Nige.

It was early evening but already dark. We arrived at the FUP, forming up point. I opened the boot of the kit van, grabbed the ballistic shield and got my shit together. The Glock has a lanyard that attaches the weapon to your belt. If you were running, got in a bundle or dropped it for some reason, the lanyard stopped your Glock from going very far. Before every dig out, I always unscrewed the bolt and detached it from the Glock. I didn't want the lanyard catching on furniture or a door handle at a critical moment.

I had seen it happen in training and on live jobs and had no intention of being 'that guy.'

The stick formed up, and off we set. Now, unless you have lived the dream at 19, you would be unaware of the Trojan mantra, '19 don't use lifts', for a host of obvious tactical reasons, which I won't bore you with. The ability to get from A to B under your own steam, carrying kit, was another reason the highest fitness levels are required for entry into this world of guns. The venue was on level six. If you count the basement, that's about seven floors. That's a lot of floors, carrying a lot of kit. With each floor the kit got heavier; you could hear the breathing of the stick getting louder and louder as we all sucked in as much air as we could. Arriving at level six, Kev called a halt. This wasn't his first rodeo. Everyone, including me, took a moment to refocus. Breathing under control, the stick spoke in whispers. The method of entry (MOE) team re-checked the Ram, the hydraulic door opener. Thumbs up from Kev, nods of affirmative from the stick. I waited for the pat on my shoulder from big Nigel. Pat received I walked the team in. Shield on my left arm, Glock in my right hand, I closed down the front door. Stopping just short, I made room for the MOE guys as they set up the hydraulic ram and placed the enforcer close at hand.

This stage of the dig-out is known as the dance steps, and for good reason. Sometimes ten or more officers and a bloody huge Trojan dog, usually an Alsatian, can find themselves on a walkway designed to be wide enough for a mum with a baby buggy. We move around one another in silence; in the dark each movement is precise to avoid noise or bumping into an officer covering a window or 'tactical opening,' as we called them. It's precise; it must be. Often before a job, if it's pre-planned, the team will practise the dance steps at the base. over and over until it's choreographed like a dance. Get it. On a pre-planned job, you often know what you have to work with; on fast-time ones, it's a classic suck-it-and-see situation. The ability to come up with a plan on the hoof made Trojan what it was and still is.

The tension in these seconds is palpable, as you wait for the MOE team to give you the nod. I was new still and totally in the zone; focused on the front door, on my role and not screwing up, I felt big N lean forward. "Kev,"

"Yes," what words of wisdom would he impart, what tactical nuance would leave his lips?

"Kev, chicks really dig this shit." Before I had time to burst out laughing, the Ram came to life, the motor tearing the silence and the door to shreds. The second the ram starts, everyone shouts at the top of their voice, "Armed police, armed police." This aggressive shout is intended to tell the suspect we are not rival gang members, drug dealers, etc., coming to kill him. If he then decides to engage us and shoot, he can't say in court he thought we were the bad guys. The shout also tells everyone nearby, in flats or on stairwells, wherever, to keep the hell out of the way.

The door breached, the MOE team stay low and get the hell out of the way. In those critical seconds with the door now open and me stepping forward to plug the gap, they are on offer. They stay low and move fast; the shield man and his number 2 get where they need to be. Once in the doorway, it's all down to you as number one. The rule is 'one voice,' my voice. Every number one has his or her own pattern; this was mine. "X, we know you are in this flat. We are armed police officers. Come to the front door with nothing in your hands; you will not be harmed. Do it now." Silence, you wait, you let the words sink in. On another occasion, you may say the house is surrounded, but six floors up, I didn't see much point. I repeat the challenge this time, though: "X, we know you're inside; come to the front door with nothing in your hands. I must warn you; we have a police dog and will send it into the flat if we receive no reply." Silence, then movement. The hallway led to a series of closed doors; one of them cracks open, two open hands appeared through the gap. "Don't shoot, man, don't shoot." Contact made; I feel the Taser officer joining me. I tell the suspect to walk out into the hallway, to move slowly, to interlock his fingers and place his hands on the top of his head. I tell him he's doing great; he won't be harmed. X walks into the hallway. I tell him to keep moving towards me, to keep his hands on his head. I can see my Glock torch dazzling him, that's just what I want. A few feet from the door I get him to turn around and walk the remaining distance backwards. As he closes the gap, I withdraw a few steps, keeping my Glock out of arm's reach. This movement allows the arrest team to take hold of the subject, cuffed they move him away from the front door; in that instant, I step forward and once again plug the gap.

All that remained was to search the flat and hand it over. The job went well. I enjoyed being number one and the responsibility that comes with it. During my career, I would hazard a guess I was number one more times than anyone in the department's history, but only because no one was dumb enough to stay on the cars for eighteen years. As we were putting the kit away, big N offered one final pearl of wisdom: "I like you as my number one."

"Why's that big N?"

"Being so little, if you get shot, it will be easy to step over your body." Everyone cracked up; I smiled my appreciation.

Years later I was on a daytime dig-out in Brixton, not far from the nick. Y was wanted for a series of violent gun-enabled robberies; the local task force had only gone and located him. Everyone wanted him nicked ASAP; he posed such a high risk that a daytime job was given the green light. This created a few more problems than normal. At 2am the suspect is probably tucked up in bed, along with the rest of the estate, the risk of the job being blown is much lower. Today, it was the middle of the school holidays; the estate was alive with people getting on with their lives. Speed would be critical if we were to pull this off. We had to be kitted up ready to move the moment we hit the forming up point (FUP). I was number two on the stick, armed with my 5. We made quickly made our way to the staircase then up onto the landing where the plainclothes officers had eyes on the front door. They withdrew as we closed it down; suddenly a front door, one before the target address opened, and out walked a small child holding some action figures. He sat down on the walkway and started to play with his toys, and then he saw us.

With number one covering the door, I lowered my 5 and knelt. I put my fingers to my lips, making a shooshing sound. He nodded back at me and smiled; I started to smile too. This kid was so cool. I now pointed for him to go back inside; he nodded, still smiling. He picked up his soldiers and walked back into his flat, giving me a wave goodbye as he shut the door. In a flash I was up. I wasn't tempting the gods on this job; we pushed on, setting up on the suspect's front door. Seconds later all hell broke loose as we shouted armed police as the door went in. The suspect surrendered, house searched, job done, we headed back to the FUP, but not before I knocked at the kid's door. Mum opened it and let me have it with both barrels. How dare we bring guns to her home? Her son was terrified, etc, etc. I listened patiently all the while her son smiled and waved from the sofa. Pissed off with her histrionics, I looked past her and gave him a Trojan thumbs up. He returned the favour, like I said, cool kid. "Take care buddy," and I was gone. On the drive back to base I suddenly thought of that armed cop in my front garden all those years ago, look at me now, I wonder what he would say.

Back now to my early days up north. By now I was driving as well as running comms. Each role could be a piece of cake or an absolute nightmare. As Dickens wrote, it was the best of times or the worst. I took to running a job on the radios like a duck to water. Some officers look at the radio like it's about to explode in their hand. A fear of speaking on the radio was and still is a 'thing,' as more and more officers arrive with less and less experience. It must sound ridiculous to civilians, but some officers' mouths disconnect from their brains when they hit the transmit button. Nowadays the roles in the car are a little different, but back in the dark ages, the good book of ARV tactics stated that upon arriving at the RVP, the driver must set up control. The operator hands over his notes and the radios and deploys to the incident with the maps officer. The reasoning being that the driver will be tired and stressed after driving to the job. Whoever thought this was a good idea had clearly never met the type of officer 19 had behind the wheel: full of testosterone, yes; tired and stressed, not a chance.

The practical implications of this role reversal were that the poor driver now gets lumped with one of the most difficult and thankless tasks in the world of armed policing: running control. Back to the good book, every job must have a control. 19 was the only armed department in the UK that ran cars three up, but I am happy to stand corrected on that.

WATCH AND REACT

The thinking being, if only one car arrived on the scene, two officers could contain the address, and one could set up control. This system worked brilliantly; it put armed officers into the mix right from the off. Not sat in their car waiting for further armed units, units which were often not even available. Back to the driver: he or she has been getting updates from the operator on route; it's the same for maps in the back. You're super busy, but all the while comms is drip-feeding you updates. Pulling up on scene, the three of you have a quick powwow, and then it's down to the driver to run the job. If it's a big one, they could find themselves coordinating the arrival of other Trojan units, including the kit car, as well as local officers, dog section, the helicopter, the LAS, and possibly the LFB, and if the shit really hits the fan, getting the CTSFO teams and negotiators involved. What a palaver. Take it from me, Trojan officers are masters of multitasking.

It's Springtime; the birds are singing, the sun was shining, and the day was full of promise, or so I thought until Ecky took a call to Barnet. A male in an address with a firearm. That was about the gist of it; Ecky was all over comms, on route he laid out the story. The informant sees a male with a gun enter the flat next door. Lots of noise and shouting. The informant wants to talk to the police and is giving real time updates on the landline, so this is probably for real, not a hoax. We arrive on scene; I take the radios and the clipboard from Ecky, I put my earpiece in, I can now chat with my crew on the back to back, and off they go. The venue is a flat, in a high-rise block, the plan is to get eyes on the address, an internal covert containment. Basically, they get to the landing and watch the front door. They stay covert, awaiting the arrival of further armed assets, but are close enough to react if the shit hits the fan. They can also provide intel to control, crucial stuff, like the best route in,

WATCH AND REACT

the construction of the door, and the atmosphere in the premises. So far, so good.

The local Duty Officer (Inspector) arrived on the scene; these were the days when borough Duty Officers were trained to run firearms calls. Arriving at the RVP, they would take command guided by the skipper in the base room and by the officers on scene. I introduced myself and started to ask what resources he had available. Straight from the get-go I'm getting a bad vibe. The Duty Officer is acting like it's his last day before retirement, he's gone all Danny Glover, Lethal Weapon. He was distracted, mumbling, fidgeting, clearly, he would rather be anywhere, other than standing here talking to me. He's giving a great impression of being on the verge of a nervous breakdown.

"Where are my Sergeants? Where are my Sergeants?" I see Trojan One's car arriving along with another car; with that, all hell breaks loose. My earpiece crackles into life: "SUPPORT." It's Ecky, and he's no flapper; the Duty Officer has had enough and literally runs and jumps into his car and disappears off into the distance. Trojan One arrives. "What's going on, Kev?" I'm at a loss; suddenly a swarm of people comes pouring out of the block. Chaos is now taking hold.

"What floor are they on?" Shit, what floor are they on? I didn't ask at the handover, and I hadn't asked the guys inside to confirm. Big mistake. Not wasting another second, the crews ran into the block to back up the armed officers. Soon normal service was resumed, with no one injured, thank God. When the informant called police, he failed to mention the venue was a drugs address. The flat was full of punters, druggies and the hangers-on that you find in such places, a real mixed bag of humanity. Apparently, a few customers decided it was time to leave and walked straight into the armed officers watching the front door. At that moment, World War Three broke out; the occupants of the flat started to flee, and two armed officers found themselves surrounded. It was Custer's last stand. Only the arrival of the Boss and the team saved the day. No one was arrested, and no gun was recovered; it was not my finest hour. It wasn't my first control, so I should have been all over it; sadly, I wasn't. The boss called everyone together for a chat. then said to me, "Kev, where is the Duty Officer?"

"I don't know, Sir; he drove off."

"He drove off."

"Yes, he drove off, Sir." I thought it best to start saying, Sir. Trojan One ended the huddle and suggested we return to base for a debrief. The drive back to base contained little or no chit-chat; I was deep in thought. Just how bad was my control? As I walked into the base, Johnny Orange put his arm over my shoulder. "Bit of career advice: it's going to get messy. You are in for a grilling, so just apologise and keep on apologising, ok" John wasn't wrong; I got ripped to pieces. Everyone had something to say about my performance, and none of it was good. At the end of the firing squad, the Boss went around the room asking each person to sum up their thoughts. Boy, oh boy, they didn't hold back. My catalogue of crimes too many to list, too embarrassing even now to put to paper. Debrief over, everyone went for a cup of tea, then back on the road. I walked into the yard and for the first time in my life understood why people smoke.

Sadly, this was not the end of the matter; the Boss went to see the local Duty Officer, who buggered off and gave him both barrels, he then had me back in for another chat. That job wasn't the last time I would be dragged over the coals at a debrief; I knew the golden rule: you can make a mistake; just don't make the same mistake twice. This was classic 19; no one gets a free pass, not the new guy, not the old sweat. The following day a rather sheepish-looking officer called Kevin Healy walked into the base; he was nervous as hell, but he needn't have been. Everyone was over it; things got said, lessons were learnt, and the team moved forward. My lesson: when you're wrong, you're wrong; take ownership, don't hide, and never lie. I mention this because I have witnessed debriefs where officers have attempted to shift blame onto others and have been economical with the truth; these officers are not forgiven. Wherever you are, Johnny Orange, thanks for the advice.

The worst debrief I ever endured was on overtime; in fact, it was so bad that afterwards, if I was asked to do overtime with this team, I would happily have gone to the shops, purchased a pen knife, whittled a wooden spoon to a point and stabbed myself in the eye just to avoid it. My list of mistakes was considerable, but basically, I ignored the golden rule: never say never on Trojan. So, when I arrived at a call in Wembley and was informed the suspect was on the run from prison and was sitting drinking in a pub on a busy high street, I stupidly assumed we would wait until he left the boozer and do a foot strike. Well, the Skipper arrived at the RVP and made the big call to dig out a busy pub. I had never done this before or since, but he was in charge; to add to my woes, somehow it landed in my lap to run the job, and I didn't know a single person there. The heavens opened; the crews all stayed sat in their cars and let me walk up and down the street in the pouring rain. Tapping on windows, asking officers' names and designating roles, it was a total clusterfuck, and to make matters worse, I forgot to get a dog. In my mind, we were never sending a dog into a crowded pub. Stupid decision by

WATCH AND REACT

me. The job went live; the suspect got arrested, and we returned to Wembley for a debrief. When they had finished ripping me a new one, which some of my colleagues enjoyed just a little too much, I only had one thing to say. I thanked them all for going out of their way to help me get the job up and running, my tone thick with sarcasm. That job really knocked my confidence. As much as I felt that I was thrown under the bus, I was the master of my fate; I let it unravel, and I had to shoulder the blame. It would never happen again.

By the time I retired, debriefs bore no resemblance to the ones I endured; maybe that's for the best; I'm not sure. I know one thing: I don't bloody miss them.

WHEREVER I LAY MY HAT

One evening whilst out on patrol the base called me direct, "Kev, bad news mate, looks like your flats been burgled can you make your way home, local officers are on scene." I was a bit shocked; a police flat being burgled that's a first. Arriving home, I saw the front door ajar, the lock damaged. Two local officers were waiting for me with a guy in plain clothes who it turns out was one of my neighbours. It was he that discovered the door wide open and the flat turned upside down or so he thought. I thanked him, then walked inside with the local coppers. It soon became apparent I hadn't been burgled; this was how I chose to live. There was no furniture, no computer, no bookshelves, no pictures, no personal effects, no objet d'art. An inventory or the flat would have read bed, sofa, telly, fridge. As for the front door I had come home weeks earlier rather the worse for ware and couldn't find my keys. I didn't have the money for a lock smith, so I did what I had done a hundred times on calls, I forced entry to my flat by shoulder barging it open. The lock was old and didn't take much persuading. Leaving the flat after that I used a piece of folded cardboard wedged between the door and the frame to secure it. Somehow today my door wedge failed. Oddly, I wasn't embarrassed in the least, I had nothing to be ashamed of, my kids wanted for nothing, and it seems I had unwittingly invented minimalism, get me. The look on the young officers faces was priceless. I thanked them for popping by then wedged the door shut and went back on patrol. They went off with a good story to tell on parade the next day. My two colleagues pissed themselves laughing. At the end of the shift Trojan one asked if it was true, I lived in a crack house.

That story of my flat and my lifestyle may sound a wee bit sad, but to be honest I was a happy soul of sorts. It's my good fortune that my natural disposition is to see that glass half full. Yes, I missed my children terribly, I balanced that against them being with their mother, living in a lovely big house, in a safe rural environment. Of course, I was financing this, but I had no complaints, it was my duty after all. This explains why I was always broke, my kids wanted for nothing in stark contrast to my own childhood. My police flat was a life saver, somewhere I went to get my head down between shifts, but it was never a home. If I'm honest I was over the making a home gig. Ten long years I had tried that and look how that worked out. I clearly wasn't cut out for it, I did my best to be a good dad, nothing came before my children, but as for being a husband, a partner, a soul mate do me a favour, I carried way too much baggage around. I thoroughly embraced this new lifestyle and freedom, I enjoyed my own company, I was wise enough to know boozing it up wasn't a good career move and you can only spend so long in the gym. To burn up some of my free time I started going to the cinema during the day. I became a member of the Ritzy cinema Brixton and loved the bohemian atmosphere of the place. Wandering in to watch just about everything and anything. I got to know the staff, but they didn't get to know me, I would never let on I was a cop. Over the months I developed my routine, cinema ticket, coffee, plumb cake, take my seat. Sitting in an empty cinema was my idea of heaven and woe betide any late arrival who sat within twenty feet of me.

Be it drinking alone, watching a film, or sitting in a Portuguese restaurant eating tapas with a beer I was ok with solitude. At work I was always with my crew, I loved the banter, the gossip, the piss taking. That and doing the job kept my mind focused and my thoughts positive. I didn't have time to think, which considering the state of my personal life was a good thing. Karate had taught me the mind controls the body, the mind can be your best friend or your worst enemy, I decided it would become my bestie. I created a persona that worked well for me. I never bitched about my ex, money or my divorce, never a bad word and if a mate on the car commented on the cards I had been dealt, I brushed it off, saying I still had my hair and boyish good looks, I refused to get twisted out of shape. This positivity made me a lot of friends and I think it helped others when their lives fell apart, which seemed to happen a lot in the police. Was it because I was the oldest guy on team, who knows, but people trusted me and opened to me. I couldn't believe it, Kevin Healy the agony aunt.

Life now decided to send me a curveball. I was asked to return to base and have a meeting with the Superintendent. My crew were full of questions; Big N didn't pull any punches. "What have you fucked up now, Healy?" In all honesty, I was at a loss. I left my crew in the canteen and headed to the fourth floor. I knocked on the Superintendent's door and was invited in. What followed is enough for me to look up the definition of surreal, and yes, surreal cuts it. The Super had in front of him on the table a folder, a very large folder bound with string and the word confidential stamped across it. "Kevin, I have to inform you that for the last few months you have been the subject of an investigation, the allegation being one of money laundering." If I had been a Disney character, my jaw would have hit the floor, my eyes would have shot across the table on springs, and tiny little birds would be flying around my head chirping. I was lost for words. "You can relax, Kevin; you're in the clear. No case to answer, in fact. Looking at the file, there's no evidence at all to support the allegation."

For the first time in my life, I was lost for words.
Eventually I came to my senses. "Can I see the file?"

"Sadly, no, I'm sorry."

"Can you give me a clue what this is all about?"

"it's connected to your divorce and financial irregularities."

With that, he picked up the file and put it back in a drawer in his desk. "So, what now? I asked".

"Well, Kevin, it's done and dusted. I have to say this is a bit of a first."

For you and me both, I thought. I left his office utterly bemused; a few phone calls later, I joined up the dots and solved the mystery. My ex-wife's legal team could not get their heads around, how I, a lowly paid police constable, lived in a three-bedroom flat in Belgravia. Going through my accounts, they were clearly confused that I shopped in the Kings Road; they saw receipts from John Lewis, Russell and Bromley and a host of other West End stores. Not happy that they achieved their goal, utterly humiliating me in court, they went on to contact the relevant authorities, voicing their suspicions as to my finances. The DPS, Department for Professional Standards, would have saved themselves a lot of time and energy if they had visited my 'luxury apartment.' My postcode was courtesy of the Met, and the shopping trips, Christmas and Birthday presents for my kids, all of this had been taken out of context by a legal team wanting a pound of flesh. When I gave evidence in court, they relentlessly berated and bullied me; eventually, utterly drained my tank empty, I bent over and started banging my head on the witness stand. I found myself involuntarily humming a tune that was getting a lot of airplay at the time. 'I think I better leave right now,' classic Will Young. It seemed strangely apt. The Judge, a man of compassion, seeing I was at the end of my tether ordered me to stand up straight, I was a professional witness. I passed a handwritten note to my solicitor, just five words: THEY SHOOT HORSES DON'T THEY.

The issue of living in Belgravia was resolved for me a few months later. I received a letter informing me that my tenure was up, and I was to vacate in the next few weeks. I dragged it out for a month or two, but eventually I bit the bullet and quit. It wasn't much of a wrench. Brixton, here I come. My sister owned a house there and generously offered me a room; God bless her. They say things happen in threes; I got invited into the office to see the boss. I walked out a few minutes later a South officer. I didn't see that coming; was becoming my epitaph. The logic was unmistakable; someone had to move South. I was one of the last people to join the team; I lived South of the river, and I was a driver. Swampies, here I come.

I had made friends, I was starting to fit in, I was learning fast, and then the rug was pulled from under my feet. I moved my kit South, said my goodbyes, and so a new chapter began. What I knew about South London you could write on a spliff. When my new buddies found out I lived on Lima Delta, Brixton being identified as LD in the same way the Hill was BH, they couldn't believe their ears. It was pointed out to me that south cars spent most of their day on Lima Dangerous, as it was fondly known. How did I feel about living on a Trojan borough? In truth, I couldn't care less. I didn't join the police for a quiet life, now did I. Brixton never failed to live up to its reputation in so many ways, both good and bad. One afternoon we decided to park up outside the Ritzy Cinema and drink our coffee. This was a risky call; you're sitting in a marked police car,

WATCH AND REACT

taking five, which acts as a homing beacon to the weird and the wonderful. True to form, a well-known local prostitute approached the car and started chatting. I should point out the distinction between Hollywood's idea of a sex worker and the tragic reality. To put it kindly, Julia Roberts, she was not. She was however a very funny lady; all was going swimmingly until she decided she needed the toilet. Without further ado, she climbed on top of a street bin and emptied her bowels in broad daylight, still chatting away to us. A member of the new Brixton elite, white, young and middle class, came up to my window and demanded, "Are you going to allow that? Do something." Oh boy, was she knocking at the wrong door. "What do you suggest I do?" The bright young thing thought for a moment. "I don't know; you're the police."

"Yes, we are, and the last time I looked, they didn't issue us with toilet roll." My nemesis shook her head in disgust. Happy her virtue signalling was done for the day she wandered off to tell her friends how she had stuck it to the man. Give me a sex worker with loose bowels any day; maybe I should rephrase that.

One Brixton Duty Officer, the Inspector in charge of the borough, did not like seeing ARVs driving around; I think we made him anxious. To him we equalled trouble, and to be honest, I did see his point. Sadly, for him, he went way too far in his efforts to keep us away from calls. A car with a firearms marker was being followed by a local unit. The marker linked someone in the car to possession of a firearm. Markers were great if they were up to date, which sadly often they were not. I was driving, heard the call and got Bear on radios to offer up our services to carry out the stop. Quick as a flash, the Duty Officer was on the radio: "No, thank you, Trojan; it's old intel. Stand down." By now we were behind the local police unit; not wanting to step on anyone's toes, we watched as they lit up the suspect with blue lights and two tones. The bandit car responded immediately and stopped. I pulled up alongside the marked police car; the driver gave me the nod that all was cool, and we drove away. As I turned left onto Poynders Road, not 50m away from the stop, I heard over the radio, screams and shouts for urgent assistance and then the shout "Gun."

I had already done a U-turn and was back with the local officers; the passenger of the bandit car had produced a bloody gun and was now out on foot. We gave chase across a car park and into a block of flats. My heart was blowing up; I had just run a few hundred metres flat out in boots and body armour. My crew, Bear and Stretch, were top lads and were already pointing guns at areas of danger, i.e., places the suspect could hide. Methodically, the three of us cleared level by level until we had only the top landing to clear. It's for moments like this that you join Trojan; it's as risky as it gets, pure adrenalin. We arrived at the last landing, hiding in a recess was the suspect. He was Tasered in an instant and detained. As I walked back to the car, I saw blue flashing lights signalling the arrival of multiple cars, armed and unarmed. This was the Met at its best, a call for urgent assistance, and everyone started heading to help. We handed over the prisoner who I found out had just been released from prison, so guess where he was heading. The gun was recovered and thank God no one was shot. The Duty Officer had given birth to kittens and looked a broken man. He thanked us for our help; no one felt the need to say, "Told you so." That's as close as it gets, I guess.

Driving along Coldharbour Lane, Dave D saw police struggling with an aggressive male. We stopped the car to help, just in time as it happened. The subject went to push the female officer. In a flash DD had his Taser out and was red dotting the aggressive male. To red dot someone is to turn on the Taser, which activates the red dot, which shows up on the person you're pointing it at. The male did not approve of our intervention, letting us know his thoughts on the Met police in no uncertain terms. Things were escalating; that was until DD explained what would happen if he did anything stupid. "Mate, if you kick off, you will be doing the electric boogaloo all the way to the nick." The mention of the electric boogaloo caused all parties to pause for thought. This was Brixton after all and a stone's throw from Electric Ave. The big aggressive male is laughing his socks off, what could have been a drama de-escalated, and all parties went home in one piece, which made for a nice change.

The sheer diversity of Brixton is something to behold. I was walking through the market after a foot chase when I saw what I thought was one rather large banana. Being a lover of the benefits of this fruit, I stopped at the market stall and purchased one. The stallholder handed it to me and started chatting about life, love, and traffic wardens when he stopped mid-flow and burst out laughing. It was not a banana; it was a plantain, and Muggins was trying to peel it, which was never going to happen in a month of Sundays. The stallholder is now calling to all the other traders in his thick Jamaican accent, "He thinks it's a banana; man thinks it's a banana." Now all the stallholders are cracking up, and I am laughing too. What an idiot. That's the day-to-day reality of a Brixton or a Hackney or any inner-city borough. One minute you're chasing suspects; the next, you're laughing at yourself with the locals. This may sound odd, but I loved living in Brixton. I loved policing it; every single day it tested your perceptions. The challenge is to keep your head, do your duty and go home in one piece.

All deaths are a tragedy; I've lost count of the times I've heard this spouted by the media, politicians or community groups. I can't say I always agreed. Often the victims of violent deaths were bad men who were more than happy to do bad things to further their criminal lifestyle. Revenge shootings, punishment killings, kidnappings, and sexual assaults – nothing was off the table. When innocents were caught in the crossfire, it only confirmed to me the ruthless nature of these young men, and they were always young men. One shooting stands out. In the early hours of February 6th, 2007, two gang members broke into a flat in Peckham looking for an associate who they believed had stolen money off them. The gang were carrying out cash-in-transit robberies and were convinced their intended victim was asleep in bed. Entering his bedroom, they shot the victim four times with a Mac-10 machine gun before fleeing. The intended victim was out selling drugs in a nightclub; the male they shot was his 15-year-old brother, totally unconnected to any form of criminality. His kid sister alerted the emergency services and then stood and watched her young brother die. This shooting shocked the public and drew a lot of media attention.

I was on early turn when I got a call to get two cars to Peckham 'on the hurry up'. The main suspect has been housed. I was in the alpha car and running the show. The murder team using technology I won't go into had a rough location but couldn't tie him down to an address, so no fast time dig out. Keeping two ARVs hidden in broad daylight on a busy housing estate is no mean feat, I can tell you; the hours dragged, then "Trojan, he's on the move in a car, no index." Still, we waited; until we had a registration or make and model, we were in the dark. Tension grew. "Come on, come on, get us the bloody reg." On cue the surveillance team transmitted the street name, then the make and model; we were now racing after the target. The car was located,

WATCH AND REACT

and a full-on option two played out. The suspect gave up without a struggle; he got thirty years for the murder, but as good a job as it was, no one was that elated. The whole operation summed up the sheer waste of life that happened daily on the streets of South London.

This wasn't my only run-in with a Mac-10 submachine gun. The firearm was being moved to an address for collection by a gang member. The courier was a young mum in her early twenties, pushing her new-born baby in a pram. The firearm was wrapped in a blanket in the tray below the child. Surveillance watched her leave her home address, as she neared Lordship Lane, we were given the nod to take her out. No one on the job wanted to point guns and go in 'full Trojan' on the stop; for Christ's sake, she had a kid with her. However, we didn't have control of her partner, the hero that let her move the weapon. If he turned up as we moved in, then things could get messy. We all agreed low-key until things went pear-shaped. As we pulled up alongside her, I saw the look on her face; I thought she was going to throw up. She was a kid, a poor kid, somehow in possession of a loaded Mac-10, that could see her get seven to ten years inside.

We put a bubble around her, located the firearm, and left it in place for the make-safe officer to do their magic. An unmarked car rolled up; she was arrested and driven away with her toddler in tow. I never found out what happened to her. I didn't want to; it would only be bad news, and I was tiring of bad news.

"Shots fired at Streatham ice rink." Arriving on the scene, we located the victim, a sixteen-year-old shot on the ice. Total bloody chaos inside the sprawling old building. Lockers ripped open; property stolen by hordes of youths' intent on taking advantage of the situation. Trying to make sense of all this are police officers desperate to save a young life. The lad died; he was 16. We searched the building, but the suspect was long gone. Just another call in South London.

Sometimes the victims bite back, as was the case in a flat just off the Wandsworth Road. Only minutes from the base, we turned out post haste to an aggravated burglary; the suspect was still on the scene. Screaming up to the address, an emergency search was authorised. We located the venue, a council flat, the door open and blood everywhere. The victim was sat in the kitchen, battered and bruised but alive and certainly not bleeding out. Lying on the floor was the suspect who had clearly bitten off more than he could chew. The victim, who was no mug, disarmed the burglar and, in the melee, stabbed his attacker more than once by the look of it. First aid commenced; everyone was covered in blood. It was one of those jobs. Rather unconvincingly, the victim said he had no idea whatsoever as to why someone would break into his home, in broad daylight, and attack him. Not being a budding Poirot, I left the scene none the wiser as to what the hell that was all about.

Trojan officers face unbelievable scrutiny from the media and the public. I have no intention of going all political and weary, but it should be mentioned just how many lives we as a department save. We arrive, often well before an ambulance crew, and get to work. The person we are working on is often part of the criminal fraternity, a gang member, drug dealer, etc. We don't hesitate for a second; the effort put into saving that life is incredible. I have lost count of the times I have worked alongside the helicopter emergency teams (HEMS) as they crack open a chest cavity, to massage a heart, or to stem a catastrophic bleed, all the while you're there in the thick of it. The victim's injuries are often a testament to bad life choices. At one shooting the victim had been blasted with a shotgun; we escorted the ambulance to the hospital, acting as security. Rushed straight into theatre, I followed. "Who the hell are you, and what the hell are you doing in my theatre?" The room was full of doctors and nurses in scrubs and me. Ouch! The nurse in question was purple with rage; I thought she might have an embolism. By contrast, I was in body armour not washed in five years (that's a lie, in 18 years, I never once washed my bod, I was the Febreeze kid) and mud-covered boots; I cut quite a dashing figure. "Get out, get out, get him the hell out." This was one nurse I wasn't going to ask out for dinner. I will conclude by saying the subject survived, though I can't speak for the nurse.

TROJAN 97

The South base, as already mentioned was located slap bang in the middle of a housing estate in Union Grove Clapham. As estates go, it wasn't Fort Apache the Bronx that dubious title went to the portacabin police station in Thamesmead. The architect of this concrete hell hole must have taken his inspiration from Hitler's bunker. Surrounded on all four sides by high-rise blocks, a posting to Thamesmead was the equivalent of getting orders to report to Stalingrad. The local youth liked nothing more than to drop white goods from a great height onto unsuspecting panda cars and police vans. I think they called it a community police station. It's gone now, I wonder why?

97, the South base was a shock to the system, the gym was so antiquated, Time Team could have done a show on it. The locker rooms were old offices with a mix and match of rusty lockers. The parade room, was the TV room, was the dining area, was the octagon when testosterone flared up. The South teams were small in number, they only had to provide two cars a day per shift plus a South kit car, which was crewed by a skipper and his driver. On any given day you could parade eight officers, if there were spares i.e., an officer not on a car, you rang the base room and waited to be told if a space existed on a north car. If you were lucky no space was available, you then were admin which meant training, paperwork and finding something to do which usually meant going home but keeping your phone on in case you were needed. The South base was like kryptonite to senior officers, who were known to go giddy and lose their superpowers if they attempted to cross Tower Bridge. This state of affairs suited the gentlemen of the South just fine.

WATCH AND REACT

Each relief had its own unique style, but the South took this to a whole new level. By far the toughest relief was D. Each one of them was a 'lump,' as in big and aggressive. I have never known such a short-tempered group of officers in my career. On overtime with them, the driver swore at me so much I started to wonder if he had Tourette's syndrome. I was actually doing a good job; God knows what would happen if I got us lost. Coming in for early turn, you took your life in your hands if they had been night duty. D relief would be slumped in chairs, lights out, catching up on some sleep after another hectic night. As you picked your way to the locker room, you did well not to wake them. Stepping over outstretched legs in the dark was no easy feat, in such a confined space. If you woke one of them, pray it wasn't a driver, because a set of car keys would be heading in the direction of your head. I felt sorry for the criminal fraternity if D Relief got hold of them. All that said, I loved working with this team; they were brilliant.

A relief believed they were the best relief bar none and made sure everyone knew that. The team had several eccentric individuals who could only exist South of the water. One of the team smoked a large pipe which he would produce when you least expected it. Puffing away in the yard staring off into the distance lost in thought. I was reminded of black and white pictures of the Battle of Britain, RAF pilots awaiting the next wave of Heinkel's.

E relief had a few elder statesmen such as Jules a Welshman who called me boy but did so in such a charming way you could never be offended. He loved to drive but refused to get in a BMW, far too much technology, for him, it was the Omega every time. Being front wheel drive, it was a driver's car, Jules loved nothing more than arriving on scene sideways, with maps upside down, head in a sick bag. Magic my old mentor from the Hill, Larry, who my mum met on a call one day in Croydon, she thought he was "A terribly handsome man." Junior were Gareth and Andy both who had less service than me but had longer on the unit, good guys. Andy looked like a Confederate Civil War General with his long goatee beard and was well into his military history as for Gareth he was a quiet man, an excellent operator and shot. No matter what you thought of your colleagues you always had to remember each person had passed the course. The toughest course the Met had to offer and every one first time, which was a big deal back in the day. In time, Dan would join from the counties and bring an irreverence to all things Met police which we all loved, he was also an excellent ARV officer which helped. DD would arrive with the introduction "I only applied because I was bored on nights," this went down like a lead balloon. What DD lacked in tact, he made up for with brains, a great sense of humour and a disdain for training which I loved about him.

Keeping us all under control were a couple of skippers, who as expected were very good at their job. One however stands out. Paul, Paul was a giant, well over 6 feet tall heavily built with a mop of black hair. His genetics must have come straight out of an East German Laboratory. He was a natural athlete and a born leader, SO19s very own Jack Reacher. In all the years I knew him I never saw him flap, stress, or drop the ball. He was the consummate professional, he led by example, he led from the front, qualities I respected, we all did. He demanded respect by his actions not his words, which was handy because he didn't say a lot but when he did the room fell silent. I fell out with him a couple of times over the years, job related stuff. I regret these bust ups, sadly we never got to sit down one to one to put these issues behind us. He was a great skipper and a good man; with this character he moulded a great team.

My first call was with Jules and Larry, and it was a humdinger, male shot in an address, the base gave the tactic straight to scene to save life. That was it, no added extras, get there and do what you need to do. Arriving on scene the three of us entered the house the front door being open, lying on the stairs was the victim, shot in the stomach at point-blank range with a Shotgun, he was a mess. Larry shouted for me to clear upstairs, and he would clear the ground level, Jules remaining with the victim. It took seconds, it wasn't in the book not in those days anyway, now it's called an emergency search. I shouted, "Level 2 clear," Larry confirmed "Level 1 clear." Jules had cut away most of the victim's clothing and was doing his best to stop blood flowing from multiple wounds not made easy by the victim's screams and thrashing around. Scene secure we called forward the LAS who were parked nearby. These were the days you could actually get an ambulance in London. The local duty officer arrived with his team, Jules gave the handover detailing our actions at the address, and that was that for us, we mounted up and headed to Leicester Square for coffee and a cake. I called the base room with the result and the job was put to bed.

In those days, there just wasn't the time to be weary about jobs. Trojan One didn't call us up, neither did the South Skipper. We were trusted to do our job and move on. A few days later we took a call to a group of men forcing entry to an address armed with guns and knives. Now this type of call was a bit suspicious. "Guns and knives" sounded a bit like overkill to me. We then got an update: "Trojan, we are getting a lot of calls on this one." OK, I thought it might be pucka. From the base "Gents straight to the scene." As we pulled up, I heard screaming coming from inside the address. As we closed down the front door, about five or six white males came out to greet us. One with the thickest Irish accent you could imagine, calm as you like, said "Good morning lads and what can we be doing you for?" Ah, the traveling community did have a way with words. With that, a neighbour shouted from the bedroom window, "HE HAS A GUN." We had little choice. We put in armed challenges, they hit the deck. A female voice in the house started screaming, and a baby started wailing. After debriefing the Irish contingent lying prone on the floor, clearing the address, two cars, and a bloody caravan, and speaking to the homeowner, it appeared it was all a huge misunderstanding. I came to learn travellers have a lot of misunderstandings. To be sure, no one was the wiser as to what the hell was going on, least of all us. Everyone was searched for a gun, but none was found. The traveling community never talked to the police and the neighbours knew better than to get involved officially. I called the base with the result, two words to describe the mayhem: "No offenses."

"Biggin Hill, where the fuck is Biggin Hill? Is it in the Met?" I was driving around Croydon when Andy took the call on the main set. A male was stabbed at an address with no locals to deal. Trojan in the early days didn't do knife calls, but if we did, 'they would probably be the best knife calls in the world'; we were far too busy. If we were nearby, no drama, we would help, but the general feeling was that when we were on borough, we dealt with knives without Trojan, so let the locals deal unless they specifically asked for us. The venue was a farm; I didn't know we had farms in the Met. The dual carriageways of Croydon gave way to country lanes; no GPS in the car meant the poor map reader was getting thrown around like a rag doll, as I drove flat out down winding country lanes. Eventually, we arrived on the scene; sure enough, the victim, a male, had multiple stab wounds. He staggered out of the house, collapsing in front of me. Bleeding puncture wounds evidence of the assault; the suspect was still in the venue. The suspect was his wife. The first rule of first aid is danger, as in, make sure there isn't any. Well, a disgruntled wife with a knife spells danger in my book. We cleared the ranch-style house, moving silently from room to room. This was her home; she knew every inch of it, where to hide, and where to ambush us. I should say it was incredibly tense, but actually it was great fun. Searching for an armed suspect who was hiding really gives your day purpose. This isn't bravado, I bet; if you surveyed 19, every ARV officer would want that call. It never crossed my mind that I could be injured; I never gave it a second thought. Eventually, we cornered the lady who instantly gave herself up. First aid involved cutting off the victim's clothing to reveal his wife's attempts to turn him into a human sieve. Plugging a series of puncture wounds as well as some very deep slashing cuts as we waited for the LAS and local units. Once again, a quick handover and then a blue light run to Brixton to another gun call. Not once at any of these calls did anyone say we saved a life or think about a pat on the back; we were just doing our job and thinking ourselves lucky to be allowed to do it.

Never take a call for granted; I learnt that years before at the Hill, sadly, 19 appeared to have its fair share of Mystic Meg's. Calls would come out, and you would hear them chipping in, "that's a hoax call," "false alarm," "fireworks," etc. I hated hearing this stuff; it was contagious. Soon you would hear new guys spouting this tosh, old sweats before their time. Sat in the Lewisham canteen, a call came out: "Kids running and pointing guns, in a street just off Coldharbour Lane, Brixton. We took the call, but my driver didn't exactly bust a gut getting to the car, and when he did, he drove like Miss Daisy. In his defence, we only had one call, and he played on that: "Come on, be real, only one call to guys with guns in Brixton; do me a favour." Eventually, we arrived on the scene, and what a scene it was. Shell casings littered the street; a blood trail ran off towards a private gym. Residents started appearing, giving versions of the shoot-out they had witnessed. One bloody call, I thought, as I radioed the base asking for a second car; we were going to have to clear the gym. The base skipper told us to do a 'walk-through'; now I hated walk-throughs, and most people I worked alongside did too. The problem is, it's not one thing or the other: you're just visually clearing an area. It's not a search; you don't go opening cupboards and searching under beds or clearing lofts, etc. So, what's the point? When you leave, you can't hand on heart say someone isn't hiding or indeed lying injured inside.

When I say private gym, you're probably imagining your local family-friendly Virgin Health Club or David Lloyd, maybe something with a pool and a crèche. Well, stop right there, amigo; the sports facility we were about to walk through was a private gym for very serious dudes. Dudes whose size was less down to protein shakes and broccoli than to the stuff they were injecting; simply put, they were beasts. Beasts who, to a man, were not fans of the Metropolitan Police and SO19 officers were top of the list. The degree of hostility was apparent from the second we walked inside; all our questions to the receptionist were met with a blank stare. As to the recent events in the street, as well as the owner of the blood all over the car park, we were met with silence. Ignoring the lack of community goodwill, we commenced the walk-through. Fortunately for me, my reflexes were still pretty good; I ducked as a basketball flew past my head with some serious intent behind it. We cleared the gym as best we could, but it was a tricky proposition, especially as one bodybuilder the size of a double wardrobe refused to stop training as I walked gingerly around him. His knees were bandaged, his elbows were bandaged, and his wrists were bandaged. The last time I saw that many bandages on one person, it was at a Boy Scout first aid assessment. Completing his last set, he threw the bar down with a clanging of metal plates. He screamed in my face, "MOMMA, MOMMA, I do it for you, momma, I do it for you." He was fucking huge, he was pumped, and he was as mad as a box of frogs. This was one of those moments when a Healy wisecrack could have got me killed; I kept my gob firmly shut. The blood trail was a dead end; often if you find blood at a scene, you get a call that a person has presented at the hospital with gunshot wounds. That's the signal to dispatch a car to A and E, to secure the wounded party and to provide armed protection for the hospital staff. No such call was forthcoming, so whatever happened to the injured party, God only knows. As for gym membership, no one asked if they did police discount.

These calls were typical of a day down South; a couple of cars covered this huge area, and it was brilliant to be part of it. I was never any good at paperwork, be it files for a prosecution or putting reports on the intelligence system. CRIS, if anyone remembers it, was the Met's first computerised crime reporting system. To log on, you had to swipe a card, put in a password, and if you inputted something incorrectly, the computer would make a "Ping" sound. I was so bad at inputting reports that the machine sounded like it was playing jingle bells on a glockenspiel. Trojan saved my sanity; the most paperwork we ever did was an Incident Report Book (IRB). We wrote these up after each job, but only if we used force, so in truth, after most jobs. Pointing a gun at someone is an assault, in our case a legal assault, which we justified in our report books. Years later the books went out the window, mostly because they were getting lost or damaged or whatever, and so we would knock out statements on the computer and then e-mail them to the officer dealing with the job. I had years of statement writing under my belt; my days at the Hill were invaluable, but as a custody sergeant once said, "Healy, you're a good street cop, but you lose all interest once you arrive in custody." I loved the chase, the roll arounds, but as for sitting in an interview room listening to "No comment" fifty times, please God let me die. So, what I am trying to say is this: 19 was made for officers like me, who enjoyed a mix of physical danger and mayhem but went weak at the knees if we had to complete a file for court. All in all, I was loving being a Southy.

The base may have been infested with rodents; it may have been a nightmare to get to on public transport, but it was located near Clapham and its multitude of bars. After the last early turn before lates, we South officers would head to the watering holes it offered. Often when the lads called it a day, as married men who wish to stay married do, I would remain in Revolutions or All Bar One, drinking and making new friends. I lived in Brixton just up the road, so a meandering stroll home wasn't exactly taxing. When my team discovered I was walking home drunk late at night on Lima Dangerous, they had kittens. Only once did I almost come unstuck; it was the early hours in some back street. A car pulled up, and the passenger asked for directions. My spider sense told me this was cobblers; as I weighed up how this was going to play out, the driver and rear seat passenger got out of the car. This was escalating fast; even being a highly trained ninja was not going to get me out of this situation unscathed, I sensed. As if by magic, the dark street became illuminated with blue lights as a police car pulled up alongside the parked car. The police car was a south night duty ARV; the crew didn't know it was me, not until they were right on top of us. The guys who had got out of the car were back in it in a flash and off down the road. The ARV operator shouted, "You ok, Kev?" I called back, "All good, no dramas," and with that, they were high tailing it after these suspicious characters, who bit off more than they could chew. I couldn't stop smiling the rest of the way home. This near miss didn't change my drinking habits one bit, which says a lot about how much of an idiot I have been.

An often repeated saying on 19, back in the day, was that the North got more calls, but the South got real calls. Now having worked both North and South, I could see there was some truth in this statement. The North ran more cars because they got a greater volume of work; however, the South did get its fair share of shootings and a lot less hoax calls. Talking of real calls, we ran to a male shot in a flat not far from Brixton Nick. We arrived at the block and got buzzed in by the porter; we ran up the stairs and knocked at the front door. The caller had stated the suspect was long gone. Walking into the flat, I was surprised at how many young women there were inside and even more surprised by their state of attire. It was 10 am on a Sunday morning, and no one seemed to be wearing any clothes. As distracted as I was, I did locate the victim who was sitting on a sofa, his hands holding his groin. Moaning and rocking to and fro, this guy was not having a peaceful Sunday; even in the dimly lit room, you could see the large blood stain soaking through his jeans. The girls in the flat were all talking over one another, telling us a Black guy broke in, shot the victim and fled. We called for the LAS to come up and join us; whilst we awaited their arrival, we convinced the victim to remove his hands and let us have a look at the injury.

"How bad is it, man?" The victim, a Black male with dreads aged about thirty, was staring up at the ceiling, not wanting to view the train wreck that had once been his penis and testicles. Andy replied, "I've seen worse; try and relax." Seen worse! where I wondered, the Texas Chainsaw Massacre. The LAS ran into the room, all green jumpsuits and excitement at being at a shooting. The excitement on the young paramedic's face didn't last long as she attempted to convince the victim nothing vital was missing; if you discount a testicle on the ceiling and a chunk of penis in the sink, nothing was. No arteries were hit; in truth, he was a very lucky fella and lived to 'fight' another day, so to speak. A few days later, we were sitting in the canteen in Streatham nick. A local DC came over and asked if we were at the shooting. He went on to explain the working girls in the flat came clean later and admitted he had the gun down the front of his trousers, and when one of the girls started undoing his zipper, it went off, the gun that is. Well, how's that for an own goal?

WATCH AND REACT

THAT'S NOT BRAVE

I have banged on about my early years on 19, when we were autonomous. Compared to today, when a 999 firearms call comes in, it often doesn't even make it to the cars because the information has been interrogated in the Pod and gets not declared. Sadly, more and more calls got the dreaded not declared, sometimes rightly, sometimes wrongly. I will talk more about the Pod later, but back in the day we had a base room, and if someone said "Gun," 19 sent a car. Easy, really. If it turned out to be nonsense, guess what? Nothing happened. If it was Pukka, then someone was likely to get a gun pointed at them, and rightly so. The base trusted the cars to make the right decision based on what they found on scene.

Keeping this in mind, it was night duty; Dave, Gareth and I were punting around Lewisham when over the local radio we started hearing about a guy locked in a room with his kids, threatening to kill them. Clearly, the base wasn't aware; we headed to the scene, located the block of flats, the car park was crowded with police cars. The address was a small new-build development. Walking inside, I found the local Duty Officer and some of his team as well as the Inspector and skippers from the Territorial Support Group, the TSG. Add to the mix Mum and friends; it was one crowded flat. So, what did we have? Dad, ex-military, had some form of mental crisis. Armed with two large kitchen knives, he has taken his two young sons into the bathroom, locked the door and told his wife he intends to kill them and himself. Local police were called and decided this was above their pay grade; the TSG were called as they were trained in forced entry and dealing with knife calls in buildings. However, 19 should have been called because the big book of police tactics says if you have hostages, then this falls into the remit of an armed op; these two kids were hostages, and there was a threat to life. To put it bluntly, a gun beats a knife; this was a Trojan call all day long.

The Duty Officer and his section sergeant were deep in conversation with the TSG boss; I was about as welcome as a cold sore on prom night. I introduced myself and pointed out this was a 19-job and that we would now take over running the call. Inspectors don't like being told what to do by PCs, but as the saying goes, tough shit. I informed the base what we had; the response was, "Crack on, lads." A local officer was first on the scene and was talking to the suspect through the closed door; he had a good rapport going, so I told him to continue. This officer was doing a great job, and a few years later I was not surprised to see this same officer sitting in the base, a new arrival on 19. I like to think our actions that night convinced him to join us.

The suspect stated he was going to kill the kids at midnight, and the clock was ticking. Only a door separated us, I could hear the suspect praying, the young boys crying filled me with dread. He was going to kill them, and we had to stop him, if these kids were to see their mother again we had to act fast. Between us we formulated a plan to get in that room and save the boys. The toilet door was outward opening, we got a hooley bar to crack it open. The hour was getting close, the mood of the suspect even more erratic, and the tension in the tiny flat was like nothing I had yet faced, it was time. The door was breached. Dave and I leapt into the room to grab the kids; Gareth, armed with his MP5, was to hold the door and take the shot if the suspect went to harm the kids or indeed us. In a flash I found myself standing one foot in the bath struggling to hold the knifeman's wrist, fighting to gain control, Dave doing the same. The next few seconds were a blur; the children were plucked to safety. No one got stabbed, and no one got shot. Mum was crying, her boys safe; the local duty officer thanked us, he didn't have to explain two dead kids and Dad shot by police to the Commissioner, let alone the media. It was a great job, and one that today just couldn't happen. Back to the big book of firearms operations: when you have hostages, you call negotiators, we didn't; you call an SFO team. The base did but they were deployed on a job. You negotiate, negotiate, negotiate, and the SFO teams trained in hostage rescue do their thing if it comes to life and death. Coming in for our meal break, in the early hours, the team asked, what have we been up to? "A hostage rescue." Word got out what we had done; it was tea and medals all round, and we got 'written up'. Job speak for a commendation.

The ceremony was to be held at The Royal Hospital Chelsea, the home of the Chelsea Pensioners. The recipients were from across all departments of the Met. I was the proud dad, in my tunic with my kids, having given the triplets Max, Sas, and Fire a day off school to share in the memory. As I sat waiting for our award, we listened to what the other officers and civilians had done to warrant being there. My son Max was clearly not impressed. An award went to a guy who fixed a radio issue; Max shook his head. Next up, a team for community relations work. Max had had enough and blurted out, "That's not brave Dad." I couldn't agree more, son. Were they not just doing their job? Then again, weren't we? Max was not just impressed with our job; what about the unarmed borough officers tackling a man armed with a machete? They did a great job; Max approved of that one. I had to agree; that took guts. The event over, I got a photo of Dave, Gareth and I with our wives and kids. This job only confirmed the amount of trust placed in ARV officers. Not one supervisor

WATCH AND REACT

from 19 attended the call. We saved those kids lives I am adamant on that point and as for dad he came away unscathed, a bit bruised and battered but alive. This was a job well done.

The base room had to be dragged out of the dark ages, or so the College of Policing model demanded. From the ashes rose the Pod, based at Lambeth HQ deep in the bowels of the earth. Surrounded by traffic Pods, DPG Pods, squad Pods, and protection Pods, the days of individuality of being apart were over. The new location came with rules: no drinks or food in the Pod. Sod that, was the general reaction. To add to my disgust, you also had to do a Pod course to use the computers and radios. How had we come to this? The location was chosen to provide absolute security; nothing would stop the Pods from getting their message out, not even a Russian warhead. Sadly, the planners hadn't counted on a dodgy plumber and a sewage pipe cunningly located behind a false ceiling, directly above the Pods. It burst, spewing raw sewage in all directions, and so closed the Pods, temporarily. So much for a Russian warhead.

The closure of the base room was the end of an era for 19 officers. Never again would you hear over the ARV channel, "99 back gates, please." The base room was the beating heart of the department. I lost count of the times I sat on my swivel chair watching a movie, drinking a coffee, feet up on the counter. Talking nonsense with Kev or Gareth, leaping into action when the phone rang, or MP transmitted "Any North Trojan unit". Change may be inevitable, but when it came to policing, I found change was often for the sake of change, with little or no practical benefits. Secretly I had my suspicions the move had darker motives. Some senior officers seemed to have a bee in their bonnet about the way we conducted ourselves. Did they

WATCH AND REACT

want to make 19 just another department? Special Branch was no more; the same was true of the Flying Squad. What lay in store for us?

Another bitter winter blew across the UK; I thanked the baby Jesus that bad people tended to stop shooting one another when it got cold and icy. It makes running away from the police that wee bit trickier. A grim freezing night duty driving around Croydon made you question why you didn't try harder at school. A traffic unit was behind a car involved in a domestic; that's not a typical traffic call, a second traffic unit is now involved. Curious, very curious, I thought to myself in between thoughts of a warm bed and sleep. It transpired the suspect in the car had abducted his child from Mum. The child was a baby, not a newborn, but way too young to be away from Mum. Traffic put in a two-car stop with the intention to get the child somewhere safe. This plan fell at the first hurdle; the suspect intimated he had a knife, telling the cops to back off. This was now 19 territory, cars started making 'progress' to the scene. Job speak for driving very FAST.

Arriving on the scene, I saw the suspect's car sandwiched between two traffic cars. Very quickly other Trojan units were on scene and began negotiating with the male. Jamie, who had been on the team a while, took the lead with this and was doing great; his ability to get his message across was the talk of the team. As a newbie, he would sit on parade and take great care and attention as to the preparation and ingestion of his sandwiches and banana. His meticulousness upset the more Neanderthal members of E relief. The next time he sat to eat, he discovered his lunch box had been tampered with. The ham sandwich had the ham removed, and his banana, well, the less said about the banana, the better. Looking across the table with fire in his eyes, he spoke the immortal line, "You don't mess with a guy's lunch box." This classic one-liner was a green light to the team; it was now open season on that little box of treats. Jamie had to eventually give up bringing a packed lunch. He is now a priest, vicar, or God botherer somewhere. I say this with a huge amount of love and respect; he's a wonderful individual, and I count him as a dear friend, someone I would do anything for. So back to the story, Jamie is doing the talking, a natural communicator.

This call had all the potential to go horribly wrong. Dad is armed; the weather is atrocious, with a bitter wind cutting through you, and then it started to sleet. It was as wicked a night to be deployed as I can ever remember in all my years in the job. The baby was wrapped in a blanket, but the car engine was turned off; it was freezing inside the cabin. Dad was one volatile individual erupting without warning; young Jamie has his work cut out. The ambulance arrived along with paramedics. Eventually, the negotiators arrived and do what they always do: stand back and let Trojan continue building bridges. 19 officers do a lot of talking; just ask any of the poor sods who had to work with me for twelve hours. ARV officers must be good communicators; it's essential in the role, keeping people from doing crazy shit that may get them shot. Talking them down, getting them to surrender, this is a skill and explains why 19 may run to thousands of calls each year, but how many ends in shots fired by police, on average, one a year. That tells you how good the boys and girls are at keeping the lid on things. This call and its potential outcome drew the Duty Officer from Croydon as well as Trojan One.

Calls were being made to the local hospital asking how long an infant could survive in these dropping temperatures, but any answer they gave was pure guesswork. The driver was told to turn on the engine to get the heater going, but his behaviour was so erratic we couldn't be sure he might not try and ram his way out of the roadblock. Hours ticked by; no one wanted to make the big call. It was now so cold you could hardly feel your hands, let alone your fingers. The ARV officers took turns sitting in a warm police van; we all knew at some point we would be deployed. Frozen fingers and triggers are not a good mix. Eventually, the word went out that if we didn't act now, that child would die of hyperthermia. No one was smiling now; a plan was formulated. Officers were designated to smash the windows to gain access but also as a distraction, one officer was to grab the child, and one to Taser the driver by means of dry stunning. This involves pressing the Taser against the person, creating contact, and then discharging the Taser, incapacitating the male. Lastly, one officer had firearms cover because if Dad went to hurt that child, he was going to be stopped. Everyone had an important role, and come zero hour, they did their job. With a nod from the boss, 'CRASH,' the windows go in; the guy is Tasered, and the child is out and whisked off to the ambulance. The suspect is dragged out, prone on the ground, secured, job done, no loss of life, and fuck, am I cold. My job in this controlled melee was to deal with the driver, and even though I got tasered a wee bit, it was worth it.

We drove to Croydon to debrief and warm ourselves up, we then decided to stay indoors the rest of the night. We had earned our pay that night, and who knows that little kid is running around somewhere, oblivious to the danger they were once in and the hell of a night they gave us.

The Christmas period is an odd one. No one wants to get nicked over the holiday period, but once Santa has eaten his mince pie and buggered off up North, the gloves are off. Brixton was having a series of violent carjackings. The suspects were two Black males, both armed with large knives; if you read the briefings on these two, it was clear they were a scary proposition. It's night duty; at 7 am, I plan to collect my kids from my sister's, and away we go visiting family in Norway. I was crewed with Paul, the skipper, and a new officer, a young female called D. I for one had my mind on other things than crime; getting the kids on that plane involved a lot of moving parts, and I was not going to be off late. The skipper, out of the blue, said, "Kev, that Vauxhall Astra that was carjacked earlier, it's behind us." I looked in the rear view mirror to see the Vauxhall with two Black males seated in it about twenty metres back with none for cover. It was a case of who would blink first; they did, pulling a violent sharp right. I was already doing a U-turn and was after them. I turned left and saw their brake lights ahead; the road had speed humps, but neither of us was slowing down. The skipper went to the main channel, putting up the pursuit, I focused on the bandit.

For the next few minutes, I pursued the bandit (we don't chase anymore; it gives the wrong vibes to the public) around the back streets, and then suddenly we were on a nice bit of straight road. I was flying down Abbeville Road towards Acre Lane when the bandit lost control in front of me. The Astra hit the kerb at the junction of Crescent Lane and went airborne, cutting a telephone kiosk in half, going straight through the 8ft brick wall and missing a very large tree by inches. It came to a halt in a garden and promptly caught fire. The skipper, D and I, ran to the burning car expecting a full-on tear-up; instead, we extracted the two suspects who did not put up a fight. Probably due to the fact two airbags had deployed in their faces. Not wearing their seat belts must have added to the trauma of the collision. Dragged clear, other units arrived and doused the flames. The car still contained a boot load of Christmas presents; the victim's kids would be happy to see them again. Mum and Dad may not feel the same about the car, though.

A Traffic Sergeant was on route; a police pursuit culminating in a crash, injured parties and a tonne of damage was right up their street. The traffic skipper couldn't care less; we caught two badass carjackers and recovered the Christmas presents. As I awaited their arrival, I surveyed the scene: two bad guys on stretchers, being treated by the LAS; a smouldering car; a demolished wall; and a phone box that now looked like a transformer. I was thinking to myself, Nice one, Healy, good job, when I troubled to look at my police driving permit and realised it wasn't signed. This was bad; driving a police vehicle with a permit missing the correct dates and signatures was a big deal, a discipline kind of big deal. This was your classic hero-to-zero moment; that is, it would have been if Night Duty Trojan One, no names, came over and said, "Everything ok, Kev?"

"Not really, sir," I quickly explained my predicament; all my paperwork was in order; I just forgot to get it signed that night after parade. With that, the Traffic Skipper pulled up. "Quick, hand it over." The boss took my permit and signed the relevant parts, furiously scribbling as the Skipper got ever closer. Handing it back to me, he walked into the path of the traffic officer and told him what an amazing job we had done, not that the skipper looked in the least bit interested. The gods smiled on me that night in the form of a Trojan one who trusted his officers and was prepared to do some nifty accounting, safe in the knowledge that I wasn't pulling a fast one, which I wasn't. The boss is retired now, so, Sir, wherever you are, thanks a million.

WATCH AND REACT

That was not the end of the evening; everyone involved had to parade at Brixton for a debrief. The room was packed and buzzing; the carjackers had done three or four jobs in just a couple of days, and so this was a fantastic result. Into the room walked Superintendent Musker. Well, well, the borough commander doing a night duty with the troops – you don't see that very often. He handed the crew and I handwritten notes thanking us for the brilliant job we did that night. The firsts kept on coming. He then stood in front of his officers and praised our courage and professionalism in detaining such violent, dangerous men. That pursuit and its climax were great fun, but in truth, it was just another job to join all the other jobs. Within a few hours I was sat with my children flying to a snow-covered Oslo, the four of us excited to be together, not a care in the world. Once again, I had managed to keep all those plates spinning, but for how much longer would my luck hold, I wondered. My kids were soon fast asleep; only then did I allow myself a little shut-eye, ever vigilant, their safety always my primary objective.

CRASH BANG WALLOP

It snowed overnight, and so the British transport network went into meltdown. I was up early with my route planned. Train to Gillingham, Dorset, collect car at station, arrive at the kids' school no later than ten am. Plenty of time for a mince pie, a hot chocolate, and to find a front row seat for the kid's first nativity play. I promised I would be there, so that was that. Sadly, a freak weather front was planning on turning me into a liar. What's worse than a no-show dad? The train crawled out of London, meandering west through Basingstoke and Woking, eventually arriving in Salisbury. It was about then that I noticed the snow, deep white snow, not the melted slush in London. The train travelled at a reduced speed and eventually crawled into Gillingham. By now I was beside myself; I was cutting it so fine, my timing's all out the window. I jumped into my brother's car, lent to me for the day, and sped off in the direction of the kid's school. Sadly, my eagerness to arrive on time overshadowed the other driving rule, 'arrive alive'.

I was driving a car I had never driven in appalling conditions down country lanes that were evidently a death trap, well, not to me but to every other road user doing 20 mph. The lanes got narrower, the gradient steeper, and the road more treacherous. It was inevitable I would crash, and boy did I do it in style. Rounding a tight bend, I was faced by a brewery delivery lorry. It was crawling up the steep hill I was flying down. I saw the lorry far too late, hit the brakes, forgetting all my police driver training, hitting the lorry head-on. The impact smashed all the windows in my car; my head hit the steering wheel, stunning me. The car seemed to bounce off the front of the lorry and come to a halt in a deep muddy ditch. I got out and collapsed onto the tarmac. The crew of the lorry ran to my assistance just as my phone began to ring. Dazed, I took the phone out of my pocket and stared in wonder as it played the tune YMCA; some very baffled faces stared back at me. I found out later Dave D had changed my ringtone as I was leaving work late the previous evening. I got to my feet, apologised for the crash, then blurted out, "I will be back; I have to go to my kid's nativity play." With that I began to run down the hill to the school. It was about a mile, but I was on autopilot. I don't remember much about the journey; all I know is that a short while later I was sitting in the assembly hall, waiting for the curtains to open.

The pianist commenced playing, the choir began singing, my headache throbbed in time, and lo, the nativity play commenced. I saw my two girls, one an angel, one a shepherd with a fuzzy beard, and then my son with a beaming grin appeared. If I had died then, I would have died happy; I had kept my word. Not even the sight of my ex-wife and her new partner could ruin this moment. I must have been in shock or concussed or both.

The story of the nativity play highlights the lengths I was going to, trying to be a good dad. I thought nothing of finishing a night duty, getting a train to Dorset, having the kids all day, dropping them off, then jumping a train back into town and doing another night duty. The lads on the team thought I was nuts. Looking back, yes, I was, and yes, I would do it all again; it was worth it, but it almost killed me. Overtime became a huge part of my life; without it, I couldn't exist. It was a good job I was relatively young and fit because I was always on the move, be it doing my day job, overtime, raising my children and all the while attempting to stay fit and healthy. That, my friends, is some juggling act.

WATCH AND REACT

The call asked for two Trojan units to head to Brixton on the hurry up. A vehicle three up, at least one armed with a firearm, is on route to shoot X. It was the middle of the afternoon, and Brixton was buzzing. It was baking inside the car; the air con was busted, and the three of us were suffering. The Bravo car was driven by Gringo, a lad from another relief who sported the sexiest moustache in the department. We had hardly ever spoken, but when we saw one another, we always gave one another the nod. The nod that says, 'You're alright.' The bandit car was in front of us, passing Morley's department store, heading towards Streatham. I was the lead car; we were too close to the bandit to use lights and two tones, so we were running a two-car convoy in stealth mode.

As I approached the bridge at the junction with Atlantic Ave, the lights turned green. I pushed through only for a white van to appear from nowhere and hit us head-on. The accident investigator later ruled the white van had raced to beat the lights, screwed up, went through on red and turned right into Brixton Road. Well, you know what happened next. Andy, who was upfront on radios, had his MP5 rammed into his face; Mark in the back smashed his knee, and I bounced my head off the door window. Dazed and a little shaken I turned my head to see Gringos car pull up alongside ours. What happened next, I say with enormous pride, I gave him a thumbs up and shouted, "GO, GO, GO." He smiled back, then hit the gas after the bandit. I got out of my car, which was a mess, walked towards the van, opened the driver's door and called the driver every name under the sun. Walking back to my car, my legs gave way, and I collapsed. My next memory is of a lovely young Black girl giving me a bottle of water; her kindness was in stark contrast to the whooping crowd that had gathered to see the injured police officers.

The young lady worked in Marks and Spencer's. Her kindness is something I will never forget. Andy shouted, "They are out on foot." With that, my brain unscrambled. The three of us started to run, hobble, limp towards the suspects who, as luck would have it, ran straight towards us. How we did it, I don't know, but, in a blink, the suspects were prone and in cuffs and never got to shoot X, and that was something I was proud of then and now. Reality bit me in the arse when the ambulance took the van driver to hospital but told us we had to make our own way. The ARV was a wreck; my crew and I were a mess, and to put a cherry on my cake, Gareth the skipper informed us we should all be in for night duty the next day. He had to be kidding, right? He wasn't.

Traffic skippers and Trojan are like oil and water; they just don't mix well. Traffic has a certain reputation, hence their nickname, Rats. Police vehicles are a visible representation of the service. Traffic cars are the Rolls Royce of the fleet, immaculate in every way; the Trojan fleet of Vauxhall Omegas and BMW saloons were, by comparison, a very poor relation. Like a journeyman boxer's face, the cars carried the scars of every brutal encounter. The state of the ARVs was a constant reminder that Trojan played by their own rules. The rat Skipper who attended my collision was typical of the breed; he couldn't care less that I was on a firearms op and about to stop armed suspects. He had his job to do, and that involved being as weary of a jobsworth as I ever met. Thankfully my ordeal ended when I got shipped off to hospital.

Roughly a year later I attended court to give evidence regarding the collision; police cars don't crash, we collide. The defendant was charged with a host of motoring offences and decided the best way to tackle the problem was to defend himself. Well, he had clearly watched a lot of US courtroom dramas because he accused me of lying, moving the cars prior to being photographed, jumping a red light, and tampering with evidence. The list went on and on; he really went the whole nine yards. It was quite a performance. At one point I almost shouted "You can't handle the truth." By contrast, the police accident investigator was rather dreary, as he only dealt in facts. The hearing that day was being heard by a lay bench of three upstanding members of society. Who, with a little training, get to sit in judgement over hard-working, professional police officers? These three unwise men were utterly clueless. I say this because after hearing the evidence, they summed up by saying, "Sometimes accidents just happen, and it's no one's fault."

Spilling a cup of tea – now that's an accident. The defendant wrecked a police car, hospitalised three officers, lied to cover up his mistake and walked away scot-free. So much for justice. The poor Traffic Skipper sat shaking his head, staring at the ceiling. As I was leaving the court, he came over to say goodbye. "Well, I retire in a couple of weeks, thank God. I don't think I can sit through another clusterfuck like that." We shook hands, and I wished him well. He may have been a rat, but he was done; he had made it to his thirty, and rat or no rat, you deserve a round of applause in my book. His parting shot was to give me three points on my police driving permit. Thanks, skip about that round of applause.

Sophia was triplet number three, three because she was the last triplet delivered. She, like so many young girls at the time, was obsessed with Bratz dolls, a fad that was sweeping the country. I hated the look of the dolls, but what did I know? Sophia desperately wanted the Bratz bike, an item so sought after that every shop I visited was sold out. I mentioned this around the parade room table and was astounded by the response. My teammates, my friends, set out to find me that bike. Cars headed to all four corners of the capital. Imagine the looks they must have got: three armed officers walking into Toys R Us asking to purchase a purple Bratz bike. I couldn't believe their kindness; nothing was too much trouble, and sure enough, Dave D located one. Not happy to stop there, he then built the bike for me, as I knew nothing about such things. Dave D is now an Inspector and has a great career, but I will always remember my friend building my daughter's bike in the base and helping make my little girl's dream come true. The big day arrived; I gave her the bike, I thought she would explode; she was so excited. I rang Dave and put her on the phone. "Thank you, David. Happy Christmas." It broke my heart, and from his croaky reply, I think he was pretty moved too. For giving me that memory, I love DD. Thank you, Dave.

Not all armed stops were high speed; crewed with DD and Andy, we took a call to an armed robbery at a corner shop in Peckham. The suspect had decamped on a Motability scooter, approx. speed 5 mph. It wasn't long before we were behind the suspect; we decided against putting up a pursuit on the radio even though he was failing to stop. I pulled up alongside him; DD got out and turned off the engine. In the basket was a silver kids laser gun, two bottles of whisky and some Ferrero Rocher. To this day I'm not even sure if he got nicked; I know we didn't lay hands on. A disabled alcoholic with a ray gun certainly raised a few eyebrows on the handover.

Clapham, I always thought of Clapham as a safe space, somewhere to chill, but near enough to the South Circular to respond to calls on the outer boroughs. Only minutes from Brixton, a regular haunt for south ARVs. Drinking a coffee parked up on Clapham South Side, a hand slapped the window. I spilt my drink all over my lap; not happy, I turn to see a partially naked young Black lad pulling at the door handle. Jumping out of the car, I see the young man is covered in cuts and bruises; he's begging for help. We get an ambulance running whilst I try and figure out what the hell is going on. The lad has been held hostage in a flat, burnt with an iron and cigarettes; he escaped by jumping out an upstairs window. He was a mess. For the life of me, I couldn't get him to tell me where the flat was or the suspects descriptions; he was way too scared to give up his attackers. In the end he was carted off to hospital accompanied by some local officers. I got back in the car and resumed chatting about winning the lottery, the usual stuff. This was how real life played out; our victim had pissed off the wrong people, and this is what happens to you. I didn't give that lad another thought; next week it could be him abducting a rival gang member, cutting off the odd finger or toe. The paying public love a 'mockney crime caper', with all its witty banter, loveable rogues and lashings of violence. All to a sexy, cool soundtrack, do me a favour. South London crime was about as sexy as a weekend at Pontins in January, with your gran.

By the time I retired, acid was the new weapon of choice. Not content with knives and guns, our client base now decided to include corrosive substances in their armoury. Where did that leave police officers? We were all vulnerable. As a firearms officer, could you justify shooting a subject armed with a squeezy bottle? I was lucky; I only attended a couple of acid attacks before I retired, one in, of all places, Portobello Road. Rival gang members, a road rage incident, absolute madness. Running to the incident I asked for tactical advice from the pod, "Not declared, locals to deal." By the time we arrived on scene, both sides had made their escape. Even though it wasn't declared, we still rocked up. How could we let borough officers face this threat without backup? Continuation Training appreciated the problem, writing a training package to get us all on the same page. Taser wasn't the silver bullet some hoped it would be. The risk of the suspect going up in flames couldn't be discounted. Boohoo, I wasn't alone in the opinion that if you carried acid on the street, then you were in play. My Healy rules of engagement accepted that the bad guys would have guns and knives. Brilliant, that's fine by me. Acid attacks, on the other hand, seemed so cowardly to my archaic sense of honour and duty. The Magnificent Seven may not have been so magnificent if Steve McQueen was armed with a Jif lemon squeezer.

THAT ESCALATED QUICKLY

You never see it coming, the big call or the huge fuck-up. You can be the most squared-away operator, but circumstance, luck, fate, karma, bad drills, call it what you will, are waiting in the long grass to get you. The 11th of April 2012 was one of, if not my, darkest hours. I had been on 19 for roughly eight years; I was a sound operator. I was mentoring new guys; I was one of the first batch of newly trained Operational Firearms Commanders, OFC for short. I had proved myself tenfold on jobs; in some people's eyes, I was a bit of an elder statesman. I was 49 years of age, ancient for ARV ops. In my defence, what unfolded was not down to arrogance or growing too big for my boots; I just got distracted and I paid the price.

Unconnected events contrive to screw you. 19 had purchased new body armour, not good body armour, but it was new, and we all had to wear it. I didn't like the new bod and held out until my original body armour started to fall apart. As with all new kits, it was stiff and uncomfortable, I hated how it sat on my frame. An added annoyance was my Taser, which I carried in a pouch that was held by Velcro to my bod; it just didn't sit right and kept coming loose. On the day in question, I was early turn sat in the yard; I was sat in the operator's seat, and the Taser pouch came loose. Annoyed, I got out of the car and placed the Taser pouch on the roof of the car. Everyone in the history of 19 up until the introduction of the X5s put their Taser on the roof. This was not a unique act on my behalf, but from the media reaction, you would have thought I had put the crown jewels in a cement mixer for safekeeping. More about the media later.

As I messed around with my bod, Smalls, a new member of the team, engaged me in conversation, along with Bear, another new guy. We were all chatting away, soon it was that time, time to get out and do some patrolling. I got in the car, and we headed out. An hour or so later we met up again at Brixton for breakfast. As we gathered around the table, I looked at my bod, and to my absolute horror, the Taser pouch wasn't there. Initially, I looked at Smalls, Kingy, Bear, and Matt, thinking it was a practical joke, but the look in their eyes told me I was screwed. Everyone was great; we got back in the cars and re drove the route, but there was no sign of my taser. For a good hour or two, everyone was out looking in the side streets around the base, but no joy. I even drove into the London Fire Brigade (LFB) base, which was only around the corner from our base and on the route, I travelled, but no joy. It was time to tell the boss and take my medicine.

"Any Trojan unit, any Trojan unit," Not now, please, God, not now, I prayed as we drove to Camberwell to an armed vehicle. On route, the information changed, and the suspect was housed off Lyndhurst Grove SE15. The job went live, and I found myself on white/red containment. My head was in bits; I had no desire to be on a job when I knew what awaited me. Next, I get a tap on the shoulder: "Kev, you're one on the stick." Come on, give me a break; I've lost my Taser. I am royally in the shit; my mind is blown, and you put me number one. This is where I had to walk it like I talked it. I grabbed the shield, set my mind and focused on the job at hand. The search went off without incident, and I thank God that it did. Can you imagine if I was confronted at that address by an armed suspect? Me being me, I would have got the job done, but given the choice, it was best the address was empty of gunmen. Dig out, put to bed, it was time for the real drama to begin. The Boss and I sat down; I detailed everything that had happened. She was amazing.

Kath was the first of the three female Trojan ones I was fortunate to have in my time in the department. Kath passed the bad news up the food chain, ending on the commissioner's desk. I did what a childhood spent watching heroic movies demanded I should. I offered to hand in my blue card and resign from the department. Falling on my sword seemed the only honourable way out. Kath told me to shut up and not to worry; it would be fine.

The shift came to an end; I said good night to my team. Night duty was in, and it was clear the word was out. I was getting a few pats on the back and nods, all of which were really kind but didn't even touch the humiliation I felt. The Chief Inspector Operations arranged to meet me at 6 pm at Leman Street. Kath refused to go home and headed north with me; my Boss was a legend. Entering his office, we sat down; the enormity of my screw-up hit me full on. The Chief informed me I was suspended from ops, and that came from the top, the very top. My fate was out of my hands; if the Taser was used in criminality against a member of the public or a police officer, my job, let alone my 19-year career, would be in jeopardy. On the spot I offered to resign; I loved 19, and I didn't want to harm its reputation. The Chief Inspector was a great guy; he told me to sit tight. Hopefully it wouldn't reach the media, and fingers crossed it would be handed in. I looked at Kath; she was in tears, and that my friend was the quality of my Boss. I bloody loved her for that.

I woke the following morning and decided to get the hell out of London. As I walked into Waterloo station, my attention was drawn to the giant media screens. Staring back at me was Eamon Holmes, sat on a sofa in a TV studio. The text of the conversation was appearing across the screen. Firearms officer leaves Taser on car roof. Holy shit, the game was up. The media, and notably social media, ripped me apart. It's hard to read negative stuff about yourself, and boy, was I portrayed as a total numpty. This hurt. I sat on the train planning what to do with my life after the police gave me the boot. Around 9 am my phone started to ring, and it didn't stop. The call usually started with "Tell me it's not you." For two days I stayed in a hotel and waited for bad news to get worse. As I sat in a rental car waiting to collect my kids from school, my phone rang. It was my skipper, Paul. His voice was serious. "Kev, your Taser has just been used in a cash-in-transit robbery; a couple of guards are injured." I dropped the phone in my lap; the news couldn't have been worse. As I fumbled to pick it up, I heard his voice: "Kev, Kev, Kev, Kev."

"Hey, Skip, sorry I dropped the phone."

"Jesus, we thought you had topped yourself," and that's when I heard the laughter and everyone shouting abuse at me. It was a wind-up, a brilliant heart-stopping wind-up; the Taser had been handed in. "Kev come back; all is forgiven." When I stopped thanking him for the news, I hung up and, not for the first time in my career, started to cry. I was still suspended and awaiting my fate, but I could face that, no one was hurt because of my stupidity, and that was all that mattered.

A few days later I returned to Leman Street; I didn't know what to expect. I was told to report to the Chief Superintendent. Walking through the base, people shouted my name, "Healy you loser," and "Kev have you seen my Taser?" You get the drift, poking fun, taking the piss, but all good-hearted, no one enjoying my humiliation. I had to laugh along with them; even if I was out on my ear, what a way to go. I knocked and entered; the Chief Super and a couple of other senior officers were having a coffee break, all very relaxed, not at all what I expected. "So, Kevin, you will be wanting this."

I looked at my blue card sitting on his desk. "What a few days you have had, eh? How are you feeling?" With that, the other two chipped in, taking the piss and inviting me to sit down and join them. This was not on my radar. I politely declined the offer to take a seat, the Chief, seeing I was a tad nonplussed, put me at ease, it went something like this, "Kevin, all I hear about you are good things, the common theme being you are 19 through and through; from the top down, no one wants to see you punished. I hear you even offered to resign; we can't have that, can we?" And with that, he handed me my blue card. "Good luck, Kevin." Hey presto, the others stood, and we all shook hands, and I floated out of his office.

Back on duty, walking in the yard, I was met at the gate by Kingy, Bear, Smalls, Foxy and the rest of the gang, who told me the car was kitted up. Turning the corner, I saw the BMW parked up with every bit of kit they could find squeezed onto the roof. I still have the photo of that kitted car. The humour and loyalty of the girls and boys that made up my team kept me sane at a dark time. You don't get adventures like this on civvy street; it's the job, and what a job it is.

The final chapter of this saga concludes with the fact that a fireman found the Taser and took it home. When news of the loss went viral, he called police, stating he thought it was a bicycle repair kit. A car was dispatched to recover it; my thoughts on his actions are best left out of print.

ARV, continuation training, finally caught up with me. Asked to run and do a diving forward roll onto a crash mat, whilst clutching a blue plastic MP5, probably wasn't what the doctor ordered at my age. The reasoning behind this peculiar request, "Spetsnaz, bloody do it, get going." These were not our normal ARV instructors; we had been handed over to public order instructors for officer safety training. Sadly, they had their own ideas about safety. As I leapt, gazelle-like, into the air, I dislocated my knee and snapped my patella tendon. Take your pick; which one was more excruciating? I lay on the crash mat screaming in agony, my cries for help drowned out by "You Sexy Thing" by Hot Chocolate. Music always accompanied these sessions. Taken to hospital in an ambulance, I laughed the whole way, high on Entonox. I left a few hours later, leg in plaster, struggling on crutches, who's laughing now.

I was screwed; no work meant no overtime. I needed to be back to work yesterday. I now commenced a rigorous rehab programme involving sitting in the pub sulking. It would take six months to recover, maybe longer at my age, the young physiotherapist informed me. We shall see about that young lady you're talking to, Healy; watch this space. Months passed; I worked that knee to death. I had to get back to ops; I had four kids and an ex-wife to feed. Eventually, after much pushing from me, the date for my OH referral arrived. My knee strapped up, I headed for the meeting expecting an intense examination. Was I ready? Not a chance; the knee wobbled like a blancmange in a wind tunnel. To give myself any hope, I purchased a knee brace with more metal bars than a window at Strangeways. What follows does not cover me or OH in glory. I entered the examination room to be met by an Australian lad straight out of Neighbours, with long blonde curly hair, a huge smile, and a golden tan. He was gorgeous. We spent the first ten minutes discussing the chances of being eaten by a shark on Bondi Beach. I bloody loved this kid. Wearing track suit bottoms to conceal the brace, he didn't even look at the knee. When he asked me to hop on it, I hopped on my good one as he sat typing with his back to me. So far, so good. It was time to run; this was the moment of truth. The machine was bust; I couldn't believe it. The belt kept jamming on the running machine; there was no way it was safe to use. I assured him I was fixed, and that very kind young man gave me the benefit of the doubt, and that was that I was back on ops.

During my enforced sabbatical I was posted against my will to the intel office; in the immortal words of TEAM AMERICA, "We have no intelligence." This career move did not go well; before I could take up the position, I had to attend Hendon to become a briefing officer. Travelling on the tube with my leg in a brace was no fun; arriving in the classroom, I was in a foul mood. Each student went through the ritual of "Hello, my name is? and I want to tell you about my cat Mr Tibbles." I remained seated, informed the class I was only there because I was broken, and couldn't wait to return to operations. The lead instructor was a retired shot, loved firearms and spent the rest of the week sat beside me sharing war stories and completing the training for me. I left Hendon, a fully trained briefing officer, nationally accredited to boot, absolutely clueless how to do my job.

Nina, who ran the intel office at 19, was a straight shooter; within a day, she had me sussed as a fraud. I was tasked with making the office staff tea and coffee and not a lot else. Paula who ran duties would throw sympathetic smiles my way when Nina admonished me for messing up another one of her intel slides. Unfortunately, Nina had to go away on a course, leaving me in charge. I could see the fear in her eyes; I promised her I wouldn't let her down. I was tasked with sending a briefing document to the Commissioner's office, detailing 19's fine work over a twenty-four-hour period. Nina went through the whole process step by step, even sticking post-it notes on my computer as an idiot's guide. Assuring her the office was in the safest of hands, she departed.

Coming in the next morning, I set to work. By 0800 hours the document was ready; I hit send and then headed off for an extended breakfast. Later that morning the phone rang; it was Commander X. "Is this Kevin Healy, the officer of great daring and charm?" From his tone I ascertained he was unhappy. "Yes, it is, and how can I help this fine morning?" What followed was one-way traffic, as a very senior officer with anger issues explained in no uncertain terms that a career in intelligence was not for everyone. It appears I sent a blank document, having first deleted all the intel. Eventually he calmed down enough for me to explain, I was only in the intel unit due to injury, though not a brain injury, as he assumed. Warming to my obvious charm, he congratulated me on my profile; an officer of great daring and charm had infuriated him initially, but now he understood I was an ARV officer flying a desk with a busted leg. He couldn't have been nicer. I would like to say we parted friends; though he did reiterate I shouldn't be allowed anywhere near a computer, I agreed wholeheartedly. Two days later I was reassigned.

Being back operational was where I needed to be and not just to pay the bills. 19 gave me purpose and direction, and I needed that. I could have milked the knee for as long as I wanted, maybe even got myself a nice admin job at training or on the purple team, the office that runs ARV admin. Playing it safe wasn't me; like a moth to a flame, I fought to get back on the cars knowing full well that one day I could get burnt but not really caring if I did.

As an OFC, you had to be able to manage a crime scene as well as the officers working alongside you. A late-night call to a stabbing in Croydon was a good test of my OFC skills. Arriving on the scene, the house was in darkness; suspects had forced entry and stabbed all the occupants before escaping. The motive, as always, drugs. The house had no electricity; we carried out the emergency search by torchlight. Happy no suspects remained, I set about triaging the scene. I had four victims stabbed, each in a different room. I called out for medics and thank God we had four on the search. I directed each medic to a room with a victim, assigning them an extra pair of hands off the stick to assist. Happy that things were now under control, I made my way from room to room to check each medic had enough medical equipment; to my surprise, some of the rooms were still in darkness. A few of the guy's torches were dead; I couldn't believe it. I was now lending my torch and going round borrowing more. No one died that night; the team did a great job even getting commendations, though I didn't, which did make me smile. I debriefed the guys about the torches. I wasn't impressed, but it didn't take the shine (sorry) off a good job. I will bet no one ever went out with a dead torch after that.

WATCH AND REACT

CATCH ME IF YOU CAN

After years of pleading for a uniform fit for purpose, the ARVs finally got their wish. The Chinese have a saying 'be careful what you wish for.' Those Chinese must have been on the clothing panel. After years of looking at designs, talking to suppliers, seeing what other forces were going with, they finally came up with something the Commissioner approved of. Wow, as disappointments go this was up there with Jack winning free passage on the Titanic. We had hoped that we would get something sexy in black, like our county counterparts. What we got instead was blue shirt and trousers, that made us look like garage hands, the boys and girls who look after the cars. The 'new' blue uniform was rubbish and boy did we get some stick when we started wearing it. My biggest gripe was the trousers. They were so tight on the legs and backside that sat in a car all day you lost circulation in your lower half. I had had a vasectomy, coming back to work the pain was excruciating, everything was packed so tight down there, like a tin of sardines. The cheap material created enough static electricity to power a Tesla.

Many were unhappy with the shirts, which were way too baggy on the arms. In a department where every day was arms day, baggy shirts would not pass the fashion police. So began the unspoken act of taking in the sleeves. Most did it sensibly, some spent more time in the gym. Me, I upped the curls and ordered smaller shirts. I jest about the smaller shirts but not about the amount of arm workouts I was doing. Years would pass before the commissioner gave the green light on a proper tactical uniform. Black and very tight fitting, it suited the more svelte younger officers down to the ground, me, a man reaching my twilight years in policing nodded my approval and sucked in my gut. "Hold on a minute, it's only comes in long sleeve," we were all devastated.

Another change that altered the image of the ARVs was the introduction of the leg holster. The SFO teams had been using leg holsters for years, clearly because they were fit for purpose. We on the cars wore hip holsters, which wasn't a drama when walking around, however when sat in a car, the holster pressed against your body armour, and this led to back pain issues. A more serious problem was caused when your body armour pressing down on the holster, released the 'sentry,' which secured your Glock in place. The unfortunate officer would get out of the car to find his Glock was not secured. This was not cool. Eventually, leg holsters were issued, and I for one loved mine. The beauty of the leg holster was the ease of draw: no more hand coming unnaturally up to the hip and the little lean to the left so that the body armour on the right side raised to give you room to draw. To those who carried back in the day that little lean of the body became instinctive, part of the muscle memory of being an effective operator.

The trusted MP5 was gone, we were now armed with the G36. Now this was a sexy bit of kit. Folding stock, aim point, two mags that sat side by side, a new round, no more 9mm. Every officer was to have a minimum number of hours of training called 'contact time.' For the life of me, I can't remember how much training we were supposed to have; in my case, it wasn't long enough. I had to go to a catch-up class, as I was at court when my team did the training. The instructors had been giving the same lesson for weeks, and it showed. Sat in a classroom, we stripped the weapon, put it back together and repeated until we were competent. We then headed to the range to get some 'rounds down.' Now I am not someone who picks up new skills quickly, and after living with the MP5 for years, I found the 36 a whole new bag of tricks. The sighting system threw me completely; with the MP5 you shot over iron sights, now I had an aim point. To those who are not in the know, it's a battery-operated red dot sight that's attached to the rails of the 36. I found this new way of shooting hard to come to terms with, not helped by the fact the instructors wanted us to do a classification shoot – no pressure! Well, they got their wish, and it was a clusterfuck. The hitting the target bit was straightforward enough; it was the mag drills, the reloads, the stoppages, and cocking the weapon. These things take practice, you must develop new muscle memory and forget the MP5 drills. All this takes hours of repetition, and in my humble opinion, we were not given enough time; hence, the classification shoot going to rat shit. Maybe it was my age I was over 40 and this dog struggled to learn new tricks.

Day to day the jobs kept coming and no two jobs were the same. Crewed with Andy and Dan we took a call to Bonneville Gardens SW9. The call was to a female being dragged into an address at gunpoint. It was the middle of the day; the sun was out so you would expect a pedestrian or two may have witnessed the incident but only one call was made to police. I drove the length of the street, which was in a really nice area, no one flagged us down. The informant didn't give a house number, so it was a needle in a haystack job. For some reason, I parked the car in front of a school and the three of us got out to take a sniff around. From a classroom window what I can only guess was a female teacher was pointing at the block in front of us. Alarm bells began ringing. The houses facing the school were Victorian red brick bay fronted apartments set over four or five levels. Walking into the front garden of the block I heard a window open looking up I saw a black lady roughly sixty years of age leaning out the window. She had her fingers to her lips and looked terrified.

A second car arrived and deployed to join us. Hoops got the drift straightaway and ran to get black containment on. The old lady disappeared from the window only to return holding a young child maybe six years old. What happened next was truly unexpected. Whispering as she called down, she told me her daughter was being held in a back room by men with guns. She was in the living room with the kids. Reacting to this news everyone was filling in the gaps, pointing guns and covering the tactical openings, all apart from me who was standing looking up at the open window. Dan set up control and asked for more cars, not that I knew any of this at the time, because my attention was drawn to the young child now climbing out the window. Granny now held his wrists lowering him down to me. Not being the tallest I couldn't reach the child, so she did what all good Grannies do, she let go without warning. "Fucking hell lady," I caught the kid putting his feet on the ground as Andy grabbed him and took him to cover behind parked cars. The drama wasn't over, Granny appeared at the sash window with a second child this one was younger than the first. Before I had time to say "You gotta be shitting me" she had him out the window and commenced lowering him down. With no warning, she dropped the child, she clearly had great faith in me, I caught the little fella, staring into each other's eyes I'm not sure who was more shocked. Andy grabbed the kid out of my arms and got him to safety.

Now if you're thinking this is far-fetched check this out. Granny only appears with a third child and this one is the youngest. He was tiny, Granny had him out onto the ledge, then as before she dropped the kid. Thank the sweet baby Jesus, I caught him. All the while this crazy drama unfolded, I was aware of Clive kneeling a few feet away covering me with his G36. The stage was set for one final act. Granny who was a big lady climbed out onto the window ledge. In that moment the immortal words of John McEnroe came to mind "You cannot be serious." The lady was not the most agile and she had little room to manoeuvre and so the inevitable happened, she fell. If you have ever stood in the outfield on a cricket pitch, as the ball drops from the heavens like a bloody cannon ball, you had no desire to catch, you will know how I felt. Granny fell like a bloody lead weight. I had no chance of catching her safely, even so, I threw myself under her to help break her fall. Sadly, my efforts were in vain, she cracked her head on the window ledge of the ground floor flat.

She was well and truly out for the count I grabbed her under the armpits and dragged her to safety leaving her in cover by the control car. The look on Dan's face was priceless. He now needed an ambulance on the hurry up not to mention a babysitter. I ran back to white containment and joined a few of the lads. In a matter of seconds, the plan was formulated. The victim was inside with gunmen, and we feared for her safety, we were going in to rescue her. No call to the base, no authorities, we acted. A stick was formed, we closed down the front door and using the enforcer smashed our way in. The suspects of which there were three surrendered one by one and the female was rescued. By the time I exited the building, the street was crowded with ARVs an ambulance and local officers. What I remember most about that day was the smile on the faces of the crew. What a job, never in the history of 19 had anything like this happened it was a one off. I was so proud of our actions that day, the motto 'fill in the gaps' was never better exemplified, everyone did their job no time to overthink it, no time to over plan it. we just reacted and got the right result. Years later Clive leaving on promotion told me it was one of the bravest things he had seen on 19. The way I stood under the window unable to protect myself, putting my life on the line to save those kids. The fact that Granny was prepared to drop her grandkids out the window and crack her own skull open showed how seriously she took the threat.

Dear reader, I promise I never felt brave then or now, Clive's kind words felt good to hear but I knew everyone on that job would have done the same without hesitation. I thanked God the nickname 'the child catcher' didn't catch on, it just sounded so very, very, wrong. Months later we received commendations for our actions, the best thing about the day was the free buffet and going on the piss afterwards with my team. I found out later the victim was a drug dealer, she owed money and these men had come to collect. Would they have hurt her, I'm saying yes. Did our rescue solve her problems I guess not. That's the reality of that world.

Seeing dead bodies in the police is part of the job. For the most part, it's sudden deaths involving the sick or the elderly. In the world of 19, I got to see people die a violent death and that is a very different proposition. Watching the moment, the lights go out is something that I learnt to bat off. I don't wish to sound blasé but how else do you think cops, nurses or firemen learn to keep it together? Attempting to remain immune to what I saw, I often forgot the victims had people who loved them. One of the most painful incidents I attended that did break through my wall of indifference was a honey trap killing in Deptford. A girl is used to lure the victim to an address with the promise of fun and games, instead, they are met by a rival gang member, love rival, drug dealer, a honey trap.

On the night in question, the victim arranged to meet a girl at her flat. Knocking at the door expecting his sweetheart, he was met instead by a gunman who opened fire, shooting the victim multiple times at point-blank range. Somehow, he managed to escape the block and make it back to his friend who was sat waiting in the car park. Eyewitnesses said the car pulled away only to stop a little further up the road; the driver then pushed the victim out of the car. Whatever his motives, he then got out and removed his dying friend's jewellery and cash before speeding away. This is the law of the jungle; maybe the driver was in on the hit. Maybe he realised he was now top boy.

We arrived on scene, and I immediately recognised the victim as a regular on our briefings. A young gang member in his early twenties, he was routinely armed and linked to a series of violent offences. This was a bad lad, a career criminal. The LAS, as usual, were at an RVP waiting for us to secure the area; as a result, we commenced first aid. He was alive just about; we were doing everything we could to stem the flow of blood and keep him that way. The paramedics soon joined us, and side by side, everyone went to work. Suddenly he started to convulse, vomiting up the contents of his stomach. "He's had his last takeaway," the paramedic commented as rice and Christ knows what poured from his mouth. I watched as he fought to stay alive; he did not want to die; he wasn't ready to check out, his eyes pleading for help; there was nothing I could do.

We left the scene to the LAS and headed for Deptford. Nick, to write notes. As we sat in the writing room surrounded by local officers all chattering away over tea and biscuits, we could hear the activity at the crime scene over the local radios. Suddenly a scream, then another, then another came over the airwaves. As I write, I am taken back to that night and the look on the faces of the cops in that room. The screams were so full of horror, so haunting, that everyone stopped what they were doing and fell silent;

WATCH AND REACT

you could have heard a pin drop. The local skipper, a grey-haired old-timer, looked at me. "That's his mum; she's on scene. What a fucking world." Seeing her son lying lifeless in the street must have torn her world to shreds. My thoughts went to that poor woman and the nightmare she was now living through. Her screams left the room silent. Coppers are hard; that's a given, but no one said a bloody word. Everyone in that little writing room would remember that night for a very long time; when does it all start to become too much? I had kids; I had sons. That mother's scream took me close to finding out.

Weeks before I retired, I was on the wind down; I honestly thought I was done with death and mayhem. It was the time for those who follow to deal and get their hands dirty. Surely, I had done my bit. Driving through Blackheath, I saw blue lights ahead, and the dual carriageway was backed up with traffic. Laughing to Richard, I turned on the noise and went to see if we could help; however, my primary motivation was getting out of the jam. Lying on its side was a motorcycle; a short distance away lay a body. It was a busy junction, so it didn't take a rocket scientist to work this tragedy out. I didn't want to get involved, so I left it to the locals but offered our services if required. For some inexplicable reason, I went to look at the victim. A young Black man in his twenties, he was handsome; his face was unmarked, his eyes open, there was no sign of pain or fear. Walking away, I saw the motorcycle had a screwdriver rammed into the ignition. Stolen? I didn't care if it was, his mum wouldn't care, and the people who loved him and lost him wouldn't care. That was the last death I saw in my time on 19, and it told of another young, wasted life, so many now, way too many to count.

CONTINUATION TRAINING

A common criticism thrown at Trojan officers by our less than impressed over worked colleagues; is the idea we drive around all day from one coffee shop to the next. Waiting, on the one call of the day to justify our existence. If you search social media ARV officers, come in for a lot of leg pulling from our unarmed colleagues, some of it is pretty accurate to be fair. What outsiders don't appreciate is the fact that just because you passed the course doesn't mean you're now a 'made guy, or indeed girl' In fact, it's quite the opposite, the pressure really comes to bear. Not only do you have to prove your worth to your team, but continuation training wanted their pound of flesh as well.

Every six weeks the coach would arrive at the south base, here we would join our north colleagues, for the slow congested drive down to Milton our home for the next two days. As a new member of the team and remember in 2003, I was the new kid on the block for quite some time, all eyes were on yours truly. It was expected and rightly so that I would volunteer to take part in every training scenario, no watching on the side lines, oh no I was in the thick of it from the off. The upside of this, I got so much out of the two days, be it vehicle options, or foot strikes, I was jumping out of cars chasing instructors being the 'stooge' who loved nothing more than to go off script and see where it took us. All the while I was being observed by the training team, I was also being observed by my new Trojan one and Skippers, not to mention the relief who weighed up my performance and fed back their thoughts. The numbers training was small, the team was less than 30 strong all told. I was involved in everything, there was nowhere to hide, I was in the spotlight. This environment though stressful and exhausting was the best thing that could have happened to me, though I'm not sure I would have said so at the time.

The two days were intense, I quickly discovered the best way to deal with the rigours of continuation, was to treat it like the last few days of the ARV course. I was being assessed and I had better perform. The training team was a mixed bag of ARV instructors on attachment to Milton along with a sprinkling of SFOs. Also, along for the ride were a few City Police Firearms Instructors who didn't always see eye to eye with their 19 counterparts. One of them was called Lenny, not his real name, he was a big lump, with a lot to say, most of it negative but worst of all he kept calling us ladies, which I did find rather annoying. I wasn't the only one who tired of his banter, one day he pissed off the wrong person and received his just rewards more of that later.

Arriving at Milton we headed for the 'continuation classroom,' here we drank tea, ate biscuits, and watched PowerPoint presentations outlining how the next two days would scope out. That first meeting up in the classroom was always great fun. The whole team got along so well, jokes and piss taking bounced back and forth, but it was all done with such respect for one another, no digs no cheap shots. It was great catching up, the Thames was the only thing that divided the bases. A lot had to be crammed in, but we all expected to be in the bar for a beer around 9 pm. Each cycle would involve a series of 'stances' which covered searching, vehicle stops and shooting. Searching was the old one-to-four system that always led to arguments and some pretty intense debriefs. Being new I kept my mouth shut and just got on the stick. On one memorable occasion, Lenny the City instructor, was upstairs in a search house making a real nuisance of himself as the stooge, acting the bad guy going off script and pushing his luck with experienced officers who didn't stand for much nonsense. Finally, enough was enough, Lenny rushed the stick dishing out blows and throwing his weight around, one of the team grabbed him, lifted his T-shirt and fired several paint rounds into his belly, you could hear the scream back in the City of London. He was not amused, in fact, I thought he was going to explode, he was on the verge of kicking off. He had to be led away to help him calm down but that's what happens if you push too far. Remember we were doing it for real every day, taking multiple calls every day, pointing guns every tour of duty. We were busy and the older sweats took no shit, as the new guy they looked after me but only as long as I got the job done. As for Lenny, he calmed down eventually and after that wee incident no more talk of ladies, by the way the shooter was my old mate Magic from the Hill he hadn't changed a bit.

Paint was used as an excellent learning device, because paint rounds bloody hurt. I was shot in the head on an ambush drill, the round hitting me smack in the forehead, it broke the skin and quickly got infected which the team thought hilarious, I looked like I was growing a third eye. Blank ammunition had its place, but paint found you out, especially on house searching. The instructor would be hiding somewhere in the building and we the ARV officers would search to contact. Once contact was made, we would endeavour to negotiate a safe surrender. Of course, training had its own ideas on how things should play out. No two searches where the same, shots would be fired, the suspect would break out, the suspect would shoot one of us, suddenly we would have to go into Casualty evacuation and ballistic first aid. Coming out of the search house at the end of a search you quickly discovered who wasn't in cover and who didn't use the shield correctly as red and orange paint smudges betrayed your poor drills. I for one found the training so spot on and so realistic that real life was often so much easier than training. The training wing took us out of our comfort zone, stretched us, got us to think often outside the box. The result, you had a team who were not scared to use their initiative and make decisions on the hoof.

On a job everyone was equal, it was the same at training, rank did not exist, decision making was everyone's responsibility. Years later the introduction of the Operational Firearms Commander, OFC, would impact the status quo, bringing with it a lot of good but also some negative fallout as some new officers, not all, but some looked to the OFC to make all the calls and in effect dumb down the role of the ARV officer. M the Boss along with the Skippers trained alongside us, took criticism (we never got praised) without a word of dissent. As role models you couldn't ask for better.

Vehicle options and searching were intense but fun, I was with such a great group of officers I never stopped laughing. Debriefs could be long brutal affairs but shit sandwiches seemed to be dished out evenly across the relief so I had no complaints. I was here to learn and show I was worth my place on a car. This brings me back to my initial point, every officer who moans about Trojan having an easy life doesn't understand, you are under the microscope, all the time. I had to perform on jobs, every job, no one gave me a pass, but training took this to another level, if you fucked up and it was a safety issue be it an ND (negligent discharge), sweeping a colleague, accidentally pointing your weapon at a friendly or shooting a suspect without due cause, boy oh boy you were for the high jump. I lost count of the times; I was sat in the bar relaxing over a beer to hear someone I knew had lost their blue card and with it their authority to carry a firearm. Losing your ticket was bad enough, what training decided to do with the culprit could be career changing and in some cases 19 closed ranks and the officer was gone. It was brutal but it was fair, perform to the highest standards no exceptions. This level of scrutiny kept the public safe, no one made it past training if they were a liability.

Every cycle, we shot on the range, every second cycle we classified. Nationally ARV officers only had to classify twice a year not 19, we maintained standards by doing it every 12 weeks. To add to the pressure 19 made up its own classification shoot, incorporating the standard ARV shoot used nationally mixed together with a few shoots training saw as invaluable. On top of this it was a dual weapon shoot, you fired your primary weapon the MP5 ditched it and reverted to your Glock. Distances from the target were further than required nationally and time to engage targets were reduced. All in all, you had to be switched on the whole shoot, if you went to sleep mentally or zoned out you would fail. I found it bloody intense and was often soaked in sweat by the end of the 100 round shoot. Did I mention the pass mark was 90%, nationally it was 80%. At one shoot, I dropped five rounds scoring 95%, as I sat in the canteen eating lunch the Boss and Kev pulled up a chair and suggested I get some extra range time in, 95% was not acceptable. Nothing was easy, we did everything the hard way, I lost count of the times I heard the words "train hard fight easy." The anti was raised when a new head of ARV continuation was appointed. An SFO he was not a fan of the ARV reliefs, his first command decision, was to make all officers classify in full operational kit, helmet, goggles, gloves and body armour containing extra ballistic plates. The ARVs rose to this challenge without complaint, we just got it done and sure enough, no one failed, so I'm not sure what he hoped to prove. I never failed a classification; I came close a couple of times over the course of eighteen years but always pulled it together. The stigma attached to dipping the shoot kept everyone on their toes.

On top of shooting the MP5 and Glock, you had to re-classify in the Taser and the Baton Gun. The Taser was hilarious because someone always managed to electrocute themselves. As for the Baton Gun, because we rarely handled it after the ARV course, I always managed to mess up what was fundamentally a big old load of sharp metal. On every shoot I would manage to cut the bridge of my nose, how I'm not sure even to this day, bad drills, I guess. In 18 years, I never once deployed with it though now it's on every car I'm told.

As the years passed, 19 grew exponentially and in my humble opinion suffered growing pains. Suddenly we found ourselves with way too many officers on each cycle. The time allotted for training was still the same but with more people involved actual 'contact time' went down, where you may have got to do five vehicle options you were lucky to do two. This went for searching and foot strikes. Everything was becoming a rush and here is a controversial opinion. Some officers, if they so wished, had ample opportunity to take a back seat and coast letting others do the heavy lifting. Suddenly I was training with people I had never met, but were on my team, coming from one of the four bases that had now sprung up. The close knit family feel was gone and with it some of the elan that made 19 so special, to me anyway. Experienced officers voted with their feet, I was used to seeing the cream rise, Trojan One, Kev and a host of excellent officers had already made the jump to SFO, or training. Now, more good cops were looking to 'head upstairs,' to the Teams or do the cadre (the instructor's course) I remained, new officers arrived, they would need mentoring, training learnt to cope with ever increasing numbers, but it was different now and I wasn't sure if I liked what I saw.

Why didn't I jump ship? Why didn't I apply to become an SFO? Was I too old in my forties, was raising triplets too much of a commitment? I can't hide behind these excuses; I didn't apply, because, in the words of Dirty Harry "A man's got to know his limitations." I never thought I would be good enough.

I slowly started to dislike training not because of the personnel, but because of my own insecurities about my ability. In the early years, you're an unknown, the instructors see you every six weeks, for a few hours and your easily forgotten. After eight, ten, fifteen years everyone knew me. Kevin Healy the perennial ARV officer. The new guys looked to me to be excellent to lead from the front and why shouldn't they, I was the oldest of old sweats. The instructors expected me to be all over each scenario because I had been there and printed the bloody T-shirt. To be fair to the instructors many of them would tap me on the shoulder, "Kevin you have done enough today drop back let others have a go." This respect for what I had done was much appreciated but inevitably you also got the new instructor, not a lot of service, sometimes only a few years on the cars, who had gone training nice and early, for reasons known only to them (easy life). This individual would pull me up on a decision I made or a tactic I used. I would smile and say to myself ok let him have his moment in the sun.

A vehicle exercise was going badly, the suspect wasn't coming out of the car because the Skipper doing the Extraction was making a dog's dinner of it. The stooge then started to drag the Skipper into the car attempting to grab his Glock. Now if this happened in real life the suspect

WATCH AND REACT

would be tasered and extracted very harshly if you get my drift, but you can't use that level of force on an instructor otherwise they would all end up in hospital. Using restraint meant you can end up looking a dumbass, good instructors know where the line is, and they play up just enough to test the officer but not enough that things escalated. I was on the periphery but couldn't stand by and watch this cluster fuck. I ran over grabbed the instructor in a headlock and started to strangle him while simultaneously dragging him out. He was pissed off with my intervention, but it did stop things going to rat shit. I kept the hold on until he calmed down and then I kissed him on the top of his head and let go. I expected a world of pain, but no one said a word to me, I'm guessing by this stage in my service everyone knew I would play the game giving 100% but wouldn't tolerate cheap shots. Even though I never abused it, I believed I had enough credit in the bank, to stand up and call foul without the risk of my blue card being shredded. The threat of losing your blue card kept many a mouth firmly shut. Maybe it was my age, my service, my experience on the cars but when I did challenge a behaviour or an instructor's peculiar bullshit theory on getting into a loft, I found I was listened to and not shot down in flames.

The pressure I put on myself to perform at training was always a huge weight on my shoulders. Why? Because continuation training never stopped, never went away, it was always there at the back of my mind, waiting to ambush me. What's bizarre is the fact I was very good; sometimes at training I was bloody amazing, if I do say so myself, but I never got to enjoy the good bits because of that voice: "Don't get cocky, kid." It must be amazing to be that confident and full of self-belief, taking it all in your stride. What's absolutely nuts is the fact that come the day of the races on live jobs with loaded guns and armed suspects, I was in my element, chilled and at ease, nothing phased me: compare that to the days leading up to training when I would be racked with anxiety. Eighteen years I put myself through this self-inflicted mental torture; I must be the definition of a masochist. The journey home on the bus, training over, I would be like a man reprieved, laughing and joking with my teammates until the stress and its release would hit me, and I would be out for the count.

The introduction of operational firearms commanders (OFCs for short) added to my workload. Now when a call came out, the Pod would call me direct: "Kev can you OFC this one?" Fair enough, but if I was the only OFC on duty, that meant I was constantly in demand, and trust me, planning and activating firearms operations is a very serious business with dire consequences if things turn bad. Fortunately, I had a team around me that would arrive on scene and do everything to assist me without me even asking. Containment would go in, a stick order would be sorted, a safe route in a planned, as I discussed the intel and tactics and everything else that goes into briefing your buddies on digging out an address or stopping armed suspects in a vehicle. When it went well, which for the most part it did, then I felt pretty good about life. To run a firearms operation taking out bad guys, and you're the one who makes the big calls that can be immensely satisfying, but boy, it's pressure too because if shots are fired and people are hurt, the world is looking at you, through those 'hindsight glasses' worn by judges, barristers, members of Parliament, the press and last but not least the British Public.

During my time at the Hill, I discovered I could lead people, and more importantly, they seemed happy to follow me. I have never read a self-help book (obviously), or indeed any of those 'Leadership for Numpties' or 'Men Are from Mars, Women Wish They Would Stay There' books.

Taking charge at a crime scene came naturally to me, as did getting a grip on a firearms call. Leadership for me was all about leading from the front, by example, deeds not words. After I retired, I was given a book called 'The Face of Command'; the author talks about how military leadership has changed through history. I discovered the theory of heroic leadership. This was the period when a king had to be at the front of the army, sharing the risks with his followers. This acceptance of danger, leading the vanguard, was expected of them; it came with the territory, being the boss. Leonidas at Thermopylae, Henry V at Agincourt, Custer at the Little Bighorn and me, Kevin Healy, the Angel Town estate in Brixton. To lead, you must have credibility, and to get that, you have to get your hands dirty. One things for sure you won't get it sat in the kit van checking your Instagram account.

I loved leading a team on an op. I loved it because I knew I was good at it; I loved it because it allowed me to test myself over and over and, in doing so, gain the respect of my peers. I loved it because at last, I was proving all those sarcastic teachers and all the put-down merchants wrong. My team trusted me. I did everything in my power to live up to the trust they placed in me. This was the huge conundrum that I lived with daily. I loved leading from the front and had no issue at all with taking risks and making decisions. I must have appeared to the outside world as one switched-on operator, but when the drama was over and the pressure was off, the nagging doubts would resurface. Trying to control that negative voice in my head was and still is a daily battle. That I had the strength to overcome my fears and doubts must say something about me; I'm just not sure what. I do know this; the OFC role was not for everyone. Passing the course is a great tick in the box; doing the job for real is another story. A friend of mine, S, left 19. He started hating coming to work because he dreaded being called upon to OFC. He was not alone in this.

Continuation training must be tough; it must test you, and it must put you in the spotlight, however uncomfortable that makes you feel. I treated training as if I was on an ARV course under continual assessment, expecting no favours. This mindset I passed on to anyone who would listen. The role of the OFC, though not for everyone who joins Trojan, will always attract those who relish a challenge. Obviously, I am only speaking for myself when I say I dreaded training whilst at the same time fully appreciating its importance. Always trying to do my best, taking the lead and giving 100%.

So, to every borough officer, traffic PC, schools liaison officer, etc., grumbling about Trojan and how easy they have it. Please feel free to apply but be careful what you wish for. The boys and girls parked up on Clapham Common, drinking an iced venti caramel macchiato and scoffing a warm pastry, have earned the right to be there, so cut them some slack.

WHEN THE SHIT HITS THE FAN, WE DON'T RISE TO THE OCCASION; WE FALL TO THE LEVEL OF OUR TRAINING.

WATCH AND REACT

TIME FLIES

The Olympics came and went; not a lot else I can say about that. We on the cars saw the Olympics in terms of a great adventure and an opportunity to earn some serious overtime. As far as adventures go, I found it a dull affair, and as for the overtime, it never materialised. I have a picture somewhere of me holding the Olympic torch – well, a copy that was doing the rounds and somehow ended up at Bexleyheath Nick. The advent of marine training meant I spent a few days protecting London from imminent terrorist attack, sitting on a police boat sunbathing. Marine training was a good idea; the Thames was a great way to access the city, and so an armed presence with modified tactics became another skill set the ARVs needed to learn. Cross-decking, getting off one fast-moving boat onto another fast-moving boat, was the sexiest and most dangerous element, and I enjoyed that a lot, especially as I can't swim the length of a paddling pool. Truth be told, I wasn't even marine trained, but don't tell anyone; water and I didn't hit it off from my Hendon days, so I never volunteered for marine training. Lo and behold, I rock up to the base to be informed I'm on a boat for the day.

Obviously, it's a mistake, but there wasn't anyone to swap with, and it's the Olympics, and everyone is busy. I grabbed my kit and drove to Wapping to the Marine unit base, put a life vest on and got on a boat. Simple, really. We 'drove' up and down the Thames on a nice big boat called a Targa; all was cool until the CTSFO team turned up; they suggested we do some training to keep us shipshape. Next thing I know, we are taken off the nice safe Targa and put on a boat called a RIB (rigid inflatable boat). Holding on for dear life, as we roar up and down the

Thames, bouncing off the waves being thrown all over the place, and I can't bloody swim. The Rib is black, it's sexy, and it goes like the blazes, so of course the teams (CTSFOs) must have one. I had not seen this coming; next thing I know, we were closing in on the Targa, with the intention to 'board her'. Boarding her! BOARDING HER! Hold on, I am not Jack Sparrow. 'It was time to 'cross deck' me hearties,' all I needed was a cutlass in my mouth and a parrot. Oh dear, this is going to be interesting. I had never even seen the manoeuvre done, let alone practised it. Well, it's a bit late now, Kev. Up I get, join the stick and follow the guy in front of me. Next thing, the nose of the rib bounced up onto the deck of the Targa; everyone was jumping ship. It's my turn; the Rib is battling to stay in contact with the Targa, and I'm battling to stay in contact with my breakfast. I leap from the rib landing like Bambi on ice on the bouncing deck. Nothing to it; the Rib disengaged, and off we headed for breakfast at a feeding station on dry land. Looks like I'm marine trained, tick in the box, really.

The highlight of breakfast was queuing up to collect snacks. Every single Met police officer who has ever been on Aid feels their heart sink upon hearing the word 'snacks'. A cardboard box containing sandwiches, crisps, bottles of water and chocolate bars, historically a Mars, though by the end of my career the chocolate bar was a pale imitation of a Mars. A single skinny Twix – do me a favour; who wants to tackle terrorists on a Twix? As I collected the snacks for my team, the CTSFO in front of me, with no hint of irony, asked for his "rations". Rations! Bloody hell, where are they heading to need rations? Maybe if the Rib hit an iceberg, they may all be cast adrift for days with only a limp ham sandwich, prawn cocktail crisps and a panda pop to survive on. You just had to love the CTSFO teams, as they were now branded.

WATCH AND REACT

The Sheer size of the Games demanded the Pod got an upgrade, it now looked like the set of Minority Report. A giant interactive flat screen dominated. I was banned from even looking at it. Arriving for my tour of duty, Officer King appeared to be running the Mets entire firearms operation single-handedly. Clearly, I was surplus to requirements; bored, I roamed from Pod to Pod getting into mischief. Suddenly out of nowhere I found myself face to face with Commissioner Hogan-Howe. "Why are you not wearing a tie? Where is your name badge, what is your name?" Not even a hello; I thought northerners were famed for their warm welcome. His bagman loitering at his shoulder looked more worried than I did. I opened my mouth to respond, but before I could verbalise my thoughts, the base skipper appeared from nowhere, pushing me sideways out of the line of fire. Was he saving my bacon, or was he scared to death of what I might say? The Skipper now took the heat, talking absolute bollocks about our state of readiness. I made a tactical withdrawal, hiding behind the flat screen, I knew it would come in handy.

My only other moment of note involved answering the phone to a senior military officer, he informed me the surface-to-air missiles on Blackheath were in place, and he had the contact details and call signs for the Pod. My response: "Fire away."

The games over, rumours started circulating about the introduction of a new shift pattern. Rumour turned to reality, and the reality was that 19 needed to lose a relief. Not enough bums on seats and an attempt to reduce the overtime bill. I never in a million years thought E Relief would be the one to get the chop, but sure enough, I came in for night duty to see some very sad faces; the news was out; we were it. Each of us had to choose a new relief. I didn't care, so I left my decision to the last and ended up on F Troop, as they were commonly known. The end of E relief was a sad day, and no amount of beer at the team wake could wash away the disappointment. I had mentored so many officers on the team that it felt like I was losing family members; that's how close we were. People talked of reunions, but they never materialised; we were cops after all, not graduates. My goodbye to my team came in a special edition of the newsletter I had been writing for the last couple of years. Pod news, as I titled it, was my own underground, mildly subversive attempt at jabbing the finger of fun at a department that sometimes needed to laugh at itself. Each edition mildly mocked the Commissioner Hogan HOW! it had a letters page, angry of the South Base, caption competitions always featuring CTSFOs, and Milton, renamed Miramar after Top Gun, always came in for stick. I started it when I was forced into taking a Pod course and found the monotony of working the Pod unbearable; only then did I hit on Pod news.

Once written, I sent it to friends who passed it on, sometimes to the wrong person. I never got disciplined for my efforts, but on one notable occasion, I was driving a Superintendent to a meeting at the yard when he asked out of the blue if I was the same Kevin Healy who thought he was Ian Hislop. After a few seconds, the penny dropped. I went bright red and sat in silence as he burst out laughing, admitting he had read a few editions and rather enjoyed them. In my final editorial, I talked of the friendships I had made and the way we operated as a team, describing us as being quiet professionals. A line used to describe the SAS. Not for one moment did I think of us breathing the same oxygen as these men, but we did share one similarity: the desire to do the job without ego, no drama, and no fuss – the quiet professionals. This hit a nerve with a few of the team who to this day say how moved they were by my description of a group of men and women from hugely varied backgrounds who, by circumstance, were thrown together and somehow created bonds of loyalty and respect that shaped how they carry themselves as police officers.

My first parade with F troop, left me feeling, all was well with the world. Sat around the table were some of the most unruly, funniest, larger than life characters you could ever hope to meet. The Skippers and the Boss were spot on, everyone was so welcoming, I knew I had landed on my feet. F troop it turned out also had some fantastic ARV officers.

It was November, and I was well and truly homeless. My housing situation was now critical. All bridges had been burnt; I couldn't live with my sisters. My mum would put me up, but no self-respecting male my age lives with Mum, do they? Girlfriends were another stopgap, but asking, "Do you own your own property, and do you like kids?" isn't a great chat-up line on a first date. The base was now a no-go area, plus it was bloody freezing sleeping in the cars. Necessity being the mother of invention, I called the Met police property services, as they used to be called before the Met sold off every bloody bit of real estate. I spoke to a lady called Melanie Spooner; I will never forget this lady; she saved my life. I explained I was homeless; it was Christmas, well, almost, and could she help? She asked when I joined the service; I told her 1991. She then informed me that I had joined the Met before the Sheehy enquiry, an enquiry that changed police officer housing regulations. Being pre-Sheehy meant I was entitled to police housing until the day I retired. Well, this was the first I had heard of it. I had requested a section house room years before but was told to jog on by some bureaucrat who didn't know a thing about police regs. After years of nomadic living, I had a home at last. Section houses were constructed all over London in the 1930s, built to house young officers close to their station, at a time when pay was terrible; nothing's changed on that front, sadly.

I will never forget the day I moved into the Gilmore section house. Armed with two washing bags full of clothes, I rang the buzzer, and a guy in his late 60s opened the door; his name was Les, and he ran the section house. We would become great friends Les and I; he always met me with a South London "All right boy." He told me I was expected and asked if I had any preference on what floor I would take up residency. I didn't, so I got a room on the 5th floor; the ladies had the 4th. Cheers, Les. The section house was a thriving melting pot of young officers new to London and a hard core of older cops like me; the closure of Hendon as a residential training academy shoved new recruits into section houses; the building was packed. It contained a launderette, two gyms, two TV rooms (one for smokers), and a kitchen. Each floor had communal showers and toilets and a small kitchen for those foolish enough to attempt cooking. Located 8 minutes from the base, getting in for overtime and early turns was a doddle. Surrounded by some fantastic pubs, I was in my element. My parting advice from Les: "Boy if you own a knife and fork, don't leave them lying around." Fortunately, I didn't but I thanked him for the heads-up. Les was right about the cutlery situation; within a few weeks I witnessed two officers come to blows over ownership of a knife and fork. It was bonkers to watch but showed just how tightly wound some of the older residents were. These were cops whose life plans had not included nearing retirement, being divorced, being overweight and being functioning alcoholics. I suppose I never had a plan, maybe, that helped me in the long run. Mike Tyson once said, "Everyone has a plan until they get hit in the face." Life had clearly hit a few of my colleagues firmly in the chops.

I quickly discovered the smoking lounge was where the real action took place. Walking in, it was like walking into a pub in the 1960s, the air thick with smoke. The chairs, a mixture of sofas and armchairs, were never vacant. The boys and girls would bring in bottles of wine, tins of beer, and Cava, which was very popular for a while, and last but not least, the old favourite tequila. These were often shared around by tired, emotionally drained police officers coming off nights, or on rest days, or those who simply had nowhere else to go. The TV channel was decided by the Chinese parliament, though horror films always got a thumbs up. Not that you could hear the telly for the laughter, insults and world's worst chat-up lines. The arrival of a new batch of recruits every few weeks, many of whom were female, ensured the two gyms were in constant use. The smell in the lift on a Saturday night was always a heady mix of aftershave, perfume and alcohol. Les, who had seen it all over the years, declared, "It's like a tart's boudoir that lift."

The roof of the section house was off limits for obvious reasons, but that didn't stop a group of us from moving armchairs and a selection of weights up there. On warm sunny days, I would escape the cloying heat in my room, making for the roof. Here I would sit and read whilst enjoying the most wonderful panoramic view of London. Residents in nearby apartment blocks had the pleasure of watching yours truly weight training topless, in skimpy shorts, drinking a can of beer, all to the Top Gun soundtrack.

That first night, I unpacked, poured myself a JD and climbed into bed. Moonlight illuminated the tiny room. I surveyed my surroundings: a sink, a wardrobe, a desk, a window and a bed, all the essentials covered. The recruits were kicking a football in the corridor; someone somewhere was playing London Calling by the Clash; the guy next door clearly had his girlfriend over for the evening. All was well with the world. I had a bed and a roof over my head, and no one was taking it away from me. Years would pass, residents came and went, but I was a constant. There were times when the place was so empty it felt like a ghost ship. The number of Christmas holidays I spent there I lost count of, to be honest; they were challenging times. Christmas alone is tough. The lowest of low points was finding myself out of booze on Christmas Day and no shops open. Going through my presents, I discovered a kind soul on the team had got me a box of chocolates: 36 dark chocolate barrels, each holding a different liqueur. With great care and precision, I sliced the heads off the barrels and poured the contents one by one into the glass that normally held my toothbrush. Crème de menthe, cherry brandy, orange this, rhubarb that. Job done. I gave my festive cocktail a stir with my trigger finger. The concoction was never going to be anyone's favourite tipple, but it did the trick, I think, because the rest of the evening is rather a blur.

One thing I learnt about myself: I was a born survivor. When we lost our home, we moved into a council house miles from my school. We were the only Irish Catholic family on the estate. We were the only kids that wore a school uniform with a bloody blazer. I may as well have had a target painted on my back. To get to school I had to take a bus, a train and walk a mile. I was eleven; the school run wouldn't be invented for another thirty years. In the 70s, parents didn't care how you got to school; they were far too busy dealing with a three-day week and the Cold War. Getting to and from school was like the movie The Warriors, my uniform, my gang 'colours.' My school was named after the Douay Martyrs, a group of religious fanatics killed for their religious beliefs, I knew how they felt. I had to survive this journey ten times a week. Like a salmon swimming upstream to mate, the Grizzlies were waiting, and this little salmon was more than happy when a brother salmon took the heat. My radar was highly sensitive to danger, and danger loomed at every turn. Sat on the bus, my mate wearing his new Parka, it was the time of the Mod revival. Johnny Agga, he of the hair lip, dropped a lit cigarette in the hood. In seconds it went up in flames, along with a patch of my mates' hair; after that he sat downstairs with the old ladies. Me, I was constantly 'eyes about,' not a bad grounding for policing.

In the interests of historical accuracy, I couldn't let Johnny burn my mate alive without a pointless, futile response, now, could I? Standing at the top of the stairs, I called out, "Agga, you're one ugly motherfucker," then threw him the finger. Knowing Johnny was now at DEFCON 1, I flew down the stairs and out onto the pavement, thanking God the doors were open. I stood looking at the bus as one of the top windows slid open. Somehow, he squeezed his enormous head out; he then conjured up the evillest ball of phlegm from the depths of hell and spat at me. I was frozen to the spot, watching mesmerised as it arched its way towards me, landing on the top of my head. The bus erupted. Johnny smiled. "See you tomorrow, Healy." With accuracy like that maybe he should have joined 19.

Please don't think I tell these anecdotes in the hope of some sympathy; far from it, one of life's victims I am not. I bloody loved my time in the Section House; in many ways, they were some of the happiest years I can remember, but of course, you have lows, and what better way to trigger melancholy than Christmas? The hours I spent alone did give me time to reflect. What conclusions did I draw lying on my bed staring at the ceiling? Firstly, I recognised the positives: I had a place to live, the kids were doing well at school and seemed well-adjusted. My work – I loved my work. I felt a passion for being on 19; it was my anchor. No matter what storms raged around me, I was tethered to something solid, defining who I was and what I stood for. Health-wise, I was fraying a wee bit at the edges, but my heart and lungs wouldn't let me down any time soon, and the gym sessions were paying off. I was getting on in years, but I had never been physically stronger. Oh, and with a free launderette, my clothes had never been cleaner.

The negatives Well, let's just say that the box marked too difficult was filling up year on year. It was during my meditations on life, love, and pub opening times; that I formulated my plan to move abroad when the Met was done with me. I decided upon France; houses were cheap, the wine cheaper, and a police pension could buy me a lot of croissants. I popped into HMV on Oxford Street and purchased a Charles Aznavour CD. Best I start learning the language, I thought. The guy serving me looked like he presented the Old Grey Whistle Test; in his whispering tones, he advised I purchase an album by Jacques Brel. I found out later he was Belgian, but close enough. To complete the ensemble, I added Edith Piaf's greatest hits. Many were the nights I drifted off to sleep half pissed, emotionally exhausted from listening to tragic songs about heartbreak, unrequited love, death, growing old, first loves and extramarital affairs. Being of Celtic blood, I'm never happier than when I'm sad. Looking back, I'm surprised the young recruits didn't put me on suicide watch.

It was Saturday morning, and I was posted on a central London car, so I was not in a great mood. Things got worse when my driver, James, informed me we were to patrol in a bloody red X5. James drove out of the base, over the bridge and into Horseferry Lane. He then pulled up outside a cafe

WATCH AND REACT

and announced he fancied breakfast. Without a second's hesitation, he parked the car on double yellow lines and jumped out. I was maps; I shook my head but knew James wouldn't move the car; he was a stubborn sod. The three of us ordered our meal and sat chatting at a table awaiting its arrival. It was at this point that I noticed a woman standing beside the table looking down at us. "Good morning, you probably don't recognise me, but..." I interrupted before James told her to jog on. "Yes, ma'am, we do. Your assistant commissioner, Cressida Dick." With that, the other two sat bolt upright. "Guys, what sort of message are you sending to the public parking your car on double yellows outside this cafe? What about public perception?" Without needing a bigger hint, James was up moving the car. Whilst he was on his errand, she stood in silence staring at Michael and me, until I said, "Fancy a cup of tea, boss?" Thank God this broke the ice; she took a seat. The four of us sat chatting for the next half hour; she used the time to get the feel of the mood on 19, asking our opinions on changes being made to the department. She certainly knew her stuff. "Well, I can't chat all day, can I? You three take care and keep up the good work." We smiled back at her and then, "As for the parking offence, take this as a verbal warning." Ouch, was she joking? Probably, but it's not a good idea to piss off the future commissioner of the Metropolitan Police. What can I say about that interaction other than she was a nice lady, intelligent obviously, but what I really liked about her was the fact she was clearly shy and slightly awkward, and that showed a vulnerability I could relate to. Compared with her boss, Hogan Howe, her humility was a breath of fresh air.

Why were we driving around in a Diplomatic Protection Group BMW X5, a 'Ranger car'? It's complicated; it's not my intention to bruise any egos, but this is my take on events. The DPG back in the day protected diplomatic premises; armed officers stood on 'post' supported by mobile units, call sign, Ranger. These two-person cars were described as enhanced, whatever that meant. They were not ARV officers. The College of Policing (who in the name of God are these people?) told the Met there was no such thing as enhanced cars; they had to be ARV trained. At training, the Chief Firearms Instructor broke the news to us. The DPG (doors, posts and gates) were to be upskilled to ARV level. The response was less than enthusiastic. We were told, don't worry; they won't be search-trained, just some vehicle tactics. Relax. This was wishful thinking; the DPG officers were trained as ARV officers, 19 then swooped, and before you knew it, the DPG officers were SO19 ARV officers.

This pissed off a lot of 19 officers, officers who had jumped through so many hoops to make it to Trojan. Now we had colleagues who had got in via the back door, and it didn't feel right somehow. Lots of very good ARV officers jumped ship; some went training, some to the SFOs, and some got desk jobs. Yes, good officers joined us, but so did some who were just not cut out for life on 19. Experienced Trojan officers were now posted checking diplomatic premises in central London, and none of us signed up for that; Trojan officers are not glorified security guards. I hope this explains why we were sat in a DPG car. Thank God they got rid of them shortly after. As for us, years of experience running vehicle options, dig outs and foot strikes, we now found ourselves checking the fire alarm at the Algerian embassy. What a waste of experience, and experience is worth its weight in gold on 19. As for the brains trust, the College of Policing, how did we cope before 2012 and its inception? Just what coppers on the front line need, out of touch senior officers running around a grand old country house, Harperley Hall. "Cucumber sandwich anyone."

A gun buy is taking place in a pub off the Old Kent Road; surveillance is plotted up and feeding us live intel on the suspects. We were a little distance off on a side road, briefed and ready to go. Option two was authorised; the venue was a 'Trident pub', a location used for dealing drugs, gang meets and a host of other criminal activity. "Target is out; target is out. He's getting into a silver SUV, index 123ABC; he's the front seat passenger, car two up, car two up." We slowly started to roll; street names and directions are updated by surveillance. We are closing in. You can't afford to spook the suspect, so all progress is made minus two tones and blue lights. It's raining hard; keeping our convoy together is tough work. Suddenly the suspect pulls a U-turn and is heading right for us. "Fuck it, he's doing counter-surveillance." Once he passes our marked cars, the job's blown; take him now. Over the back-to-back, the decision is made to take him head-on, Bravo to go long; this isn't textbook. I see the target, two car lengths away: "Strike, strike, strike." I pull the wheel hard right; we skid across the wet tarmac, hitting the SUV, and with a lovely thud of rubber, bounce off the kerb. I'm shouting "Doors, doors, doors," but the crew are already out, boots on the ground, running towards the suspects. Windows are going in; I'm dragging the gunman out, shouting "Down, down, down." I pin him face down in the grit, stretching his arms down his back; I cuff him. I pat him for weapons, pulling up his sweatshirt; a silver handgun is stuffed inside a minging sock. "GUN."

Hours we sat up on that job waiting for the off. For each one that goes live, countless ones are stood down or come to nothing. I lived for jobs like these, where you adapt the plan to fit the changing circumstances, knowing the boys and girls are up to speed, filling in the gaps. No fuss, no drama, just fast thinking; the best Trojan officers had that flexibility, that adaptability. Never say never.

TERROR

The 1990s were certainly not terror-free; the threat of the IRA was a constant, and central London security patrols were the bane of all probationary constables. Thrown onto a minibus like a pressed man, I lost count of the night duties I spent walking Westminster freezing to death, thanking my Irish ancestors for ruining another set of nights. The mortar attack on Downing Street in broad daylight was both unbelievably daring, and a reminder Republicanism wasn't going away. A night I won't forget easily, I was sat in a packed briefing room in Charing Cross police station listening to officers from Special Branch giving us the latest intel on IRA methodology. One of the briefing officers was passing around the room dummy devices; mock-ups of timers currently being used by the IRA. Magic, sitting next to me, was tinkering with a clockwork timing device, with a key. like you get on a music box. Casually he handed me the box; as I took hold of it, the bloody bell exploded into life, the ring drowning out the branch officer's voice. Magic had wound the key up and handed it to me primed and ready to go. The room was stony silent as the box was grabbed out of my hands with the words "There's always one, isn't there?"

On the day of 9/11, I was at work chatting in the backyard when everyone started running into custody. Not sure what was going on, I joined the rush to find the team standing in front of the TV watching as two planes flew into the twin towers. For days after we responded to false alarms to terror attacks, but no attack came. My naivety led me to think Islamic terror wasn't an issue in the UK; were we not an example of multiculturalism at its finest? The London terror attacks on the tube and bus were a massive wake-up call. It was July 7th, 2005, and I was on 19 by this time. On the day of the attacks, I was on a rest day, and like so many officers, I called the base offering to come in. The department didn't have the cars or equipment to get us out on the street, so I sat watching events unfold on the telly. The following day I was rostered to work, and it was mayhem, call after call, nonstop. Scared members of the public calling 999, with sightings of suspicious males, rucksacks left on buses and trains, park benches – you name it, we got sent to it. The public were asked to be vigilant, and boy did they step up, no one complained, least of all, 19. The shifts were never-ending; no one minded, not because of the overtime but because we wanted to do our bit. I lost count of the times I had near misses when driving, a mixture of tiredness and pushing a wee bit too hard in an effort to get to the next scene. These were crazy days; my disbelief went through the roof when I saw the suspects were Joe Average, they played cricket and led seemingly normal lives. 52 innocent civilians died that day. The impact on Trojan, for law enforcement in general was immeasurable. We were now dealing with suspects who were prepared to die for the cause, and that was a game changer.

The Republicans were happy to blow up the UK, but always with a modus operandi of getting away and living to fight another day. Not so with this new threat, now we had to contend with religious fanatics who were prepared to die to achieve their aim. The suicide vest, SV, was now a threat we had to be prepared to face. Continuation training started giving us scenarios based around suspects in SVs, and with that, the tactical option of taking a critical shot – no more shooting to stop; now it's shooting with the sole purpose of killing the suspect stone dead, giving them no chance to detonate. Hand in hand with this went the fact you wouldn't issue armed challenges. Why would you? Training was becoming more and more complex, and with it, the need for wise heads carrying on the streets. The role of the ARV officer had been to deal with spontaneous armed criminality. The book said, 'ARVs will be deployed to persons in possession of a firearm or immediate access to a firearm or to someone who is otherwise so dangerous." The car's bread and butter was criminality, and that's straightforward enough. The book says to identify, locate, contain and therefore neutralise the threat. Easy, really. Now we had terrorists who were capable of blowing themselves and everyone else to pieces. It was time to change our tactics to identify, locate, confront. Confront? That means stop the threat and it could well be a pre-emptive shot. I wasn't kidding when I said times were changing.

At training, I saw young Trojan officers confusing their tactics, unclear as to the threat and the appropriate response. On one occasion I saw an officer talking a bomber in an SV, a suicide vest, out of a car towards him, all the time bringing himself and his crew into the kill zone. I intervened, shooting the instructor in the head. At the debrief I put it simply: is it crime or is it terror? If it's terror, then bloody shoot him, but that's training. The truth is it's not that black and white, when you turn up to an incident, males armed with knives attacking a victim, that could be a crime, gang-related crime, for example, or a robbery. On the other hand, it could be what Trojan faced on the 22nd of May 2013 in Greenwich and the murder of Lee Rigby, or the attacks in Borough market or London Bridge. Training responded brilliantly, in my opinion, to this new world order. Each cycle we trained in our traditional tactics dealing with the myriad of scenarios armed police can face. We also had training on stopping vehicle-borne bombs and attacks using vehicles to kill the public. Nothing was off the table; we were practising shooting through windscreens, stopping heavy goods vehicles and working alongside colleagues from the world of counter-terrorism. The world had changed, and we had changed with it. As an OFC, the responsibility you carried was bloody huge. An OFC, in theory, could authorise a critical shot. Think about that: a PC telling another PC to shoot a subject in the head. All based on information you may be getting from the pod, information you won't have seen first-hand, trusting the people around you to deal in life and death. Who would be an OFC? Well, me for one. Sadly, though there were times when I felt an advantage was being taken of me.

I was in Penge, deepest South London, when a call came out to a vehicle that was causing concerns, parked up at a location, in west London near Sheppard's Bush. The vehicle was giving indications it contained explosives, and local police were on the scene, but at the present time it was unoccupied. The Pod put up for an OFC to run the job; I sat listening, thinking to myself, no way is this ticking time bomb my baby. It was a North job, and I was South, very South. Add to this the North had more than its fair share of skippers and OFCs. No one volunteered; the Pod asked again, and again no reply. I could not believe my ears. I told the Spaniard to call up the Pod and tell them I was driving; I was in South London; I was miles away but would deal if no one was available. Well, Spaniard spelt this out, and I honestly thought this would shame some OFC North into responding. Well, you guessed it, total bloody radio silence, and then from the Pod. "Kev, it looks like it's you. Cheers." I drove the whole twelve miles on blue lights through busy traffic whilst simultaneously telling Spaniard to ask this or clarify that; not bloody easy. Arriving at the RVP, I was met by two kit cars containing a Trojan one and three skippers, all OFCs; I was gutted. This job had a critical shot written all over it, with me making the big calls whilst officers who were happy to take promotion stood by and avoided any flak. Eventually, after much investigation, the call ended up being called a false alarm. As I prepped to leave, one of my team commented, "Fuck being an OFC." I didn't respond; my face said it all.

We were now carrying grab bags containing extra rounds in case we got involved in a proper firefight. The weapon platforms had evolved from the G36 to the Sig to the MCX. Each one was chosen to give us the best tactical options if and when we faced bad people intent on a killing spree. The 2015 Charlie Hebdo incident saw Paris police being gunned down with automatic weapons, the suspects clearly were trained in tactics and weapons handling. Our foe was indeed becoming more formidable, and in response, our training became even more terror-related. What was happening abroad was not being ignored by those higher up the food chain. The attacks in Nairobi on the shopping mall and the hotel attack in Mumbai both resulted in hostages and large-scale fires. If 19 dealt with such an incident in the Shard, Harrods or Westfield shopping centre, what could we offer as a tactical response?

The CTSFOs are highly trained and bring a lot to the party, but the reality of every terror attack so far was ARVs were first on scene. Maybe the worst case scenario was the roaming attack; in preparation for this event, we were sent to iconic London locations to get some idea of the venue and scale of the problem. In truth, how valuable these visits were is open to debate. The team visited the Shard, and the head of security showed us around. I came away none the wiser as to how to deal with an attack, but I did know, I wouldn't want to be in one of the luxury high-rise apartments if things started going bang. I wasn't the only officer who thought of the twin towers. For me, you can talk plans, and building layouts, and security systems, but ultimately if the shit hit the fan at one of these sites, we would rock up and deal and work it out on the hoof, just like we always did. My theory on the subject was put to the test when a lone male walked into St Thomas's Hospital stating he had a bomb. I Arrived on the scene with a couple of cars; control was up and running, the Pod declared the call, I led part of the team into the huge sprawling building, the first job: secure the lifts and get control of someone in charge. I couldn't shut down a bloody hospital now, could I? Could I? This was another first for yours truly; lifts locked down, I posted armed sentries, organised search teams, and off we went hunting a man with a bomb. The team were amazing, taking floor by floor, leapfrogging one another, everyone in sync. Ben was OFC new in the role; he was nailing it, even taking on some hospital administrator who demanded to know why armed officers BLAH, BLAH, BLAH.

As the search played out, I realised from the look on everyone's faces they were loving it, not a moment's thought for personnel safety. I should clarify at this point I am talking about the team, not the patients and visitors who looked a tad concerned, though the nursing staff seemed very pleased to see us. As luck would have it, the suspect was located in a waiting room. I arrived at the entrance with Tom X; the room was packed. If he was going to go bang, now was as good a time as any. "This is why we get paid the big bucks, Tom," he smiled back, and with that, we closed him down and dealt with him. It was a hoax; he had made the threat but came to regret that decision. The operation was stood down, and we returned to base for tea and medals. I sat in silence throughout the debrief. It wasn't my show; this was a young team forging its own identity. I looked at the faces of all the volunteers, all happy to accept risk and danger, and I felt overwhelming pride to be in their company.

2017 was a watershed year with multiple attacks in London and the terrible events at the Manchester Arena. However, it was the events in Paris in 2015 that changed 19 forever. The highly coordinated attack involved suicide bomber's multiple locations and culminated in the attack on the Bataclan and the taking of hostages. I sat in bed watching the events unfold on my phone, genuinely shocked at the carnage. The final toll is 130 dead and nearly 400 wounded. The memory of the shield officer taking rounds was amazing to see in a European capital city and is something I will never forget. I, for one, expected a reaction from the Met, but no one could have imagined the eventual outcome.

The Commissioner and his team had a meeting with 19; at that meeting, senior 19 officers were asked if this attack was mirrored in London, could we cope? The answer was a resounding no; someone in the room, when asked how many cars you would need to deal with such an attack, came up with the magic number X. (I heard this story from a friend, who knew someone, who once saw the Commissioner riding tandem with Theresa May, so it must be true). That ladies and gents initiated the biggest recruitment drive in the history of the department. Adverts went out inviting firearms officers nationwide to come and join 19. Internally, Met officers were invited to apply, some still on their bloody probation. I was not happy with this new policy. What I saw as elite, the Commissioner wanted to turn into just another department. What about experience, maturity, and a proven track record? All of this went out the window. How would the reliefs cope with the influx of newbies, mentoring them, getting them up to speed? No one seemed to care. How would training find the instructors and locations to train them? What about the size of the vehicle fleet and having enough advanced drivers. All in all, the logistics element went out the window.

Uplift, as the programme was called, got officers through an application process and onto a course at Milton. As expected, the course weeded out the unsuitable, but some of these were seasoned armed officers from the counties. Pressure was exerted to get the pass rate up, causing tensions between the instructors and those asking them to ease up on standards. Suddenly you could fail an element, get a second chance, fail the next stage, get a second chance, fail, search, and get another chance. It was getting ridiculous. As for the county uplift, that too had major issues. On one course, every single officer bar one failed, and these guys were already supposedly fully operational ARV officers. Training for us went out the window; Milton was now fully booked, and so we, the actual ARV reliefs, were shipped out to train on military ranges on the South Coast.

Accommodation was a hotel room, which was fine, but we were now travelling further distances to and from training, reducing contact time. Add to this the increased numbers training, meant you were standing around waiting your turn like a bloody conveyor belt. It was not good, not good at all. One negative that had to be addressed was shooting. You could find yourself on an outdoor range in bloody December, an Arctic storm blowing in from the English Channel, shooting in the pouring rain at a paper target that may or may not be there when you walk down range to score. I shot in sleet and snow and gale, not amused at the direction training was taking. On one occasion the weather over the two days was so awful that by the end of training I was in a terrible physical state; within a couple of days, I was in hospital on a drip. I was the oldest guy on ops; I was the longest-serving guy on the cars, and boy, it was taking its toll.

Eventually, things calmed down, numbers grew on each team and a lot of the new faces were top notch operators. C relief South (F Troop, re branding) gained four county officers; Chesney, the only one to pass his course, hence the nickname Chesney, (the one and only) you work it out. Stu and Chris were quickly accepted, not least because they were top lads and great to work with. The fourth left within a few months; he struggled to fit in, the nail in the coffin declaring to the team, "I'm just a guy who loves too easily." Shit, if I had said that on day one, I think Ecky would have shot me. The young man returned to his home county; we wished him well. Uplift continued; the reliefs came to terms with the new world order, and I learnt that excellent armed officers did exist outside the M25.

WATCH AND REACT

GROWING PAINS

The speed at which 19 grew took all of us by surprise. The Pod was now staffed by a Metro Alpha, an Inspector who was a trained Firearms Commander. Their role, to declare or not declare a call and ultimately decide if we deploy or not. This, in theory, should have been dandy; sadly, it wasn't. The quality and experience of these officers of Inspector rank varied hugely. The Pod was also staffed by a Sergeant who was a tactical advisor; their role was to work with the Metro Alpha to make the right call. Again, it would be great if they got on and trusted one another, the Inspector being prepared to listen to a Skipper, which some clearly struggled with. The Pod then had at least one PC who was Pod trained, and finally a civilian was added to the team to run checks on intel off the computer system. The base room of 2003 bore no resemblance to the Pod, and that, ladies and gentlemen, was not always for the best. Any system on paper can be made to look good; however, add human nature, ego, or call it what you will, and the system didn't always function as it should.

One problem was the threshold that was used to deploy an ARV; it could vary so much from day to day that I couldn't honestly tell what decision the Pod was going to come up with. Sadly, the sit-on-the-fence approach prevailed in some quarters, and so we would get a situation where the Metro Alpha would not declare a call but ask you to run anyway to be in the area just in case. What sort of tactic is that? I often found myself going to the borough radio link and asking follow-up questions that would, on occasion, confirm we should be attending, supporting our unarmed colleagues. Informing the Pod of this, you can imagine it put a few noses out of joint. Bust-ups with the Pod were not uncommon to the point it felt like some Metro Alphas just didn't trust us to get on scene and make good decisions. Why would you join our command if you were, by nature, risk averse or pissed on rank? (unable to take advice from officer, junior in rank) I should clarify there were top-notch Metro Alphas running the show, but sadly, some believed if you ignore it long enough, it will just go away.

The two-base system was now gone, and with it, the single Trojan One. 19 now had four bases, and if you counted Heathrow, we had five. The two Trojan Ones worked, one North and one South; did they always agree? Of course not. Did this cause issues? Of course, it did. The reliefs were full of Skippers; some were OFC trained, some were awaiting a course, and some had failed and awaited a second go, aware that a second failure meant, do not pass go, do not collect £200, adios back to borough. Many of these new Skippers were hands-on, running the show; some however decided that they would skirt around the edges and do as little as humanly possible, because of the growth spurt, this behaviour went unnoticed by the powers that be. Rightly or wrongly, we now had more cars, maybe too many; the crews needed jobs, but fewer deployments were now the norm. 'Not declared' equalled less experience being gained. New boys and girls could wait months for a vehicle option or a dig out. The mentoring period had to be extended often because officers were not getting the opportunity to test their skill set. In my mind we grew too fast to the point the department were scavenging for kit for new officers because we didn't have enough uniform.

Was it me? As someone who remembered the old base room and the constant flow of work, maybe I was living in the past, not evolving, not accepting change. I did ask myself, was I becoming a dinosaur, and we all know what happened to them.

WATCH AND REACT

On a sunny Saturday I was driving around Lambeth when the local link came to life. More units to a male armed with a knife inside a shop. We contacted the Pod to be told they had seen the call, not declared, locals to deal. Fair enough, but on the local radio link, shit was getting very real; I thought, sod this, we are going. We arrived on the scene to see a large crowd outside the shop; they were shouting and screaming for us to get inside and hurry. Entering the little store, I was met by bloody carnage; two males, both covered in blood, were fighting, both struggling to get hold of a very large kitchen knife. Bottles of drinks, milk and foodstuffs, cans and tinned foods were scattered across the floor, making it bloody slippery. The two of them were falling on top of one another, slipping and sliding in every direction. One of the men grabbed the knife; my Glock was already out. I was shouting armed challenges; this is all happening in milliseconds. I hear "Taser, Taser," and one of the males rolls away in agony. Local officers are now helping separate the two; it's absolute chaos. I then see the Asian male has a slash wound to his neck that is millimetres from the artery. The paramedics are now arriving on scene, and I am still none the wiser as to what the hell is going on. Stu, one of my crew, is holding a bandage to the neck of the victim, the tasered male is now in handcuffs and being led away. Total bloody bedlam, not declared, SERIOUSLY!!!.

When everything calmed down, I got the full story: the suspect entered the store and started to steal some items. The Asian shopkeeper attempting to stop the would-be thief, suddenly finds himself facing a male with a knife, a bloody big knife. He stabs the shopkeeper in the head, then proceeds to slash the shopkeeper's neck; the shopkeeper is now fighting for his life. The criteria for our deployment covers suspects who are otherwise so dangerous; bloody hell, surely this comes under that heading. In truth, if we had been driving by, we would have just self-deployed, as we can do if the need arises. Did someone in the Pod look at the call, see the word knife and think locals to deal with it, no going to the local link, no follow-up questions. Well, a knife is bloody dangerous; should we have been sent? Taser is not infallible. I have seen officers miss the target; yes, it does happen. Stress does that. The barbs can fall out, the suspect is wearing a heavy outer coat, and it has no effect. The list is endless. For that very reason, Trojan always deployed conventional firearms with less lethal. It's a pity that some senior officers risk assessment was so poor that they can casually ask 'locals to deal' without taking a moment to appreciate what that could result in. Was it better to have a few coppers hurt than shots fired by police? You cannot afford to be blasé about these things; the Pod has a duty to get the right resource to the incident and then trust the Trojan officers to deal. It's all about trust.

Of course, this is just my slant on events; maybe the Pod was dealing with multiple calls, rushed off their feet dealing with firearms incidents, and this call slipped through the cracks. It's possible the controller inputting the information didn't appreciate the serious nature of the call. Who knows? I certainly don't have an axe to grind. My experience of Metro Alphas on my team was excellent; Julian, Claude and the gang really did a great job, but were they the exception or the rule?

Going home that night, I got a call on my mobile from the Metro Alpha. Was I ok? Did I need to talk with OH? Did I need a day off? I chose to believe this was a welfare check because the officer in question was concerned. As for my crew and I, we bloody loved it, it's why you join the service in the first place, a life was saved and a high-risk situation put to bed, working side by side with our borough colleagues. Do I need to see OH? do me a bloody favour.

I have mentioned we have authority to self-deploy; this allows ARV officers a great deal of flexibility and ultimately saves lives because you're dealing with an immediate threat, not calling the base for authority to do so. A great example of this took place in Wandsworth near Waitrose. I was radios, up front, dreaming of my lottery win, my driver chatting away, maps struggling to stay awake; it was a quiet day. Suddenly, I see a guy armed with a knife chasing another male. They are running between moving cars and causing quite a scene. Andy and I are out in a flash chasing the pair. As we reach a parade of shops, the guy with the knife turns only to be faced by two armed officers, both pointing Glocks in his face. He hits the deck, and we cuff him. The whole job was dealt with in under a minute. I suddenly realise the backdrop to this drama is a very upmarket, well-known estate agent. I then double realise the staff are all lying on the floor under tables like a scene from the Blitz. I give them all a friendly wave, and they take this as a signal to get off the floor and return to work. The manager then pops out and offers us a coffee and thanks us for making his team's day; they bloody loved the excitement. Well, it's nice to be appreciated. That's a very straightforward example of having armed officers patrolling the streets, ready at a moment's notice to deploy and snuff out a drama before it becomes a crisis. I should also like to add, if there is anything cooler than running through traffic, bouncing off car bonnets, with a gun, chasing an armed suspect I don't know what it is.

Another example of ARVs being in the right place occurred on a night duty, and I was in a two-person car with PB. As we drove around the Tulse Hill estate, we saw smoke billowing from a ground-floor flat. We found the front door open, and a few of the residents stood outside in nightgowns and pyjamas. What choice do you have in these situations? You have to go in and clear the address. PB didn't hesitate; in he went, with me a few steps behind. The flat was filling with acrid smoke; to make matters worse, there was no electricity, the only light coming from the flames that had engulfed a rear bedroom. PB was clearing rooms; I went into a back bedroom. It was clear of people but was starting to go up in flames. I thought I could dampen them with a towel lying on the bed. God knows what it was made of, but it went up like a bloody flame thrower; now the bed and the curtains were on fire as well. I wasn't helping much, was I? Discretion being the better part of valour, I withdrew, happy no one was left inside. The LFB (fire brigade) arrived on scene and started doing their thing; I gave them a courtesy nod, and we left. It was only once we were in the car that the smell of the smoke hit us; we started coughing our guts up, eyes running. The big film at the time was 'End of Watch,' a cop drama; the two heroes shared a line, "Do you feel like a hero?" As we drove back to the base, I said, "Hey, PB, do you feel like a hero?" He burst out laughing, "Hell, yeah, I feel like a hero." We didn't deploy as gun cops in Tulse Hill but in our role as coppers with a duty to preserve life.

No good deed goes unpunished, the saying goes. As I found out one rainy night in Soho. It was around 2200 hours, and a female officer's voice came over the radio. She was calling for assistance, and being a top cop, she got the road name across the airways. We were just around the corner, but the road was blocked with traffic. The three of us were out in a flash; the driver is always last because he must turn off the engine and check the car is locked. I was sprinting after my crew when the driver of a car parked on the offside of the road opened his door; I had no warning and hit the door frame, which sent me flying like a kid over the handlebars of a bike. I hit the cobbled street so hard my jaw made a crunching sound. The next thing I know, I'm being pulled to my feet by my body armour, and a voice was saying, 'Healy, you tosser, you had best not have damaged that door". Focussing, I saw the guy helping me up was a dog handler mate of mine called Gavin, and it was his bloody car door that sent me flying. Both laughing, we ran the remaining hundred yards to the fight. By the time we arrived on scene, half the Met was there, and the female officer was safe and well. With the adrenaline rush receding, the impact of my impact hit me, and I could hardly walk. My hip and elbow were cut, my trousers torn, and a lovely graze ran down my forearm.

Walking back to the car, I got a round of applause from a group of lads drinking outside a pub, who had seen my tumble. As luck would have it, an ambulance was parked beside our car, and a paramedic came over to say hello. Upon seeing my injuries, she decided to give me a once-over, so to speak. By the time I got out of the ambulance, my knee and forearm were bandaged, and the graze on my arm, cleaned. I thought it best to return to base, I was truly broken. As I exited the car in the yard, a Skipper I didn't know, new to 19, wandered over in his gym kit, drinking a coffee. He asked if I really needed to go home, as we didn't have a driver for my car. I stared at this individual, good gym session, was it? I now telepathically transmitted my thoughts, just two words, just two words, just two words. Going red in the face, he clearly read my mind. He now made a tactical withdrawal. By this stage of my career, I was tiring of Skippers who didn't attend calls, didn't monitor the radio and didn't care a toss for the welfare of their officers.

WATCH AND REACT

DOGS

Man's best friend can often be the Trojan officer's best friend. I have always loved dogs, though I'm not sure my feelings are reciprocated. When we get the nod to dig out an address, control starts getting each duck in a row. The kit van, an ambulance, and local officers for cordons, but first on the list is a Trojan dog. A Trojan dog is usually a bloody great big Alsatian trained to work alongside firearms officers. The handlers wear body armour and helmets, 'lids,' mirroring ours, because they will, by the very nature of the role, be right up front where the action is. The dog acts as the armed officer's eyes, well, nose in truth; either way, the dog is invaluable, a potential lifesaver. As an armed officer, your first contact with a Trojan dog is on your ARV course, the search element. The first thing you must do if you are designated dog support is to introduce yourself to the dog handler and the dog. You find out both their names, and you ask the handler, can you pat the dog? I always did, in the hope it would reduce the risk of Mutley taking a chunk out of me, if things went pear-shaped. A dog is not a machine and can be just as erratic as any human, no matter how well they are trained.

After introductions, it's time to get on the stick. When the front door is breached, armed challenges are shouted into the address. As OFC, I would, give the occupiers plenty of time to react. If I got no reply, I would inform anyone hiding inside that we had a dog and would be sending it in. At this point in the proceedings, many a hardened motherfucker decides they would rather surrender than be bitten by Fido. Straight away you can see the dog is helping clear the venue before we even enter. Once the occupiers are out, I would send the dog in again, because, dear reader, never say never on Trojan. One diehard could still be inside waiting to ambush the stick. While the dog is sniffing around from room to room, the stick is silent; only the voice of the dog handler can be heard encouraging the dog "Go find him." The dog stopping by a door or bed and barking is the first indicator we may have a subject inside. Usually, at this point, the dog handler gives you the nod that the dog has had a positive contact. The dog is called back and put on its lead. This is bloody vital; only once it's on the lead and dog security shouts, whispers, "dog secure," would I, as an OFC, decide my next option. For me, it's another shout into the address, telling the subject we know they are inside; the dog found them. Again, this could be the cue to surrender, but sometimes there's no reply, and that's when we start to earn our money clearing the address.

Dogs are not infallible, but I have personally never had a dog indicate a contact only to find the address empty. Though I have had a dog go through a building and indicate nothing, only for the team to find the suspect hiding inside. The trump to us having a dog is for the occupiers to have a dog. We won't put a dog into an address if a dog is already inside; it's a recipe for disaster. Sometimes the occupier will lock their dog in a bathroom or kitchen and then vacate, allowing the search to advance, but with the issue of a dog in an uncleared room to be resolved, not ideal, but that's what OFCs get paid to do: make decisions and resolve problems. Ultimately, it's not a good idea to have two dogs in an address. A dog being a dog, it's not unusual for the police dog to eat any cat or dog food left out in a bowl, you often hear it chomping away until the handler gives it a few stern words, and that usually does the trick. On one dig out we breached the door to find a lovely Jack Russell facing us. We didn't know the dog was inside, so the Trojan Dog was put back in the dog van. The handler returned with a noose to control the dog, but it ran into a bedroom and lay on the bed panting merrily as Jacks do. The handler whispered to me, "The suspect is in or under that bed." The Jack Russell was inadvertently giving us a positive indicator. I put in a challenge to the effect of "I know you are in the bed; do you want to come out now?" After a pause for thought, the bed came apart, and the suspect climbed out of his hiding place.

Sometimes the door goes in, and you are confronted by a hostile individual with his hostile dog. On the dig out in question, the suspect, unfazed by the armed old bill, told us to come and get him, whilst stroking his trophy dog. A huge bloody thing, the head the size of a bowling ball. I was number one on the stick and covered the suspect with my Glock. Upon seeing this beast, I whispered to my number two, "If that dog goes for me, shoot it until it stops moving." I had no intention of letting this monster rip anything vital off. This raised a few chuckles from behind me, but I was being deadly serious. Suddenly the bloody dog came straight at me, so fast that my number two couldn't get a clear shot and not risk shooting off my toes. The Taser officer filled the gap zapping the dog; the beast gave a huge yelp, ran around in circles, then proceeded to defecate all over the hall floor, up the walls, on the doors, on the sofa, the armchair, and the TV stand. Things had just got messy. The owner went crazy, chasing his dog around the flat, slipping in the mess, sliding across the floor, screaming abuse, making the beast even more scared, and that equalled more poo. Well, I thought to myself, next time the police come around, he will think twice about not coming out. The smell was unbelievable; the suspect crawled out on his hands and knees, and I thanked the baby Jesus I wasn't prisoner reception. As for the dog, the handler got his noose around its neck, and from then on, he was a sweetheart – the dog, not the handler.

WATCH AND REACT

As part of our role as armed officers, we have the unsavoury task of destroying animals in pain. The kit van carries a shotgun which is used for this purpose. Skippers, for some reason, get the shotgun course, but in the latter years of my time on 19, PCs started getting trained. I was not a shotgunner and had no interest, I couldn't face harming an animal. The Big Book of Firearms says we can be used in the humane destruction of animals which are dangerous or suffering unnecessarily. Trust me, watching a dog being put to sleep with solid slug ammunition is not pretty and as for humane. One evening we took a call to a dog going berserk in a house in west London. Arriving on scene, we were met by a dog handler and a couple of paramedics. The dog in question was locked in the kitchen; it had bitten several family members. The Daily Mail would describe it as a devil dog, an illegal fighting dog that should never be a family pet, but sadly the public can be unbelievably thick. The skipper and I walked in to see Satan, not his real name, lying on the kitchen floor. Upon seeing us, it goes batshit crazy; I had seen enough. The dog handlers refused to deal, citing a fear of death and/or mutilation as his defence. After a powwow, it was decided the dog had to be destroyed. The Skipper loaded the shotgun; I stood by as backup. The door to the kitchen was of the stable variety, which was handy, as this allowed for a safe shooting position, but in truth, I wasn't convinced Satan couldn't clear it if needs be. The Skipper dispatched the dog, but it was brutal to watch and took several rounds. Even with my ear defenders on, my ears were ringing. Job done; the kitchen looked like an abattoir. The wretch of an owner wandered in asking about cleaning up the carnage; the Skipper pushed past him, "Not our problem," and with that, we departed. The Skipper owned two dogs and was clearly upset carrying out this duty. I wanted to punch the twat's lights out, a nation of dog lovers, my arse.

Searching lofts is always a tricky proposition. Tradition demands that the smallest officer on the stick goes up. Now getting into a loft if it has a suitable ladder is a piece of cake. Compared with teetering on a banister rail, one foot on a colleague's shoulder, getting a bloody big shove and you're up and in. Now try this manoeuvre holding a Glock, trying to cover points of danger; it's not easy. Add body armour and your lid, and it can be a bloody nightmare. Being short, two jobs often fell to me: shield officer and loft specialist. I made up the bit about the specialist. I have climbed into countless lofts and only once found someone hiding, but that doesn't matter; you can't declare a building clear until you can swear on a pile of Men's Health magazines it's clear. As an OFC, your reputation depends on it, and more importantly, lives could. So, what has this meandering line of conversation got to do with dogs? One day a guy on the team decided, Let's innovate; Trojan loves to innovate. He convinced the dog handler to put the dog on the shield, then we lift the shield up to the hatch and the dog goes in; hey presto. I wasn't convinced this new K9 tactic was a winner but kept my mouth shut. The dog was a bloody huge Alsatian, and it was less convinced than I was. Not happy to be on the shield, imagine its surprise when it got lifted above head height; it went bloody crazy. All those years of dog training disappeared out the window; it leapt from the shield and bit the officer who suggested the plan on the arse. Medic! Of course, Muggins still had to clear the loft.

One tactical option available to armed officers is to do nothing. At the call-in question, a couple who lived in a one-bedroom flat over a shop decided they needed a dog to make their lives complete. If a breeder wanted to create an antisocial lethal weapon with paws, this dog is what they would have come up with. How they got it home is a mystery; within a couple of days, it was eating the furniture and going nuts being locked in all day. For some reason, the owners called the police. The dog section declined to get involved, and somehow it bounced to us. I entered the flat to hear it eating its way through the kitchen door, howling like the Hound of the Baskervilles. I asked the owners what they expected us to do, to which the male replied, "Shoot it, man, we can't get any food, and we are starving." I asked if it had injured anyone, which it hadn't, so I gave him the good news: we were leaving; that dog was his problem. He was furious and started swearing at me, and then came the line of the day: "Yo bro, what are we going to do about dinner?"

"I would go for a takeaway, bro."

Dogs are also a brilliant tool when containing an address. If you have a containment position at an address, that can't be covered by an armed officer, that could lead to a breakout. The good old dog can be kept out of sight to catch 'runners,' from the address. The golden rule, and every copper worth their salt knows this, if you're chasing a suspect and the dog is let off to pursue, for God's sake, stand still, because that dog could easily confuse you for the suspect, you can guess the rest. Twice I have seen this happen on both occasions; I was glad it was them, not I. A dog bite is not to be sniffed at; no pun intended. As a final observation on the wonders of police dogs, one must have some sympathy for the dog with the worst job in the Met, the semen dog. I think that's enough on that subject, don't you?

LIFE IMITATING ART

Often after a job, someone would comment that the vehicle stop, digs out, etc., felt like a training exercise, this went to show just how in touch the instructors were with our reality. Sometimes, though, you would run to a job so oddball that you had to go home and bore your family members with it. Here, dear reader, are Kevin Healy's top three WTF (what the fuck) moments. At number three, we got a call to some disused railway arches in Bermondsey. It was around midnight. The text of the call described a man in a sports car pointing a gun at a second male. Sounds good so far, two males, one with a gun and mention of a high-powered car. We pulled into the road that led to the arches; we went for the silent approach, not wanting to spook the gunman. Out on foot, we approached the archway only to see it bathed in white light. I then saw the suspect: a tall white male, athletic build, dark hair, black dinner jacket, bow tie. He looked like James Bloody Bond. The sports car was an Aston Martin; it was Bond or at least a very good imitation. The second male was a photographer. The new Bond film was coming out, and this was an advertising photo shoot for some glossy magazine, using the Bond brand. I introduced myself: "The name's Healy, Kevin Healy." Well, obviously, no one pointed a gun at anyone, and Mr Bond showed us the replica firearm he was using for the 'shoot', as they say in the world of photography. I was disgusted to discover it wasn't even a Walther PPK. Result: no offences, but a few words of advice.

At number two, A few years back, if you visited central London as a tourist, or for a day out with the kids, or maybe for a romantic break with your loved one, I would guess you would have seen the yellow aquatic landing craft used to ferry tourists up and down the Thames. The company that ran the show was called 'Duck Tours'; their amphibious landing craft were a regular sight on the river. Would you believe it? A member of the public walking on the Embankment saw a passenger on the landing craft pointing a gun at the driver. On route to deal, we get this cracking piece of tactical advice. Wait for it to leave the river; once on dry land, carry out a vehicle stop. Thanks for that; the last time I looked; we weren't issued oars. I am running scenarios through my head; Husband finds out his wife is having an affair with the driver of a Duck Boat and decides to shoot him. Boyfriend finds out girlfriend is having an affair with Captain of Duck Tours and decides to shoot him. To be honest I have a very limited imagination when it comes to calls like this. Though a disgruntled tourist, unhappy at the exorbitant cost of tickets, decides to demand money back at gunpoint, did cross my mind We shadow the boat until it heads for dry land; this is the moment. We pull up alongside the craft; I leap out, looking up at the passengers, and see a guy in a white dinner jacket, bow tie, dark hair, and athletic build. It's bloody James Bond again. After a few questions, I discovered it's a James Bond experience Duck Tour, very popular with the Japanese. The passengers are clapping, lapping it up, thinking we are part of the show. I gave them my best bow, a few choice words of advice to the crew, and we were off, result, no offences.

At number one. The last thing you want at six in the morning is a call an outer borough, especially if it's been a busy night. A call came out to Croydon, an outer borough; a real drag, we are getting off late. The story: Officers under attack from a knifeman going berserk. Well, ladies and gents, that is right up our street. I gathered my crew and set off; it was a Sunday morning, and progress was good; nothing on the road to slow us. Pulling up at the

RVP, I was struck by the houses, all detached and all worth a bomb, not the sort of street we usually end up in. The local area car was parked, blocking access to the road. I wound down my window and asked the driver where the suspect was and how come they were sat in the car. The driver, obviously pissed off with my question, informed me their Inspector had ordered all his officers to remain in their cars and avoid the suspect. Well, I had never heard that tactic before; it's right up there with run away. Ok, fair enough; I got him to reverse and let us drive towards where the suspect was last seen. The station van then pulled up; same story, they were staying put. We got out of the car; nothing much was going on, a typical Sunday morning in suburbia. The first hint that things were going to get interesting was when the driver of the van pointed over my shoulder and said, "He's back, Trojan."

I guess my crew and I saw the suspect at the same time. Not the biggest guy in the world but 'distinctive' in his own subtle way. He was holding a bloody huge kitchen knife with blood all over it. To add to the drama, our suspect was wearing a hockey mask, just like Jason in Friday the 13th. I pointed my Glock at the suspect and told him to stand still and drop the knife. Jason was clearly working from a different script, ignoring my shouts to stop and drop that bloody knife. Still, he advanced towards me, his head lolling slowly from side to side. Where is Jamie Lee Curtis when you need her? It's understandable to feel work-related anxiety at times like this. Not me; I had to fight the urge to laugh out loud because my number two, an ex-Para and man of choice words, chipped in, "You didn't tell me it was bring your kid to work day?" The timing was perfect, you just had to see the funny side. A few steps closer, 'Zap,' the suspect was tasered as soon as he got in range, dropping to the floor. He was cuffed, and then the big reveal: removing the mask, we found our knife man to be a teenage kid, just like in the movie. The backstory: Mum and Dad are away for the weekend; son does way too many drugs and flips out, attacking his girlfriend who, though injured, escapes out into the street, and that's when the police got involved. There you have it, three examples of calls that were outside the norm and made for good banter around the parade table.

Before I move on, I feel I must give an honourable mention to one call that I would think no one on 19 has ever faced. Sat on parade talking nonsense as we would and loving every inappropriate second of it, a call came out; a male armed with a shotgun entered Brockley Park. The informant believed the male was going to commit suicide; living in South London, I knew how he felt. We jump in our cars and head to the location. Being a big open area, we asked for the helicopter to assist with the area search; it was unavailable; they were watching James Martin boil an egg or something equally as important. The cars entered the park from different locations and commenced a pincer movement Rommel would have been proud of. Out on foot, we closed down the area where the male was last sighted, then through the trees and hedges I see a white male with something in his mouth; I edge closer, it appeared a little bit long for a shotgun, and then I heard it, a strange droning sound. At that moment my earpiece came to life: "Have you guessed what it is yet, cobber?" I then heard a word I never thought I would hear spoken on 19. "Didgeridoo, guys, he's armed with that thing Rolf Harris used to play." I decided it was time to break cover, the risk of being killed by a didgeridoo, being one I was prepared to take. Long story short, a young hippy guy wanting some 'me time' liked to sit in the park playing his didgeridoo. Beat that, Australian ARVs.

19, deal with armed suspects every day of the week, 365 days of the year. 99.9% of the time, it's the same result: suspect detained, no shots fired. The training and pressure testing, that Trojan officers go through, is one reason why potentially lethal situations are resolved quickly and safely. Trojan officers are bloody good because we get so much exposure to real gun crime. We are not traffic cars who 'double hat' as ARVs; Trojan has one purpose: to deal with armed criminality in all its various guises. So, just how do you get baddies to listen to reason? One tool at our disposal is the use of good old fashioned Anglo Saxon swearing. I was lucky, swearing was something I mastered at a very early age.

Verbal domination of a subject is the goal, and that often involved using some very aggressive language. The suspect must feel completely overwhelmed. They are staring down the muzzle of a MP5, with only one option, comply. The public, media and a few senior officers don't get it. Of course, it's not pretty, it's not very Dixon of Dock Green. It's a necessary evil, just like having armed units in a service where officers patrol unarmed, and long may it remain so.

A few years ago, training got the nod from on high that we had to tone down the bad language. The crop of TV documentaries highlighting our work, showing 19 officers in full voice, probably didn't help. The result, when at training, we swore less to keep the instructors happy. Once back on the street, the air was blue with armed officers giving it their all. What follows is an example of muscle memory on the subject of strong language. A delegation from a very wealthy Middle Eastern country visited Milton to observe us in action. A fact-finding tour with the intention of possibly creating their own ARV unit.

WATCH AND REACT

The scene is set; we are to stop a car with two suspects and carry out an option 2, this involves extracting both occupants at gunpoint. Just before we commenced the exercise, an instructor reiterated, "do not swear," for fear of upsetting our guests and potential clients. The crews all nodded, Yep, we are on board; you can trust us. ACTION, we follow the car, and at the chosen location, the stop goes in, and hey, frickin' presto, the air is filled with every expletive you can imagine, all screamed with full gusto. It was a total full-on bash-up; the instructors in the car were dragged out as if they had real guns. It was a great stop, in our eyes anyway. Our guests, however, looked on in absolute horror. With the call "Car clear," the exercise ended, the bemused entourage clapped the most half-hearted, emotionally disturbed clapping you ever heard. The instructor looked like his daughter had just told him she was joining Isis, and no, we did not get a letter of appreciation. As of writing, the Middle Eastern nation is still assessing the use of ARVs.

To reiterate, the course prepares you well; the subsequent calls you attend help you grow in experience, but the thread that runs through everything you do is common sense: the ability to take in information and react in a proportionate way. You can't teach common sense, and it's unbelievable how uncommon it is. That's why the recruitment of proven officers, and the retention of the best is vital if 19 is to maintain the standards set by those who came before. 19 has no place for the red mist of overreaction; deal with what you see, and if you do that, you can't go far wrong.

PEAR-SHAPED

Most of the time, things go to plan, most of the time. If it's a pre-planned job, it often is still reasonably spontaneous. You come in for night duty to be informed by one of the skippers that an address needs digging out. A squad or a borough team will have a warrant; they have housed a subject, and the only way to safely arrest this person is by means of an armed operation. Working backwards, the door usually goes in around two or three am. You want it to happen when everyone is fast asleep in bed, reducing the risk of compromise. What's a compromise? Anything that can let the subject of the operation know we are about to put their door in. You can have a self-inflicted one, such as a member of the stick's mobile phone ringing as we were setting up around the door, and yes, that did happen; at 2 am, it sounds like bloody Big Ben, or one of the team leaning on the suspect's car, setting the alarm off, and yes, that did happen. Or you can have an external factor such as the suspect opening the bedroom window to smoke a fag, only to see a stick of armed officers heading their way. And yes, that did happen.

The briefing takes place around midnight. This allows the Recce team a few hours to get into plain clothes, secure an unmarked car, drive to the address, recce it and the surrounding streets, return to base and then formulate a plan. Once the plan is agreed, it's on to PowerPoint to write up the operation, draw maps showing the RVP (rendezvous point), the FUP (forming up point), containment points and a host of other tactical considerations. At most, you will have three officers doing this. By midnight, if all is on schedule, the officers involved, including outside agencies such as the LAS (ambulance service), are sat in a room awaiting the briefing. That is how a pre-planned job can end up in your lap as an OFC; it's bloody hard work. Always keep in mind the aim of your plan is to deliver armed officers to a front door to arrest a very dangerous individual. Put simply, the plan must work. Of course, shit can happen – 'the best-laid plans of mice and men' – and that's where contingencies come in, but sometimes even the most detailed plan can go pear-shaped, as in the blow-up in your face. Follow me down memory lane, as I describe a few challenging incidents that test the best of us.

I was on a dig out in Hounslow; I sat through the briefing and found I was to be black containment, in a service road that ran at the rear of a row of terraced houses. So far so good; I saw from the map my 'route in,' which was straightforward. I arrive at the FUP (forming up point); it's around 2 am. I don't have any kit to carry, such as a ladder or ballistic blanket, which suits me fine. With a nod to the OFC, I head off into the night and quickly find myself at point 12 black. A lovely concrete wall gave me 'cover from view,' as well as ballistic cover. I whisper into my radio, "Black containment in," soon followed by white. With this, control, asks for radio silence, the stick starts to advance. I am standing in the pitch dark, no moonlight, not making a sound, when I hear movement to my right in a garden. It can't be the suspect escaping; I could see the black door (back is black in the world of Trojan) through a broken gate, and it has not opened; the house is still in darkness, as you would expect. Rats, maybe; no, too big; a badger or a fox, perhaps, but no, dear reader, it's a bloody great male, dressed in black from head to toe, known to you and me as 'Billy Burglar.'

To be fair, I'm not sure which one of us looked more surprised. Yes, I do, and he looked even more surprised when I pointed an MP5 in his face and whispered, "Get on the fucking ground." He didn't need to be asked twice. In my earpiece, I could hear the OFC telling control, "Stick at the front door." This was not the time for added distractions; I needed to be doing my job covering Black. I got my cuffs off my body armour and threw them to my new best friend. I got him to put one cuff on, then to lay face down, I pulled his arms together and secured the other cuff. I was hoping to God he didn't kick off and compromise the job and thank God he didn't. I now whispered very politely in his ear, "Don't you dare fucking move, ok?" He nodded his agreement. Now I was on my jack, and the door is going in 'The jobs gone loud,' as we say. I have one foot on my burglar's back pressing him into the ground, just to let him know I am still there. I can hear the armed challenges; the light from the team's torches shine through to the back garden. I watch as level one, then level two, last, the loft gets cleared. It seems to take ages, but probably no longer than usual. The whole time my friend keeps nice and still, not a peep. Finally, I hear the all-clear over the radio. I give it another thirty seconds, then let control know I need a few local officers to my location. Job done, adapt and overcome. At the debrief, no one even mentioned my heroics, least of all me. Just part of being 19.

Working with a team on overtime, I was given black containment on a dig out in Lambeth. The briefing officer said, "Ok, Kev, you walk along this road, and you will come to a gate on your right. It will be unlocked. Open it, and you will be in a communal garden. We will leave glow sticks on the ground that will lead you to the black, Take a ladder; it's a high wall." Sounds simple enough, I think to myself. Zero hours arrives, and I leave the FUP and head for the garden gate; sure enough, it's open. In I go, shutting the gate behind me, but no glow sticks to guide me, nothing. Some kids may have been in the garden and nicked them. Shit, shit, shit, I'm thinking as I carry my collapsible ladder, trying to work out the correct address.

Finally, happy I am in the right place, I set up the ladder. I climb up nice and covertly; I now cover the rear of the building. In my earpiece, I hear the stick setting off. I hear they have arrived at the front door; here we go. I hear the door frame smashing and the shouts of "armed police", but unfortunately, I'm looking at the wrong bloody house. You have never seen anyone get down a ladder so fast in your life. I now sprint in the dark towards the chaos I am meant to be covering. I arrive, put up the ladder and start pointing my gun in the direction of the right bloody house. Fortunately, no one broke out in black; I got away with it. The suspect was nicked. As I walked out into the street, I saw a group of kids on bikes throwing glow sticks at one another. I never mentioned my little problem. What was the point? I was on overtime and didn't want to rain on anyone's parade.

The best plans have as few working parts as possible; with this in mind, I was nominated to get a black containment on an address that looked tricky on paper. The OFC was aware of this and so allowed me and John plenty of time to get in place. We were taking two ladders, as we had to climb several walls; garden hopping, as it's known, is never easy. Try doing it in the dark with two bloody ladders and an MCX you're 'long,' swinging around your neck. We arrived at the first wall, about 8 ft high, brick construction: that's good. Ladder up, climb, drop the second ladder down the other side, and hey presto, we are in garden one. We gather the ladders and head for the next wall; wall-located the ladder goes up the same routine, dropping the second ladder on the other side, and down I go into Garden Two. As I get halfway down, John's boot dangling in my face as he is sat atop the wall, I hear a deep growl, and it isn't my buddy. We both freeze. Silence. Ok, I start to move again; the growling, this time longer and meaner, I freeze. The door to a conservatory is open. Who leaves a bloody door open at night and then, that growl again, this time longer and more menacing?

It's at times like this that teamwork is everything. "After you, Kev, go shut the door." I look up at John; he's smiling down at me. I had no choice but to tiptoe across the lawn and slowly close the door, all the time waiting to be ripped apart. Reaching the conservatory, expecting some XL Bully to leap out, I faced instead a furious-looking Chihuahua. Seeing me, it ran indoors, through the cat flap. Thank God for that. Once the door was secure, John came down off the wall. On that job, we climbed over three walls, got into position, set up our ladders and didn't disturb the environment, which is no mean feat, and sure enough, the bloody address was empty.

Standing on a ladder armed to the teeth, covering a rear garden on a daytime dig-out, I felt the ladder move. I looked down to see an elderly couple looking up at me. "Hello, would you like a cup of tea?" And sure enough, Mum was holding a tray with a China cup and saucer and a selection of biscuits. As politely as I could, I explained I was a tad busy; they looked at one another, then Dad said, "In that case, would you like a sandwich?" I fell in love with this couple on the spot. I thanked them profusely but declined. "Well, constable, we will be inside watching; this is better than loose women." I wanted to say there's nothing better than loose women, but I don't think they would have appreciated police humour. As I packed up to leave, they opened the garden gate and wished me well, but not before giving me that cup of tea and Hobnob.

The shortest dig-out I was ever on consisted of forming up a stick and getting the go, go, go, only to be fifty feet up the street when the skipper stood us down; the warrant had been obtained for the wrong address. Stand down.

WATCH AND REACT

My funniest dig-out took place in Croydon; after a row with his mum, the subject took her hostage. To be fair, we've all done it. Threats were made to harm her and burn down the building. It was a terrible night: rain, high winds and bloody freezing. I stood on white containment in view of the suspect; he was armed with a blowtorch shouting abuse at Mum as well as officers – all very dramatic. When I say 'blowtorch, a more accurate description would be 'one of those devices you use to caramelise the sugar on a crème brûlée. Deadly in the hands of Jason Statham, fortunately we weren't facing the 'Transporter,' our guy was more Mr Bean. The suspect came to the window and took an immediate dislike to my face. He then disappeared, only to return with a Henry Hoover, and proceeded to threaten me with it. My team pointed out I was in danger of being 'sucked off,' which must be a first at a dig out. The male was eventually arrested; Henry was unharmed.

Now if we all agree that pre-planned jobs can go pear-shaped, what chance do spontaneous jobs have? By spontaneous, I mean those jobs that happen without warning. Fast time, responding to a threat happening now or in the very near future. The husband, on route to kill his wife's lover at his place of work call. The male seen putting a gun in the glove compartment of his car call. The idiot pointing a gun out his bedroom window at passers-by call. This list is endless; they happen every day, and if declared, cars start rolling. You arrive at an RVP chosen by maps; it's got to be near enough to react but out of view from prying eyes. The OFC now starts coming up with a plan whilst the containment officers are briefed and, on their way, to secure the venue. Over the bonnet briefings were something I was very comfortable with, much more so than pre-planned. Probably down to my nature, I hate overcooking things. In fact, if it's an emergency search, fast time, or getting in to save life, the briefing can be two words: "on me." This was the 19 I loved. I excelled in the fast time; it held no fears for me. Sadly, I was involved in a fast-time job that went so wrong people in high places were asking difficult questions.

Sat in the base, it was a miserable dark winter evening; the Pod called, officers in an OP, (observation post) had been 'blown,' job speak for being spotted. The target was wanted for murder. The very real fear being he may decide to 'take out' the officers in the OP. This was a threat to life call, a get-there-and-fix-shit-fast call. Arriving at a huge housing estate in Lambeth, with a complex layout of flats, we spent an age trying to locate the correct block. The plan was to simultaneously secure the OP as well as contain the suspect's address, getting between him and unarmed officers. Both venues were located, so far so good. More units arrived; a stick was formed. I was on containment covering the front door and was very happy to see the stick coming down the corridor, the OFC, a guy I knew well and very capable. All set, the door was breached; the shield officer, Dan, stepped into the void and covered into the hallway with his Glock. The suspect was called to identify himself, which he did by running up to the shield officer and telling him he was going to stab him. I for one believed him; he was one very, very angry man, and having his door smashed in did not help his mood. Dan stood his ground and started negotiating, but the suspect, who I will now call Peter Parker, was having none of it; he was losing the plot. Peter Parker ran upstairs and then proceeded to climb out of a window and start scaling the outside of the block like Bloody Spiderman. I watched with a mixture of horror, what if he falls? and a hint of FUCK, he's escaping. Up and up, he climbed, and we could do nothing to stop him.

The block was huge and had a flat roof, once on it, he was gone. The Helicopter was called but was not available. No dogs were available to track. What the fuck just happened? This was bad and just got worse. Calls started coming in, a man garden hopping further up the street, then calls he was at an address, and so the confusion grew. The OFC reacted brilliantly, deploying officers to gardens and even searching a few houses, but all to no avail. No one lost their head; everyone stuck to the task for hours. I personally must have searched three houses and any number of gardens, but in my heart, I knew we had lost him. All units were eventually stood down, and we returned to base. As we drove back, one of my crew made a joke about what had happened; I ripped him a new one. Did it not occur to him, we had lost a guy wanted for murder, who may, or may not, have known we were on to him, but boy did he know now. This was going to go up the food chain fast. How we had screwed up, and what if our suspect hurts someone? Now, that's down to us. This was bad, and I was right. That night I got a phone call from an Inspector asking me to explain how we lost the guy; he was asking because someone high up at the Yard was asking. "The team was a bloody disgrace," I was informed by an instructor who didn't realise I was involved; I was part of that team. What can you say?

This was a classic example of an OFC thrown under the bus. A job came out, and we responded. We did everything we could with limited resources. The OFC took it on the chin, and life moved on, but it left a few scars. The next time applications came out for an OFC course, no one was crushed in the rush. This is the reality of life in the cars, the risks you face and the decisions you make based on limited information and all the time the clocks counting down.

THE LONGEST DAY

A wise man once said Under stress you don't rise to the occasion; you sink to the level of your training. Well, no one had trained harder or longer than me.

I was posted on a Central London car, which was a drag, checking Embassies, going to alarms at Diplomatic premises etc, not why I was on Trojan. My crew were good guys and a good laugh, so every cloud. The morning was sunny, and I was maps, which had a twofold advantage. One, maps in central London were a doddle, and two, I could catch a little power nap at some point. I started to hear chatter on the radio. Cars were running to Lambeth; local officers were threatened at an address by a male armed with a handgun. The second I heard the call, I knew we were going; my crew, like me, were never going to sit in central London drinking coffee while the team were dealing with a subject who had pointed a gun at unarmed officers.

We arrived at the RVP and were kitted up and ready to go in seconds. Control gave us the location and pointed us in the right direction, and we were gone. A call of this nature is described as a siege; no third person is involved, no hostages in the address, just the suspect. The building was a block of flats, typical of 1930s design, with long open walkways giving access to flats. Set over three floors with access via a central staircase, they are in every city in the UK. The type of housing you see in all those 1960s British kitchen sink dramas, giving the viewer gritty realism. As I got to the landing, I was met by a few of the team who had arrived first on the scene. The plan was to close down the front door and make contact. A stick was quickly formed; we pushed forward, setting up around the door and covering the windows. The front door was missing a tiny wood panel; this allowed some vision into the flat and assisted communication. The stick that day was made up of officers who I will not name to protect their anonymity but who I have to say I was lucky to be surrounded by on that crowded walkway.

The siege was now well and truly underway; the subject had no intention of coming out, and we had no intention of leaving. The residents living next door, below and above were asked to evacuate, for their own safety. Additional cars arrived, filling in the gaps as they appeared. A siege is a very labour-intensive operation. Control was now up and running the show. Numerous officers were tasked with running the radios, drawing up plans and sorting the logistics. These things last as long as they last: the endgame, the safe surrender of the suspect and no one injured. How long this can take is anyone's guess. The Hackney siege of 2002 lasted 15 days. The negotiators now arrived on scene and attempted to create some form of dialogue via mobile phones.

Armed officers started rotating roles to allow for rest breaks; it was bloody baking now; everyone was getting water down them. Soon the CTSFO teams arrived; they commenced planning for their involvement if required. The scene was a hive of activity; I took a half hour break, using the neighbour's flat to rest my legs and take on some fluid. My rest break over, I returned to the walkway and took up position as number two supporting the shield officer. We stood chatting, talking about a million unrelated subjects, as you do on jobs: it helps keep perspective and allows the blood pressure to remain nice and low. Time moved slowly, the stick rotated, everyone shared roles and responsibilities. I was so lucky; after E relief was disbanded, I doubted I would get the same buzz, but C relief, the old F troop, was made up of some formidable coppers, both male and female.

The negotiators now made the tactical decision, to withdraw us from the front door, and move us back along the walkway out of sight. Why we did this, I don't know; Officer A had been doing a great job so far, getting the suspect to talk, to build some sort of rapport. Withdrawing, we lost that essential human connection, but move we did. The Skipper that day was one of those Sergeants that I had huge respect for, always at the front, always taking charge, making the tough calls. He was on the walkway; it was good to have him there.

The hours dragged, and the conversation slowly dried up, leaving each one of us alone with our thoughts. That was until someone cracked a joke, and we were all 'back in the room.' Humour, dark and morbid or juvenile and daft, these are the valves that release the stress and happen on every job. The buzz of being on the stick, only feet away from an armed male focuses the mind, but it's also bloody draining. That's where professionalism, determination, character, grit, pure bloody-mindedness, call it what you will, kicks in. It's something inside each one of us; it keeps us focused, keeps us sharp, and you must be sharp to do this job. As I chatted with the shield officer, it was obvious he was as chilled as I was; we had both been here countless times. I knew he was on the same page; he always was. As we spoke, our eyes never left the front door. The Japanese have a word for this state of mind, zanshin, relaxed alertness, to be completely in the moment but calm. The radio came to life with another update from the negotiating cell: "He's coming out; he is surrendering." That was it: no surrender plan, no further instructions, nothing.

WATCH AND REACT

From where I was standing, I didn't see the door open, but in an instant the subject was out on the walkway, standing squarely in front of me, pointing a black handgun directly at me. I heard gunshots as I simultaneously fired two shots from my Sig. The male was falling to his right; he was down. If you blinked, you would have missed the whole thing; it all happened that fast. Who lives and who dies is decided in a heartbeat. The skipper on my shoulder was pushing me forward along with the shield officer, closing the male down, kicking the gun away from his hand; we were on him in seconds, I was kneeling in his blood, cutting his clothing away, revealing several gunshot wounds. He was groaning in agony and writhing around on the floor. I have never felt calmer in my life. Someone grabbed the strap on my body armour and pulled me up to standing. A clear, calm voice, it was Pete: "Kev, we got this." Pete was always so chilled even now; I stood looking down at my friends doing everything to stem the flow of blood, using all their training to save a life. Year upon year I had trained for this very day, but now, in the moment, my thoughts were not of me or my actions; they were ones of overwhelming pride and respect for the team, my team and I was walking away. Only now did I realise the shield officer had also engaged the subject; someone handed me a balaclava to hide my face from the press, I was now out in the sunlight, the shield officer by my side. I winked at an old friend as I climbed into an ARV; he joked about it months later. That wink told him I was ok; I was still me, calm, in control. Seven hours the siege lasted and resulted in shots fired. Hours later my legal rep asked how I felt. I wish I could have thought of some Bond-like quip, but nothing came. I sat staring back at him and wondered what my wife would say. We had been married just six weeks.

After discharging your weapon, a post-incident procedure is declared, a PIP. Today it has a new title, but ultimately, it's just the same drawn-out ordeal; everyone wants a piece of you, and you have no choice but to go along with it. writing an initial statement detailing your actions, being seen by a doctor, taking legal advice and a host of procedures, all under the watchful eyes of the DPS, Department for Professional Standards, the police who police the police. Also tagging along was the IIPC, now called the IOPC, Independent Office for Police Conduct; add your Fed Rep, and you have quite a circus. The whole saga finally concluded on the morning of the following day. Two of us had discharged our firearms; I was in no doubt my actions were lawful and necessary and justified and all the other words that scream, yes, I did the right thing; I did my duty.

The sun was up, a new day; we both got the nod we could go home. I was physically and mentally done in. The senior 19 officer involved in the case was speaking with our Fed Rep, asking how we the principal officers were getting home. Our Fed Rep, the man who supposedly had our backs, suggested we get the tube, as they were now running. My buddy and I stared in bewilderment at our Rep. I was lost for words; in fact, that's not true; I had two, but what was the point? We had now both been on duty for twenty-four hours and awake God knows how long. The Chief looked as bewildered as we did; he then explained to our Rep in no uncertain terms, that cars would be arranged to get us home. End of conversation. A short while later I shook hands with my fellow principal officer, and we went our separate ways. An ARV drove me home; the crew didn't ask, and I didn't tell. These were the rules 19 was built on. Home, I thanked them and watched them drive away. I knocked at the front door to be met by my wife. The last time I saw her, we had been arguing as I left for work. I think we both felt terrible about that. I was a bit emotional; the lack of sleep combined with seeing my wife and the drama I had played a role in, hit me hard, harder than I thought it would. I went to bed but couldn't settle; eventually, I slipped away, my longest day finally over.

Months would pass before I was cleared of any wrongdoing and given the green light to return to operations. I used this garden leave to see my kids and drive my wife crazy hanging around the house. Before returning to ops, you have two final hurdles to jump through. First, you must speak with OH, Occupational Health. One of their highly trained staff would interview me, and decide through a vigorous assessment of my faculties, if I was ok to return to the world of guns. The date arrived, I attended ESB, Empress State Building, for my evaluation. I wasn't in the least bit concerned because, from experience, they were often more screwed up than I was. I arrived on time, but she was late, very late. Eventually, a lady walks into the waiting room still in her coat and hat, carrying two bags of food shopping and asking if any of us present was Kevin Healy from SO19. I raised my hand, the other OH referrals stared at me, 'that's the shooter then.' She told me she would return, then disappeared through a door and didn't return. I was on the verge of walking out when she finally strode into the office and asked me to follow her.

Sat in her office, I was not impressed. She asked my name and didn't give hers, not until I asked, but she did explain her husband didn't appreciate how tough her job is and that getting the kids to school was a daily nightmare she could do without. She asked if I had children; I said four, but I could have said I was raising Martians; she wasn't listening. Fiddling with her phone, distracted, uptight, wasn't this how I was meant to behave? At last, she asked the big question, the one that breaks you down to reveal your inner demons. "So how are you feeling?" Pause "Kevin" Had she really forgotten my name? I stared back at her, weighing up my options; she was clearly ill-equipped to be sitting across from me. I felt sorry for all the officers who would come to her seeking help, only to be met by this emotionless vacuum. She didn't give a shit about me, so I set my mind to autopilot and said the right things. Yes, I'm sleeping well; yes, my family life is dandy; yes, I can still get an erection; and no, I don't dream about putting my Glock in my mouth and pulling the fucking trigger. I was out the door in under half an hour; my car MOT takes longer. One down, one to go.

I arrived at Milton and headed for the instructor's office. I was met by a couple of guys I knew well who took me on the range to shoot. Sometimes after a shooting, the officer can become what is known in the trade as gun shy, nervous around firearms. I wasn't that officer; I shot my rounds and hit the target. We all drank tea and chewed over the latest gossip. It was good to be around these people; I felt like I was home again. I was back on operations; I was fifty-two years of age, still at the sharp end, competing with lads and lasses half my age but still wanting more. I was approached by several instructors and senior officers who pointed out my age and the fact I had done more than enough to prove myself. Time to step sideways; it was in my best interests, and they were right, of course, but that voice in my head kept nagging away at me. See it through to the end; finish this thing you started. I had considered becoming an instructor. I knew I had a lot to offer, plus I loved moulding ARV officers, the next generation. Bloody hell, I had been mentoring new people for well over a decade and knew I was good at it. My shooting, however, was never going to get me on an instructor's course, not unless I put in hours of practice, and that just wasn't me. I was old, but I certainly wasn't past my sell-by date, I told myself. A few weeks later, arriving at a call in Downham, a youth saw me getting out of a car and shouted at my crew, "What's this, bring Grandad to workday?" I saw my reflection in the rear-view mirror, my beard now silver, my hair going grey. deep wrinkles around my eyes, I had become an old man, and I hadn't even noticed.

Five more years I would remain an armed officer. The yearly fitness test got tougher no matter how hard I trained. The injuries spoke to me on cold, damp days as I stood on containment or organised a stick. My mind, however, was still sparking. I had experience, and of course, I was one tough bastard; I had proved that. I still had my Irish charm and gift of the gab. My mother once said in her soft Limerick brogue, "Son, you're the kind of man that things happen to." I told her I don't go looking for trouble; she laughed at this, "Then, son, you were born under a dark cloud." My mother prayed for me every day; Christ is her saviour and safety net. Me? I worked without one.

MY LAST RODEO

I married Kerry; I swore I would never remarry, but I of all people should have known the Trojan mantra: never say never. Kerry was a police officer working in intelligence, though what she saw in me makes me doubt the vigour of the recruiting process. We moved in together, and I started to live like normal men my age. By that I mean sitting down at a table and eating a cooked meal, sharing your day with your partner not a bottle of JD, going out as a couple, doing the weekly shopping, planning a holiday, cutting the lawn, fixing things (badly), and all the other normal husband stuff. It took some getting used to; if I am honest, I had been flying solo for so long it felt strange to be we instead of me. Within a few weeks of the big day, I was a principal officer. I wondered what she must be thinking of her decision now with me sat at home pondering my fate. I won't say much more about this new chapter other than that I was the best thing that ever happened to her. Truth, I think you can guess that Mrs Healy kind of saved my life. She was religious, attended church, and I started to go as well. At first, I went to be supportive, but gradually I came to enjoy my weekly visit to the big man. I would block out the priest and talk to him directly about my kids, my life, and the bad things I had done, and for one hour a week, I would keep my big mouth shut and reflect. Kerry, my wife, gets me. She understands what this life can do to you; she holds my hand when I struggle to cope, when the memories whirring through my mind become a little too real, childhood, Cal, triplets, the job, my dad, what a journey. Sitting side by side in church, she can sense if I am getting a bit frayed around the edges, and that's her cue to reach out.

WATCH AND REACT

I was now a real elder statesman. I was well into my fifties, and somehow, I was still operational, still early, lates and nights. I asked for no special favours from my Skippers or at training; my pride wouldn't allow it, but boy, was I falling apart physically. My eyesight was on the decline, I wore glasses as a matter of course. My injuries piled up, because they never had time to heal. My right rotator cuff was in tatters, and once my body armour was draped over my head, I had little intention of taking it off until I went off duty; the mechanics of removing it were excruciating. My knee was a creaking, jarring mess; climbing ladders, jumping over walls, all things I routinely did, would haunt me later when I was driving home or lying in bed. The worst thing, though, was the cold foot chase. When you're young, jumping out of a car and chasing a suspect down is great fun. After a certain age, the muscles, joints, tendons and ligaments are not so forgiving. Imagine if, midway through this sentence, with no warm-up and no stretching, you had to jump up and sprint 100, 200, or 300 metres flat out, and then point a gun at someone, or struggle with them. It would be interesting to see how you cope.

I decided the only way to compete with the ravages of time was to live like a bloody monk. I would get up at 4 am, drive to work, and be on the running machine before 5. Run over, I would punch the heavy bag or hit the weights; this would get me up to just after 6 am. Shower, kit the car, book out guns, and be on parade, a live wire ready to rock. The downside of my new programme: by midday, I was a shattered wreck. Catching power naps when my crew was having a break. So much for competing, eh? Not a chance. This was how the last five years of my career played out. If I was early to turn, I was in bed by 10 at the latest. I was living like an athlete but without the results. Why? Because I forgot to account for two crucial facts. The first, sitting in a car, hour after hour, day after day, kills you. The days of nonstop Trojan calls were a distant memory. The Pod killed that golden goose. Sat in a car, your body getting soft, trying to avoid eating crap; it's a killer. Ageing had given me the metabolism of a tortoise. The second I was fighting the sands of time. The harder I trained, the more I got injured or aggravated the old injuries. Growing old literally kills you. 30 years of shift work are meant to reduce your life expectancy, or so the science says. Now, in my opinion, that depends on the officer and the regime they lived by. If you are overweight, as many cops are; eat badly at ridiculous times, as many cops do; and have to deal with the stress cops face, all of this on shift work, then yes, you probably are going to die prematurely, sorry. I chose to stay at the sharp end; on ops, no one forced me to, so I duly sucked it up and ate my greens.

A stark reminder of my mortality was being asked to mentor a new guy. In walks 6'3 of solid muscle; he was built like Arnie in Terminator. Only a test tube in a Russian lab could account for this physical specimen. I took one look at this guy, and in the words of Custer at the Little Bighorn, "You got to be shitting me." The fact that this giant was a polite, humble individual as well as operationally spot on left me feeling rather redundant. Nicknamed Chandelier for reasons I won't go into, he was the last officer I ever mentored, not that he needed much guidance from me. Turning up at jobs with this unit, I would often smile to myself at the reaction he received from both suspects and our unarmed colleagues. He was starting out and was blessed with all the gifts; I was shutting down, and what few gifts I had were fading fast. It had a duality about it which seemed right somehow. I was being replaced by a bigger, stronger, faster model, and rightly so.

WATCH AND REACT

Examples of my decline started to sneak into my work. Driving to a job, I was the lead car of a convoy of three. Over the radio one of the crew from Bravo made a joke about my car's speed or lack of it, to be precise. Jokes like this are never jokes; it was a hint to put my foot down. The fact it came from a new guy who was a non-driver hurt my pride; in my defence, I had my foot to the floor. It was an old-ish X5, and that was as fast as I could get it to go. After the call, more jokes about me driving like Miss Daisy. I went off somewhere nice and quiet and had a word with myself: was I now holding on too tight? I was nearing retirement; was I easing off because I wanted to avoid anything that could screw up my exit plan? Most officers at this stage of their careers are shining a seat with their backside in an office, and I don't blame them one bit. From then on, I made a conscious effort to push hard like I always had. I hated the idea that the team thought I was coasting. I should add that I was never the fastest driver in the department. I was quick, I was safe, and I was smooth, and smooth goes a bloody long way with your crew. The real speed merchants were brilliant drivers like Dave R or James Mc. My God, what they did with a car was amazing, fortunately I was a good passenger, never worrying about my safety even if we went airborne, which did, on occasion, happen.

The Ageing process is cruel, as I found out, driving around Lambeth when a call came out to a stabbing outside a garage on Tulse Hill. It was early afternoon and a lovely sunny day, not that it mattered what sort of day it was on this borough. We pulled up at the scene; a large crowd had gathered, and local officers were commencing first aid. My crew, Chandelier and the Prince of Persia, were both medics and ran straight to the victim. I went to the boot, grabbed the first aid kit and laid it out beside them. The victim, a young Black male, had multiple stab wounds and was barely conscious. The two lads were doing a great job, and I was filling in the gaps feeding them equipment. Soon Paramedics were working beside them, all with one goal: to save this man's life. A Paramedic handed me a sealed bandage to open, I wasn't wearing my glasses and couldn't find the serrated edge, indicating the opening to tear. I handed it to the Prince, who had it opened in a flash. This was the first and last time this ever happened to me. The young lad survived, and in no small part due to the brilliant work of the ARVs, namely my crew. This was the last commendation I was awarded, for saving life. I couldn't tell you where it is; I didn't collect it; I didn't feel I covered myself in glory that day. These were the standards I set for myself and expected of the team around me.

One of my final vehicle options demonstrated everything that was great about life on the cars as well as the risks. I was OFC; the job involved stopping a car three up, the occupants on route to an address containing suspects and a firearm. The car may also contain armed individuals. Speed was everything; the second the car was dealt with, we would form up a stick and flop onto the address, just off Clapham High St. It was rush hour, it was pissing down, and the surveillance team were struggling. Suddenly we are at 'state amber,' we were in play, three cars in convoy, battling through heavy traffic, the glare of headlights and spray cutting visibility to nothing. My driver Al is doing a fantastic job keeping up. We were close, so no blue lights, no noise, just gutsy overtakes and pissed-off members of the public. Surveillance drops out of the follow; we are in 'pole position.' A quick check: Alpha, Bravo and Charlie are set. "State red, state red, strike, strike, strike, strike." My driver goes for the overtake, forcing the bandit vehicle to come to a standstill. Everyone is out, windows are going in, suspects are extracted; it's so bloody slick, the shout goes up, "Car clear." What now? Fill in the gaps, gather the team; someone has let the handbrake off on the target vehicle. The engine's still running; it shoots forward, crushing my legs against a tree. Fuck, it hurts. I thought I may have broken my leg; my dodgy knee is screaming at me. No time to waste worrying; I limp back to my car, waving away my concerned teammates. "Mount up, let's go," we are on route to the address. In the street I give a quick over-the-bonnet briefing to the stick, and off we go, Trojan One; Claude has just done her first option 2, armed extraction and is now on the Shield; the door goes in, and suspects detained. Premises searched, one Shotgun recovered and three more arrested. A great job: the team was brilliant, and me, me, I am pretending it's just a scratch. That job was everything I joined for and more: the stress of being the OFC, the fear of fucking up, ruining a squad job, worrying about the team, people I loved being around. Getting the stars to align isn't easy, culminating in a debrief with no tears. I remember the faces: the Boss, Big Al, Tom X, Adrian, V, Harry the …. and the rest. What a team! I went home happy, if a little broken. It was worth it.

"So how does a Chinese guy eating a penguin cause all this?"

"It's a Pangolin."

"That's what I said, penguin."

It was this clash of intellectual heavyweights that first alerted me to the unfolding crisis, sat in the canteen at Lewisham, officers were huddled around the TV watching updates from China. I didn't take much notice; within months, the biggest threat to hit the UK, the planet since the Second World War was upon us. We were now wearing face masks on patrol, and using hand wash, all aimed at defeating COVID. On parade we were told to sit further apart, genius, however, at the appointed hour three of us would get in an ARV, patrol for 12 hours, breathing each other's air. Dealing with borough officers, the LAS, and the public, it did seem all rather disjointed. Training rose to the occasion; no, it wasn't stood down for the duration of the Pandemic. Instead, we all got our own bedroom and staggered mealtimes. If anything was going to save lives, staggered mealtimes was it. I had learnt a long time ago that an Asteroid strike on London, an imminent alien invasion or the melting of the Polar ice caps would not stop continuation training. Of course, I caught it; eleven days I lay in bed convinced I was dying. In my state of delirium, I considered writing my will, only to realise I didn't own anything, I promised myself if I made it, if I pulled through, I would drag my credit rating up to very poor. I survived, as for the credit rating. Slowly life returned to normal or has it.

I once saw an interview with Brian O'Driscoll, the rugby legend; he explained he knew the game was up when a young opponent left him for dead on the pitch. In that moment he knew it was over. I woke one day and just knew it was time, no doubts, no what ifs, this was my BOD moment. I had several months left, but my blue card and driving permit all ran out, 6 weeks before I was due to retire. I spoke to my wife and gave her the good news: I was calling it a day; she supported me 100%. Kerry was convinced I would deliberately get involved in something controversial on my last day, just so I could put off retirement. I asked for a meeting with Trojan One and requested that when my authorisations ran out, could I go on garden leave until the big day? Claude was a true star and gave my plan the thumbs up. I had no desire to put myself through another classification shoot, and the thought of two days of training did not excite me; I had reached saturation on that point.

Japanese companies, when retiring a long-serving member of staff, have a system where the employee goes from a five-day week down to four, then gradually down to three, then two, until they are mentally prepared to leave. The wise old Japanese realised that this gives both the employee and his family time to gradually adjust and come to terms with life after the company. I was copying my Japanese counterparts; what they were doing over 12 months, I was doing in two. Having made the decision, I wrote the date in the calendar on the fridge. I was totally at ease; my mind was made up, and, in my heart, as well as my head, I knew it was time.

One of the final hoops I had to jump through, before I headed off to the happy hunting grounds, was something called an exit interview. Anyone leaving the department was asked to have a chat with the big cheese who runs 19. It was a two-way street; the boss thanked you for your service, and the departing officer gets the opportunity to get a few things off their chest, if they felt so inclined. For the record, I did not feel so inclined. Why? Because no one is changing 19 on the say-so of a constable, that just doesn't happen. Waiting for the Boss to finish a phone call, a random Superintendent stuck his nose out of an office and asked what I was doing loitering in the corridor. Loitering, indeed, that upset me straight off. I informed him I awaited my exit interview. The Superintendent informed me he had done 32 years in the job and had no intention of retiring any time soon. He then told me with no sense of irony if he could still do the job, so should I.

I looked at this leader of men, heavily overweight and out of shape. He certainly hadn't done 30 years of earlies, lates and nights. He didn't work Christmas Day, miss his kid's birthdays or his wedding anniversary. When was the last time he was assaulted on duty? When was his last foot chase? The toughest decision he would make today would be whether to have another slice of cake with his afternoon coffee. It was hysterical that he could somehow compare his office job to the role I performed. The fact he did showed just how out of touch he was, just like so many senior officers. Of course, he would keep on working, taking a nice big pay cheque every month, minus any risk, other than a possible heart attack. For those of us on the front line earning considerably less, shouldering huge responsibility, and always having the risk of serious injury hanging over us, retirement and pension were hard-earned and certainly not a done deal.

A part of me wanted to jab him in the chest and point out a few realities; even now as I write, I feel my blood starting to boil. However, I held my tongue not because of his rank; I had squared away more than a few senior officers in my time, or because I didn't want to blot my copybook. I just couldn't be bothered. To me, he may have once been a cop, but that was a long time ago. The Chief Super suddenly appeared at my shoulder, shook my hand and whisked me away into his office. The meeting was brief and relaxed, just what we had both hoped for, I guess; I was presented with a framed certificate thanking me for my service, and just like that, it was over, and I was walking out of Leman Street for the last time.

My last shift as an armed cop arrived. Life doesn't end with a bang but a whimper, someone clever once wrote. Well, that guy was right. My last call, I ran from the Embankment all the way out west to Hounslow, the classic guy seen with a gun in the street. We arrived; we did an area search, result, no trace, and then it was a slow drive back to base and de-kit. I stood in the unloading bay looking at the Glock I had carried for eighteen years. Odd to be parting company after so long, after so many adventures. Booking in my Glock and MCX, the armourer shook my hand and wished me well. I headed to the kit room, putting my body armour on the shelf marked Healy, trying not to well up. The numbers flew around in my head: eighteen years on the cars, thirty years operational. How did I manage to keep my job with my gob? Eighteen years of classifying, four weapons platforms, nine Trojan ones, and two shots fired. Two ARVs written off, three changes of base, two marriages, four kids, hospitalised seven times, complaints I lost count of that one. So many memories, so many friends, so many moments laughing on parade. That's what I will miss, I thought to myself, that hour each day on parade when I sat with my peers, guys and girls half my age, listening to their stories and their adventures. The piss-taking, the random acts of kindness, the mocking of everything that wasn't us, 19. I knew nothing would come close to replacing this world; 19 had become my home, and I'm not ashamed to admit it.

My final day arrived; I entered the base and was met by a wave of kindness. Matt Twist, my old skipper from my days at the Hill, walked on parade. I almost fell over, as did Trojan One and the Skippers; Sergeant Twist was now Commander Matt Twist. He pulled up a chair and joined the team banter, even risking a brief Q&A session. Drinking tea, he talked of our time working together and won the room over in no time. We shook hands as he left and wished each other well, and that dear friend is the JOB. Speeches were made, and I was presented with an array of gifts that now hold pride of place in my gym. Obviously, I was moved to tears. I stood looking at the faces who had come to say goodbye: my co-shooter at the siege, now a skipper going for his Inspectors; a host of old friends, now CTSFOs; and some instructors. Some who had moved to pastures new on promotion. Every face a memory, a bust-up, a roll around, a foot chase, coffee on overtime, sweating in the gym, a vehicle option, continuation training.

Claude unveiled a small plaque to commemorate my time in the department. Inscribed on it the words MO ICHIDO, Japanese for, 'just one more.' I often used that expression when I trained. One more punch, one more kick, one more blow. It also has a deeper meaning to me, to carry on, never quit, deal with what's in front of you. It summed up my career, my life. I can take it; I won't break. Just one more.

I now live in France, and it's almost five years since I last wore the uniform. I had to get away from London and start a new adventure – something big, completely alien and challenging. I now keep myself busy renovating an old 'Maison de Maître,' a master's house, in the Vienne, just outside a mediaeval town called Montmorillon. Nothing of note happens here; the farmers go about their business battling the elements and EU farming regulations whilst showing absolutely no curiosity towards the English couple who moved into the 'Petit Chateau,' as our home is known locally. I love the peace, the silence that's only occasionally disturbed by a tractor or the French military blowing something up at their base a few kilometres away. I have discovered a love of nature and marvel at the abundance of wildlife that surrounds us. Wild boar and deer wander into our garden; hares so large they must be seen to be believed eat our vegetables, which I don't begrudge them; we all have to survive.

Winter has taken hold now, and it's getting colder every day. I pass my time in the barn chopping logs for the wood burners that heat our home. It's great exercise, though my shoulder injury often likes to remind me of my past life. I own two chainsaws, both of which have attempted to kill me, and maybe one day they will, because sometimes I'm that daydreaming boy again, my mind wanders, and I'm back on duty, leaning over the bonnet of a car, planning an op, the faces of my friends staring back at me, and I feel my heart beating that bit faster because once, a lifetime ago, I was Healy 19, an officer of great daring and charm.

Finally dear reader I leave you with this. Finishing my story, I needed someone to proofread it, someone who could tell me just how bad it was. This dubious task fell to an English couple, Lin and Willy, who live in a Hamlet a few miles away. I wouldn't have blamed them if they thought English was my second language. Being lovely people, they agreed to add a few commas, full stops and the odd capital letter. Day and night they laboured; I felt their pain. They are an extraordinary couple, married fifty years, parents to four wonderful girls they have crossed the globe in search of adventure. Sitting listening to tales of their bohemian lifestyle I have to say my life feels very safe in comparison. Blessed with kind hearts, good brains and a wonderful sense of fun, being in their company is a delight. Out of the blue they informed me Lin had written a ballad about my life, taking my story as inspiration. I was embarrassed and humbled in equal measure. I listened in silence as she read it to Kerry and me. When she had finished, I knew I had to use it. I decided that her poem was the perfect way to put this three-year journey to bed. When I started writing, the house was a building site, and Kerry and I were far from convinced France was for us. Today the house is finished, and we don't regret for one minute the leap of faith we took.

To those of you who worked alongside me, I don't need to tell you I am no saint and certainly not sent from Heaven. My greatest hope was that by putting pen to paper, I would immortalise the men and women who shared my journey. Crumps, Magic, and Scott all played a role in getting me started; E Relief and then later F Troop gave me a home. I hope you enjoyed being reminded of those great days when we chased danger with a smile on our face.

And so, without further ado, I give you.

KEVIN FROM HEAVEN

Kevin was sent from hevin,
I am so sure of that.
He loves to eat Kerry s bakes,
And is amazing at combat.
Pretty adept up a ladder,
Great with a sack on his back.
Kevin was sent from hevin,
I am so sure of that.
Kevin's written a book on cops,
Such a wonderful read.
Am sure it will get published,
Success for him indeed.
Kevin was sent from hevin,
Driving a car at high speed.

Mama brought him up well, for sure,
But his da fecked off, so he grew up poor.
A childhood so tough, so raw.
Kevin is a mighty oak,
Rooted firmly to the floor.
Sorting conflicts, dodging bullets,
Giving chase to crooks galore.
Kevin was sent from hevin
Of that I am so sure.

Kevin likes to exercise,
(doja, achi, choku, suki)
Take his villains by surprise.

WATCH AND REACT

Kevin was sent from hevin,
Fully in police disguise -
Take 'em down, no matter their size.

Kevin and Scott make their connection,
Out on patrol, people's protection.
From lurchers, raiders, thieves and crims,
Out in the dark, committing their sins!
Healy known as Kevin was
Certainly sent from hevin.

Healy moved to Notting Hill,
On the job he honed new skills.
Arresting addicts, chasing cons,
Evictions, warrants, on and on.
Now policing is not an easy job,
The taking down,
The occasional swab.
Kevin came down on a
Thingamabob.

The firearms unit is where Kevin
Belonged.
An easy fit, full of grit.
Take no shit.
Definitely Kevin's role,
Out and about, on patrol.
Dealing with those masses,
Cars he sometimes crashes.
Kevin was sent from hevin,
Wearing a pair of glasses.

Many years passed by,
Children grown, 'twas time to fly'
To fairyland, a warm blue sky.
Tall buildings replaced by trees,

Birdsong surrounds him,
A man at ease.
Kevin resides in a house so grand,
Still finds himself in demand.
Chopping logs, walking dogs,
Finding frogs, epilogues.
Long roads, sunny skies, check-in,
Ventures for the future begin.
Kevin without question,
Was sent from hevin,
Of that I am so sure.

Lin Mann

WATCH AND REACT

GLOSSARY

A

AFO authorised firearms officer.
ARV armed response vehicle.

B

BANDIT bad guy/girl.
BELT RIG officers' belt (can hold cuffs, asp, mobile phone etc).
BOD body armour.

C

CARRYING to be armed with a firearm.
CONDITION ONE firearm loaded ready to go.
CTSFO counter terrorism specialist firearms officer (upskilled SFO).

D

DIG OUT armed containment and call out of a suspect from an address.
DPG diplomatic protection group, now called something else.

E

EAR DEFENDERS worn on range and dig outs. To save your hearing.

F

FIELD SUIT very expensive raincoat not waterproof in my experience.
FNG the new guy on team.

G

GLOCK 17 side arm issued to AFOs fires 9 mm round.
G36 assault rifle designed by Heckler and Koch.

H

HARD STOP term used by non 19 officers to describe a vehicle option.
HUNTER UNIT call sign for Heathrow ARVs.
HOOLEY BAR used by MOE to force entry.

L

LID ballistic helmet.
LONG slang for longarm such as a rifle,

M

MCX assault rifle designed Sig Sauer, (mission configurable weapon).
METRO ALPHA inspector managing firearms incident.
MP5 semi-automatic carbine fires 9 mm round.
MOE method of entry,

N

NICK police station. (before they were all sold off)
ND negligent discharge of firearm.

O

OFC operational firearms commander, PC or a Skipper, role to plan, brief, and lead armed officers on an operation.
ONE FOR COVER using the vehicle in front of you to conceal your presence.

P

PELTORS ear defenders.
PIP post incident procedure.
POD the modern version of the base room (soulless underground bunker devoid of humour and cakes).
POLAC police accident, see bad day at the office.
PROT protection officers, think Kevin Costner/Sandra Bullock Miss Congeniality.

R

RAM hydraulic door opener used by MOE.
RANGER call sign for DPG enhanced cars.
RIFLE OFFICER think sniper.
RAT traffic officer easily identifiable in white hat.

S

SCD serious crime directorate. Squads dealing with serious organised crime.
SFO specialist firearms officer.
SNURGLE covertly get into containment without waking up the whole estate.
SLP self-loading pistol.
SLT senior leadership team (senior officers).
STICK team of armed officers used in search of address.
SWEENEY old name for the flying squad, re branded SCD7.
SWEEPING to accidently point your firearm at the friendlies.

T

TACTICAL CONTACT using police vehicle to stop bandit vehicle.

THIRD FLOOR folksy name for home to the CTSFOs.

T I target identification (used to designate points on premises).

TROJAN call sign for ARVs.

TSG territorial support group, public order trained identified by always getting out of the carrier wearing their hats, and pulling clip on ties off in lift.

W

WIO weapons issuing officer.

X

XRAYS the bad guys.

Y

YANKIES innocent members of the public.

WATCH AND REACT

WATCH AND REACT

Printed in Great Britain
by Amazon